**"Why did you d[o] . . . [His]
voice was a low g[rowl.]**

"Do what?"

"Volunteer us to organize the auction." Color rose in her cheeks. "I have a sick *bobbeli* to care for. When am I supposed to work on this? And with you, of all people."

Her anger pierced him. When had their love turned to such bitterness?

"I thought you'd want to be part of it."

"I have no desire to do anything with you."

"Simon and Sylvia are counting on us." *Ja*, it would be difficult to see her on a regular basis, but maybe they would discover a path beyond the hurt.

"I suggest you volunteer someone else. It won't be me." She turned to leave.

He caught her by the elbow. "Won't you reconsider?"

"Leave me alone, Elam. Because of what you did to my brother, you're the last person in the world I would ever organize an auction with." She yanked free of his grasp.

This time, he let her go.

That one mistake, that one accident. Could she ever pardon the man she had once loved?

Bestselling author **Liz Tolsma** loves to write so much it's often hard to tear her away from her computer. When she closes her laptop's lid, she might walk her hyperactive Jack Russell terrier, weed her large perennial garden or binge on HGTV shows. She's married to her high school sweetheart, and together they adopted three children. She's proud to be the mom of a US marine.

Alison Stone lives with her husband of more than twenty years and their four children in Western New York. Besides writing, Alison keeps busy volunteering at her children's schools, driving her girls to dance and watching her boys race motocross. Alison loves to hear from her readers at Alison@AlisonStone.com. For more information, please visit her website, alisonstone.com. She's also chatty on Twitter, @alison_stone. Find her on Facebook at Facebook.com/alisonstoneauthor.

LIZ TOLSMA

The Amish Widow's New Love

&

ALISON STONE

Plain Outsider

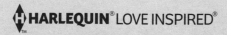

If you purchased this book without a cover you should be aware that this book is stolen property. It was reported as "unsold and destroyed" to the publisher, and neither the author nor the publisher has received any payment for this "stripped book."

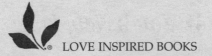

LOVE INSPIRED BOOKS

Recycling programs
for this product may
not exist in your area.

ISBN-13: 978-1-335-47011-9

The Amish Widow's New Love and Plain Outsider

Copyright © 2019 by Harlequin Books S.A.

The publisher acknowledges the copyright holders of the individual works as follows:

The Amish Widow's New Love
Copyright © 2018 by Christine Cain

Plain Outsider
Copyright © 2018 by Alison Stone

All rights reserved. Except for use in any review, the reproduction or utilization of this work in whole or in part in any form by any electronic, mechanical or other means, now known or hereafter invented, including xerography, photocopying and recording, or in any information storage or retrieval system, is forbidden without the written permission of the editorial office, Love Inspired Books, 195 Broadway, New York, NY 10007 U.S.A.

This is a work of fiction. Names, characters, places and incidents are either the product of the author's imagination or are used fictitiously, and any resemblance to actual persons, living or dead, business establishments, events or locales is entirely coincidental.

This edition published by arrangement with Love Inspired Books.

® and TM are trademarks of Love Inspired Books, used under license. Trademarks indicated with ® are registered in the United States Patent and Trademark Office, the Canadian Intellectual Property Office and in other countries.

www.Harlequin.com

Printed in U.S.A.

CONTENTS

THE AMISH WIDOW'S NEW LOVE   7
Liz Tolsma

PLAIN OUTSIDER   209
Alison Stone

THE AMISH WIDOW'S NEW LOVE

Liz Tolsma

To my sisters, Carolyn and Elaine.
Thank you for all the love, support and fun
throughout the years. I'm privileged to have
gotten to be your big sister. Love you guys!

Acknowledgments

Special thanks to Richard Dawley of Amish Insight
and Judy Cook from The Woodshed Amish Tours
in Augusta, Wisconsin, for your help and
knowledge about the Amish in Wisconsin.
I so appreciate everything you taught me!

I, even I, am he that blotteth out
thy transgressions for mine own sake,
and will not remember thy sins.
—*Isaiah* 43:25

Chapter One

Naomi Miller crossed the Masts' side yard between the house and the barn, her brother Aaron beside her, bumping over the ground in his motorized wheelchair, the smell of new-cut grass assailing her. The shouts of the young people playing volleyball engulfed her as they cheered for each spike and every point gained. Near the metal shed, a group of teenage girls huddled together, white prayer *kapp*-covered heads bent together. Bunches of laughing boys hugged the barn's back wall.

Her stomach knotted. Years had passed since she'd been to a singing. She didn't belong here. This was all for her brother. That's the one reason she came. He should be a part of the gathering.

Aaron tightened his shoulders and twisted in his chair, his broad-brimmed straw hat askew. "I shouldn't be here."

"Nonsense. We made a deal. If I came, you would, too."

"But they'll look at me funny." He pounded on his unfeeling, useless legs.

"People here are used to the chair. And at least you're

single and have no children. How does it look for me, a widow with an infant son, to be at a singing?" Wait, did she hear Joseph crying? *Nein*. She shook her head. Her son remained at home with Mamm, safe and sound asleep.

"At least you—"

"Enough of that. We'll both have a *wunderbaar* time." She swallowed hard. Maybe it wouldn't turn out to be a lie. But her gut clenched when a picture of Joseph flashed through her mind. She wiped her sweaty palms down her dark purple dress. What if Mamm couldn't get him to eat enough? What if he had trouble breathing again? Maybe Aaron was right. Maybe this was a bad idea.

He lifted his hat from his head and mussed his blond curls. "No girl is going to want a man in a wheelchair. That's why I haven't been to a singing since the accident. I wish you would never have suggested this to Mamm and Daed."

She did, too. But what was done was done. "Which young lady do you have your eye on?" If she concentrated on Aaron, she might get through this night.

He turned to her. "Can we please go home?"

"Out of the question. Mamm and Daed would be disappointed if we didn't stay for at least a little while. So if you don't tell me who you're going to sit next to, I'll pick out the prettiest girl and bring her to you."

All the color drained from his face until it matched the color of Mamm's bleached sheets. "You wouldn't."

"Don't make me show you I'm serious." She couldn't quite force a smile to her lips.

"Hold on. You don't want to be here either."

He'd always been too perceptive. "What makes you think that?"

"When you used to come to singings, your face would light up. You loved these gatherings. I don't see that in your eyes now."

"It's not the same." Not since… *Nein*, she couldn't think about all the terrible losses. But Aaron had given her an out. "Fine, we can leave. I'll get the buggy and be back in a moment."

"*Nein*, I'll get it. I don't like the way you drive. Much too slow for me." Daed had modified Aaron's buggy with a ramp so he could roll in and out. He liked to spur his horse to trot as fast as possible. "You can stay. I think Solomon Mast wants to drive you home."

"He may want to, but he's not going to. I'm not interested in him. Or in anyone for that matter. It's only been a year since Daniel died." When she spun around to go to the buggy, she hit something. Someone. Hard.

The masculine scent of wood and horses enveloped her. The man grabbed her upper arm and prevented her from falling. The warmth of his hand seeped through her dress's cotton sleeve. "Be careful." His deep voice resonated in her ears.

She stared into eyes the same green as the spring grass beneath her feet. For a moment, she forgot to breathe, the wind knocked out of her. Then she drew in a gulp of air and stepped back. "I'm sorry. I wasn't watching where I was going."

"Are you alright?"

She nodded, and lost her breath again. She knew those eyes. Much too well. Naomi's heart throbbed in her chest as she took in the man's straight reddish hair and his ruddy cheeks. "Elam Yoder. What are you doing here?"

"Hello to you, too." His words were strained. He wore Amish clothes. Dark pants, a light blue shirt and a straw hat.

"You've come back?" She worked to keep her voice as controlled and distant as possible, even as she trembled from head to toe. How dare he show his face in this district again.

"I have."

"Why?"

"Because of Daed's stroke. He needs my help around the farm until Isaac can sell his ranch in Montana and get home. So I'm here."

Aaron piped up behind her. "Hello, Elam."

"Aaron. It's good to see you. How are you?"

"Just on my way home. This isn't for me." He nodded in the barn's direction where a clutch of young women giggled at what the young men said.

Elam shuffled his feet. Seeing Aaron must make him uncomfortable. All the better. He should be uneasy. Should be ashamed of himself.

"I'll go to the barn with you, if you'd like." Elam took a step in Aaron's direction.

Naomi jumped in between them. "That won't be necessary. This wasn't a *gut* idea for either one of us. We'll be going now."

In the distance, footsteps crunched on the gravel driveway. Not some latecomer strolling up the road. Quick, light steps. Running. In the fading daylight, she made out the shape and size of the figure. Her younger brother, Samuel.

He slid to a halt in front of them, panting, sweat dotting his brow. "Mamm sent me for you. Joseph woke up and is fussing, and she thinks he's running a fever. His breathing is raspy."

A cry rose from her chest, but she trapped it in her throat. "Is he okay?"

"I don't know. Mamm just wanted me to get you. She didn't say anything else, but I think you should hurry."

Her entire body turned cold. "Let's go." For her son's sake, they had to be fast. "Aaron, get the buggy. Joseph's labored breathing isn't *gut*. The doctor told me to bring him right in with any kind of respiratory problem."

Before she could move, Elam grabbed her. Oh, the temptation to sink into his arms for comfort. Instead, she squirmed in his grip. "My *bobbeli* is sick. I have to get home to him."

Elam held on to her. "I still have my truck. I fixed it, and my license hasn't expired. Let me take you home."

If possible, her heart rate elevated. "You want me to put my life in your hands?"

"It will be faster."

She'd heard the crash that night, right in front of their house. She couldn't wipe the sound of crunching metal out of her mind. Aaron's screams. "I can't. I can't trust you. I will never trust you again."

Naomi's voice was as icy as the pond in January. Elam shivered. Both at her words and the sight of Aaron in his wheelchair. The young man worked the controls on the chair, spinning around until the wheel caught on a rock. He was stuck.

Stuck in the wheelchair Elam had condemned him to. Every muscle in his body clenched. After three years, the vivid images hadn't faded. Neither had the tinkling of shattered glass. Nor the echoes of Aaron's cries of agony.

He had stripped this man of his vitality and relegated him to a life of struggles and pain.

"Come, Naomi, Joseph needs you." Her brother Samuel tugged at her arm.

Elam shook his head. He'd heard Naomi had married Daniel Miller. What, then, was she doing at a singing meant for singles?

Naomi snapped to attention. She massaged the end of the string of her prayer *kapp*.

"We could get to the clinic faster in the truck. I know I was rebellious when I was young, buying a truck and a cell phone when I was thinking about leaving the Amish. Only you held me here. That and the fact they couldn't kick me out because I hadn't been baptized. But I don't have my cell phone anymore, so I won't be distracted. You can trust me. The truck is in our barn across the street. In a few minutes, we can be on our way."

They didn't have Rumspringa here like back East, but Elam had come close to it. "Sam, go home with Aaron. I'll go with you, Elam, on one condition. You have to drive slowly. But get me to Joseph as fast as possible."

Elam gave a two-beat laugh. "I'll try and do the impossible." Not giving her time to change her mind, he sprinted down the gravel driveway and across the street to his daed's farm. He flung open the barn door, his footsteps reverberating in the silence as he went to his truck.

In the Englisch world, he had needed it to get around. He slipped inside and retrieved the key from under the floor mat. As he slid the key into the ignition and turned it, he drew in a deep breath, his heart pounding. He had thought his truck-driving days were behind him. The engine roared to life.

He shifted into Drive, stepped on the gas and pulled from the barn. Naomi hadn't changed. Big, almost purple-blue eyes in a heart-shaped face. A delicate nose. How she tugged on her *kapp* string when she was nervous.

His breath stuck in his throat. She had turned her back on him after the accident. They had been planning their wedding, but she refused to listen to his apologies. Refused to hear him out. And less than a year later, she had married someone else.

And where was Daniel? Shouldn't he have been with her? Or watching their son?

As his headlights swept the road in front of him, they illuminated Naomi, who stood at the end of the drive. He stopped in front of her, and she climbed into the backseat.

"You can sit up front." He adjusted his rearview mirror.

She buckled her belt. "This is where I always sit in a car." Like she would do with any Englisch driver. That's what she treated him as. An outsider.

"Where do you live?"

"At my parents' house." She gripped the edge of the seat.

Had they retired to the *dawdi haus* already? They weren't old and still had young children. Wouldn't Daniel have his own place? Nothing about Naomi made sense. "So, how old is your *bobbeli*?"

"Three months."

"Daniel must be worried if he sent for you."

The roar of silence filled the truck cab.

"Naomi? Did you hear me?"

"My husband died almost a year ago."

Elam blew out his breath. How awful for her. "I'm sorry. I didn't know."

They passed a few farms, bright white light spilling from the windows of fancy *Englisch* homes. Softer, paler light flickered from the plain white Amish houses. He glanced over his shoulder. "That must have been hard."

Naomi swiped away a stray tear. "It was. He fell from a roof. But Joseph was a wonderful surprise. His coming eased some of the hurt. I'll have a piece of Daniel with me forever."

He returned his attention to the road. Daniel always had his eye on her. Elam shouldn't be surprised she'd married him. Unable to forgive Elam for his one mistake, she had moved on with her life. Had turned her back on what they shared and became another man's wife. The pain that pierced his chest startled him. That part of his life should have been far behind him.

He shook his head. Such thoughts were useless.

He didn't have time to dwell on this information as they soon arrived at her parents' home and her father's woodworking shop, where he had once worked. Before he could come around to help her out, she unlatched the belt, slid from the truck, and slammed the door shut. He jogged behind her to the house, the *bobbeli's* weak, raspy cries reaching them as they crossed the front porch.

A moment after entering through the kitchen and into the living room, Naomi was at her mother's side.

Sarah Bontrager rocked the infant in a well-worn rocking chair, and Naomi's sister Laura was at their mamm's side. Joseph coughed, deep and tight, the sound tugging at Elam.

Sarah wiped the *bobbeli's* perspiration-dotted brow. "You got here fast. That's *gut*. He was fussy, so I picked him out of his cradle. The heat of his body radiated through his clothes. When he hacked, such a terrible cough, I sent Sam for you right away. I can't get him to eat either."

Naomi felt her son's forehead and widened her eyes. "We need to get him to urgent care. Now. With his heart condition…"

Sarah cradled Joseph. "Laura, tell Daed to run and call Frank Jameson and see if he can drive. Naomi and I will get Joseph ready."

Elam stepped from the shadows. "No need. My truck's right outside, warmed and ready to go."

Both women stared at him with open mouths, as if he'd appeared out of thin air.

Sarah stood from the rocker, handed the *bobbeli* to Naomi and then clenched her hands. "Elam Yoder. You still have that truck?"

That truck. The one that had caused so much damage. They would never let him forget. Not this family. Not this district. He stepped back. "*Ja*, I do. I brought Naomi from the singing. I can take her."

"No need." Naomi shook her head so hard it was surprising it didn't fly off her shoulders.

And her mind was made up.

She hustled by him into the kitchen, and he followed. From a peg by the back door, she grabbed a diaper bag. "Frank Jameson can be here in less than fifteen minutes. There's no reason for you to make the trip. The doctor might send us to Madison."

She was that afraid of him? Would his actions from that night haunt him forever?

The little one coughed. "We're wasting time debating this. If you go with me, I can have you there fifteen minutes sooner than Frank."

Naomi's daed entered the kitchen from the hall. "I'll go phone for Frank."

Elam suppressed a sigh. "If the *bobbeli* is so sick, you shouldn't waste time."

"And let my daughter and grandson end up like my son?" Leroy Bontrager crossed his arms, jaw tight.

Naomi's hand trembled as she brushed her boy's cheek. "He's so warm."

Joseph gasped and coughed.

"Let me take you. Please. I can help. I want to."

She glanced away from him, then back in his direction. "I don't know."

"Naomi."

She gritted her teeth. "Fine. I'll get Joseph's blanket, and we can leave. Mamm, you'll come with me, right?"

"Of course." Sarah entered the kitchen, her sweater already in her hands.

Leroy stepped to within inches of Elam. "If anything happens to any of them, I will hold you responsible. You be careful with that truck. They are precious cargo. This is only because the need is so urgent."

Naomi placed the *bobbeli* into the car seat on the hall floor. His face. Wide-set eyes, thick lips and a flat nose, all positioned in a round face. His Englisch boss at the construction company had a daughter like that.

He called it Down syndrome. What a burden for Naomi to carry, on top of losing her husband.

The object of his thoughts tucked a fuzzy blue blanket around Joseph then swept up the car seat by the handle. "We're ready. Let's go. Do you know the way?"

"*Ja*. Don't worry. We'll be there soon."

"It can't be soon enough." A tear trickled down Naomi's cheek.

Elam held himself back from wiping it away. She wouldn't allow him to comfort her.

Sarah rubbed her daughter's back. "We must trust God to do what is right."

Elam held the door open for the two women. As he turned to shut it, he caught sight of Leroy, who glared at him.

Elam shivered and then stepped into the chilly Wisconsin night.

Chapter Two

Naomi stroked her son's hot, damp cheek with one hand and clung to the edge of the truck's back seat with the other as they raced toward the clinic. Joseph cried weak, pitiful mews, stopping only to catch his breath, which he did far too often. Her throat burned. "Can't you go faster, Elam?"

"I'm speeding as it is. We're in town. Not far now."

The trip had taken much too long. Why did the clinic have to be so far? The dim glow of the streetlights illuminated Joseph's red face.

Mamm reached over the car seat and patted Naomi's hand. "Don't worry so. We'll be there soon. You just drive careful now, Elam."

He clung to the steering wheel and peered out the windshield. At least he heeded Mamm's instructions.

After another eternity, they pulled into the parking lot. Elam rolled to a stop as she grabbed Joseph's car seat and hopped out, Mamm sliding out the other side.

"I'll park and be right—"

Naomi slammed the door.

By the time she carried her wailing child inside

and registered him at the desk, Elam had joined them. Why had he come? Better for him to stay in that truck. Mamm was here.

The waiting room buzzed with activity. Sick children. Some virus or bug must be going around. Maybe Joseph had picked up his illness from one of the children at the church service two weeks ago. Mamm calmly sat on one of the chairs on the far side of the room. Probably praying.

Elam sat across from her, clasping his straw hat with his big, work-roughened hands. She paced the room and jiggled Joseph on her hip. Elam patted the chair on his left. "Come sit, Naomi. You're going to wear yourself out."

"I can't. What's taking them so long?"

"Fretting about it won't make them call you sooner. Now sit. I can hold Joseph if you want a break."

"Nein, denki." The harsh words flew from her lips, but she would not give her son to him. Never. "I'm sorry, Elam. I shouldn't have been short just now. I am thankful for your help tonight."

She moved the car seat from the chair beside Mamm and sat. Joseph's little body melded into hers. She kissed his burning cheek.

Elam peered at Joseph. "Does he often get sick?"

"The doctor said if he got a respiratory infection, it could be very bad. He has a hole in his heart, and that is not good for his lungs. I don't fully understand, and it's hard to explain. It's dangerous for him to be sick." Like always, he managed to get her to open up. To share her heart. She couldn't allow that. He'd broken it once before. She wouldn't give him a chance to do it again. She pursed her lips together.

A nurse dressed in bright blue scrubs emerged from the doorway to the side of the desk. "Joseph Miller?"

Naomi gathered Joseph's diaper bag and stood. She and Mamm followed the nurse into one of the small rooms and sat in the chairs beside the little desk.

Naomi leaned over, willing her hands to stop shaking.

Julie, as the nurse had introduced herself, took Joseph's history, his blood pressure, his temperature and his pulse, and typed everything into the computer. "So he hasn't been sick that long?"

"A sniffle or two this morning, but I didn't think anything of it. I put him in bed before I went out. My mamm was watching him, and she sent for me not too long afterward to tell me he was crying and wouldn't eat." She shouldn't have left him. It was her fault he got so sick. Mamm pulled her into a side hug.

"Any tugging on the ears?"

"Not that I've noticed." Naomi forced the words around the lump in her throat.

Mamm patted her hand.

"Cough?"

"Yes, deep and tight."

The questions went on. Mamm sat beside her until Julie finished. "The doctor will be in soon. If you need anything, just holler. I'll be right down the hall."

As the nurse closed the door, Naomi worried the hem of her sleeve. Mamm rubbed her shoulder. "He'll be fine. He's made of sturdy stuff."

"I'm scared." Her insides quivered.

"I know. But God is watching out for him."

"I could lose him." More tears streamed down her face.

"I know, my daughter, I know. But the doctors will take *gut* care of him. He will be fine. You'll see."

Mamm's words washed over her, but her stomach still tightened. "Even with Aaron's accident and Daniel's fall, I never felt like this. So helpless. So frightened of being alone." She nestled Joseph against her, the one good thing in her life.

Dear God, don't take him from me. I can't stand to lose him.

Naomi kissed her sleeping son on his cool cheek and pulled up the blanket to his chin, careful not to rock the cradle and wake him. Now, with several doses of antibiotics in him, his breathing was once again normal. Such a scare he'd given her the other day. Denki, *Lord, that he's well.*

As well as he could be for a child with a hole in his heart.

He puckered his blue lips and puckered his mouth in his sleep. With one more kiss, Naomi slipped out the bedroom door.

Mamm, a basket of laundry in her hands, met her at the bottom of the steps. "Ready for your first day back at the bakery?"

Naomi's stomach churned. Other than the singing on Sunday, she hadn't been away from Joseph since his birth. And look how that had turned out. "I don't want to leave him. What if he needs me? He did when I went to the singing."

"Laura and I will be here all day. You'll be across the street. His getting sick had nothing to do with you leaving him. It's *gut* for you to get out of the house, even if only for a few hours of the day. If you don't, you'll go stir-crazy in no time. And a happy mamm makes for a happy *bobbeli*."

"Still…"

"Off with you. Take your mind from your worries for a while. Go, before I make you iron all of this."

Naomi tried to smile at Mamm's joke. Ironing was the worst form of torture. "I'm going, I'm going. Anything to avoid that." She gave a slight chuckle. "But you get me if Joseph needs me for anything at all. Anything."

"I will." Mamm kissed her on the cheek in much the same way she had kissed Joseph. Her tight muscles relaxed a little bit.

Before she knew it, Naomi stood on the threshold of the walkout basement's back door leading to the downstairs bakery. After drawing in a deep breath, she stepped inside, warmth enveloping her, the yeasty aroma of bread, doughnuts and cinnamon rolls welcoming her.

She hadn't been here as an employee since Joseph's birth. The people, the routine, the work had brought her a measure of comfort after Daniel's death. Perhaps Mamm was right. Maybe being here would keep her from worrying about her son, even if only for a few hours.

Rachel Miller, her sister-in-law and best friend, scurried into the hall. "Naomi, welcome back. How *gut* it is to see you." She wrapped her in a hug. "How is Joseph doing?"

"Fine now. But that illness was one of the scariest things that I've ever had to experience." Joseph was her precious only child. His sickness could have been serious, even life-threatening.

"The Lord is gracious. And it is *gut* to have you beside me again, even if it's only a few days a week."

They entered the kitchen, and Naomi stared at the stoves lining the walls, the big sink in the back and the large metal table in the middle where the women did most of their work. Rachel squeezed her shoulder. "Are you okay? You sure you're up for this?"

She had to be. "*Ja*, except it's almost like I'm dreaming. But Mamm says it's *gut* for me to get out of the house for a while, and the money will help with the repairs to the *dawdi haus* so I can move in there. Have a measure of independence."

"Whatever the reason you came back to work, I'm glad you're here."

They set to their tasks, Rachel kneading dough that would become pretzels, and Naomi kneading seven-grain bread. Before long, the rhythm of the work settled her.

"You crazy old man, what are you doing?" A voice carried from the back room.

Naomi turned to Rachel. "Is that Sylvia Herschberger?"

"Sounds like it."

"Just getting this flour you wanted."

Naomi chuckled. "*Ja*, that's Simon answering her."

"Let me help you with that."

Elam? Was that his voice? Her stomach fluttered in her midsection. Which was ridiculous. He had helped them when Joseph got sick, but that was all.

"Watch out."

Boom. Crash. Bang.

"Simon!" Sylvia screeched.

Naomi wiped her hands on her apron and scurried to the back room. "*Ach*, Simon, oh no."

The older man lay on the floor, his right leg jutting out at an odd angle. Elam pulled a ladder off him. Sylvia stood over her husband, wringing her hands. Flour covered all three of them and the floor. Dust floated on the sunlit air.

Naomi hurried to his side. "What can I do? Tell me how to help."

Elam's green eyes widened when he saw her. "We'll need an ambulance."

Rachel reached Naomi. "I'll run down the street to call for one."

Naomi knelt beside the gray-haired man, his hat crushed underneath him. "Simon?"

"Oh, my leg." He spoke the words through gritted teeth.

"I told you not to climb up there for the flour." His wife paced the room stacked with large quantities of baking supplies, her black shoes leaving prints on the dusty floor. "Why didn't you wait for Elam to get here to do it?"

Elam motioned for Sylvia to stop. "That doesn't matter. Right now, let's get him comfortable while we wait for the ambulance."

Sylvia wiped a tear from the corner of her eye. "There are pillows and a blanket on our bed upstairs." She wobbled on her feet.

"I'll get them. And you look like you need a chair." Naomi held her by the arm. "Lean against the wall. Will you be okay while I grab a seat for you?"

Sylvia nodded.

Elam placed the ladder against the shelves. "I'll help you carry everything."

Naomi opened her mouth to object, but shut it right away. Instead, she followed him up the stairs. "Why are you here?"

"I could ask you the same question." He opened the door to the family's living quarters.

"I'm trying to scrape together some money to repair the *dawdi haus* for myself and my son."

"And Simon asked me to make a few new picnic tables for the Englisch to sit on when the weather's nice. The ones they have now are unsteady and falling apart. They're giving me a chance to prove myself and show people I'm serious about returning. I'm hoping it will lead to a new business venture. How is Joseph, by the way?"

She popped into the Herschbergers' bedroom and pulled a couple of pillows and a red-and-blue wedding-ring quilt from the bed before returning to the kitchen, where Elam grabbed a chair. "Fine. And once more, *denki* for what you did for us when he got sick."

"I'm happy I was at the singing to give you a ride." His smile was tight, like he forced it.

They descended the stairs and returned to the Herschbergers. Naomi knelt beside Simon. "Here you are." She lifted him enough to slide two pillows under his head, and then covered him with the quilt. Elam helped Sylvia into the chair.

Simon grasped the coverlet, his knuckles turning white. "Guess I'm going to have to go to the hospital."

Naomi took care not to hurt him when she straightened the quilt over his twisted knee. "You've broken your leg. And done a good job of it. Let's hope that's all."

"How long do you think I will be out of commission?" Simon groaned.

"Only a doctor can answer that." What was taking that ambulance so long?

A furrow appeared on Simon's brow. "But the auction is coming up."

All the air rushed from Naomi's lungs. That auction was to raise money for medical needs in the district. Like for Joseph's surgery. And Aaron's ongoing expenses. Simon did most of the organizing. How would they pay for anything without the funds the event raised?

Elam peered out the door. "I hear the siren. The ambulance must be just down the road. You hang on."

Simon winced as he nodded. "And you and Naomi will take over coordinating the auction."

"You want us to do it?" Elam spun around to face inside.

"You'll do a fine job. I won't have to worry with the two of you in charge."

Elam hawed for a moment. "I'm not sure."

"Make an old man happy. Let me rest well."

Simon couldn't be serious. "*Nein*, we can't." They couldn't.

"She's right. It would be too—"

"Nonsense. You can make it work."

Elam shifted his weight from one foot to the other. "Fine, we'll do it."

A bolt of lightning couldn't have shocked her more. "We will?"

Chapter Three

The sirens wailed as the ambulance raced from the bakery's parking lot, carrying Simon Herschberger to the hospital, his wife at his side. Elam relaxed his shoulders. His friend and mentor was in *gut* hands now.

He turned to walk up the driveway, back to his wagon loaded with lumber for the picnic tables. The crowd of curious Englischers dispersed, some to their cars, others into the line for their baked goods.

Naomi scurried in front of him, blocking his path, her hands on her hips. "What did you do that for?" Her voice was a low growl.

"Do what?" His innocence was an act, one she was sure to see through.

"Volunteer us, me, to organize the auction. How could you do that without consulting me? Do you know how much time and effort that takes?" Color rose in her cheeks. "And I have a very sick *bobbeli* to care for. One who needs surgery as soon as possible. When am I supposed to have the time to work on this with you? *You*, of all people."

The shine in her face got his blood to pumping. Her anger pierced him. When had their love turned to such bitterness? He peered around. Several of the Englisch stared at them. "You might want to keep your voice down." He nodded in the direction of the bakery.

She whipped around and then turned to face him, the red that had graced her cheeks dissipating.

"That's why I said you and I would put it together. Much of the money raised will go to pay Joseph's medical bills and my daed's. You're as invested in this as I am. I thought you'd want to be part of it."

"I have no desire to do anything other than sew a few quilts and bake a couple of pies. Besides that, leave me out of it."

"Simon and Sylvia are counting on us." *Ja*, it would be difficult to see her on a regular basis, but he could find a way to do it. Couldn't she? Maybe they would be able to discover a path beyond the hurt.

"I suggest you volunteer someone else. It won't be me." She turned her back to him once more and started for the bakery.

He caught her by the elbow. Why he did it when she had just lashed out at him, he couldn't say. "Won't you reconsider?"

"Who's making a scene now?"

He bent to her height and whispered in her ear, the clean scent of soap tickling his nose. "Please assist me. I'll do most of the work."

"Aren't you helping your daed on the farm? Since his stroke, I think he'd need you." She kept her gaze forward.

"I am, but Isaac will soon be back to take over the day-to-day operations. You know farming isn't my life's calling."

"Go build your picnic tables, Elam, and leave me alone." She yanked free of his grasp and scuttled to the kitchen.

This time, he let her go.

He scrubbed his face. Would he ever live down what

he'd done years ago? It had been an accident, and she had turned her back on him when everyone else did. Then and now it seemed she couldn't pardon the man she had claimed to love. He lost himself in the work in front of him, sawing and screwing and sanding until he shed his jacket and wiped sweat from his forehead, the day warm for early spring.

The line of customers stretched out the door, around the path, up the steps and into the parking lot. Naomi and the others inside would be busy. But he glanced up as a group of Amish women exited through the back door. And there Naomi was, in the middle of the bunch, a slight smile touching her lips as she reacted to whatever Rachel said.

He averted his gaze. Bumping into her so much made being back in the district more difficult. Part of him still loved her as much as when he left. But another part of him ached at her hard-heartedness. Motherhood added a soft roundness to her face, color to her cheeks, straightness to her back. Though he had first thought she hadn't changed, she was not the woman he left behind.

"What are you doing there?"

Elam sucked in a breath. Rachel peered over his shoulder as he screwed two pieces of wood together. "You want to scare a man to death?"

"*Ach*, it's not that easy to frighten you. If I had really wanted to, I would have snuck up even quieter." Rachel stood with her arms crossed.

"So you were trying to give me a heart attack. Isn't it enough we've had an ambulance here once already today?"

Naomi tugged on Rachel's arm. "Come on, let's have some lunch. The other girls are already sitting down to eat. It's busy, and they'll need us back soon. Especially with Sylvia not here."

Rachel nodded at Elam. "Why don't you join us?"

"*Ja*, I need a break." Elam wiped his hands on his pants. "Let me wash up, and I'll join you."

A scowl appeared on Naomi's face. Well, she may not be happy about it, but that wouldn't stop him from getting a bite to eat. More than anything, he wanted her forgiveness. Everyone's forgiveness.

After a stop in the washroom to scrub his hands and face, he joined the girls at a table away from where the customers ate their baked goods. Still the crowds stared, giggled and even pointed.

The only spot available was on the end of the bench, right beside Naomi. He plopped down, and she scooted as far away from him as possible, knocking elbows with Rachel as she unwrapped her sandwich from the wax paper. Rachel scraped some dilly chicken salad onto a paper plate and handed it to Elam.

He ate a few bites before turning to Naomi. "When would be a *gut* time to get together to work on the auction? I can speak to Sylvia when she returns from the hospital, find out what Simon has planned and what we still need to do. Maybe tomorrow night?"

"I told you I'm not working with you. You volunteered for this. Take care of it on your own." Her words were so icy, her breath should have puffed in small clouds in front of her.

"Wait." He grabbed her by the forearm. She winced and pulled away. Should he press the matter? *Ja*, what did he have to lose? He had promised Simon. "You haven't heard the best part yet."

"There's more?" She hugged herself.

"We can make it the biggest, most successful auction yet if you tell your story about Daniel and Joseph to the newspapers across the state. The Englisch will flock here to buy quilts and furniture and baked goods, all to support a widow and her little son."

She clenched her fists and sat back, almost tilting off the bench. "You want me to do what?" She almost screeched by the end.

He closed his eyes and grimaced. Once again, he had managed to anger her. He couldn't seem to do anything else.

A cold sweat broke out all over Naomi. "Absolutely not." She kept her voice low to avoid drawing attention from the bakery's customers for the second time today but stern enough for Elam to be clear about her desires. "I will not help you with the auction. And I will not, under any circumstance, go to the papers." She wadded up her sandwich wrapper and stuffed it into her bag.

He opened his eyes, and a vein in his neck throbbed. "After all this time, are you still so angry?"

Her thoughts scrambled in her brain like eggs in a frying pan. How did she identify this burning in her chest? Anger? Or something just the opposite? "So much has changed since the night of the accident. So much that can never be undone. Don't you understand?"

"I do. But you once claimed to love me. Didn't that mean anything? Can't you forgive me?"

She breathed in and out, the back of her neck aching. "You ask too many difficult questions. Ones I don't have the answers for, that I may never have the answers for. I'm dealing with my husband's loss and my son's serious illness and disability. Isn't that enough?"

The other women gathered the remains of their lunches and meandered inside to resume work. Naomi rose, as well. With a brush of his hand against hers, time stood still. Just like years ago, her knees went mushy, and she thumped into her seat. She nodded at Rachel to stay. Her friend shrugged and bit into a peanut butter cookie.

Elam plowed ahead. "The auction is just a couple weeks away. If you're going to tell your story to the papers, we have to contact the reporters soon. You want to give their readers enough notice so they can make plans to come here."

"It's bad enough to have these people here, staring at us. We're nothing more than a tourist attraction." She motioned wide, her gesture sweeping over the lot packed with cars, one pulling up the gravel driveway every couple of minutes. "But to encourage even more of them to come, that's not a *gut* idea."

"What are they going to do?"

"Disrupt our lives. Mine has been stretched and changed until I don't recognize it. I don't need any further interference." Couldn't he go away and leave her alone? Just leave her in peace? "Why are you even back in the area? Do you want to bring the Englisch to us?"

"*Nein*, not at all."

But he had abandoned her. When she'd gone to him for comfort, he had left. And hadn't returned until now. "Don't you miss the friends you made out there?"

"I missed the Amish much more."

"And your family? How do they feel about you being back? Won't they miss you when you leave again?"

"I'm home to stay, Naomi."

She couldn't help but be doubtful. *Forever* didn't mean much to him.

He stabbed his plastic fork on his plate. "Listen to me. The most important person to you in your life is your son, *nein*?"

"*Ja*, that's right."

"He's beautiful, Naomi. Such a gift from the Lord. All you have left of Daniel."

Rachel stared straight ahead, her eyes filling with tears. "My brother would have done anything for his little boy."

"He would have been a *wunderbaar* daed." Naomi patted Rachel's hand.

Elam nodded. "Parents are like that. They would make any sacrifice for their children. Even though I'm not a daed yet, I know I would walk to the moon if I thought it would help my children. Isn't giving Joseph the best chance at a happy, healthy life worth anything you might have to do to make that happen?"

Tears now clouded Naomi's eyes. The way Elam had of putting things… "Of course. That's why I'm working here. That's why I take him to the doctor, why I walk the floor with him at night, sing to him, love him. But there are things I can think of that I wouldn't do."

"Wouldn't you do anything that was legal, moral and ethical?"

"Maybe." Every time Elam came near her, she couldn't think straight. He spoke with pretty words and was very convincing. If he were Englisch, perhaps he would be a lawyer.

"All you would have to do is sit down with a couple of reporters and tell your story. Tell them how much you love Joseph. What he means to you. And the good the auction does, not only for your son, but for people like Aaron and Simon and my daed."

All of her muscles tensed. She couldn't cry. Wouldn't let him see how much he affected her. But the back of her throat burned.

Why did God have to take Daniel? Why did He have to make Joseph so sick? And why had He brought Elam back?

"Fine, I'll think about it."

Chapter Four

Naomi lifted her face to the sun and breathed in the scent of warming earth. Mamm, about to make an oatmeal pie, had found herself out of brown sugar. With Joseph down for a nap and the weather this warm and beautiful, Naomi offered to walk to the bulk food store. What she didn't tell Mamm was how perfect the timing was. She and Elam had a meeting with Sylvia to pick up the information Simon had put together for the auction.

She hadn't found the courage yet to tell her parents she was working with Elam. Forcing the words through her lips shouldn't be this hard. But she held back. They would not approve of her spending time with him, though they had no basis for worry. She would never let him worm his way into her life again. Once this auction was over, she would steer clear of him for the rest of her life. She would have to tell them sooner or later. Nothing stayed secret for very long here. But she would hold off as long as she could.

A slight breeze tugged at her dress. She shouldn't enjoy this taste of freedom as much as she did, but every now and again, it was nice to not be Naomi the widow, Naomi the mother of a child with special needs, Naomi the bakery employee, but just Naomi. As a small blue car whizzed by, she jumped to the side of the road.

In a few days, the early daffodils would be in full bloom. Tulips' leaves peeked above the ground. The buds lining the tree's twigs were about to burst open. Spring.

Amid the back-and-forth calls of the cardinals in the trees came the clip-clop of a horse's hooves. Which of her neighbors was out and about? She turned and groaned. *Nein.* Not him.

Elam held the horse's reins in one hand and waved at her, a smile deepening the creases around his mouth. "*Gut morgan*, Naomi. I'm glad I found you." He slowed Prancer, his shiny black buggy horse, to keep pace with her. "I stopped at your house to pick you up, and your mamm told me you had left already. She said you were on your way to the store, but she didn't know about the meeting."

Naomi sucked in her breath. "You told Mamm about it? You had no right to do that."

He pushed back his straw hat. "How was I supposed to know you didn't tell her?"

"Well, I mean, you should have, it's just that…" She sighed. Elam was right. She shouldn't have kept that information from her parents. But when she got home, she would have to see the double disappointment on their faces. "Fine. You weren't at fault. But I didn't ask for a ride."

"I know you didn't, but I thought it might be nice."
She kept walking.
"Naomi."
The clicking of the horse's hooves behind her halted.

Elam's footsteps approached. "Come on. You can't stop talking to me forever."

"*Ja*, I can."

"See, you already spoke three words."

Despite herself, the corners of her mouth turned up. He always did have this way of making her smile, of keeping her from being too serious. That's one of the things she loved about him. *Had loved.* Didn't love anymore. But he did have a point. She stopped. "Fine. You win this time. It would be silly of me to walk when you're going that way."

Once they were both settled in the closed buggy, Elam clicked to the horse, and they trotted off. Several times, she caught him glancing at her from the corner of his eyes. Finally, she had to say something. "What do you keep looking at?"

"Can we agree to be civil to each other? At least while we work on the auction?"

"I'm always polite."

"Glad to hear that." His words were clipped and short. Had she offended him? How, by being cordial?

She didn't have time to mull over the thought as they arrived at the bakery. They slipped around to the back, went up the stairs and knocked on the door. Sylvia answered, a few salt-and-pepper hairs escaping from under her *kapp*. "*Ach*, how *gut* to see both of you. I was just dozing off, so forgive how I look. Let me put the kettle on for some tea."

Even though Elam entered, Naomi stood firm in the doorway. "We're sorry to disturb you. Please, go back to your nap. You must be exhausted."

Sylvia waved her in. "Nonsense. The place is too quiet without Simon. I just sat down with my sewing to give my old bones a rest, and I can't keep my eyes open."

"How is he doing?" Naomi brushed shoulders with Elam as she entered, a shiver racing through her. Once inside, she stood a few feet away from him.

"Grumbling that the hospital meals aren't as good as mine and that the nurses don't let him sleep. In other words, he's much like his old self." A twinkle sparkled in Sylvia's blue eyes. "Another few days there, and then he'll be my problem. Now, Simon had something he wanted me to give the two of you. Sit at the table, and I'll be right back."

She hustled out of the room as Elam and Naomi took their seats, Sylvia's basket of needles and thread on the table, small scissors and a pair of pants beside it. Naomi shifted her feet. "We shouldn't be bothering her."

"She told us to come. We won't stay long, just enough to get Simon's notes. I do have another surprise for you, though." He winked, and her cheeks burned. Why did her insides flutter when he played so coy with her? Daniel had been gone only a little over a year.

Naomi rose, drew an old, stained mug from the cabinet and set about making tea. Even if they wouldn't stay to enjoy it, Sylvia would benefit from a cup.

Before the kettle whistled, Sylvia lumbered in, a large cardboard box in her hands. "Oh dear, I didn't realize how heavy this was." She plunked it on the table, worn from many family and community meals.

Elam stood and peered inside. "What is all this?"

"Everything Simon says you'll need to finish the preparations for the auction. You'll find his contacts for the auction house, the list of donated items and whatever else you might have to have. I don't know exactly the full contents. He always handled every little detail, so you might have quite a job on your hands figuring out what is what and what you need to do."

Naomi brought over the steaming cup of tea. The sweet fragrance of chamomile was homey. Her muscles, tense since Elam had driven up behind her, relaxed. She set the mug in front of Sylvia. "Elam will get it straight. Don't you or Simon worry about a thing. Enjoy your tea, and we'll leave you in peace."

"You've only just come."

"And now we must go. We have Aaron's old wheelchair, the one he used before he got the motorized version, so if your husband needs it, let us know."

"*Denki*. You really are too good to an old woman like me. And you, too, Elam, for doing this."

"I'm grateful to Simon for giving me a chance to get back into the district's good graces."

They said their goodbyes, Elam carried the box out and Naomi started down the driveway so she could get to the grocery store.

"Hey, where are you going?" Elam made his way around the Englisch in their usual long line for baked goods.

"I told you. Mamm needs brown sugar."

"But I'm going to take you to see a surprise. Have you already forgotten?"

In the same way the women ogled the new baby in church, the Englisch watched Elam and Naomi. She squirmed under the intense scrutiny. This is why she didn't really want to speak with the papers. She didn't want to be any more of a spectacle to the Englisch.

With no other choice, she marched to where Elam waited with his buggy. When she got close enough, she hissed at him. "In the future, please refrain from shouting at me in public. Or anytime at all. I have to be on my way. Joseph will wake from his nap and be ready to eat."

"I won't keep you long, I promise. When we're finished, I'll run you to the store and then home. You'll be back sooner than you would have been had you walked everywhere."

Maybe if she gave him what he wanted, she could be rid of him faster.

Probably not.

With a sigh, she climbed into the buggy.

After a short ride from the bakery, Elam reined Prancer to a halt near a tree on the far side of the parking lot in front of the large, rectangular red-and-silver metal pole barn used for auctions. Most of the time, the Englisch used it to sell their produce.

Naomi hadn't cracked a smile since they left the Herschbergers'. And she pulled her frown down farther as they sat in the buggy and stared at the building. What could he do to get her to grin? "What do you think of my surprise?"

"I'm supposed to be surprised?"

"You didn't think I'd bring you here, did you?"

"As far as surprises go, it's about as good as an unplanned root canal."

A hearty chuckle burst from Elam, and even Naomi gave a soft laugh. *Ach*, so much more like it. "Point taken. Next time I surprise you with something, it will be better. I promise."

"Why are we here?"

"Because my mind has been whirring since Simon asked us to finish the plans for the auction. I have so many ideas, but I need your help." He jumped from the buggy.

Naomi climbed down before he could assist her. "There's not much to do. We set up the bakery items over there, the plants and such here, the tools there and everything else inside. Like it's always been done."

"That's fine, as far as it goes, but we have to think bigger and grander if we want to raise more money. Like maybe having one of those shaved ice trucks I've seen at the county fairs. If it's a hot, sunny day, that should bring in an extra boost of cash."

"I'm not sure. Shouldn't we limit our offerings to Amish-produced items? Isn't that why the Englisch come? They can get shaved ice everywhere."

"But it would be a big seller. We have to continue to add new offerings and change things around, or we won't get repeat customers from year to year."

She shook her head and pulled her eyebrows into a deep V. "While it's fine to search for ways to improve the auction and increase proceeds, those who come are looking for a uniquely Amish experience. They wouldn't appreciate seeing a vendor they could find at any county fair. We've always done things the same way, and it's always worked. Have you changed so much you don't remember?"

He huffed. Naomi was the most stubborn woman he'd ever met. Time hadn't changed that. "Can't you see how *gut* this will be for the auction?"

"And slowly, you'll take away everything Amish about it until it's like any other craft fair. I think including a silent auction for those who don't like to bid with others watching is a much better idea."

"And I think I'm going to find out how we go about getting a shaved ice truck."

"Whatever you want to do is fine with me." She waved as if dismissing him. "You have my blessing. Can we go now?"

He deflated a little. "I thought you'd be more excited."

"This is your project, not mine."

"Why won't you help me?"

She faced him, red blooming on her cheeks. "Why not? You're kidding me. You really don't know the answer to that question? Let me tick off the reasons for you. My brother and his permanent disability. Your leaving me. My humiliation in the district when you took off. Isn't that enough?"

He stepped back. "It was an accident, Naomi, nothing more than that. I never set out to harm your brother. Or you." Maybe putting this together with her wasn't the best idea in the world. But like it or not, they were stuck on the project. "I was young and foolish. And scared. And you turned your back to me, refused to even listen to me. But as we work together, you'll see I've grown up. Give me the chance to show you that I'm not the same man who left three years ago." His heart banged in his chest.

She paced in small circles, her focus on the gravel at her feet. "I'm sorry to have gotten so angry with you." She kicked at a stone with her bare feet.

"Can we put aside our differences long enough to make this work? Neither of us wants to go to Sylvia or Simon and tell them we can't do it."

"You're right."

"Does that mean you'll partner with me?"

"Partner, no. Give you a helping hand from time to time, fine. I give up, because you'll pester me until I agree."

The way she said it was almost like he was a bully. "I don't want to pressure you."

"I said fine. I'll make sure the quilts come in and get organized, along with the donated items. And arrange the bakery sales. What else?"

He sighed. One major obstacle overcame. They spent the next few minutes reviewing a list of items that needed to be taken care of, one he'd written up last night while the gas lamp hissed overhead. With the box from Simon, the list was sure to grow.

"Is that enough for now? I don't want to overwhelm you since you have Joseph to look after and your job."

"That will be *gut*. I'll let you know when I have this finished."

"One more thing. The papers. You never answered me if you would go to the press and share Joseph's story with them. It's sure to bring in many more tourists. The story is moving and should compel the Englisch to come and buy our products. Raise more money."

Naomi rubbed her prayer *kapp* string between her fingers. "There are so many needs in the district right now. Like Simon. He'll need help, too. And your daed."

"All the more reason to sell as much as we can. What harm will it do? We'll tell them no pictures. No Englischer will even know it's you."

"They won't?"

"If the paper wants the story, they'll have to publish it anonymously."

"They'd do that?"

"I believe they would."

She scrunched up her forehead. "Can I give you my answer in a few days? I have to think."

"Sure. But don't wait too long. We'll need time for the interviews and for people to make their plans." A streak of lightning and a quick crack of thunder brought Elam's attention to the sky. When had the thick, black clouds rolled in? A gust of wind pulled his straw hat from his head and sent it skittering across the parking lot. He gave chase to it, several more bolts of lightning brightening the now-dusky afternoon.

He and Naomi raced for the buggy. She fell behind.

"Ah." Her cry cut through the rolling thunder. "Elam."

He turned. She'd fallen, her bare shin scratched and bloodied. The first fat drops of water fell to the gravel. He hurried and helped her up. While they ran, he kept a hold of her, the rain pelting them. They finally reached the buggy, the fierce wind buffeting it, and it swayed side to side. Now soaked to the skin, they climbed aboard.

Naomi shivered, and he pulled her to himself. They used to be close like this.

A streak of light. A deafening crack. The ground shook.

Kaboom.

Naomi shrieked.

The tree they were next to split in half and crashed to the earth, missing the buggy to each side.

She trembled in his arms.

He held her close and whispered against her cheek. "Hush now. We're safe."

But would his heart ever be?

Chapter Five

Only the clinking of silverware on the dinner plates broke the silence around the Yoders' large farmhouse table. Mamm loaded Daed's plate with another heap of creamed corn. He grasped his fork with his left hand, his right one paralyzed by the stroke, and tried to shovel the vegetable into his mouth.

Much of it ended up back on the plate or in his lap. He grunted, the right of his mouth downturned. "Can't even eat properly." He thunked his fork onto his dish, pushed away from the table and reached for his walker.

Elam jumped to his feet and grasped his daed by the elbow to help him to stand.

Daed shook him off. "I don't need your help. I'm capable of getting out of a chair."

"I just thought it would be easier…"

"Easier. That's what you always want, isn't it?"

Elam scrunched his eyebrows as he stared at his daed. When had the lines formed around his eyes? When had he become an old man? "I don't understand what you mean."

"You run away when times get hard. Now you're back, but for how long? A week? A month? A year?"

"You know I'm back to stay. I came to give you a hand until Isaac returns, but I'm not leaving the district again."

"I don't need your help. We could manage just fine."

Mamm shook her head as she carried the dishes to the sink. "*Nein*, we weren't managing at all until Elam came home. How would the crops get planted if not for him? Don't be a foolish old man. We need his help." She turned and smiled over her shoulder. "He came on his own, volunteered to do this. Let's not turn him away."

Elam sucked in a breath. Is that what Daed wanted to do? Open the door and give him a shove outside?

"Nobody said anything about that." The muscles on the good side of Daed's face strained as he pulled himself to a standing position. "Just didn't ask for his help." He shuffled out of the kitchen, the back door slamming behind him.

Mamm returned to the table with a dishrag in one hand. She patted Elam's cheek. "Don't be so glum. I hate to see you sad like this." Many laugh lines crinkled around her eyes and mouth. Over the years, she had plenty to be happy about. And plenty of heartaches to cry over.

"He barely tolerates my being here. Even across the table from me at dinner, he glances my way only when necessary. When Isaac returns, he'll be happier."

"That's not true. He loves you."

"You can't convince me."

"He's afraid he's going to lose you again. He couldn't stand that, you know."

"Why does no one believe that I'm staying put?"

"Give them time to see you're sincere. When troubles come and you face them head-on, then they'll trust you."

"And can they forgive me? Forget the past?"

Her face softened, and she stared at a spot behind him. "That I cannot answer for anyone else."

When she set to washing the dishes, he wandered outside, the early spring evening cool. Daed wasn't on the porch. Where could he have gone? In the short time Elam had been home, he'd built a ramp so Daed didn't have to negotiate the stairs. Mamm had thanked him. Daed had not.

A light shone from one of the barn's windows, the one that held Daed's office. Elam walked down the porch steps, across the dusty yard and into the barn, the odors of hay and cows as familiar to him as the smells of Mamm's apple pie. The animals munched their dinner, lowing songs to each other. On a bale in the far corner, the new litter of kittens mewed.

He entered the office through the open door, Daed at the desk, scratching in the account books with a pencil, his lips drawn tight as he struggled to use his left hand.

"Do you have a few minutes?"

Daed grunted, not even glancing at Elam. "What is it you want?" Even with therapy, his speech remained slurred.

"I'll do those figures for you later."

"I'm capable. There may be much I can't do anymore, but writing is one thing I can. And figuring numbers."

"I just thought…" This was getting off to a terrible beginning. Best to start over. "What do you have against me?"

"Nothing. You're my son. But sometimes, I wonder.

You always were…" Daed squeezed his eyes shut and furrowed his brow. Sometimes he couldn't recall the word he needed.

"Independent."

"*Ja*, and stubborn and strong-willed. What are you doing here? Why did you truly come back?"

Elam's windpipe tightened. "I missed this place and the people. And it was time to stop running, to face up to what I did. I didn't realize that making amends would be so hard."

"You can't walk back into people's lives and expect them to let go of what happened like that. You—" Daed pointed straight at Elam's heart "—have to prove yourself."

Isn't that what he'd been doing? How long was it going to take? So far, he hadn't made headway with anyone. Including Naomi.

"Time and hard work. That's what you need."

Had Daed heard his thoughts? Elam puffed out a breath, then spun on his heel and left the office and the barn. He stood in the farmyard and stared at the multitude of stars in the sky. In the city lights of Madison, they got lost. Here, they were almost close enough to touch.

In order to show the people of the district he wasn't the man who left, he would have to start with Aaron's family. Already, he had upset Naomi. He shouldn't have dismissed her objections to the shaved ice the way he had. If he admitted so to her, perhaps they could work together better.

Aaron sat in a wheelchair for the rest of his life. If that's the amount of time it took for Elam to make amends for the accident, then that's how long he would work for it.

* * *

Naomi pressed her nose against the window of Frank's van. Joseph was peacefully sleeping in the car seat beside her. In her hand, she held the information for his surgery. The one he needed sooner rather than later, according to the information the doctor had just shared. Naomi leaned over her son and whispered. "Dear God, protect my baby. Make him strong. Make me strong. Help us get through this."

Elam was correct. This year, there were many medical needs in the district. Much as she hated to admit it, she had to work with him on the auction. He was going to bring Simon's box and meet her at her home to go through it. She would have to be as nice to him as possible. They would get nothing done if they argued.

She rubbed her upper arms. The way Elam held her during the storm warmed her through and through. For a brief glimmer of time, she was safe. Cared for. He watched out for her.

But Aaron would always be a reminder of what happened that night Elam betrayed her trust. He'd broken her brother's body and her heart. She wouldn't let Elam back into her life. No matter that Simon threw them together to organize the auction.

Maybe Elam did have a point about the papers, though. Perhaps if she gave them an interview, people would be interested and would come from all over the state to the auction.

Her palms dampened at the thought of having to talk to the reporters. What would they ask her? What would she say?

Just as Frank turned into the driveway, Elam pulled

his buggy in behind them. She unbuckled Joseph's car seat and stepped out with a wave to Frank.

Elam came toward them and tickled Joseph's tummy, and the now-awake *bobbeli* squealed. "I hope the doctor had nothing but good things to say."

"She said it was time to schedule the surgery. He's going to have it in July."

"That's *gut*, isn't it?" He grasped one of his black suspenders.

"*Ja*, I suppose." So why did her head ache?

He touched her arm. She stepped away. "Please, don't."

Nein, she couldn't rely on him for help and comfort. But her chest ached. Some nights, alone in her room, she cried herself to sleep. How much lonelier it would be when she moved to the *dawdi haus*. "Come in. We can start sorting through the papers."

He grabbed the box from his buggy and followed her into the house. Mamm took Joseph and Naomi and Elam settled at the table, the large box between them.

He cleared his throat, and she gazed at him. An uneven red flush mottled his neck. "First of all, I want to apologize for the other day."

"You…you do?" Why did her stomach dip the way it did?

"*Ja*. I shouldn't have dismissed your ideas the way I did. That was inconsiderate of me. You make a *gut* point. This is an Amish auction, not an Englisch one. All the other items we offer come from our communities. We should forget the shaved ice truck."

"Having a hard time finding a vendor?" She flashed him a playful grin.

The red creeped into his cheeks. "Well, now that

you mention it." He chuckled, his coloring returning to normal. "I'm not incapable of seeing reason. You were right. I was wrong."

Warmth seeped into her chest. The old Elam rarely admitted his mistakes. "*Denki* for your apology. Offering a cold treat on a warm day was a nice thought. Is there an alternative to the shaved ice?"

Elam stroked his clean-shaven cheek. "Your family makes the best ice cream I've ever had. Just vanilla, but there is a secret ingredient in there, say not?"

"There is, but you want to make ice cream? How are we going have enough for all those people?"

"That's a good question."

"Multiple machines hooked up to generators?"

He grinned, and her arms broke out in gooseflesh. She focused on the pencil in her hand.

"That's a great idea. Maybe someone in the district has a large-capacity churn."

"I'll ask around at the church service next week."

For a long while, they sorted through the papers, Naomi jotting notes on a yellow legal pad, filling several pages with people they needed to contact, payments that had to be made and ideas they had.

She could almost close her eyes and imagine that the past three years hadn't happened. Almost. His deep voice washed over her and lulled her.

Elam's words broke into her into thoughts. "I'd like to make some furniture pieces for the auction. I was hoping your daed would let me use his equipment. I have an Englisch friend who has a workshop in his garage, but I want to construct them the true Amish way."

If Daed allowed Elam to work here, she would run into him every day, just as she had when he was Daed's employee. Did her hands tremble because of dread or excitement? She had to say something to him, but what? Surely not that she was happy he'd be so close. "Well, I hope the meeting with him goes well. I think we've reached the end of the stuff in the box. I should feed Joseph before he fusses."

Elam rose and filed the papers away. "And what about the newspapers?"

She locked her knees to keep them from knocking together. "Go ahead and contact the reporters. I'll speak to them."

"I have the letters ready to put in the mail. Would you like to read them first?"

"*Nein.* Just send them." Before she changed her mind.

Chapter Six

The tang of pine and the sweetness of maple permeated the shed where Leroy Bontrager ran his woodworking shop. As Elam made his way through the building, he glided his hand down a length of quarter-sawn oak that had been sanded to a mirror-like smoothness. The whir of the gas-powered table saw welcomed him home. *Ja*, this is where he belonged. Construction, as he'd done while away, was building. Woodworking was creating.

"Hello, Leroy, are you here?"

Naomi's father entered the main room from the back. He wiped dark stain from his fingers onto what must have been an old shirt. The heady odor of varnish hung about him. "Elam. Why are you here?"

Not the start he'd been hoping for given that first meeting between them. Maybe this wasn't the best idea. "You're hard at work, as always." Several kitchen chairs sat in a row along one wall, as did a couple of book-shelves and a large dining room table with well-turned legs.

"Of course."

"Daed told me you hired Solomon Mast to help after I left."

"Aaron gives me a hand as much as he can, doing a few things from his chair. But I can't run this place with the two of us. Solomon is a *gut* man, but still learning. He puts in a hard day's work, and I appreciate that. But he doesn't have the eye, the insight that you..."

Had Leroy been about to compliment him? "Naomi and I have been working on the auction. She said they've set the date for Joseph's surgery."

"That's *gut*." Leroy dug in his pants pocket, but didn't produce anything. "Then the boy can grow strong. I can teach him to sweep the floors and get me my tools. Maybe to do a little staining."

"That was always my least favorite part of the job." Elam chuckled.

Leroy didn't. "I have an order due tomorrow that I have to finish. What can I help you with? You didn't come here to make idle chatter."

Elam swallowed hard. "You're right. I don't want to take up your valuable time. I'd like to build some things for the auction for Joseph's—" Elam drew in a deep breath "—and Aaron's medical expenses. Could I use your equipment? Your saw and sander and things like that. In off-hours, of course."

Leroy stroked his graying beard, his eyes narrow.

"When I ran away, I left you in the lurch, down an employee. And I caused your family a great deal of suffering and pain. What I did was foolish. Stupid. I can't go back and undo my mistakes, but I would like to move forward. To somehow make up for the accident. And for breaking Naomi's heart."

Leroy took a seat in a rocking chair, one with simple rungs along the back. As he examined Elam, he rocked.

Elam's throat closed so he had a difficult time drawing a breath. "Please, I'm asking for your forgiveness."

Leroy shot to his feet, the chair still moving behind him. "Forgiveness? That's what you want? The Amish way is to forgive, and so I have. *Ja*, right away, in my heart, I forgave you. But forgetting. That is another matter. Every time I help my son in and out of his chair, I remember. Every time his mother massages his useless legs, we remember. Every time I see the sadness in my daughter's eyes, I remember."

Elam hunched his shoulders and rubbed his temples. "For a long time, I avoided my problems, thought they would disappear if I wasn't around to see what I had done. Life doesn't work that way, though. The accident, Aaron's condition, my promise to Naomi, all those weighed on my mind every day. I'm glad you forgave me. And I understand that you can't forget. But if we could only move forward. Repair the damage between us."

Leroy fisted his right hand and pounded on the table. "Repair the damage? Can you fix my son's broken back so he can walk again? Not even the Englisch doctors with all their fancy medicines and expensive therapy can do that. He will never take another step again. Never. And what about his chances of marrying and having a family? Do you realize you've robbed him of that, too?"

Elam staggered back three steps. His chest burned. "What can I do to make it up to you?" The whispered question reverberated in the room.

"There is nothing."

"Daed, I need to flip that end table so I can finish staining it." Aaron rolled in from the back room.

Leroy narrowed his eyes, his jaw tight. "And he can't do it because of you."

A weight crushed Elam's chest. "I know." He turned to Aaron and strode toward the back. "Let me help you."

The heaviness of Leroy's stare pressed on Elam's shoulders, but he didn't flinch. Instead, he followed Aaron to the staining room. "Can I ever make it up to you?"

Aaron pointed to the half-stained table. "I don't hate you."

"Glad to hear that." Still, the young man didn't even glance in Elam's direction. "I shouldn't have done what I did. It's my carelessness that put you here. That stole your life from you." He struggled to draw a breath.

"This is my life now. I have to accept it. Nothing will change it."

In other words, nothing Elam could ever do would be enough. He stared at Aaron's atrophied legs. His stomach clenched. He moved the table.

"You're a talented young man. I've seen your work. Your injuries shouldn't prevent you from doing what you love." He shifted his weight from one foot to the other. "I'll be going. See you later."

When he reached the doorway, he turned. Aaron reached for a can of varnish on a shelf just out of his grasp. He pushed himself up, but it wasn't quite enough.

He couldn't manage a simple task like taking something from a shelf. Elam returned to Aaron and handed him the can.

"Denki."

"Anytime. And I mean that. If there is ever anything

I can do…" But what would there be? He left the shop and made his way back to the buggy.

The home's screen door slammed, and Naomi descended the porch steps toward him. "How did it go? Is Daed going to let you use the equipment?"

Elam shrugged. "I didn't stick around long enough for him to answer. He says he's forgiven me but can't forget."

"Forgetting is impossible."

Could he ever change their minds?

The next afternoon, Naomi tiptoed down the stairs, then held her breath as one she stepped on creaked. After twenty minutes of rocking, her very tired *bobbeli* had finally given up the fight and drifted to sleep. A few seconds passed. No sound from the bedroom she shared with her son. *Gut*, she hadn't wakened him.

The kitchen sat quiet. Mamm had mentioned working in the garden this morning. From the counter, Naomi drew the wooden box that held all of Mamm's recipes printed on three-by-five cards in her own neat script. Many bore stains from the ingredients used in them. With twenty-five years of cooking and baking to her credit, Mamm didn't often use the recipes anymore.

Where was that one for ice cream? Naomi should have memorized it herself, but couldn't remember how much of the special vanilla it called for, the secret ingredient Elam mentioned when they decided to make this instead of the shaved ice.

The back door clicked open and shut, and Naomi peered up as Mamm entered the kitchen, wiping her dirty hands on her apron. "What do you need from there?"

"The recipe for ice cream. I can't find it in my own box, and I'm not seeing it in yours."

"It should be in there."

Naomi rifled through the cards but still couldn't locate it. "How much vanilla?"

"Two tablespoons, one of each flavor."

"*Denki.* Now I have to multiply that by how many ever batches we're going to make for the auction before I run to the store to make sure Marlin can order it and get it here in time. And everything else we need."

Mamm pumped water at the sink and scrubbed her hands. "Daed and I have been talking about this auction and your working with Elam. We don't like it. Remember how you felt when he walked away? He hurt your brother and broke your heart. It's not *gut* for you to spend so much time with him."

A lifetime had passed since she had harbored any feelings for Elam. *Ja*, she had been devastated when he'd left, not willing to stay and face what he'd done, not willing to fight for a future with her. But now she was older and wiser. This time, she would guard her heart better and wouldn't lose herself to his charm.

"Naomi, have you heard anything I've said?"

Mamm's question snapped Naomi to the present. "Don't worry. I'm not the same naive seventeen-year-old I was when I fell in love with him. Joseph is my main priority. And the only reason I'm working on this auction. Simon volunteered us without asking, and I couldn't turn him down."

"Daed doesn't want to forbid you." Mamm futzed with untying her apron, her back to Naomi.

She couldn't have heard right. "Forbid me? From what?"

"Seeing that boy."

"He's hardly a child. Nor am I."

"Just because you're an adult doesn't mean you can sass your mamm. You're under your daed's protection once more. Elam's actions tore him apart. He loves you so much and doesn't want to see that kind of pain in your eyes again."

"They're making progress on the *dawdi haus*. Soon, I'll be back on my own." Maybe having her freedom again wouldn't be such a bad thing.

"But you still need someone to watch out for you." Mamm turned to face her, faint lines fanning from the corners of her eyes. The cares of the world etched those wrinkles.

Naomi scraped the chair back and stood, her chest and cheeks warm. She bit back words stronger than her earlier ones. Working hard to keep from stomping across the kitchen, she marched outside. The screen door banged behind her, maybe a little too hard.

Life wasn't fair. It wasn't fair that Elam left her. That Daniel died. That her parents treated her like she was still a child.

Out in the farmyard, she kicked at a stone on the gravel driveway. Her breath came in small gasps. Sure, working with Elam on the auction hadn't been her idea, but she had made a commitment. And despite her parents trying to tell her what to do, she had to see this through.

Chapter Seven

Naomi pushed Daed's favorite brown chair into the first-floor bedroom and then shoved the couch along the living room wall, as out of the way as possible. She had fed Joseph, but he hadn't nursed long before he fell asleep. And he had struggled to get the milk into his tummy, breathing hard, sweating.

If only the surgery day would hurry and get here. But then again, if it would just take its time in coming. She could lose her son.

She shook the thoughts away. The women would be here in a few minutes to finish this quilt for the auction. Every spare second she had between the bakery and Joseph, Naomi worked on the list of items that needed to be done. She had sketched out where everything would take place and was compiling the list of donations. Many nights during the past week, she had worked until Daed turned out the lamp over the table.

The roasted scent of coffee filled the kitchen as she entered. Mamm drizzled a glaze on the coffee cake while Laura pulled a batch of oatmeal cookies from the oven. Naomi swiped one and popped it in her mouth.

"I'll get Sam to help me set up the form, but is there anything else you need?"

Mamm motioned to the cabinet next to the sink. "You could set out the plates and silverware. Laura, when you finish there, go find your brother. I saw him heading to the barn not too long ago, probably to pester those poor cats."

Naomi got busy with the chore Mamm gave her. "I'm sorry about storming out the other day."

"I'm sorry about what I said. Sometimes it's easy for me to forget you're a grown woman." Mamm hugged her. "I know none of this has been easy, especially with Elam back. We have to trust that you know what you're doing. Your daed and I can't forbid you from doing what you feel is right."

"*Denki*, Mamm. You do have so much wisdom to impart, and I need to keep that in mind."

Mamm drew away and untied her apron. "Well, now, we'd best finish getting ready."

Before long, feminine voices and laughter floated from outside as the quilting party arrived in several buggy loads. Sam came in among them and set up the frame while the girls and ladies enjoyed a cup of coffee. Before they even sat to work, Joseph cried.

Naomi hurried to his room. She picked him up, his few curls damp with sweat. "Oh, my *bobbeli*, don't tell me you're getting another fever." He nestled against her neck and cried all the harder.

His cheek was cool against her skin. "What is it, little one? So unhappy you are." She walked the small room with him, but it took a good five minutes to quiet him. "And now you're awake, so I don't know how much quilting I'll get done."

She brought him from the bedroom, patting his back to stop his wailing. "Look who wanted to join the party."

The women rushed to him, fawning over her *bobbeli*, who gave a contented yawn. Were his lips bluer than usual? Was his heart condition getting worse? *Nein*, it must just be the blue from her dress. Sylvia took him from her arms and cooed over him.

Talk swirled around Naomi. "Have you heard how Leah Byler is getting along with her twins? *Ach*, I can't imagine having two toddlers and two infants at the same time."

"What are you planning for your garden this year?"

"Simon came home from the rehab center yesterday, say not? Must be good to have him home."

"I've heard tell that you and Elam were seen riding in a buggy together the other day."

At that statement Naomi stood up straight. "He took me to the store so we could order what we needed for the ice cream."

"So it's true, that the two of you are working together." Bethel Byler shook her head as her bony fingers pulled her needle through the fabric.

Naomi gulped as each of the fifteen ladies stared at her. "Simon Herschberger asked us to help. I couldn't turn him down."

Fourteen pairs of lips tightened. All but Sylvia's. "Naomi has been so sweet to our family since Simon's accident. She checks in every time she works at the bakery and swept my floor the other day when my back was giving me trouble. In all my life, I've never run into such a helpful young woman."

Maybe a hole would open in the wood floor and

Naomi could fall through to the cold, spider-filled basement. Anything would be preferable to this. "Really, it's nothing. I'm glad I can do it."

"I, for one, don't know how you can stand to be around Elam so much," Eva Miller said as she bent over her work, the set of her jaw firm.

"It's not like I volunteered or—"

Joseph's wails saved her from having to defend herself. She grabbed her *bobbeli* from Sylvia and swung around to hide in the kitchen.

Too bad Elam stood in the doorway, blocking her path.

Fourteen gasps sounded behind her. And her traitorous heart missed a beat.

"Hello, Naomi." Elam's voice was low and tight.

She needed that hole in the floor more than ever. Surely he had heard some of what the women had said.

"Hello there, young man." Elam rubbed the top of Joseph's head, and the child calmed.

She backed up a few steps to put some distance between them. "Joseph's fussy, and I have to—"

"He doesn't look the least bit upset to me." Elam waved a piece of paper in front of Naomi. "I came to bring you some news."

Joseph had to pick that moment to gaze at Elam and break into a toothless grin. Naomi sighed. Just when this day couldn't get any worse. "What is it?"

"The Eau Claire and Madison papers wrote back to us. They both want to interview you. And the best of all? The Milwaukee paper wants to do a feature. A big spread in their Sunday edition."

The women behind Naomi murmured. "What is he talking about? Newspapers? Big-city *Englisch* ones?"

Naomi's mouth went dry. How could he have blurted out the news in front of everyone? "I… You shouldn't… I mean…"

She clung to her child and fled up the stairs.

Elam stood in the living room's doorway, gazing at the staircase where Naomi disappeared. Why had she run away? Why wasn't she willing to listen?

A gaggle of women, all seated around a quilting frame, stared at him as if he'd grown a mane and a tail. "I… I…" Speechless wasn't his usual condition.

One of the older women, Ruth Zook, the bishop's nosy spinster sister, scraped her chair back and marched to stand in front of him. She wagged her arthritic finger. "Just who do you think you are, barging in here, upsetting that poor, sweet girl? Hasn't she been through enough? And what is this about newspaper interviews?" She shook her head. "Being away hasn't taught you anything. You always were one to charge ahead and do whatever you wanted without thinking about it."

He wiped his damp hands on his broadcloth pants. "She agreed to speak to the reporters to bring more buyers to the auction—the one that's raising money for her son's surgery. And we plan to do it anonymously. No one will know who she is, just what the funds that the auction generates is used for."

Naomi's mamm shook her head. "I don't want to see my daughter hurt more than she already is. Isn't it enough that she's working long hours to help you?"

Sylvia stood and sidled next to Ruth. "Simon asked Elam and Naomi to finish organizing the auction for him. He trusted Elam with this job, so let him do what Simon has asked, whatever he feels is best."

Ruth puffed out her cheeks, expelled the air and whirled to take her seat.

"*Denki*, Sylvia." Without her and Simon, he wouldn't have anyone in the district on his side. He owed them a great debt. Elam lowered his voice. "I don't know what I did to send Naomi running like that." He rubbed the ache in his chest.

"She is a young mother with a very sick *bobbeli*. That's emotional. Be kind and supportive. She needs you more than she realizes she does." Sylvia patted his upper arm before returning to the rest of the women.

Elam's head swam as he left the house. Naomi should have been happy about the newspaper interviews. They had talked about it. She'd agreed to speak to the reporters. Had she changed her mind?

He kicked at a larger stone in the gravel driveway on the way to his buggy. He'd have to talk to her later, when the rest of the women had gone home.

Elam hitched Prancer and gave a half-hearted cluck to the horse, who then plodded down the street. He didn't go directly home, but meandered the quiet country roads. Gray clouds hung low in the sky, and a chilly wind buffeted the bravest of the daffodils.

When he paid attention to where he was, he found himself down a dirt road and at Miller's pond. He'd come here every chance he'd gotten as a boy, a fishing pole in one hand and a Styrofoam container of worms in the other. Large trees surrounded the small lake, a few weeping willows dipping their branches into the pond. A foggy mist rose from the water's surface. A large, smooth rock sat at the pond's shore. The kissing rock, most people called it. Many young Amish had their first kisses here, stolen pecks on the cheek as early teens.

He had been among them. Naomi had been the one and only girl he'd ever loved. He doubled over and rubbed his head under his hat. Young, cocky, a braggart, he thought nothing bad would ever touch him. Though he dabbled in the Englisch world by buying a truck and a cell phone, he intended to join the church, marry Naomi and settle into the way of life his ancestors had lived for hundreds of years.

And then that one night happened.

Nothing would ever be the same. Had he been a fool to come home? A fool to believe the district would welcome him with open arms? *Ja*, probably. What was he doing here other than torturing himself and everyone around him?

No doubt, many in the district believed it would be better if he left, if he went his own way. Isaac would be home soon.

The auction. He had promised Simon he would organize it. And so he would.

But after that…

The temptation to run pulled at him. But if he left, he would never have the chance to redeem himself. Or to gain Naomi's forgiveness.

What was the right thing to do?

Chapter Eight

As Naomi stood at the kitchen window washing the lunch dishes, Mamm wrapped her in an embrace. She sank into Mamm's arms.

"You're exhausted. I heard Joseph crying several times last night."

Naomi sighed. "He's hungry, but he isn't feeding well. He struggles so for breath." Her voice caught. "He needs that surgery. Soon."

"Stay home from the bakery tomorrow and rest. You don't need to be on your feet for so long after walking the floor all night with a sick child. Sylvia will understand."

"Sylvia has her hands full with Simon home. And now that the weather is nice, the busy season is starting. She can't spare me."

"And here comes another one of your obligations. After what happened the other day, you'd think he'd be too ashamed of himself to show up here."

Naomi peered out the window. Elam unhitched Prancer, led him to graze in the field and made his way to the house. That's right, they had to sign the contracts with the auction house and order the tents they would need. But after the reaction of the women to her going to the papers, her midsection clenched. She smoothed down her apron and cringed at the streaks of raspberry jam down the front of it from the sandwiches she had made. Well, she didn't have time to change, so it would have to do. She hustled to the door and let in Elam.

He lugged a large box and plunked it on the kitchen table. When she crossed her arms in front of her, he sobered. "First things first. I want to apologize for the other day, when I blurted our news in front of the other women. I know what a private person you are, and I shouldn't have done that. The letter from the Milwaukee paper had me excited, and I didn't contain it well. Can you forgive me?"

"You're always asking for forgiveness."

"Will you give it?"

"It doesn't matter. I'm not going to speak to them."

He creased his forehead. "But we talked about this. For your son, Naomi, and your brother, and all the others, you have to tell your story. I promise to be with you every step of the way. They won't use your name or anything. No one will know it's you. One article in each newspaper, and it will be over. Think about your family."

"That's all I think about. My son is very, very sick. He's not sleeping well. He needs that surgery." She clenched her jaw.

"Even more reason to go through with the interviews. I have the meetings set up. To make it easy for you, everyone is coming in a single day."

Outside the window, a cardinal flitted from the maple tree nearest the house to the big oak along the road. If only she could fly away like that bird. "Fine. One time. Nothing after that."

"And Naomi?" He touched her arm. "Can we move on from this misunderstanding? At least enough to work together?" His voice held a note of pleading.

What choice did they have? Simon expected their help. If they didn't do it, who would? "If you will promise me one more thing."

"What's that?"

"Think before you speak."

"It's never been one of my strong suits but something I'm working on." He tipped his head and gave her a lopsided smile.

At his boyish expression, she almost laughed. Almost. Instead, she sat on the bench at the table, and he joined her.

"What is all this? I expected a folder, not so many papers."

With a shrug, he pulled a folder from the top of the box. "This is what we need for now. Later on, we'll get to what the rest of the box contains. Here's the contract for the auctioneer. Read it over and let me know if you see any problems."

She rubbed her gritty eyes, but the words blurred on the page. And her brain couldn't make sense of the legal wording. After only a minute or so, she handed the papers to Elam. "This is nothing but gibberish to me. If you think it's fine, go ahead and sign it."

"Simon told me it is the same as last year, so I think we'll be okay."

All of the sudden, the world spun, and Naomi grabbed the table to keep from falling over.

Elam dropped the papers. "What's the matter? Is something wrong?"

Nausea accompanied the bout of dizziness. "I don't feel well."

"Let me get you a glass of water." He jumped to his feet and returned in short order. "Here, this should help."

She sipped the cool drink. *"Denki."*

He gathered the papers. "We can finish the rest of this another day. You're quite pale. Maybe you should lie down."

"Nein, I'm fine. We can finish."

"Are you sure? I don't want you to overdo it."

She motioned for him to return to his seat. As he brushed against her on the bench, her arm tingled. He slid away, putting some distance between them, cleared his throat and rummaged in the box. Was he uncomfortable? Did these same feelings that coursed through her make him uneasy, too?

Her mind whirled. "You know what, let's forget about the auction today. I'm too tired to be of much help."

"Then I should leave you to rest."

Nein, for whatever reason, she didn't want him to leave. "I have to feed Joseph in a little while, and then he'll nap, so I can sleep then. There's something I want to show you first."

"Are you sure? I caught your mamm's eye as I came in. She's none too happy about my being here. If I don't let you rest, I'll irritate her even more."

"I'm a grown woman. If I want to show you something before I lie down, then I'll show you something."

Was this what a year of widowhood did to her? Made her stand up for herself?

Elam slapped his thighs. "Alright, then, what is it you want to share with me?"

"Come on." She stood and led the way to the door between the main home and the *dawdi haus*, peering over her shoulder to speak to Elam, still not understanding the pull to show him this. Maybe to prove to him she had put the past, including him, behind her and was moving forward. Without him. "Since Grossmammi died two years ago, it's been empty. But it's the perfect solution for me. I can be close to my parents yet live my own life with Joseph."

"Do you really want to be alone?"

The answer was *nein*. She didn't want to live by herself. Then again, she had been a married woman, had run her own home, and she missed that part of her life. "I can't rely on them forever. That's not their job." She turned the doorknob and entered.

The stale odor of cooking oil still hung in the air. There, in the corner of the living room, Grossdaadi had relaxed in his olive-green armchair every evening, the sweet smoke from his pipe curling around his face. And over there, where the kitchen table had once been, Grossmammi had served chicken soup every Saturday evening, the warmth of it filling Naomi's belly.

"Daed has torn out the cabinets. The boxes sagged, and the doors didn't hang right anymore. So many stains colored the ceramic-glazed sink that, unless you knew it had been white at one time, you wouldn't be able to tell."

"A nice, new kitchen will be *gut*." Elam rubbed his flat stomach. "Will you make me a blackberry tart once you move in?"

The reference flooded her brain with memories. "Like we had at Miller's pond the summer before we were supposed to get married?"

"*Ja.* The best I've ever had. Better than my mamm's, though I'd never tell her so."

Naomi chuckled. "The wind blew so hard that day, it knocked your hat off more than once."

"Glad I'm a fast runner, or I would have gone home hatless. What a scandal that would have caused."

"Or you might have had to go for a swim to retrieve it."

"And then I kissed you." Elam leaned closer.

She bent toward him. His lips had tasted like blackberries that day, tart and sweet at the same time. What innocent times those were, when the world was nothing but *wunderbaar.*

Elam pulled her close, so close his breath tickled her neck and shivers coursed up and down her spine. She drew in a deep breath.

And then he backed away. "I'm... I'm sorry. I didn't mean to..." His face reddened until it resembled a ripe tomato.

Her stomach flipped and dipped and did a little dance. He'd been about to kiss her. And she would have let him. He was the one who broke it off. Why?

Never mind the reasons. Kissing him would have been a terrible mistake. She grabbed at her skirt and continued the tour. "The wood floors need to be sanded and stained. In the hall, Grossmammi wore the floorboards almost through as she paced during those long nights while cancer consumed Grossdaadi's body. Once a fresh coat of paint graces the walls, I'll be ready to move in. And start life on my own."

"Why did you show me this?"

"I... Because I remember sitting in the kitchen with you and Grossmammi when you worked for Daed. She always made molasses cookies because they were your favorites. I thought you might like to see the changes."

"Is that really the reason?"

She gestured wide, taking in the entire space. "Because this is going to be my life."

He nodded. "I think I understand." He backed up a step. "Let me know when it's time to install the cabinets. I'd like to help."

"You don't have to." Did she want him here, this close, even for a few days?

"Please, let me do it."

"We'll see when the time comes. I'm sure Daed already has men lined up to lend him a hand." After a last, sweeping gaze, she turned for the porch, clicking the door shut behind her.

"One more thing before I go. There's something in the box I want to show you."

They returned to the kitchen, standing opposite each other, the table between them. The distance she needed to keep herself from becoming overrun with her feelings for him.

He grabbed a plastic grocery bag from the box and pulled out a package wrapped in brown paper. "With Joseph's surgery coming up and all that has happened to you in the past few years, and with how I've messed up everything, I wanted to do something special for you."

Her heart fluttered, but she couldn't decipher what caused the irregular beat. "You didn't need to. I wish you wouldn't have."

"I wanted to." He held out the gift, maybe two feet wide by two feet long and six inches deep.

She unwrapped the paper. Inside was a beautiful wood box. He had dovetailed the corners and stained it a soft golden oak.

Naomi pushed it toward him. "I can't accept it."

Elam's green eyes lost a bit of their luster. "Of course you can. I want you to have it. Things will come up in your life, precious times you're going to want to remember. Mamm tells me children grow so fast. You can put papers in there, maybe little drawings that Joseph will make, or the lock of hair from his first haircut. His first pair of shoes."

She relaxed her shoulders and took it from him. "You did a *gut* job on it."

"*Denki.* My friend Chase let me use his tools. I wanted it to be special for you."

She blinked away the tears that gathered in the corners of her eyes. Why did he get to her like this? He had done a beautiful job. The craftsmanship was superb. He'd been so thoughtful.

"*Denki.* I'll treasure it."

He rubbed her cheek, and her knees went soft. *Nein, nein.* She couldn't allow herself to fall in love with him again.

A light mist obscured the scene outside the van's windows as Frank drove Elam and Naomi to town to order the auction flyers. Yesterday, they had almost kissed, and they shared a tender moment. But he steeled his heart, feelings washing over him. He hadn't quite forgiven her for turning her back on him. And she hadn't forgiven him for leaving. And she never truly might—which meant they had no future together.

Naomi stared out the other window, not saying much.

When they paused at a stop sign, Frank turned. "One more passenger to pick up before we get going. Solomon Mast called last night needing a ride. Something about going to the hardware store for a whetstone to sharpen his lawn mower blades."

Elam choked back the huff that rose from his chest. So far since his return, his childhood friend had avoided him, walking away at church gatherings. Now they would have to share the over twenty-minute ride. Before Elam knew it, Frank pulled into the Masts' driveway, and Solomon climbed into the seat Naomi had vacated when she moved to the third row.

"Gut morgan." Solomon directed his words to Naomi, giving Elam a brief nod and nothing more.

Elam swallowed hard. "Hello, Solomon."

His once-friend stared straight ahead.

"With the rain we've been having, the grass grows fast, say not?"

And that's what Solomon did. Said nothing.

Naomi leaned forward and whispered in Solomon's ear. He turned to Elam. *"Wie bischt du?"*

"I'm doing fine, *denki.*"

Strained silence followed, each second more like an hour. Naomi cleared her throat. "Elam made a very nice memory box for me. And he's crafting picnic tables for the auction."

Solomon harrumphed.

"You're going to have to talk to him sometime."

Naomi's soft words nearly stopped Elam's breathing.

"He broke your heart. Don't be a fool. Elam is like

a rabbit. At the first sign of trouble, he scampers away. Can you trust a man like that?"

The question hung on the air.

Elam shifted in his seat. "Don't put her in a position to have to answer such a question. You're not being fair. And I'm through running. I'm here to stay, whether you like it or not."

Solomon now turned to Elam, his red face a contrast to his light hair. "Your actions that night and in the following days hurt more than Aaron and Naomi. You broke the community's trust. And that isn't easy to fix."

Elam swiped a glance at Naomi as her face reddened. *Nein*, to put their lives back together would take work. But didn't they see he was trying to do just that? Didn't they see his heart had been broken, too?

No more words were spoken between the car's passengers, and soon enough Frank dropped Solomon at the hardware store and then brought Elam and Naomi to the copy shop. They entered, a chime ringing. No one worked behind the counter.

As they waited for the clerk, Naomi brushed his arm, his breath hitching. "Solomon shouldn't have said what he did. He didn't mean it."

"How do you know?"

"Because I believe you're going to stay."

He spun to face her, her pretty eyes the color of periwinkles, her gaze never veering from his face. She truly did. While it wasn't much, it was something. Perhaps the start of the road to forgiveness.

Chapter Nine

With each clip-clop of Sugar's hooves on the asphalt, Naomi's stomach clenched tighter and tighter as she neared Elam's home, like clamps were screwing into her midsection. She rubbed her eyes, gritty from lack of sleep last night.

And this was only the practice session for talking to the reporters. What would her nerves be like when the real day came? She couldn't do this, just couldn't. As soon as she arrived, she would tell Elam to call it off. Somehow, the people would come. Somehow, they would earn enough money for the district's needs.

The Yoders' farm came into view, the large, white clapboard house, the green roof and the blue curtains at the windows much like every other Amish home in the area. Dark pants and dresses in an array of colors clung to the clothesline as they snapped in the breeze. A horse whinnied.

She pulled in the driveway and reined Sugar to a stop. Before she could climb from the buggy, Elam sprinted from the house, two fishing poles and a tackle box in his hands. *"Gut morgan."*

What was he up to? "I thought we were going to rehearse what I'm going to say to the reporters next week."

"And so we are. But Mamm is in a cleaning frenzy, and I have a longing to go to Miller's pond. Look at the blue skies. It's the perfect day."

So was the day he took her there and kissed her for the first time, just as dusk settled around them and the frogs took up their nighttime croak. All had been right with the world then. At that moment, she'd believed nothing could ever go wrong.

And then it had.

His shoulders drooped. "This isn't easy for either of us. And I remember what happened there. Don't worry. I have nothing more in mind than catching a few small-mouth bass to fry for dinner. There's no rule that says we have to do all our work at the kitchen table. Especially not on such a fine day. Can't you smell summer in the air?"

"How can you smell a season?"

"The magnolia tree beside the house is blooming, it rained last night and the earth is plowed. The air is sweet."

"And you're a dreamer."

"Call me what you want. What do you say?"

"Fine. We can practice while we fish." She scooted over and handed him Sugar's reins, her hands shaking.

He touched them. "Are you *narrisch*?"

"Very."

"There's nothing to be afraid of. Pretend you're in your living room speaking to a cousin you haven't seen in a while, telling her about Joseph."

"What if I say something wrong?"

"What could you say wrong when you're sharing with people what has happened in your life? You're worried about nothing. And if they have questions, they'll ask. That's their job."

For the rest of the ride to the pond, Naomi stared straight ahead and clasped her hands in her lap. Of course Elam would reassure her about the meeting. He'd lived among the Englisch for three years. Plenty of time to get to know their ways. She avoided working the front counter at the bakery so she didn't have to speak to them. She hated talking to people she didn't know, and especially in English.

He pulled the buggy from the main road down a wide path and drove deep into the woods, the trees bursting with life, until the pond opened before them, sparkling in the sun. In short order, they baited their hooks, cast them into the water and sat on the dock to watch and wait.

"How are your plans for your new business coming?" She jiggled her pole, attempting to get a fish to bite. Anything to avoid talking about reporters and newspapers.

"Stalled at the moment. Isaac has sold his ranch and will return in the not-too-distant future. With your daed refusing to let me borrow his equipment and his shop, I might have to go back to working construction until I save enough for the tools I need and a place to work." He pulled in his line and fiddled with adding bait, never looking at her.

She caught the downturn of his mouth. "Will you go back to Madison?" Her words floated out in a whisper.

"When I came back, I came back to stay. No matter what people like Solomon say or think about me.

They're going to have to put up with me, because I'm not going anywhere. I tried to run from my problems, but they followed me. Better to stay here and deal with them."

"I'm glad to hear that." And she was, no doubt about it. Maybe he had changed. Maybe... *Nein*, better to not let her thoughts get away from her. Once the auction was over, they could go back to being acquaintances, people who ran into each other in the store or at church services. Nothing more. She rubbed the arm that held the pole. "Working for a boss isn't your dream, is it?"

"*Nein*. But I'll have to do just that until I can save my money." His pole bent.

"You have a bite." Naomi bounced on the dock. "Pull it in. See what you got."

"I am, I am." With a chuckle, he reeled up the line until a muddy-green fish popped above the water's surface.

"Oh, that's a nice one." The fish wriggled on the lure.

"A keeper for sure." Elam hooked him to the stringer and plopped the bass into the water. His face shone like he was a six-year-old with his first catch. "I remember how proud Daed was of me the first time I brought home enough fish for everyone for dinner. He complimented me the entire meal. Mamm had to caution him about his boasting and warn me about pride."

At his words, an idea popped into Naomi's mind. She didn't bother to think about it before blurting it out. "Won't your daed let you use a corner of his barn for your shop? That way, you can start your business as soon as Isaac takes over the farm."

"I haven't asked him. Guess I'd just rather be independent. And I'd still need the tools."

"What's the harm in talking to him?"

Elam pushed out a breath. "I don't know if I can."

"Why not?"

"Because he might say no." Elam stared straight ahead, not bothering to cast his line.

Naomi reeled in her hook. "And what if he does? You're no worse off than you are now."

For a moment, Elam was still. Dragonflies flitted over the water. Only the splash of a fish broke the silence. He turned to her, stared at her, his green-eyed gaze going to her lips.

She held her breath.

Then he shook his head and cleared his throat. "I think we'd better go."

And for the second time in as many weeks, her heart shrunk the smallest of bits.

By the time Elam finished the chores at home and pulled into the Bontragers' place, several other buggies sat in the yard. Through the open kitchen window, the boisterous voices of several men drifted on the breeze. The salty sweetness of frying bacon drew him inside. *"Gut morgan."*

The group glanced up as one then returned to eating their breakfast.

Leroy raised an eyebrow. "Naomi is dressing Joseph. She didn't tell me you were going somewhere today."

He didn't know? "I'm not here to work on the auction but to help with installing the cabinets in the *dawdi haus*. She mentioned it to me, and I'd like to put my skills to use."

"We have a full crew."

The men scraped back their chairs and stood, Solomon among them. "We'll see you over there, Leroy." With one last swig of coffee, he exited with the group.

Joseph's cooing cut the tension in the room. Naomi stepped in, her eyes widening. "You came."

"You said your daed probably had enough men, but you can never have too much help, so I'm here."

"I'm glad." A soft smile graced her face.

The *bobbeli* reached out for Elam, and he took him from her arms.

"If you're here, you're here. Give the *bobbeli* back to his mamm, and let's get to work." Leroy scraped back his chair.

A grin crossed Joseph's face, and Elam matched it. After he mussed the child's hair, he handed him to Naomi and followed her daed to the adjoining house.

Cabinets sat helter-skelter around the kitchen, a set of drawings on top of one detailing where they should go. From his tool belt, Elam produced a screwdriver, and while a couple of other men held the cupboard in place, he secured it to the wall. All the while, his mind raced with Naomi's words. Had his stubborn pride gotten in the way and prevented him from doing what he loved? But his daed had let him know with a few choice words how he felt. As soon as Isaac returned, Elam would be on his own again. Daed wouldn't want him hanging around, working in the barn.

What was it she said? That even if Daed turned him down, he'd be no worse off than he was now. True. How much rejection could one man take, though?

"Hand me that box of screws there." Solomon pointed to a white-and-blue box beside Elam. He passed the screws, and Solomon grabbed them.

The rest of the morning they worked, no one speaking to Elam other than what was necessary to complete the job. Were all their hearts that hard? If so, what chance did he stand with his daed? Why had he even come today? He wasn't proving anything to them.

Midmorning, Naomi brought coffee and Danish for the men. The two of them stepped onto the porch. "My kitchen is coming together. Now I can picture what it's going to look like."

"You'll have a nice home."

She leaned against the rail and sipped from her mug. "How is it going with the men?"

"Could be better, could be worse." He leaned beside her.

"Have you talked to your daed yet?"

"*Nein.* Not sure I'm going to."

"You convinced me to step out in faith and speak to the reporters. It's your turn to do the same."

Maybe she was right. He'd come this far. If his daed gave his business a temporary home, he could be up and running that much faster. That much sooner until he would be ingrained into the district once more.

The door banged shut behind them, and Solomon strode across the porch and down the steps before pivoting to stare at Elam. "Quitting so soon?"

He stood and crossed his arms. "Not a chance."

Easy to say. Harder to do.

Chapter Ten

Dark, heavy clouds hung over the tables spread with sandwiches, jars of last year's pickles, gelatin and pies of every imagination. The tempting array made it worth Elam's sore muscles from setting up the tables last night in anticipation of the church service and meal at his family's farm today.

If it didn't rain before he filled his plate.

Across the yard, Naomi chatted with some of the other young mothers as their *kinner* ran in circles around them. After his surgery, when he got older, would Joseph be able to chase the other little ones through the grass?

Elam repressed a sigh.

Aaron came into view, maneuvering his battery-powered wheelchair through the grass. He bumped along and skirted a mud puddle last night's rain left, then pulled alongside the table. He grabbed a plate and piled it high with food. Elam chuckled to himself. He had the typical teenage-boy appetite.

But Aaron didn't wheel himself to join the group of young men setting up the volleyball net in anticipation of this evening's game. Instead, he headed for an unoccupied spot under a large oak at the far edge of the farmyard. With each bump of his wheelchair, the plate on his lap bounced closer to the edge of his knees. Aaron, keeping his sights on the direction he was headed, didn't notice it slipping.

Maybe Elam could catch the dish. He sprinted over, but just as he closed in, the paper plate and its contents spilled to the ground.

Aaron halted as Elam sidled up to him. A muscle jumped in the young man's tight jaw, and he clenched the chair's armrests until his knuckles turned white.

"I tried to catch it."

Aaron turned to Elam with a sigh. "Guess I wasn't paying attention to my plate."

Elam bent down and scraped the sandwich and potato salad from the ground. "What are you doing so far from the action?"

Aaron returned his focus to the field beyond the barn and shrugged. A pain tugged at Elam's midsection. He'd done this to him. Confined him to this wheelchair for the rest of his life. One careless, stupid mistake. A few seconds that changed everyone's lives forever. Solomon was correct. That action impacted so many lives.

Why did he have to do it? Why did he have try to use his cell phone to call for pizza? Acid boiled in his stomach and surged up his throat. He bit back the bile. "I'd think you'd want to be over there cheering for the prettiest girl on the team."

"Like she'd ever have me in this condition. *Nein*, I'll just sit here."

"Why not with your other friends?"

"All they talk about is farming, their jobs and courting. I don't fit in with any of that. I… I haven't milked a cow or driven a plow or asked a girl home from a singing since, well, you know."

Did he ever. Elam plopped onto the ground beside him. "But you have your work with your daed. Not everyone farms these days."

"Like Daed allows me to do anything. Staining. That's it. The one thing he thinks I can handle. But I'm capable of running any of the machines, same as before. And though I may not be able to handle a hay mower, I can milk a cow. He won't see it, though. He coddles me like I'm two, afraid I'll hurt myself." Aaron blew out a breath.

"Then show him he's wrong. Like I said before, you're a *gut* carpenter. Make something for the auction. He'll see that you have a knack for it, and he'll be proud of you."

"I don't know if he'll even let me touch his tools."

If no one was watching, Elam would bang his head against the tree trunk. Then maybe the ripping pain in his soul would go away. Aaron had such potential as a woodworker. While Elam had worked for Leroy, he taught Aaron the basics. His pieces were always precise, well made and beautiful. Elam gulped. "I'm sorry." His words carried on a throaty croak.

Aaron scrunched his brows V, so much like his sister did. "What do you have to be sorry for?"

"Are you kidding? What don't I have to be sorry for?"

"The accident was as much my fault as yours."

"That's not true. I fiddled on my phone. If I hadn't done that, I wouldn't have veered from the road and hit the tree."

"And if I hadn't suggested we get a pizza on the way home, you wouldn't have been on your phone."

A bead of sweat trickled down Elam's back despite the pleasant spring temperature. "*Nein*, I won't allow you to accept any responsibility. The fault, the guilt, is all mine."

"Don't tear yourself in two. We're both to blame. If I hadn't wanted pizza, if you hadn't made the call, if I'd had my seat belt on… That's too many *ifs*. What's done is done. Much as we would like, we can't change the past."

Aaron had a point. All the wishing, all the blaming in the world didn't change what had happened. Because of him. Was this why Aaron's family could forgive but couldn't forget? Everyday life would be a struggle for him as long as he lived. "That doesn't change the fact that I'm sorry. About everything. That you can't play volleyball. That your daed doesn't trust you in the workshop. That you spilled your lunch. Let me get you another plate." Elam stood and brushed the grass from his pants.

Aaron grabbed him by the wrist. "Please do me one favor?" His voice was a low growl.

"Anything." Even one small thing that could start to atone for his sin.

"Don't treat me like a *bobbeli*. I can get my own lunch. You wouldn't offer to help me if I had two good legs. Let me do this myself. I'm the one who dropped it."

"That's a deal."

Aaron nodded, his straw hat flopping, spun his chair in a circle and headed in the direction of the much-diminished larder of food before spinning around again.

"And Elam, I'll think about what you said. About making a few items for the auction. It's only a maybe."

For Elam, that would have to be enough.

With her *bobbeli* sleeping in his car seat in the Yoders' bedroom, a lightness and an emptiness filled Naomi at the same time. So different not to have him in her arms. What would it be like when he had his surgery? How long before she could hold him?

And what if the worse happened?

Nein, she couldn't dwell on those things. She turned her attention from the group of older women chatting on the porch, a plate on each lap holding a piece of pie. Elam and Aaron huddled near the barn's far corner, just in her view. Then Aaron turned and motored to the lunch table, filling a dish with a pile of food.

Elam stood, a plate in his hand, though he made no move to eat. He stared at Aaron. What had gone on between them?

She wandered in his direction. The women would talk, and so would everyone else in the district. She stopped. Maybe it was best that she avoid him. Then again, everyone would only assume they were working on the auction. Which is what they were doing. She straightened and continued her trek toward him. "I saw you speaking to my brother."

Elam nodded but didn't turn to face her. "We had an interesting talk."

"Not to be nosy, but what was it about?"

"He told me not to blame myself for the accident. That he was at much at fault as me."

Her brother thought he bore some of the responsibility for his condition?

"But he's not. I took away games with friends and walks with girls."

What should she say? At least his guilt was coming home to rest. As it should. "He's fine at our place, where he can get around, where he doesn't have to face others in the district. But here, at Sunday services and such, he withdraws."

Elam spun on one heel, now mere inches from her, his gaze dark, his breath hot. "I will help him. I don't know what that will look like yet, but I will."

The butterflies in her stomach woke up and performed another dance. She pressed her middle to still them. *Ja*, he was sweet, and he should help Aaron. But organizing an auction to pay the bills wouldn't change Aaron's circumstances.

With a shake of his head, Elam threw off his seriousness. A grin crept across his face. "Are you ready for the newspaper interviews on Friday? We got so busy with fishing the other day, we never practiced."

"*Ach*, I haven't had much time think about them." The butterflies multiplied until there were at least three times as many. "I don't know what to say. What are they going to ask me?"

"I've never been interviewed before, but I imagine they'll invite you to tell them your story. And that's what you should do. Don't worry about being fancy and flowery like the Englisch. Just talk to them. They're people like us."

She gave a half laugh. "Not quite."

"They're not alligators. They won't snap you in their jaws and devour you."

A full laugh bubbled up and spilled out. "I never thought they were."

"*Gut.* They'll do all they can to make you comfortable. And if they ask a question you don't want to answer, you don't have to."

"*Denki* for offering to stay with me. That will make me less *narrisch.*"

"Of course." He raised the plate he'd been holding. "I'd better throw this away. Maybe I'll see you on Tuesday at the bakery. My benches sold out, so I need to make more. At least I own a saw and a screwdriver."

"That's *gut.* I'm glad your business is going well."

"In a way it is, in a way it's not. I have plenty of orders but nowhere to build what people want. For now, I can work outside at the bakery, but when winter comes, or it rains, I need a place inside, and somewhere to store my few hand tools. If my daed won't let me use our barn, I don't know what I'm going to do."

Naomi bit her lip as the kernel of an idea sprouted. He was being kind to her. And she had hurt him when she turned her back on him after the accident. Maybe she could help him.

Chapter Eleven

The loamy smell of just-tilled land filled the spring air as Elam brought Daed an after-dinner cup of coffee on the porch. Mamm had traveled to Montana to help Isaac's wife with the packing and the *kinner* as they prepared to come home, so he and Daed were like two bachelors. *Gut* thing Elam had learned to cook while he'd been away, or the two of them might have starved to death.

Daed's left hand shook as he lifted the mug to his mouth. Even with therapy, he didn't use his right hand for much.

"Are you tired? I can help you into the house."

"If I wanted to go inside, I would do it. Don't need any help getting from one place to the other."

"I was just saying…"

"If I need a hand, I'll ask for it. Fair enough?"

"Fine." Elam nodded and settled into Mamm's rocking chair. Gray and pink dusk descended, and the crickets chirped their nighttime songs. Beside him, Daed sipped his coffee.

"You have something on your mind, son?" Daed

slurred his words, but Elam understood him most of the time.

How could he share with him about Naomi when putting two civil words together in a row was difficult for Daed? "It's nothing I want to talk about. Not when I'm the one at fault."

"Again?" Daed's voice was softer than Elam had heard in a long time.

"Still." Maybe he could share what was on his heart. "Whenever I see Aaron, I'm reminded of what I did. No wonder people can't forgive me. Then I do stupid things like blurting out the news about the papers in front of that group of women."

"You gave your answer in your question."

"Huh?"

"You were stupid. You have to be smarter. Think before you act."

"That's been my problem my entire life."

"Ever since you were a little *kind*, you always wanted to do things your own way in your own time."

"Hey. You don't have to agree." Elam chuckled.

"And what about Naomi? How does she feel about telling her story to these newspapers?"

"I'm trying to help her."

"Are you sure?"

"Of course. The bishop never wants to advertise much. A few flyers around town isn't going to bring many people here. But an article in the papers around the state will increase our numbers, our sales and the money we bring in. All to help her and everyone in the district. That includes you. I thought that once I did it, everyone would see how *gut* it was."

"Sounds noble, but make sure it's what she really wants. The story is hers to tell and hers alone."

"I will." Daed was in a *gut* enough mood tonight. This was the most they had spoken in one sitting since Elam had arrived home. Maybe this was the time for him to ask Daed for a favor. "I have a business proposition."

Daed set his coffee cup on the small table beside him and gazed at Elam, his green eyes hooded, the right side of his face drooping from the stroke. "Hope you're not going to ask for a piece of the farm. It's Isaac's. You've made it more than clear over the years that you don't want any part of it. That's a bargain you can't go back on."

"*Nein*, that's not what I'm asking." Elam shivered as the pleasant evening took on a chill. "For a while now, I've wanted to start my own woodworking shop. Both Leroy Bontrager and my friend Chase taught me about the business and how to make finely crafted items. I even have a specialty in mind. Outdoor furniture. Things like picnic tables and porch swings and such."

"Go do whatever you want, then."

Elam leaned closer to his daed. "I don't have a space to work."

"Can't you continue using Chase's garage? We don't have anything fancy around here, and the bishop won't take to putting in electricity anywhere in the district, not for any reason."

A sigh begged to be released, but Elam held it in. "I don't want electricity. My aim is to make furniture the true Amish way. Like Leroy does. With gas-powered tools."

Daed wiggled his bushy left eyebrow. "You don't say. What about the construction job you used to have?"

"It's a fine job, and I know many Amish men do that kind of work. But if I have any chance at being integrated into the district, I'd like to use traditional tools. And set up business in a corner of the barn to start. Just for a while, until I can afford my own shop."

"How do I know you're going to stay this time?"

Elam drew in a deep breath. "I never planned on leaving. When I bought the truck, I didn't know what I wanted. But I fell in love with Naomi and decided that I wanted to live this life. And then, well, circumstances forced me to walk away. But I'm done running. Ready to own up to what I did."

Daed stroked his beard. "You have been working hard. And helping out. I'll have to think about it."

A throbbing pain banged behind Elam's right eye. "You tell me to prove myself, but how can I do that when you take the opportunity away by refusing to let me use the barn?"

Daed grasped the walker's handles and pulled himself to his feet. "I haven't said no. Just said I'll have to think about it. Now I'm going to bed."

"But what about using the barn?"

"Until I make my final decision, you'll have to work that construction job. You'll need the money for tools, anyway. By the time you have enough saved for them, I'll let you know. That's all I have to say on the matter."

"Did Bishop Zook say why he was coming to visit?" Naomi stood beside her mamm and Laura at their long kitchen counter and rolled out a piecrust.

Mamm measured the ingredients for the strawberry-rhubarb filling, and the tang of it filled the air. "*Nein*, he didn't tell your daed what it was about."

"And he wants all of us here?"

"*Ja*, you, me and Daed." Mamm stirred with great gusto.

Naomi draped the crust over her rolling pin and then laid it in the pie plate. There had to be more to the bishop's visit. "What are you not telling me?"

"Nothing." Mamm's face remained expressionless. She told the truth. "But your daed acted funny. Like he was holding back something. Said I should make a large chicken casserole and set two extra places at the table."

"Is the bishop bringing his wife?"

"I have no idea. Daed wouldn't give me a clue. Laura, do you have the chicken cut up and ready to go?"

"Maybe he's invited Elam to lunch." Laura dumped the casserole into the dish and placed it in the oven.

Naomi wiped her floury hands on her apron. "Why would he do something like that?"

"To give you two his blessing." Laura tipped her head and grinned at Naomi.

"His blessing? To us? Whatever for?" Now her hands went sweaty. Had Elam gone and done something else impetuous?

"I spotted the two of you the other day on the porch. You were so intent on each other, you never noticed me. And I've seen you together after church on Sundays."

"You spied on us."

Mamm plopped the sweet filling into the crust. "Now, girls, that's quite enough."

"You were in the open. I couldn't avert my eyes."

"We weren't doing anything wrong. He was talking to me."

"Whatever you say." Laura flounced away to set the table.

Naomi sighed and slid the pie plate into the oven.

By the time the casserole and the pie were finished baking, Daed and Aaron had come in from the shed and washed up, and Sam tromped in from the barn. Daed rubbed his hands together. "Smells *wunderbaar* in here. I have three of the best cooks in the world living under my roof. How much better of a life can a man have?"

Naomi glimpsed out the kitchen window as two buggies rolled to a stop in the drive. One, obviously Bishop Zook. The other... *Nein*, it couldn't be. Laura had only been funning her.

But it was. Elam stepped from the buggy and joined the bishop in making his way to the door.

With hands shaking as she turned the knob, she let them in. "Welcome, Bishop and Elam. Lunch is just about ready."

The bishop ducked as he passed through the narrow, low-roofed back hall into the kitchen, but Naomi stopped Elam from following. "What is this about?"

"I have no idea. The bishop just told me he wanted me to come here today with him for lunch."

"Then I have a pretty *gut* idea."

"You might be wrong." But Elam didn't flash his usual boyish grin. Instead, his tanned cheeks flushed.

"I told you going to the papers was a bad plan, but you keep talking me into it. Why do I ever listen?" She stomped away to join the rest of the family. The group sat and had their silent prayer. In addition to asking for a blessing on the meal, Naomi implored the Lord to keep the bishop from being too upset with them if he was here about the papers.

The potpie, the applesauce, the pickled beets and the fresh bread all made their way around the table. Bishop Zook had his plate full before he cleared his throat to speak. "I'm sure you're wondering why I invited myself and Elam to lunch today."

The bite of chicken Naomi had consumed settled like a lump in her stomach.

Daed nodded. "You're always a welcomed guest in our house, though it's curious why he is here." He glared at Elam.

"How is the *bobbeli*, Naomi?" The bishop forked a piece of carrot.

"Healthy for now. The surgery is scheduled for July."

"So I hear. That's *gut* to know he'll get his heart fixed. If the Lord wills, he'll grow into a fine young man. And of course, the auction is coming soon."

"*Ja*, very fast. With Simon laid up, Elam and I have been working hard on the preparations. I believe Daed has some special pieces he made for it this year, and I've been quilting when Joseph doesn't demand my time."

"I'm looking forward to seeing what you've done, though that's not why I'm here. I've heard some disturbing news. My sister tells me that Elam announced you were planning on sharing your story with the Englisch papers in order to get more people to come to the auction."

Naomi couldn't swallow. "*Ja*, that's true." She studied the food on her plate. Her appetite vanished.

"Bishop, it was my idea." At Elam's pronouncement, the clinking of silverware stopped.

"Why?"

Elam's voice didn't falter. "Because I know the district has a great number of medical needs this year, so many will dip into the account to pay their bills. But we don't advertise. Other auctions in the state do, but not ours. Naomi has a compelling story. If she shares it, we could make sure there is enough money to take care of everyone."

Naomi's heart throbbed in her ears, drowning out all other noise in the house. Not that there was any. She glanced up. The color of Daed's face matched that of the beets on her plate.

A muscle jumped in the bishop's jaw. He scraped his chair back and stood. "There will be no going to the Englisch papers. Is that clear? Word gets out enough. For the rest, we trust the Lord."

Elam also came to his feet. "I want to make sure the district's families have all they need."

Naomi covered her face, pain shooting through her head. She should never have listened to Elam. Why had she allowed him to persuade her to go along with his crazy schemes like he always did?

"And they will. That is my job, and the work of the deacons, not yours. You come back here having learned fancy Englisch ways of doing things. But we don't need computers or the internet or even their newspapers. People know about the auction. They come every year. We have never gone without. Don't you dare cross me, young man. To do so would be to end your relationship with this district forever." The bishop stormed out of the house, his lunch untouched, the screen door banging behind him.

Naomi had never seen him this upset, so angry that he couldn't finish his meal. Elam brought out this side in him.

Daed rose from his chair and marched to Elam, the

two of them nose to nose. "Get out of my home." The words exploded from his lips. "And don't you ever come back. You have made the bishop angry with us and have tongues wagging all over the district. How much more do you want to hurt the ones I love?"

Elam stood tall. "If the bishop would just listen to me, he would see that I'm right."

"You would put yourself over the bishop? You know more than him now?"

"Not that I know more than him, but what I'm saying is reasonable. I understand he wants to keep our district from the Englisch ways. But the articles would only bring them to the auction, not into our homes."

"The bishop has made his decision, and that is final." Daed poked Elam in the chest. "Don't involve my daughter in this anymore. If you are so determined to make such a big success of this auction, do it yourself."

"If I have to, I will. But remember that I'm doing this to help, among others, your family." Elam strode from the room.

Naomi rose to follow him. She couldn't let him leave like this.

Chapter Twelve

Elam marched from the Bontrager house, the screen door slapping shut after him. Then it slapped again. He turned, and his breath rushed from his lungs. Naomi had followed him. Why?

"Elam, stop." She, too, was breathless.

"What do you want?" His words came out harsher than he intended.

"I'm... I'm sorry about the bishop and my daed. Going to the papers was a bad idea from the start, and I should have talked you out of it. Then none of this would have happened. But they shouldn't have been so harsh with you."

Did she truly care how he was being treated? He clenched his teeth together and then relaxed them. "Why will no one give me a chance? I know all about forgiving and forgetting. And that forgetting is almost impossible in this situation, but there has to be a way to move on."

"I don't know what to say to you." Her soft, gentle voice touched him deep inside, an ache growing and spreading throughout his body. "Maybe there isn't a way. The damage is done and can't be undone. The wounds are too raw. My family has been through two terrible tragedies in the last three years, and now we're dealing with Joseph. We're just trying to get our feet under us. To figure out life."

"Is my coming back interfering with that?" She was so tiny, so fragile. He forced himself not to reach for her, to hold her as he once had. To comfort her. The hurt in her eyes stirred the tiny seed of love that had lain dormant in his heart.

She shuffled her bare feet in the soft, brown dirt. "That's hard to say."

He stepped toward her until he stood right in front of her. Touched her chin. Forced her to look him in the eyes. "Be honest with me. Tell me what is really deep inside you. Are you still angry with me? Still in love with me?" His heart slammed against his ribs as he held his breath.

"Please don't make me answer those questions. You called it unfair when Solomon asked me." She gazed at him with such intensity, he almost forgot where he was.

"I wish I could help you."

"Is that why you really came back? Did you hear about Daniel and Joseph and figure you had another chance with me?"

"*Nein.* I knew you had married Daniel, but not about his death or Joseph's birth. My parents didn't tell me much about you or your family while I was gone. They only sent me a couple of letters, and not very newsy ones. But I did return in part because of you. And Aaron." They stood face-to-face, inches apart, her breath soft and warm on his neck. "To make up for my mistakes."

"You told me this already. There's no need to go over it again."

"Then tell me if my coming back was worth it."

"The timing wasn't good."

His mouth went dry. Did he dare ask the next question? He swallowed. "Do you want me to leave?"

She pushed away from him. "That is not my decision."

"This is my home, but I'm not welcomed here."

"Did you listen to the bishop? You have always had a mind of your own, done your own thing. The last time, with that truck, it proved to be disastrous. Whatever you do, think it through, and think it through well." Her words weren't harsh but soft and determined. "Remember what the bishop said. If you are going to stay here, you must obey him and submit to the Lord's will." She kissed his cheek, gentle and short, and then returned to the house.

He could do nothing but stand and stare at the spot where she disappeared. Some of what she had said was positive. She hadn't told him to hightail it back to wherever he'd come from. She even pecked him on the cheek. What did that mean? She must have feelings of some kind for him.

Nein, he had to stop these thoughts. He couldn't allow himself to open his heart to her when she hadn't forgiven him. And when her father forbade it.

The bishop didn't approve of Elam's idea of going to the papers. He understood. Once they had opened their district to outsiders. Many came and invaded their lives. Their young people, men like him, left the faith. A few came back. Most never returned. That forced the bishop to restrict their contact with the Englisch as much as feasible.

But in this case, he was wrong. The Englisch didn't want to eat in Amish homes or set up bed-and-breakfasts on their farms. They didn't want to tour the barns or the woodworking shops. They just wanted to come and buy some furniture, some quilts, maybe a tool or two.

From inside came Joseph's little howl, like a sick or wounded dog. Poor thing. He suffered so much. Struggled. A song floated on the air. Naomi singing her son a lullaby.

Sleep, my baby, sleep!
Your daddy's tending the sheep.
Your mommy's taken the cows away.
Won't come home till break of day.
Sleep, my baby, sleep!

Sleep, my baby, sleep!
Your daddy's tending the sheep.
Your mommy's tending the little ones,
Baby sleep as long as he wants.
Sleep, my baby, sleep!

Her sweet, soft voice quieted her *bobbeli's* cries. And Elam knew what he had to do.

Naomi reined Sugar to a halt near the Yoders' side door. She hadn't intended to stop here, and in fact, didn't really want to be here. The news that she had located a couple of large-capacity ice cream churns could wait. Nothing Elam needed to know right away. But here she was.

From the open living room window, the melody of his mamm's song floated on the late spring air, a familiar tune from the *Ausbund*, the Amish hymnal. The last of the year's tulips drooped their heads, preparing to sleep until next year.

"Don't worry, Daed, I'll get it for you."

"*Nein*, I'll do it myself."

"Sit down. I'll be right back." Elam exited the barn

muttering under his breath. He kept his attention on the ground so that he almost walked right into her buggy before he glanced up. "*Ach*, Naomi, you gave me a start. I didn't expect you. Did I forget about something?"

Why did his green eyes hold the power to drive every sensible word from her brain? What had she come for? Oh, *ja*. "The Levi Millers have a large-capacity churn. That gives us three, which should be enough, I hope. What do you think?" And now she blabbered.

"That's *gut*. One less thing on our to-do list. Walk with me to the house. Daed needs another cup of coffee."

A few heartbeats passed before he turned to her. "I'm sorry about the other day. I shouldn't have made it sound like I was placing the responsibility of my future on your shoulders. That wasn't fair of me. Only I can figure it out."

The thing was, she didn't want him to go. If he walked away again, much as she hated to admit it, he would leave a gaping hole in her life. But for whatever reason, she couldn't bring the words to her lips. "What do you want to do?"

"Stay." He halted. "When I returned, it was with the intention of never leaving. But do I have a place here?"

Not trusting her voice, she nodded.

"*Denki*. It's nice to know there are a few people who don't resent my presence. My daed did say he would think about allowing me to use the barn."

"That's progress. Thinking is a *gut* thing, say not?"

"Well, you know how patient of a person I am."

She chuckled. "I remember one winter when we were still in school. Every day after class, you ran to the window to check if it had snowed yet. You didn't miss a single day."

"I had that new sled my daed made for me for my birthday."

"*Ja*, from early October on, you drove us all crazy with your talk of the first big storm."

"What's an eight-year-old boy supposed to do when he has a new sled just waiting for him? That hill behind our house was calling to me."

"And as I remember, it didn't snow until December." She climbed the porch steps.

He followed her. "Not enough to sled, that's right."

"At the right time, your daed will give you his answer."

"When Isaac gets home, he wants me to work construction and earn some money for tools. But if he'd let me use the barn, I can build tables and such with what I have."

"Well, you'll need some cash to buy tools with, so that's not a bad thing."

"I suppose not. Anyway, I'm glad I spoke with him. And I'm glad you encouraged me to do so."

Marcus Herschberger, the eight-year-old boy from the neighboring family, scrambled up the driveway, his shirttail flapping as he sprinted. Naomi chuckled. That *kind* always moved as fast as a flood-swollen creek. Maybe someday that would be Joseph.

"Elam, the postman left this letter for you in our mailbox by mistake. It says it's from—"

"Denki." Elam ripped the envelope from Marcus's hands.

"But my daed said—"

"If you go in the house, my mamm just baked a batch

of molasses cookies. But you'd better hurry, because I'm coming right after you, and I'm going to swipe every last one."

"No you won't, 'cause I'm faster than you." Marcus bolted for the house.

"Who is it from?" Naomi tried to peek at the return address on the white envelope.

"No one important." He held it behind his back as his face went pink and then crimson, and he raised his shoulders.

Anyone with halfway decent eyes could see he was hiding something from her. Who could he be corresponding with he didn't want her to know about? *Nein*, he wouldn't. "You'd better not be—"

"Elam, where's that coffee? When you promise a man you'll do him a favor, you'd best do it."

His stiff shoulders relaxed. "I have to get that before he's out here. Come in and grab a few cookies yourself."

"*Nein*, I have to go." She'd been silly to stop here in the first place. "Were we going to pick up the flyers on Thursday?"

"I have something going on that day. Friday, I think we said."

She nodded. "That's right. I'll see you Friday morning. And Elam?"

He stopped midstep and turned to her. *"Ja?"*

"Please don't do it."

He spun around and strode across the yard and into the house before she got in the buggy. Her stomach dropped like the thermometer in January. He was up to no good, that much was certain.

Chapter Thirteen

Elam drummed his fingers on the van's door handle as Frank drove him to Madison, rain splatting the windshield and obscuring his view of the greening fields outside the window. If Naomi found out what he was doing today, she'd never speak to him again.

There was only one choice. She could never find out. Not like she almost had the other day when Marcus brought the letter from the Milwaukee paper confirming their appointment. That had been too close a call. As it was, she suspected the truth.

He turned to Frank, the older man leaning forward as he traversed the rain-slicked roads. "Remember, this trip is a big secret. You can't tell anyone in the district what I'm doing."

Frank fingered his graying mustache. "I'll do my best, but I'm not going to lie. That's where I draw the line."

Though not Amish, Frank was a *gut* and upright man. "I'd never ask that of you. But you don't have to say anything more than that it's a surprise." And if anyone found out about it, it would surely be. "You can tell them you took me to buy a diesel engine. That isn't a lie. I do need to stop at the hardware store." The first piece of equipment he'd need for his shop. If Daed didn't let him store it in the barn, he'd have to keep it in his bedroom.

"Are you sure about this?"

"*Ja*, I am. For Naomi's sake and all the others. I understand the bishop's wish to keep outsiders at arm's length, but this auction is for a single day. A few hours that will benefit many."

"And you're willing to risk your return to the district for this?"

A wave of nausea turned his stomach inside out. Was he? If today's actions became public, at the very least, he stood to earn Naomi's ire forever. She had warned him earlier in the week.

And the bishop's reaction? At the worst, he would drive Elam from the district and bar him from ever returning. Since he hadn't been baptized before he left the first time, he couldn't be shunned. But Bishop Zook would come as close as he could to such an action. He had said so in as many words.

"I've debated the consequences. If I ever expect to experience any kind of forgiveness from the people of this district, if I ever hope to regain any kind of standing, I have to do something to prove to them that I'm sorry for my actions. This is the best way I can think of."

"Going against the bishop will show them you've changed?"

Elam rubbed the back of his neck. "Yes. No. I don't know." His insides churned more. "It will. I'm here to make a difference in people's lives. To better the community."

"Are you sure you aren't doing this for just one reason? To get back in Naomi's good graces?"

Was he? If that was his motivation, then maybe he needed to rethink this strategy. Because if she found out, he had no chance with her. Pictures of a blue-lipped Joseph, a broken-legged Simon, a droopy-mouthed Daed flitted before his eyes.

Nein, his motives were noble. He was doing what he had to in order to help Naomi and the rest of the district. If it took disobeying the bishop, so be it. This was for everyone's benefit.

Frank let him out at the fast-food restaurant just as the rain let up. He went inside and doffed his hat, sitting in a booth overlooking the parking lot. The greasy hamburger and salty fry aroma that permeated the place did nothing to quell the rolling of his stomach.

Maybe he should leave. Maybe Frank was right. This would only bring him more trouble.

But then Frank's white van splashed onto the street and drove away.

The first reporter arrived, a dark-haired woman wearing blue jeans and a long dark shirt. Elam came to his feet as she approached. "Hello."

She flashed him a brilliant white smile and shook his hand. "Thanks so much for agreeing to meet with me." She sat across from him. "Tell me about this little boy."

From there, the story flowed. And it flowed two more times with the other reporters. They each expressed their interest in Joseph's predicament and in promoting the auction. How could this be a bad thing?

Especially when the Milwaukee paper promised prominent coverage for it in the Sunday edition.

Once the last journalist left, he repositioned his hat on his head and walked from the restaurant. The cool rain-washed air filled his lungs. Despite what the bishop said, what he'd done here today wasn't a bad thing. Quite the opposite. So much *gut* would come from the Englisch learning the Amish were no different from them in many ways. They faced much the same struggles. They worked to keep their families strong and healthy.

As long as no one in the district found out, things would be fine.

With the sweet perfumes of sugar and cinnamon clinging to her clothes, Naomi hurried from the bakery's kitchen, through the enclosed breezeway, and to the Herschbergers' door. *Gut* thing she didn't have to dash through the rain to get here. Water dripped from eaves. What a gloomy day.

But her mission here might turn the day into a nice one.

After a few moments, Sylvia answered her knock. "Well, Naomi, what a pleasant surprise. Come in and let me put the coffeepot on. What a chilly day. Almost like fall, say not?"

"*Denki*, but I don't need any. After several hours beside the ovens, I'm plenty warm. Is Simon around?"

"I'm here. Not like I can go many places these days." He rolled his wheelchair in from the living room.

"And as pleasant as always." Sylvia harrumphed, but her eyes twinkled. So did Simon's.

Naomi chuckled. "I'm glad you're in a fine mood,

because I've come here for a favor." She rubbed the end of her prayer *kapp* string. Silly that she should hesitate in asking.

"Sit down." Sylvia pulled out a chair and motioned for Naomi to have a seat. "You know you can ask us anything."

Why did her stomach do such somersaults and flips? Simon and Sylvia were *gut* friends. They were among the few who embraced Elam when he returned. She drew in a deep breath. "Simon, you assigned me and Elam to work on the auction together." She studied her sturdy black shoes. "I have to admit, I wasn't very happy about it at first."

She glanced up as Simon stroked his beard. "I know you weren't. I saw the hardness in your eyes when you looked at him, how you walked away whenever he came close. But the Lord, in His providence, brought the two of you together when I fell. I couldn't resist. Have you had problems?"

"*Nein.* Not really. A few bumps along the way, but everything is going well now. And since the bishop forbade us from speaking to the papers, that's one less item for me to worry about." Maybe.

"*Gut*, that's very *gut*." Simon nodded.

Sylvia came to the table with the coffeepot and, not taking no for an answer, poured Naomi a cup. Then she sat down and glared at her husband. "You didn't break your leg on purpose, did you, just to get these two together? I thought scheming and matchmaking were a woman's domain."

"You give me too much credit. I just saw an opportunity and took it."

With a smile pasted onto her face, Naomi sat back

and sipped the black brew. Oh, to have a marriage like that, a home with fun and laughter, a man and a woman who loved each other in such a way. Joseph squealing in glee as his daed tickled him and threw him in the air. Her little boy curled up between them in the evenings as they read the Bible.

"Naomi? Naomi." Sylvia patted her hand and thrust her into reality. "I think you were woolgathering."

"Oh, I'm sorry." She squirmed under their scrutiny.

"What has brought you here?"

"You've already been so kind to me and Elam, but I'd like to ask another favor."

"Nonsense." Simon waved her away. "I owe you a great debt for stepping in the way you have. Both of you."

"Elam wants to open a shop that builds outdoor furniture, like the picnic tables he makes for you."

"And such a fine job he does, too. The Englisch can't buy them fast enough. He'll do well." Simon repositioned himself in his wheelchair.

She couldn't get the picture of Aaron out of her mind. Of his struggling with everyday tasks. She cleared her throat. "He needs a place to run his shop. His daed won't let him use his barn, at least not right now, and mine won't allow him to work in our shop. You have that big barn and—"

"I have the buggy horse in there and not much else. With a little rearranging, there should be plenty of room for him to work."

"Denki, denki, denki." Naomi clapped her hands. "He's spoken of getting a place of his own once the business is going, but this will give him a start. And don't say a word to him. I want to be the one to tell him."

"He won't hear it from me." Simon peered at his wife.

"And not from me either."

"He'll be so grateful, I have no doubt. How can I ever repay you?"

Simon crossed his arms and narrowed his eyes. "If I hear one more word about it, the deal is off. You just concentrate on the auction and on getting your son well."

With a lightness in her step, Naomi restrained herself from skipping to her buggy. The rain had even stopped. As she went to retrieve Sugar from where she grazed, Elam pulled in and unhitched Prancer. "Just getting off work?"

Heat grazed her cheeks, and her mouth went dry. He grinned like a little *kind*, and her heart stopped for a moment. "A little while ago."

"Hmm, sounds mysterious."

"Mysterious? Ah, *nein*, not at all." She scuffed her shoe in the mud. "Just had a little chat with Sylvia and Simon."

"You take care of yourself. I see how tired you are. The auction will be over soon, and then the surgery. I don't want you to get sick." Then the softness in his face disappeared, and he stepped back.

"I will. You, too."

He strode toward the house, and she grasped her chest in an effort to slow her pounding heart.

She would have to find a very special way to tell him her news.

Chapter Fourteen

A bead of sweat rolled down Naomi's back and between her shoulder blades. Joseph slept in his car seat under the shade of the tree. Almost everything was in place for tomorrow. The big auction. The ladies who helped her set up the quilts in the auction building had left. She turned to Elam who had come earlier to lend a hand and go over the last of the preparations. "That should just about do it until the men arrive with the tents and the truck comes from the greenhouse with the plants." She checked on her *bobbeli*, his downy head damp with perspiration.

Elam perused the grounds. "They should be here soon." He wiped a trickle of sweat from his jawline. "If it's this hot tomorrow, the ice cream will be the most popular food item."

"I'm glad it's almost over."

He sat on the lawn beside Joseph. "Why?"

"Mostly because the work will be done. We'll know how much money we have, and Joseph can have his surgery." She studied her son, his lips tinged blue, his arms and legs scrawny, all because of his heart condition.

He touched her hand, and she didn't pull away. A strength flowed from him, a surety that stilled the frantic pounding of her heart when she gazed at Joseph. "It will be fine. You'll see. He'll grow into a strapping young man."

"But what if he doesn't?" She turned to him, his eyes not twinkling with his usual mischievous gleam. "What if I lose my son?"

"Worry ends where faith begins. That's what Mamm always says."

She stroked Joseph's pale cheek. "I want to move time forward, so that the operation will be over, and he'll be fine. But I want to stop the clock's hands and keep him safe here, in this moment."

"That's understandable. You love him. I'll pray for him. And for you. I always do."

She couldn't so much as glance at Elam, or she'd cry. No way would she be able to tell him about the surprise right now.

Another buggy pulled into the lot. Sylvia steered the horse toward where they were. In the back, Simon sat with his casted leg on a pillow.

Elam helped Naomi to her feet and led her by the hand to the Herschbergers. "You're looking well, Simon."

The old man nodded. "And everything here is in order?"

Elam grinned. "It's coming together."

"Seems to me the two of you did well." Simon repositioned himself in the buggy. "Hopefully we'll have a good turnout, and the auction will be a resounding success. I knew when I put you both in charge of this you would pull it off just fine."

"I'm expecting a big crowd." Elam almost bounced on his toes. The glimmer returned to his green eyes. He was up to something. She knew him too well. Underneath his hat, he hid a secret.

Did she really want to know what it was?

Simon leaned against the back of the buggy. "Alright then, put me to work. Tell me what I should do so I don't feel like a broken wheel."

Elam chuckled, rich and deep like the spring's first maple syrup. One of the things about him she'd first fallen in love with. "You have the most important job of all, because you get to tell us what to do." He laughed again, and Simon joined in the merriment.

She turned away. Elam was a charmer, no doubt. And his charm had melted some of the ice around her heart. She steeled herself against the rising tide of feelings.

With the men here now to complete the heavy work, she collected Joseph from under the tree. Time to go home and help Mamm get dinner on the table. As she settled the car seat in the buggy, she glanced up. Aaron drove into the lot.

He waved her over. "I have a delivery here. Could you give me a hand?"

"I only have a few minutes. Joseph will want to eat soon." She peered into the back, loaded with any number of sweet wooden toy trains and three large dollhouses. "You made these?"

He nodded so hard his hat flopped on his head. "Sure did. I wanted to do my part. That's where I've been spending my evenings this past week and why I've been going to the shop early."

"They're beautiful." She picked up a train and reveled in the smoothness of it, as silky as rabbit's fur. "I'm going to have to buy one for Joseph. When he learns to walk, he'll love to pull one of these around."

"Don't worry. I have one set aside for him. No charge."

Elam strode to the buggy, whistling, his hands in his pockets as if he didn't have a care in the world. He, too, examined Aaron's craftsmanship. "They'll sell fast. You're turning into a fine carpenter."

"*Denki* for motivating me to do this, to do more than I thought I could. Certainly more than Daed thought I could."

Naomi tipped her head and stared at Elam. He had done that for her brother?

Before the sun had risen very high in the sky, Mamm pulled the buggy to a stop at the edge of the auction grounds, and Naomi scanned what the men had accomplished after she'd left yesterday. A smattering of people, a mix of Amish and Englisch, milled around the building where the quilt and furniture auction would take place. Off to the side, the men had pitched a large white tent in the grass, home to the woodcrafts and garden goods sale. Later, on the other side of the building, the tool and farm implement auction would take place. Nearby, Daed sat with the ice cream churns, waiting for the heat of the day to bolster business. And the way the sun blazed already in the cloud-free sky, they would reap a great profit.

"Sam, don't run off on me. I need help with these pies." Mamm slid from the buggy and pulled apple, peach, strawberry, lemon, cherry, oatmeal and rhubarb pies from the back.

Naomi shifted Joseph on her hip. "Hand me a few of them, and I'll get them to the bakery table."

Mamm gave her a couple to carry.

Laura emerged from the back of the buggy, loaded down with every variety. "I think that's about all. I don't care if I never see another pastry crust in my entire life."

Naomi nudged her. "You will when we have them sliced and ready to sell."

"I didn't say I would never eat another one. I just don't want to look at them." With a giggle, Laura trotted off with the bakery goods.

"*Ach*, will that girl ever grow up?"

"She's just Laura." Naomi followed Mamm to the table loaded with turnovers, doughnuts, pretzels and, of course, the plethora of pies they brought.

By the time they had everything set up and organized and the Millers came to man the table, many more Englisch had arrived, parking their cars, trucks and vans along the narrow country road, walking to the auction grounds and crowding in to ogle everything for sale.

"Isn't it a beautiful day? *Gut* thing it's not raining."

Naomi jumped a mile and almost dropped Joseph in the process. "Elam Yoder, you have to stop scaring people."

With a grin stretched across his face, he showed no signs of remorse. "Think about all we'll sell today and the money we'll raise."

Sylvia wheeled Simon over, his leg propped on pillows, bobbing his head as he took in the scene. "Not to turn either one of you vain or proud, but you've done a *gut* job with arranging the day. Seems to me the items and the sellers are in place and that the sale is running without any hiccups so far. I have to hand it to you. You might just have put me out of a job."

"Naomi, maybe, but not me. This is my one and only time to do this."

Simon frowned. "So, you didn't enjoy it, then?"

"*Nein*, it's not that. But it's best left to others. Naomi did most of the organizing, anyway. I was just the muscle power." Elam pursed his lips.

She tamped down the warmth attempting to rise in her chest, lest she get too prideful. "We worked together well, Elam. I'm surprised to say I enjoyed it. Everyone can see your effort and what a fine job you did."

"*Denki*. That means so much coming from you. Maybe…" He touched her shoulder, then jerked away, his eyes a darker green than ever.

Her breath caught her in throat, and she swallowed. "See, we didn't have to go to the papers. Word got around despite our lack of advertising, and there are plenty of people here. More than I remember in recent years."

Simon nodded. "I've never seen this place so full. Who needs that fancy internet stuff when word of mouth works so well? If you sell quality goods for a *gut* price, then you don't need much publicity. News gets around."

Elam squirmed. Like he was uncomfortable. Or guilty.

"Simon, can you excuse us? I'd like to show Naomi something."

"What are you up to?" She tipped her head and chuckled.

"Come inside the building with me."

She followed him to the large pole barn, her eyes

taking a moment to adjust to the dimness inside it after the bright sunshine. Furniture and quilts crammed the front of the building around the platform where the auctioneer would sell the merchandise. Chairs for the bidders occupied the rest of the space. Interested folks browsed the offerings. Everything was just as they had left it last night. "What is it?"

He led her to a row of three Adirondack chairs, the cuts precise. She sat in one, slid back into the depths of it and caressed the armrest. Sanded to a perfect smoothness and stained a lovely honey color. "These are beautiful."

"I'm hoping that between the picnic tables and these, I'll be able to get my carpentry shop going sooner rather than later."

Perhaps this is what he'd been hiding. She shouldn't have been so suspicious of him. She opened her mouth to reveal her surprise, but different words squeaked out. "You donated them to the auction?"

"I would do anything for you and Joseph. For your entire family." He stared right at her, not blinking, his gaze soft. When he did that, she almost believed the words he said. Almost forgot what happened between them.

She broke eye contact with him. "I want to peek at the quilts. Mamm and her friends were working on one, but I haven't seen it since it was finished." She strode away. Elam's footfalls followed her.

To keep from having to look at him or speak to him, she busied herself walking among the rows. Maybe the green Double Wedding Ring would pay for medication for Joseph. Or the red Star of Bethlehem might bring enough money for a couple of therapy sessions for Aaron. Or this Log Cabin one might be enough to satisfy a doctor's fee for Simon or Elam's daed.

Several Englisch ladies, their arms and legs bare, their sunglasses stuck in their hair, wandered among the quilts, as well. They oohed and aahed over each of them. "I might have to bid on this one." A heavier-set middle-aged woman stroked the blue Center Diamond quilt. "It's beautiful, don't you think so, Tammy? I know Bill will be upset with the amount of money I spend on it, but I have to have it."

"Gina, I won't tell if you won't." The women laughed.

Naomi turned to walk away, but Joseph grabbed for the quilt and hung on with all his might. "*Nein*, little one, you have to let go." She spoke to him in *Deitsch* while loosening his fingers from around the fabric. She glanced up.

The woman named Gina stared at her. "Is that your baby?"

"Yes." If only Joseph would let go. For one so sick, he had a powerful grip.

"You're the lady I read about in the paper. The one with the child who needs surgery." Gina turned to her friends. "That's why they're having this auction."

Naomi's knees went weak, and her mouth dried out. "You read about me in the paper?"

"Yes. It was a wonderful article about how this helps your people to get medical care. I have a grandson who needed surgery when he was little, and the story moved me so much, I had to come and support you. And look, I brought a bunch of my friends with me. What a good cause. I hope your little boy is feeling better soon."

Naomi turned to find Elam and almost ran right into him. "What have you done?"

Chapter Fifteen

With Naomi staring at Elam the way she did, her eyes wide, her jaw clenched, his stomach tumbled like a rock down a hill. Joseph whimpered as she squeezed him. "I can't believe you went behind my back like this," she hissed.

The Englisch women stared at them. The last thing Naomi and Elam needed was to make a scene in front of the customers. "Please, let's go talk in private. I can explain."

She marched out of the building, and he followed like an obedient puppy. This is what he'd been afraid of. The exact reaction he expected if she found out. How could he have ever thought he could keep it from her?

She led him from the commotion of the auction to a field behind the building, out of earshot of the crowd. "Nothing you say can excuse what you did."

"*Ja*, I went to the papers."

"When the bishop expressly forbade it? Didn't you think? Don't you ever think?"

"I thought I was doing a *gut* thing for you, for Joseph, Aaron, Daed, Simon. So many others."

"Apparently not. Joseph sticks out in a crowd. Everyone will know he is the *bobbeli* from the story. They will stare at us. I can't stand that, being a monkey in a show. I won't have it." Her voice cracked.

He lifted his hat and pulled out a slip of paper and handed it to her. "This is the article. Read it. Please. Then you will know I only did it for your good, for Joseph's, to help you out."

"Now you read the Englisch newspapers?"

"Please, Naomi, try to understand." He walked in a tight circle before facing her again. "No one here accepts me. They treat me as if I'm a criminal. Forgiven, *ja*, but still an outcast."

"So you're doing this to win favor with the district?"

"*Nein*, because I want to help you."

"This will never make up for paralyzing my brother and breaking my heart." Her breaths came in rapid succession.

His shoulders sagged. "I know. But I love you. That's what I want to prove. That I'm now worthy of that love."

"You're trying to earn it."

"Maybe."

"This wasn't the way. I never wanted anything to do with this in the first place." She crumpled the newsprint and threw it into the long grass. "You've betrayed me. Worse now than when you walked away. Please, I beg you, just leave me alone. All you end up doing is hurting me." A sob escaped her throat, and she ran toward the row of parked buggies, Joseph bouncing on her hip.

Elam stood in the field as the sun beat down on him. Despite the warmth of the rays on his shoulders and his head, he shivered. Didn't the ends justify the means? Maybe he would never win her favor. Or that of the district.

A grasshopper jumped on his shoe, sat for moment and then hopped away. It bounced above the grasses several times before it disappeared. Oh, to have the life of a grasshopper. To be so carefree as to jump everywhere you went, not worrying what people thought about you. Then again, what a solitary life.

He rubbed his temples and pivoted. Simon approached, Sylvia wheeling his chair across the grass. He waved for them to stop and hurried to them.

Simon peered over his shoulder at his wife. "*Denki.* Elam can bring me back," she whispered in his ear, and he smiled as she ambled away. "Now, Elam Yoder, let's talk about you. What are you doing here by yourself? You're missing the fun."

"I'm in no mood for fun."

"Of course you are. You always are."

"Not this time."

"What happened? I saw Naomi run off. That's why I had Sylvia bring me over here. Did you two have a spat? I thought you were getting along well."

"We were, but I did something stupid."

Simon gazed at the intense blue sky. "Are you going to share what it was?"

Elam closed his eyes, not able to look at the man who had been like a grossdaadi to him. "I went to the papers and shared Naomi's story. Without her permission."

"And I heard tell that Bishop Zook forbade you from speaking with them."

"*Ja.*" Elam opened his eyes.

Simon shook his head, just twice. "I love you like you were one of my own family, but Elam, you sabotage yourself every chance you get." Simon broke eye contact.

An emptiness swept over Elam's midsection. "I know, I know. Why can't I stop myself? I think I'm doing good for someone, and things manage to go awry."

"You don't learn your lessons. You've always been headstrong and independent, going about life your own way. Like I did, back years ago when I was a young man." Simon wiped his sweaty brow with a handkerchief. "Doing what Naomi asks you not to isn't going to win her favor. And going against the bishop's orders might keep you from joining the church and being accepted in the district."

"I know. How could I have been such a *dummkopf*?"

"Or did you hope no one would find out?"

Elam sighed and toed the ground. "Maybe. *Ja*."

"You can never cover your sins."

"So I just learned."

"You should have found that out long ago. But for some of us, me included, we have to learn our lessons the hard way."

"I think I still love her."

"And that's why you did what you did."

"*Ja*. You understand. Why doesn't she?"

"You knew she wouldn't like it. That's why you didn't tell her."

Simon was insightful, no doubt. He never let Elam get away with anything. "And why I didn't want her to ever find out. Because I wanted to help her, not hurt her."

"It's time for you to start getting smart. Woo her the right way."

"But now I have to make up for this and for injuring her brother and for breaking her heart."

Simon gave a single chuckle. "Sounds like you have a lot of work to do."

"That's the problem. I don't know how to go about it."

"Are you ready to listen and take advice?"

"What can it hurt? I can't make things worse than they are."

"That's not true." More cars roared down the street, and a few people wandered along the road to their vehicles, large wooden welcome signs and shovels painted with bright flowers filling their hands. "I know you're a *gut* man. Who else could I have entrusted the auction to? You're a hard worker. But instead of insisting on going about things your own way, think about what others need."

"That's what I did. The church's medical fund needs money for Daniel's care and Joseph's surgery, your hospital stay, my daed's therapy, among many other things. I went to the papers so many Englisch would come today."

"Fine. Point taken. Not what others need. What they want."

Elam scratched his chin. What people wanted, not necessarily what they needed? That was a new way of looking at life. "You might be right. I've been trying to win over Naomi the wrong way. And everyone else in the district." Now all he had to do was to find out what Naomi wanted and give it to her.

But what she'd said when she ran off was for him to leave her alone.

He wasn't sure he could give her that.

* * *

Naomi's heart pounded against her chest and throbbed in her ears as she sprinted across the auction grounds to the line of buggies. She scrambled inside her family's and slumped against the sun-warmed seat. She cradled Joseph to herself and cried.

"Why, oh why would he do something like that? Can't he leave well enough alone? He's come back here, Joseph, and turned our lives upside down. As if they weren't already in disarray. What am I supposed to do?"

She sat against the seat and sobbed until sweat mingled with her tears. But she couldn't go back there. Couldn't show her face around here today. People would stare at her. Already, the weight of their gazes bore down on her. She had promised to work the bakery table for a while, but she wouldn't. Couldn't. They would make out fine without her.

Nausea rolled through her midsection, and she fought to keep her breakfast inside. Joseph fussed, probably hot and hungry. "Hush, my *bobbeli*, we'll find a way to let Mamm and the others know we need to leave. We just have to do it without being seen."

"There you are."

Naomi sucked in a lungful of air, adrenaline flooding her arms and legs. "Rachel. I didn't see you coming."

Her dark-haired friend climbed aboard and sat beside her. "Sorry. I tried to make some noise, but you must have been too deep in thought."

Naomi turned toward her friend.

She touched Naomi's arm. "*Nein*, not too deep in thought. Your eyes are red and puffy. You've been crying. What's wrong?"

"Elam. The auction. Joseph. Everything."

"Elam. I should have figured he was the source of your tears. What has he done now?"

"Remember I told you about his ridiculous scheme to go to the papers?"

"*Ja*, the one the bishop put a stop to."

"Well, you know that Elam isn't always the best at listening."

"That's an understatement. But don't tell me. He spoke to them anyway. Did you know about this?"

"Of course not. After Bishop Zook's visit, I told him to forget the idea, that it wasn't a *gut* one in the first place. I never spoke a word to them. But of course, he did his own thing and apparently granted the interviews on my behalf."

"Sounds like Elam."

"And if I go out there now, everyone will stare at me and Joseph. They will feel nothing but pity for us. I don't want that. Can't life go back to normal?"

Rachel handed Naomi a handkerchief, took Joseph from her and jiggled him on her knee. "I hate to tell you, but this is normal life. Elam is back, and it seems he's not going to leave. You're going to have to figure out a way to live in the same district together."

"That would be fine if he wouldn't come around me."

"Tell me, Naomi, what is in your heart? You wouldn't be this upset about Elam if you didn't feel something for him."

"That's what I mean when I say nothing is normal. I once loved Elam. Very much."

"And he broke your heart."

"So I married Daniel. *Nein*, it wasn't the crazy kind of love like Elam and I had. But Daniel was *gut* to me. Took care of me. In a different sort of way, I loved him.

And then God took him away from me and left me with a son to raise."

"Does Elam still stir those feelings in you?"

"He shouldn't."

Rachel tucked a damp strand of stray hair under her *kapp*. "That's not what I asked."

The problem was, he did. But it wasn't good. Elam brought nothing but disaster to her family. It would be best if he kept his distance from now on. "I won't let him hurt me again."

"What are you going to do about it, then?"

"Avoid him as much as possible." Naomi grabbed Rachel by the hand. "Which means I need you to stay right beside me all the time. At the bakery and at service. You can talk to him so I don't have to."

"You're going to run into him at times when I'm not around."

"Then I'll find a way to be somewhere else, somewhere he can't come. In the kitchen. In my bedroom."

"In this buggy." Rachel laughed, and Joseph mimicked her. "*Ja*, that was funny, wasn't it, *bobbeli*? You tell your mamm that everything will work out fine in the end."

Naomi kissed her son's round cheek. "We are very blessed to have Rachel for such a *gut* friend. And you will have your operation, your lips won't be blue, and things will settle down once more. We will be happy, you and me, my precious son. I will make it so."

Rachel squeezed her hand. "That's what I like to hear. God will give you strength for each day. Elam will learn you don't care for him anymore and will go away. Perhaps another fine young man will capture your heart."

"I can't think about that, but *denki*, Rachel."

"Let me get my horse, hitch him to my buggy and take you home."

"And tell my mamm. Not why we're leaving, just that we're going. Say I have a headache, which is the truth. I'll explain to my parents once we're at the house."

Rachel left to get her horse, and Naomi eased against the back of the seat. Through the little back window, she had a view of the Englisch coming and going. Some left with nothing more than a doughnut in their hands, while others walked away with wooden garden sculptures and flats of petunias. The quilt and furniture auction hadn't yet begun.

When Joseph cried, she turned her attention to him, wiping the sweat from his broad forehead as he breathed his raspy breaths. "Just a couple more weeks, little one, and you won't struggle so much. You'll feel better and can grow big and strong."

"Naomi."

The soft voice didn't startle her. But it set her hands to shaking. Elam. And, of course, Rachel hadn't returned yet. "I don't want to talk to you."

He came around the side of the buggy. "I'm not asking you to. All I wanted to say is I'm sorry. Not just because you found out about what I did, but because I went against your wishes and the bishop's, and I hurt you again. That's the last thing I wanted. And so, I apologize. Whether you accept it or not, please know it's sincere. And now, I won't bother you anymore."

Long after the crunch of his shoes on the gravel faded away, Naomi sat in the buggy and stared straight ahead. He'd agreed to her terms. Even so, a little part of her went with him.

Chapter Sixteen

"Just a little over a month until Joseph's surgery, right?" Rachel strolled beside Naomi as they searched for a spot in the Millers' yard after Sunday service to sit and have their lunch.

"*Ja*. And I'm getting nervous." The smell of the meal, the tang of the pickles, the sweetness of the strawberries, which had set her stomach to rumbling just a few minutes ago, now set it to churning.

"He'll be fine. You told me the doctors are very good. They have done this surgery many times, so you have nothing to worry about."

"They also say there is always a risk with the operation."

"Of course they do. They're supposed to tell you that. But he's young. Babies are resilient. That's what Mamm says. They can be so sick and bounce right back."

The doctors had told her all this. But while her head knew the risks were small, her heart trembled. "He's so little. And not very strong." She stroked her boy's bony hand.

As they meandered around the yard, dodging *kinner*

racing through the grass, Rachel leaned over, nose to nose with Joseph. "*Ach*, tell your mamm that you're bigger and stronger than you look. In a few months, you'll be getting around, and she won't be able to keep up with you. She'll wish for a little peace and quiet then."

Naomi pointed to the house, the one that had been Daniel's before they married, so familiar to her. "How about the porch step? That's a *gut* place, and it's in the shade right now."

"Fine with me. I can't believe how hot it is for June in Wisconsin. I'll be a puddle in another minute if we don't get out of the sun."

The two of them settled on the step. Naomi laid Joseph on a blanket in the grass beside her feet, and he cooed as he stared at the leaves of the maple tree blowing in the slight, very welcome breeze.

"How long will he be in the hospital?"

"That depends on how well he does after surgery. Maybe even less than a week."

"How amazing."

"But I don't know how long I'll be out of work from the bakery. For sure I won't come back until Joseph is fully healed, *gut* and strong again."

"I'm surprised Elam didn't show up at the bakery to pester you this week. He comes in often enough."

"So far, he's been keeping his word about leaving me alone. I haven't seen him at all since last Saturday. Maybe I finally got through to him." She sighed. *Ja*, maybe she had finally gotten what she wanted.

"You don't sound happy."

"I don't know what I feel anymore. Part of me was disappointed when he didn't come by. But it's for the best that he stays away. He only complicates my life."

"Who does?" Aaron maneuvered his chair up the walk to where they sat.

"Elam."

"You've been sulking for over a week."

"Shouldn't I be? He went and told my story behind my back, and without the bishop's permission. How else am I supposed to act?"

"I don't know. Maybe he shouldn't have done it, but did you think about why he spoke to the reporters?"

"Because I wasn't going to cross the bishop."

"*Nein*, because he wanted to help you. And me. And everyone else. That's all. Sure, he doesn't always make the best decisions, but he always has the good of others in mind."

"That doesn't make it right." This was a battle she'd fought inside herself all week. Did his intentions make a difference in what he did? Did they make his actions acceptable? Or at least good? "But what about you?"

Aaron furrowed his light eyebrows. "What about me?"

"He may have had *gut* intentions, driving that night while ordering pizza for you, but that doesn't justify what happened. He caused the accident that paralyzed you. Others end up paying the consequences for his poor choices." She glanced at Joseph, who sucked on his bare toes.

"The accident happened because I asked him to call ahead and order."

"That's not an excuse. He was older. The one who should have known better."

Aaron leaned forward. "I don't blame him."

That is what Elam had told her. "You don't blame yourself, do you?"

"Sometimes, maybe. But I know it wasn't all Elam's fault. And he shouldn't have to pay the rest of his life for one mistake."

"You have to."

Aaron shook his head. "It's not what I would have chosen for myself, but it is what it is. I have to deal with it. You can't punish Elam. Even the state of Wisconsin only gave him a fine for distracted driving. If I were you, I'd think about the good he's done. He's trying. You have to give him credit."

"If that were true, wouldn't you be joining in with the others in your age group instead of hanging back?"

"Well…"

"You should, you know. Look, you went and made those trains. You proved to yourself you could do it."

"*Ja*, I suppose I did."

"Then you can do this. They're starting a volleyball game. Go over there. Maybe you can serve."

Aaron stared in that direction for a long moment, then sat up straight and rolled away, bumping over the uneven ground toward the group of young people.

And Elam had done this. Encouraged Aaron to start living life. Naomi set her plate aside. "I'm like a stirred pot. All mixed up."

And then Elam rounded the corner of the house. Not the person she wanted to see right now.

He marched up the path and stood in front of them. "Hello, Rachel. Naomi, I, well I've been thinking about you." He shuffled his feet, stuffed inside black shoes.

A chill raced through her. "Please, Elam."

"I know I said I'd stay away, and I will. But I have to say again that I'm sorry I hurt you. With God's help, I'll do better. I know you've already given me a second chance, and probably more than that. But I'm hoping I'm similar to a cat. You know, nine lives, nine chances."

She couldn't help but chuckle at his attempt to lighten the mood.

"I can still make you laugh. That is all I've ever wanted to do for you."

A large older man stomped in their direction, his jaw clenched, his eyes narrowed. Bishop Zook. She stood and smoothed her dark blue skirt. "Elam, the bishop is coming this way."

At Naomi's words, Elam's legs lost all strength. He leaned against the porch post for support. Of course the man would have words with him. It was surprising the bishop hadn't tracked him down on the day of the auction. "I haven't seen him since—"

"Elam Yoder. Just the man I was hoping to run into today."

Elam plastered a smile to his face and spun toward the bishop. "Well, you found me."

"Word has gotten around that the turnout at the auction was so large because an article appeared in the Englisch papers around the state about Naomi. And that you were the one who told her story."

His tongue stuck to the roof of his mouth, and he swallowed hard before speaking. "I did. She had nothing to do with it whatsoever."

"Did I tell you that you were not to speak to any reporters? To respect our ways?"

"You did. And I'm sorry for disobeying." His heart pounded like a hammer on his ribs. What punishment would the bishop mete out?

"Or are you sorry you got caught? You had no twinge

of conscience when you did this, obviously, or you would have kept your mouth shut. Once we tried opening up to the Englisch more, but that didn't work. I've striven to keep our district as closed as possible. Things are changing, so there must be some contact, but not to this extent. Not when you put one of our young women on public display." A bead of sweat trickled down the bishop's round, reddened face.

"You're right, I shouldn't have done it. When I spoke to them, I wasn't thinking." He bit the inside of his lip. "*Nein*, that isn't true. I was thinking. Thinking about Naomi and Joseph and Aaron and the others who will benefit from the extra sales. We made more money this year than in any previous year by a long shot."

"We don't set our store on the importance of money. The Lord provides."

Elam's hands trembled. "I understand. This isn't a matter of greed or personal gain, though. These bills will come. The doctors will charge for their services, as will the hospitals and therapists. Now we have a good deal of money in the bank. The Lord has provided. But just as we plow the fields and plant our crops, we do our share to see that we can pay those to whom we owe money."

Naomi touched his shoulder, and a zing raced down his back. "May I say something?"

The bishop nodded, his arms crossed in front of him.

Naomi spoke in a voice soft and gentle as the wind. "While I don't condone what Elam did, I understand his motives. He wanted to help my son and many others in the district. He only had my welfare and that of so many others in mind. In the end, it turned out fine. No one nosed around here. At the end of the day, the

Englisch all left. It's done and over with, without any additional interference. Elam shouldn't have told my story without my permission, but nothing bad happened because of it."

That zing that zapped through his spine now raced throughout his body. She defended him. He bit back the laughter that bubbled in his chest. Could it be that she forgave him?

"My word is to be obeyed."

At the bishop's proclamation, the chuckle stuck in Elam's throat. He sucked in a deep breath. "*Ja*, it is. And from now on, I will follow what you say."

"Can you?" The bishop scrunched his gray eyebrows together. "I've heard it so often from your mouth that I question the truth of it. You might say it now, but what happens the next time you want to go your own way?"

Could he follow the bishop's directives when he had this habit of running off and doing whatever he wanted, no matter what the man said? "All I can say is that I'll try."

The bishop harrumphed. "Trying is not enough. There must be doing on your part. I will consult with the elders on this matter. You haven't proven yourself to be an asset to the district. We will decide what to do about your future, whether we let you stay. For the time being, keep out of trouble. This is the last I want to hear of your antics. Do I make myself clear?"

Elam nodded, and then stared at his feet.

"*Gut.* Now, I need a piece of my wife's chocolate crazy cake." He turned and left, his step as strong and determined as when he'd marched to confront Elam.

He released a breath he hadn't realized he'd been holding. His future in the district and his life with

Naomi hung in the balance. The bishop and elders would determine his path for the rest of his days. A burning churning filled his gut. He turned back to Rachel and Naomi, who rocked Joseph in her arms. "What am I going to do?"

She straightened the *bobbeli's* lightweight blanket. "If you truly want to be Amish, you are going to have to start obeying the bishop and the Ordnung. For your sake, I hope you do. Now it's time for me to feed Joseph. Think about everything we've said today."

She and Rachel went into the house, the screen door clapping shut behind them. He sagged to the step and sat down, rubbing his temples. *Ja*, he'd heard what the bishop and Naomi said. What he was most sorry about was hurting her. That, he never intended. He'd truly meant it for her good, not for her harm.

What did his future hold? A life with Naomi or a life alone?

Chapter Seventeen

With the din of the bakery swirling around her, Naomi stood over the fryer, dropping in raised doughnuts one at a time until the vat filled. The reek of hot oil and steaming dough overtook her. Not to mention the heat, even though the cement-block basement walls kept the room cooler than the upstairs. She wriggled her bare toes on the chilly cement floor. Out front, customers would be winding their way through the tiny shop, picking out loaves of bread, pies and cinnamon rolls to consume either on the picnic tables set on the grass or once they got home.

Truth be told, it was nice to be out of earshot of Joseph for a few hours. He wasn't sleeping well. Without the aid of a doctor, Mamm diagnosed his sleeping problems. Her *bobbeli* was teething. The first razor-sharp tooth erupted last week. Even knowing what caused him to cry so much didn't make for better rest. He still had her walking the floor with him at the oddest hours of the night. She shook her head to keep awake so she didn't burn the doughnuts.

She rubbed her eyes and focused her attention on the bubbling oil in front of her.

"You'd better turn those before you have an over-fried mess on your hands." Rachel's words pierced through Naomi's groggy haze.

"What? Oh, sorry." She flipped them just in time to avoid having to toss the entire batch.

"You're clearly done in. Why don't you go home?"

"I'm not sure Mamm would let me through the door." Naomi gave a wry laugh.

"Your mamm will understand. I take it Joseph is still keeping you up at night?"

"*Ja.* Then he sleeps during the day, but I can't stay in bed. Chores don't wait until *bobbelin* finish teething. Which I hope is soon. So do Aaron, Laura, Sam and everyone else in the house."

Sylvia came up behind them and squeezed Naomi's shoulder. "I overheard that." She set her jaw. "I'm going to insist that you leave. If you doze off, you might fall in the oil."

"I agree." Rachel narrowed her eyes and frowned in a failed attempt at sternness.

"I'm not quite that tired." Naomi yawned.

"There, now I've caught you in a lie." Sylvia steered her by the shoulders toward the doorway.

"But did you see the line today? It's up the hill to the parking lot. It's Friday, people are on vacation, and the weather is sunny and warm. You need an extra pair of hands."

"You can leave your hands. The rest of you needs to go home."

Naomi couldn't help but giggle. "You have the

strangest sense of humor. That's why I love the two of you so."

"I'm glad I made you laugh. Now, if I can make you rest, my day will be complete. Go on. Rachel has to get back to those doughnuts, and I have pretzels to twist."

"*Denki* for being so understanding about everything. I will make it up to you, Sylvia." Naomi washed her hands and snuck out of the kitchen and into the narrow hallway used as a storeroom.

She opened the door to step out, ready to take a breath of clean summer air, but Elam blocked her way. She tingled all over at the sight of him. *Nein*, she had to stop this nonsense. He was not whom she wanted to run into today. She had to protect herself.

"Where are you off to? Isn't it your day to work?" He stood in front of her, lean and muscular and tanned. Her traitorous heart did a flip.

She shifted her feet in the dirt, avoiding eye contact with him. "*Ja*, but Joseph's teething has been keeping me up at night. Sylvia shooed me out and told me to take a nap."

"That's too bad. Not about your going home to rest, but about Joseph teething. Mamm has some dry rusks in the house for when Mary brings her little guy over. I'll get you some."

For whatever reason, she couldn't bring herself to tell him they'd bought some last week. "I thought you started with the construction company again."

"I did. It's tradition that the new guy on the job brings a treat for the crew. Even though I've worked with this company before, I am the latest hire, so I thought I'd bring them hand pies. Vern, another guy on the crew who brings me back and forth to work, drove me and said he'd be back after the lunch hour."

She hadn't told him about the Herschbergers' offer. Not after the fiasco at the auction. Not after he went behind her back and hurt her again.

A white van with the words *News Station* emblazoned across it in blue and red pulled into the driveway. Naomi went cold. "What are they doing here?"

Elam spun, and then fidgeted with his hat's brim. "Probably doing a story in the area and stopped by for a treat." He gulped. "I'm sure that's all it is."

But his falter told her otherwise. "Did you contact them, too?"

"They're a television station. I only went to the papers. Why would I want to talk to anyone on TV?"

"A television station?" Her mouth went dry.

A fair-haired woman stepped from the van, her dress clinging to her every curve, her lips painted a bright red. A darker man followed and reached back in for a large video camera with a fuzzy microphone on top. They sauntered toward the line of customers that snaked out the door and up the little hill toward the parking lot. The woman leaned toward the man and said something to him.

Naomi shivered. "I don't have a *gut* feeling about this."

Sure enough, the two reporters skirted the line and headed toward Elam and Naomi. She grabbed him by the arm and hissed at him. "You did this. Now undo it."

Elam kept his eyes on the Englisch couple who strode in their direction. The man wore jeans and a casual blue button-down shirt, but the woman wore a navy-blue jacket and skirt and teetered through the grass in high heels. They headed straight for Elam and Naomi, the only Amish people in sight.

Beside him, Naomi sucked in a breath and stiffened. He reached to grab her by the hand, but she pulled away, her fingers icy cold. That chill ran up his arm and straight to his heart.

He sighed. The news station probably got the idea for a story from one of the newspapers. The newspapers *he'd* contacted and given the interviews. So again, his actions would hurt Naomi. His mistakes had this way of never going away. Instead, they rose from the ash heap and haunted him. Well, since he'd made this mess, it was his to clean up. He straightened and met the reporters partway. As he reached them, he glanced over his shoulder. Naomi stood rooted in place.

He cleared his throat. "Good morning."

The woman smiled. She reached to shake his hand, and he reciprocated. "Good morning. I'm Leila Richardson from Channel 9 News, and my cameraman, Jason Turnbull. Through our sources, we heard about the auction held here a couple of weeks ago and how it was to benefit a little boy who needed heart surgery. A Joseph Miller. We believe his mother works at this bakery. Naomi is her name. Do either of you know her?"

"How did you know that? They published the story anonymously."

"I have my sources. Now, if you could point me to this woman."

"Naomi, what are you still doing here?" Rachel called from behind them.

Naomi gasped.

Leila glanced over her shoulder at Jason and gave a

single nod before crossing to stand in front of Naomi. Elam went and stood beside her. From the corner of his eye, he glimpsed Rachel duck back into the bakery.

A wide grin crossed the reporter's scarlet lips. Jason lifted the camera to his shoulder. "Well, it's nice to finally meet the woman behind the story. How is your son doing?"

"He's fine. Why are you here?"

Leila smoothed her perfectly curled hair. "It isn't our intent to intrude on your way of life. But many people are fascinated by the Amish, and the little boy's story in the paper several weeks ago struck a chord with them. A follow-up would be great. Just to let them know how he's getting on. I'm glad to hear he's well. Has he had his surgery?"

"I'm not sure I want to answer any of your questions."

Even though they didn't touch, Naomi stood beside Elam and trembled. He cleared his throat. "It's not our way to be interviewed on camera."

The man nodded. "We understand that. There are several options for conducting the interview. We could show you in shadow, so the audience wouldn't be able to see your faces. We could also just get the audio from you, and add in scenes from the area for the video. If that still makes you too uncomfortable, we could take a statement. Leila would do the voice-over, and again, we'd use shots of things like barns, cows and buggies."

"My son is very ill. He needs peace and quiet to get better, so that, God willing, he will grow into a strong man. Please, go away and leave us alone. That's all I have to say about any of this." With each word, her voice strained.

Elam took half a step in Leila's direction. "Respect Naomi's request. She didn't want any of this attention. I'm the one who went to the papers with the story. She had nothing to do with it. She lives a simple and quiet life and would like it kept that way. When I spoke to the reporters before the auction, I did so against her wishes. I'm sorry you came all this way for nothing, but there will be no statements, no interviews, nothing."

Leila stepped forward and touched his arm. He backed away.

"All I'm asking for is a brief statement as to the child's health. How is he doing? Is he getting better and stronger?"

He gazed at Naomi, who chewed on her lip. "That sounds like more than a brief statement. No one needs to know about my child. I don't even understand why they're so interested."

"Because everyone loves babies. They make the best human-interest stories. Since the public knows the beginning, they're clamoring for the end. I can't tell you how many requests I get each day for more information about the little boy. People stop me on the street and ask, not even realizing I didn't write the newspaper articles. That's why I'm here. Your interview will put the story to rest." Leila drew her lips into a pout. "It's only a small thing I'm asking."

"Not to me." Again, Naomi's voice cracked. She tightened her shoulders. "Are you a mother?"

Leila gave a laugh that was more like a burst of air from her lips. "I'm a career woman, Mrs. Miller. That's my focus in life."

"Then you don't understand my need to protect my child. Do you let the world know your business?"

"It wouldn't interest them. Not like your story."

Elam fisted his hands. There had to be something he could do to stop these people and make them leave her alone. "What, other than a story, will make you go away?"

"Just share with a small corner of the world how the child is." She leaned toward him again, her words softening to an almost-purr. "And I usually get what I want, Mr...?"

Naomi gripped his forearm with a vise-like hold. "Don't you dare even think about telling them anything."

"Now, now, my dear, there's no need for such dramatics. I understand your concern for your son. But give the people what they want, and then they'll stay away. Once their appetite is satiated, they'll be content to let you go back to your regular life. If you don't speak to someone, they'll never leave you alone."

Heat rose in Elam's chest. He fought to keep his hands at his side so he wouldn't strangle the woman. "I was wrong to ever compromise Naomi's privacy. We're done speaking to the press. And you can tell everyone who works at the other television stations and newspapers the same thing. If you would please accept my apologies, I need to get back to work." Not waiting for a reply, he grabbed Naomi by the wrist and pulled her behind him toward the door.

A strident woman's voice followed them. "Did you get all of that, Jason?"

As Elam went to turn the doorknob, he froze.

"We'll be able to piece together a statement from the mother. Good work, as usual." The cameraman's voice held a hint of laughter.

"I do always get what I want. Now, let's see if we can get anyone else here to talk."

Elam spun around as they strode toward their van. He let go of Naomi and raced after them.

They hopped inside the vehicle as he got to them. "Stop. You can't put that on TV. You need a release."

Leila rolled down her window and tipped her head to the side. "Actually, we don't. You were in public."

"Please."

"Let's get out of here, Jason."

With tires spitting gravel that stung Elam's bare forearms, the news van sped from the driveway.

He stood statue-still until it disappeared down the street.

Naomi reached him, tears streaking down her face. "They can't do that, can they?"

"Maybe they can. I don't know, but I doubt there's anything we can do to stop them." He pulled her to himself and held her close.

For a brief moment, she relaxed against him. Then she tried to pull away, but he clung to her. She pounded on his chest. "Let me go. You did this. It's your fault. How could you? How could you?"

He released her.

She stumbled backward against a tree and spat her words at him. "Go away and leave me alone. I don't ever want to see you again." With that, she fled into the bakery.

The weight of the Englischers' stares pressed on Elam's shoulders.

There was only one thing he could do. Without her, staying here was pointless. Not when no one else wanted him.

He needed to leave.

Chapter Eighteen

Naomi hid just inside the bakery's back door, taking only shallow breaths until all fell quiet outside except for the low din of Englisch voices as they waited in line.

Just like the accident, Elam's going to the papers bore consequences that continued to multiply. The news story wasn't going to go away. Tonight, her face and voice would be on televisions all over Wisconsin. When would this nightmare end? Maybe reporters from Chicago or New York would hear about the story and would want to speak to her.

She concentrated on inhaling and exhaling but couldn't get a regular pattern of breathing going.

"Naomi, there you are. What are you still doing here? Elam's out front asking for you." Sylvia wiped her hands on her apron. "*Ach*, what has happened?"

"I can't... I can't... I can't speak to him. Or to anyone." Naomi opened the door and stumbled out.

"Let me walk you home."

"I can—"

"You can't." Sylvia got that no-nonsense mother tone going. "Whatever happened has upset you something awful. You can't even stand upright. I'll help you to your place. It wouldn't do to have you hit by a car."

Out of energy to argue, Naomi leaned against Sylvia as they headed for home.

Home. The only safe place in the world. How long would it be that way? When would the outsiders come and take even that from her? She had lost so much. Her active, athletic brother. The healthy son she'd always longed for. Her husband. They had shared a deep friendship, and she missed that. The nights in the living room as he had read *The Budget* and she'd darned his socks. The easy conversation after dinner. The mornings when he'd come in from the barn and kiss her cheek as she'd handed him a cup of coffee.

Would life ever be like that again?

Elam had hurt her too many times. Over and over, he bumbled his way through life. Always sorry for what he did. But his actions left a trail of heartache.

"This has something to do with Elam, doesn't it?" Sylvia looked both ways and led Naomi across the road.

She swiped at the tears that dribbled down her cheeks. "Doesn't it always?"

"Rachel told me about the truck."

"They're going to put us on television. I didn't know they were filming when they asked about Joseph. Even though I didn't say much, I guess it was enough for them to get their story. And again, it's Elam's fault."

"I'm sorry that had to happen, my dear. But you can't blame Elam for every one of your troubles."

Naomi stopped cold at the end of the driveway. "Why not, when he's to blame?"

"He's worked so hard to gain back your trust. I've watched him these past few months. And you. You're in love with him but afraid to take another risk in letting him into your heart."

"He's already there. And that's the problem. Each time something happens, he's always sorry. Sincerely regretful for what he did. But his choices don't affect just him. He forgets about the troubles he leaves behind for others."

"That young man loves you and would do anything for you and your son. True, he often goes about it the wrong way, but he always, always has your best interest in mind. He wants to help you, to be there for you. Can't you let him? Wouldn't it be easier to bear this burden together with him rather than to walk such a difficult road alone?"

They continued their stroll to the kitchen door. "I might as well be ripped in two. *Ja*, I love him. I do. Maybe more than ever. But I'm also scared of him. Of what disaster he's going to bring this time."

"Think about why you love him. Isn't it because of everything he's done for you and Joseph? For his thoughtfulness and his protection of you. Forget about the past, forgive him of his clumsy attempts at helping you, and forge ahead with the man I suspect you've always loved. We are not promised skies always blue but a Helper to see us through."

"*Ja*, my mamm has quoted that proverb to me many times in the past few years."

"And don't forget about what Elam must be suffering. His guilt over hurting you and Aaron presses on him. I see it in his eyes, how he softens around you, but how he also sorrows over his sins."

Naomi bit her lip. Had he suffered? How much guilt

did he carry? And he walked away from her and their district. How much that must have hurt.

"*Denki*, Sylvia. I can't have a future with Elam, but you've given me something to think about. I'm done in. If I don't get a nap, Rachel is going to scold me like a hen clucks after her chicks."

Like a grossmammi, Sylvia patted Naomi's cheek. "Rest well. Things always look different after some sleep."

Naomi entered the house and clicked the door shut behind her.

No one bustled about the kitchen. The stove sat cold. Maybe Mamm would make a tuna salad or something along those lines tonight. With the heat, it would be too much to cook. The table, the floors, the counters, everything in the room was clean and tidy. Just as it should be. The way it always should be. Welcoming. Home. "Hello? Is anyone here?"

Only the steady ticking of the clock in the living room broke the silence. Where was everyone? And Joseph? She moved to climb the stairs when Aaron rolled in from the back hall.

"I thought you were working today."

"Rachel and Sylvia sent me home to take a nap. Since Joseph hasn't been sleeping well, they were afraid I would doze off and wind up in the fryer."

He smiled, the dimple she'd been envious of as a child deepening in his cheek. "In that case, it is best you came home."

"Where is everyone?"

"Mamm and Laura took Joseph and went to visit Nancy Yoder. You heard she had a baby girl last night?"

"It was all the talk at the bakery." The Amish grapevine spread that word around before the *bobbeli* was fifteen minutes old. "Did you come in for a reason?"

"Daed wanted some lemonade, if there's any made up. It's awfully hot in the shed today, even with the doors open."

"I think there is. Will you just take the jug?"

"*Ja.* And maybe whatever blueberry pie is left from last night."

"I'll get it for you." Good to take her mind off what had just happened.

"Did I see a news van parked outside the bakery?"

"*Ja.*"

"Did they stop for some doughnuts or Danish?"

"*Nein.* And I'm not sure I want to get into it."

"Did those reporters want to talk to you?"

"It's a long story that I'll share tonight so I only have to tell it one time. But in a word, *ja.*"

Aaron rolled to the table, took off his hat and set it down. "You're tired, and you need a nap, but I'm glad we're alone. If you have a minute, I'd like to speak to you."

"Sounds serious. What about?"

"Elam."

With her knees refusing to support her, she leaned against the Formica counter, chipped in a few places by years of hard use. "I don't want to talk about him."

"What I don't understand is why no one in the district or in this house, even, is willing to let go of the past and accept him."

"How can you ask that? Look at you. You'll never be able to walk again, never be able to handle a plow, never stroll with a girl by the river. Every day, you're a reminder of what happened. Of Elam's poor choices. So is that news truck that showed up today."

"We all make bad decisions in our lives. Haven't you eaten something that made you sick, goofed off instead of getting your work done, got upset with someone you love?"

"Don't we all? But those consequences aren't as severe or as permanent and don't affect people the way his choices do."

"Forgiveness is a *wunderbaar* thing, Naomi. And forgetting. That doesn't mean some reminders don't remain, but it does mean choosing to look beyond the past to the present and future. I found a Bible verse the other day that astonished me, that gave me some perspective on the entire matter. I've been bitter about the accident, but this helped me see the situation in a different light."

She stared at her brother, sitting broken in his chair. His face had lost its boyishness, replaced by a certain strength that matured him. He wasn't a child anymore, but a man. One God had given a great deal of wisdom. "What is it?"

"Isaiah 43:25. *'I, even I, am he that blotteth out thy transgressions for mine own sake, and will not remember thy sins.'* If God can forget, why can't we?"

The question hit Naomi in the gut.

Elam slammed the suitcase onto his bed, where it bounced for a moment before coming to rest. He flung open the wardrobe door, his handmade shirts hanging pressed and neat. What was the point in packing? Where he was going, he wouldn't need his Amish clothes.

And this time, he wouldn't be back.

He'd tried this before, leaving the past here to forget. No matter how hard he worked at it, he never got Naomi out of his mind or heart. He thought about her all day long, dreamed about her every night.

But staying in the district would be pure torture. To hear her voice but not be able to speak to her. To smell her sweet fragrance, but not be able to hold her close. She didn't want him here. That much, she'd made clear. She had turned her back on him once more. And the bishop was likely to tell him to leave.

He sighed. From the bottom of the last drawer, he drew out his blue jeans and a plain green button-down shirt. Beside those items sat his tennis shoes. They stared at him, almost daring him to lace them on and to walk away for good.

He squeezed his eyes shut. Did he have the courage to step through that door, never to return to live this lifestyle, even if it was one he believed in? Or did he have the greater courage to stay here and fight for his dreams and for the woman he loved?

Right now, he didn't have the gumption for either. He slumped to the floor, dropping the clothing next to himself. *Oh, God, I don't know what to do.*

Perhaps his sins were too great even for the Lord to forgive.

He heaved himself from the floor and placed his Englisch clothes in the suitcase, and then closed it with a click. If he left here in his Amish pants and shirt, maybe Mamm wouldn't be so brokenhearted.

He didn't want to know what Daed would think.

The house was quiet and empty. Daed must be at work on those account books again. This was the better way. Right now, he had to get to work. From Chase's house tonight, he'd phone Frank and have him deliver the message to Mamm and Daed.

Once in the barn, he moved to the back of the building where his truck sat, covered with a tarp to protect it from dust. He grazed over the passenger-side headlight, the area where he'd struck the tree. The accident had happened so fast.

Aaron had sat behind him, his window opened to the late-fall warmth. "You know what I could go for?"

Elam held on to the steering wheel as they bumped over the road. "Hmm?"

"A pizza. Don't you have your phone? You could call ahead to that one place that has the deep-dish kind, and we can pick it up to go. My mouth is watering." Typical for a sixteen-year-old guy.

"Sounds *gut* to me. What do you want on it?"

"Everything. Pepperoni, sausage, mushrooms, onions, green peppers. Just tell them to leave off the olives."

Elam reached into the cup holder for his cell. He fiddled to unlock it, and then with one hand typed the name of the restaurant into the search engine.

"Elam! Watch out!"

When he peered up, the tree was right there.

More screams.

The crunch of metal.

And nothing but silence.

The nickering of the buggy horse brought him back to the present. That night would haunt him forever.

He shook his head to clear the images and threw his battered suitcase into the backseat.

Daed shuffled in from the office. "Where are you going?"

"To work."

"Vern picks you up."

"He'll be here soon. I'll follow him."

"Why would you do that?"

A slicing pain cut through Elam's head. He leaned against the truck. "Let's face it, Daed. No one in the district is going to accept me. Not the bishop, not Naomi. Not even you. It's time for me to leave."

"For good?"

All Elam could manage was a nod.

"You're running away from your problems again."

Elam held his breath for a moment, then released it a little at a time. Was that what he was doing?

"It's what you always do. When you face a hard time in your life, you take off. But trouble will hunt you down and never let you go."

"What else am I supposed to do when the people here all but shun me?"

"Do you want to be here?"

"*Ja*, of course I do. I never meant to turn my back on this district in the first place. But no one can forget. And all I do is make mistake after mistake." His throat tightened, but he forced the words through the narrow passage. "It's best that I leave, so I don't ruin any more lives."

Daed held on to the truck bed with his left hand. "You haven't seen it yet, have you? You don't understand."

"What?" Elam walked in a circle, removed his hat and finger-combed his hair. "What is it that I don't get?"

"Why you aren't accepted. Why you haven't integrated into the district no matter how hard you try."

"And you aren't going to tell me, are you?" He blew

out a breath. "You're going to make me figure it out on my own, like you always have."

"Do you even want to know?"

"Of course I do."

Daed nodded. "Without raising your voice, tell me what you desire."

Elam forced himself to relax his shoulders. "I want to be a member of this district. I want to open my own outdoor furniture shop, and I want to marry Naomi Miller." The strength of that desire astonished him. He did love her. Always had. Always would. "Because without any of that, I have nothing." His stomach burned.

His gray-haired father stroked his beard with his good hand. "Then I will tell you. Come into the office."

Elam followed Daed to the back of the barn and positioned himself on the squeaky office chair.

"You've been home, what, four or five months now? You say you want to rejoin the district, but you haven't been baptized yet. Do you intend to go through with it?"

"I did. But with planning the auction and taking care of the farm, and after the fiasco with the newspapers, I didn't get around to it."

"A solemn commitment like that shouldn't be something you do when you get around to it. That should be your first priority. If you're serious, do it. Not for Naomi's sake or for the chance to be accepted here, but because you want to live and practice the Amish way of life and our beliefs." Daed sipped from a glass of water on the corner of the neat desk. "Think about that for a while. If you value this way of life, if it's what you truly want, don't leave. Stay here, make that commitment and fight for what you want."

Did he have the fight left in him?

Elam drew in a deep breath. Running away hadn't worked before. Should he stay? Could he?

"Prove yourself to be a man who faces the consequences of his actions. That's what being grown-up and mature is all about. It's what a woman wants in a husband."

Daed was right. Hadn't Naomi even told him he needed to think more? "I'll stay at least for a couple of days while I think about this. Vern will be here soon to take me back to work."

He left the barn, but Daed's words rang in his head. Was part of the reason the community—and Naomi—didn't accept him because he hadn't made a commitment to the district?

Was he ready to take that step? He loved the Lord. He believed in this way of life. The yearning he had as a younger man for the things of the outside world had faded.

Frank had a bumper stick on his van, a verse that had always made Elam stop and think. What did it say again? *"Believe on the Lord Jesus Christ, and thou shalt be saved."*

Believe. That was about it.

He brought his suitcase inside, put it away and went downstairs. While he waited for Vern, he grabbed the big, well-worn family Bible from the small table beside Daed's chair. He flipped through the book of Acts, searching for the passage. Scanning each page, he flipped them over until he came to the fifteenth chapter, in which Peter spoke to the apostles and elders. He said, *"But we believe that through the grace of the Lord Jesus Christ we shall be saved, even as they."*

There it was again. So plain. So simple. All his striving, was it for nothing? Could he ever do enough to earn his forgiveness? This verse and the one on Frank's van both spoke simply of believing.

Nothing else.

A lightness filled him, one that had never occupied his soul, even before the accident. The truth of it wcakened his knees and sent his heart scampering.

To be accepted and forgiven by God, he had to do nothing other than believe.

Headlights swept through the living room, shining on the wall behind Elam. When had it gotten so dark? He peered out the window. Large, heavy, rain-laden clouds filled the sky. Vern, strong and active despite the creeping up of years, sprinted for the house. Elam let him in before he even knocked.

He fussed with his Milwaukee Brewers baseball cap. "They told me at the bakery they'd seen you headed here. The boss has stopped work for the day. Some pretty nasty storms are expected, so we'll get a few hours off. I'll see you in the morning."

"Thank you for coming to let me know. See you tomorrow."

Vern left, and Elam thumped down into Daed's lumpy chair. Free time. Then he could go do what he should have done months ago.

Chapter Nineteen

Lightning sizzled across the sky, followed on its heels by peals of thunder rolling one after the other. Rain lashed the windows, and wind bent the trees like little old ladies.

By the light of the gas lamp, Elam read Daed's Bible, consuming the words of hope. Of forgiveness. Of reconciliation. All of that was possible with God. He closed the book and eased back in the chair, letting it all sink it. Allowing it to take root in his heart and grow.

In the midst of the storm without and the calm within, a knock came at the door. What was that? Elam rose from his chair. The knocking sounded once more, and then again as he made his way through the kitchen.

There, at the door at the top of the ramp, was Aaron. "About time you answered. Can I come in?"

Elam moved to the side and allowed Aaron to enter. "Come in."

"*Denki.* This is a nasty storm."

Elam threw Aaron a dish towel to dry off and hustled outside, pulling Aaron's buggy and horse into the barn. He returned to the house, bucking the wind the entire way. "You must be crazy to be out in this weather."

Aaron handed the towel back to Elam. "Daed needed to me to pick up a batch of drawer pulls he ordered from Paul at the smithy. Took longer than I thought it would, but I figured I could beat the storm home. Guess I was wrong. Thanks for taking me in."

"No one should be out right now. You had *gut* sense to stop."

"I'm glad the storm hit when it did. I've wanted to talk to you for a while now, but it never seemed like the right time or place. I take it your mamm went to see the new baby?"

"Isn't that where all the women are?" Elam chuckled. "Nancy doesn't have to worry about the *bobbeli* keeping her from getting any rest. The visitors will see to that, say not?"

Aaron joined the laughter. "For sure and certain. The prescription for childbirth is a casserole. The cheesier, the better."

"But that's not what you want to speak to me about, I'm guessing."

"Nein." Aaron's laughter faded away, taking his smile with it.

Elam swallowed hard. Maybe he'd heard about the run-in with the news crew. Even with the district's women occupied, word must have spread. No doubt Naomi told him before he left for the smithy.

"I've been doing some thinking about my future. What I want the rest of my life to look like. And it comes down to this. I don't want to work for my daed anymore. You've encourage me and shown me what I can do. I want more for myself."

"Why not?" Elam furrowed his forehead. "You have everything you need there, all the equipment, and your daed is a *gut* teacher. If he could show me how to be a carpenter, he can show you."

Aaron leaned forward on the couch. "That's the problem. You have some kind of idea of how stubborn he is."

Elam nodded. Did he ever.

"He won't listen to me. He's afraid the work will be too much for me, that I'll get sick or hurt. We've had numerous discussions about this. Nothing has changed."

"I know what it's like to run into brick walls with people, to have them not give you a fair chance. But what does this have to do with me?"

"Naomi tells me you want to start your own outdoor furniture shop. Make things like chairs and tables and the like."

"*Ja.*" Elam strung out the word to give himself time to formulate what he had to say next. "But I don't have a shop. No equipment other than a few hand tools and a diesel engine. My daed is just about as stubborn as yours. He still hasn't given me an answer to my idea to use a corner of the barn to get started. That's why I'm back on the construction crew. I'd love to give you a job, but right now, I don't have a business."

Aaron shivered.

Elam jumped up. "I'm not a very *gut* host. Let me pour you some coffee. Mamm always keeps the pot warm on the back of the stove." He went to the kitchen, poured a cup for Aaron and one for himself, and returned to the living room. "Do you need dry clothes, too? I'm sorry to keep you sitting in wet things."

"That might be *gut.*"

Elam got some of his own clothes and Aaron rolled to the bedroom to change. While he did, Elam paced the living room. Aaron was taking his time getting to the point.

What did he want from him? Surely he didn't want to leave the Amish, did he? Might he think that Elam would take him with him and help him find work, maybe with Chase? If that was the case, what would Elam say to him?

After a few minutes, Aaron returned to the living room.

"That must feel better."

"For sure."

"I'm still trying to guess what this all has to do with me."

"I have some money saved from working for Daed, and I'd like to invest it. In you."

Elam stumbled backward and sat in Mamm's rocker with a thump. "In me?"

"I'd like to be partners with you. We might be able to find a little space and get a few tools to get us going. If you'll have me, that is."

The world spun around Elam. He couldn't have heard right. "Why would you want to go into business with me after what I did to you?"

"Because I've forgiven you."

"But you can't forget." Elam's windpipe tightened. "You'll never be able to forget."

"I can."

Elam stared at the sandy-haired man. In the three years he'd been gone, Aaron had grown into a fine young person. Wise beyond his age. Perhaps in times to come, when Bishop Zook was gone, the lot might fall to Aaron to fill that role. Elam could see it. "You have a heart I will never understand."

"I've had plenty of time to read the Bible and think and pray. God has helped me to see many things."

"Like what?"

"That forgiveness is freeing. Putting the past into the past and keeping it there erases all the bitterness and leaves nothing but peace and joy. If God forgives and forgets, why can't we?"

Warmth ran from Elam's head to his toes. He grinned like a young boy with a fistful of candy. "I would love to have you come into partnership with me, but I can't accept your money. You need it more than I do. Later in the fall, I should have enough saved to get my own shop and equipment. But *denki* for the offer, from the bottom of my heart. And when I'm up and running, I'll hire you first thing. I can't say anything more. Your generosity is overwhelming."

"I'm not giving you the money, I'm investing it. I'd like to be equal partners with you."

Elam hugged himself. This couldn't be true. "If that's the case, I'd love to go into business with you. *Denki*."

Aaron's grin matched Elam's. "*Nein*, *denki* for doing this with me. I'm excited to get going, to be out on my own and have some independence. It's a *gut* feeling."

"What is your daed going to say?"

"That's a great question. He might be upset for a while, but he'll see in the end that it's best for me."

A little bit of the lightness left Elam. This decision had further implications, including another reason for Leroy Bontrager to dislike him.

The early evening summer air was soft, the moon large in the eastern sky, the sun touching the western horizon as Naomi drove her buggy along the quiet road. Joseph slept beside her. This moment of peace and quiet was rare. She breathed in the scent of hay and someone's barbecue. Her mouth watered.

A few more days, and she would move into the *dawdi haus*. Finally be on her own with her son. And with his surgery coming soon, she could get back to living a somewhat normal life.

She spurred the horse on. Time to get home and get Joseph settled in his crib. She glanced at him, his little mouth puckering as he dreamed. He'd want to be fed soon.

The clip-clop of the horse lulled her. And then came a thump. Her buggy tilted to one side. Oh great. The wheel must have broken. Now what was she going to do?

Leaving Joseph still sleeping, she slipped from the buggy and surveyed the damage. Sure enough, one of the spokes had snapped. She peered up and down the road. Nothing but emptiness. Not many drove this quiet stretch of street. She paced along the graveled shoulder. How was she going to get home? How long before someone came by?

Joseph woke up and wailed. She unbuckled him from the car seat and jiggled him. Tears still rolled down his thin cheeks. His cry ramped up.

No matter how much she talked to him or walked with him, he wouldn't calm down. His cries filled her ears and tore at her soul. It must be the teething. And not a car in sight. No houses along this stretch of marshy road. But with Joseph continuing to wail, she might have to hike to find a phone. She shivered.

Tears welled in her own eyes. She pinched her nose to keep them at bay, but a few managed to trickle down her face. She swiped them away. Crying wouldn't help the situation. Forcing herself to take a deep breath, she concentrated on formulating a plan. And couldn't come up with anything other than walking to the nearest home and praying the people would be kind.

Then the clip-clop of hooves on asphalt cut through Joseph's sobbing. She blinked away the moisture and cleared her vision. An Amish buggy. Who?

As it approached, the driver waved at her. Elam. How was it that he showed up just when she needed him? Or when she didn't want him. All the time, really. Strong. Reliable.

Her heart hurt. She was tired of the ups and downs of life, of trying to walk through each day alone. She was tired of pushing him away. Of being angry with him. Truth be told, she missed him.

He pulled beside her and reined the horse to a stop. "Need some help?"

Now the tears came fast and furious. Along with her son, she sobbed.

"*Ach*, Naomi." He jumped down and wrapped her and Joseph in an embrace.

She leaned into him, his strong arms around her, protecting her. Right now, she was too tired to fight it. To fight him anymore. Sylvia had said she should allow Elam to help her carry this burden. And in this moment, she would let him.

"What's wrong?"

"Everything. I'm tired of hurting, of blaming, of dredging up the past."

"Put the past in the past and keep it there," he whispered into her hair.

His soft words calmed Joseph. And her. She peered at him through tear-laced lashes. "Is it that easy?"

"Can things ever be the way they once were?"

At the pain in her chest, she sucked in her breath. "*Nein*, Elam, we can't go back to the past, no matter how much we may want it. We can't deny all that has happened."

"And neither can we move forward, can we?" With a grunt, he stepped away from her. "Why, Naomi, why? You turned your back on me after the accident, never giving me a chance to explain. Never giving me a chance to apologize. If only you had listened to me."

A groan escaped her lips. "I couldn't. Not then. Not when Aaron was suffering. And you didn't stay around long enough for me to get to the place where I could hear what you had to say."

"And now?"

Once more, she rested against him. "I think it's time to do that. To let go of it all."

His breath brushed her cheek. "Can you?"

"If I truly want to live and to love again, I have to." Her pulse pounded in her ears.

"Then I'm only going to ask you this one more time. Naomi Miller, do you forgive me for injuring your brother, for running away and leaving you, for sharing your private story with the world?"

The corners of her lips turned up. "*Ja*, Elam, I forgive you."

A truck whizzed by, one similar to Elam's, the breeze of it whipping her skirt around her knees. What was she doing, standing in the middle of the road hugging Elam Yoder? She pulled herself from his embrace. Joseph whimpered. "I put the past in the past, like you said. But there can be no future for us. I'm sorry if I gave you the wrong impression just now. Could you fix the buggy? Or take me somewhere I can call for help?"

He bowed his head a fraction of an inch and stared at the blacktop, his shoulders slumped. "Why not?"

"Please, I don't want to talk about it." Joseph revved up for another good cry. "Just get me home."

The forgiving part was *gut*. A lightness filled her chest that hadn't been there for years.

But the ache that gripped her heart didn't ease.

Chapter Twenty

With shaking, sweaty hands, Elam knocked on Bishop Zook's door. This was the last move for him to make. For himself. For the district. For Naomi.

Martha Zook opened the door, her black apron covering her round middle. Crinkles formed at the corner of her eyes as she smiled. "How good to see you, Elam."

This was the warmest reception he'd had from just about anyone in the area since his return other than the Herschbergers. Did she have some inkling as to why he was here?

"I just finished the frosting on a chocolate crazy cake. Come in and have a slice. And I'll pour you a nice cold glass of milk."

Elam's mouth watered at the thought. Martha Zook was known throughout the area and beyond for her chocolate crazy cake. She had a secret ingredient that made it the most sought-after dessert at any church function.

"While your offer is the most tempting one I've received recently, this isn't a social call. I need to speak to your husband. Is he around?"

"If the buggy's in the yard, I expect you'll find him in the greenhouse. He's probably out there watering all his little mum plants."

"*Denki.* It was good to see you."

"The offer of cake still stands. When you finish with Reuben, come back and have a piece. Don't leave it for just the two of us. Goodness knows I don't need it all."

The Lord had never granted Reuben and Martha Zook any children, but they treated the *kinner* of the district, each and every one of them, as their own. And, in Martha's case, that included Elam. He wandered across the yard, behind the barn and around the field of feed corn to the large, rectangular greenhouse at the edge of the Zook property. The bishop sold perennials, annuals and vegetables in the spring, but he was best known for the beauty and variety of the mums he brought out in the fall. Elam stepped into the warm, sun-filled building.

Sure enough, there was Bishop Zook pushing a dolly with a hug blue plastic water tank on it, dipping into it every so often and watering his plants.

"Bishop Zook."

The older man waved at Elam. "I'll be right there. Let me finish this row so I don't lose my place."

The delay did nothing for Elam's nerves. A colony of butterflies—*nein*, maybe bumblebees—danced in his stomach. His hands shook more than when he'd knocked at their door. And the sweat dripping down his face was not from the heat in the building. What if the bishop said no? "Take your time." But hurry up.

While the bishop tended to his plants, Elam paced, his hands stuffed in his pockets, until he had a neat trench worn into the soft sand.

Bishop Zook made his way down the aisle between

the flats of greens, stopping to pick a dead leaf or two. "Well, Elam, to what do I owe this visit?"

"Can we go somewhere to sit and talk?" His legs wouldn't hold him upright much longer.

"Sure. Before I left the house, Martha told me she was making a crazy cake. It must be about done. We can have a piece and chat."

"I'd rather it be in private."

"Ah." The bishop strung out the word like it had five or six syllables. "Let's go to the barn. We can pull up a couple of bales of straw."

Elam followed the older man to the barn and situated himself on a bale across from him. The straw prickled his backside through his heavy cotton pants, and he squirmed, unable to get comfortable.

"Now, tell me the reason why you've come."

When he attempted to form the words, Elam's voice cracked. He cleared his throat and tried again. "I've come to do something that I should have done months ago. Years ago, really. And I think it will affect what you and the elders decide about me."

Bishop Zook nodded, his thin lips straight, his clear blue eyes narrow. "What is it?"

If he didn't blurt out the words right now, he'd never say them. "I've come to confess that I've been wrong about many things in my life." Elam's heart hammered against his ribs faster than any man could swing a mallet.

"Go on."

"When I was a young, I was headstrong and foolish. When people call me *grossfeelich*, they're right. I am too big for my britches. I was wrong to own a truck and a cell phone. And on that one night, I was wrong to be driving and ordering pizza on that phone. Aaron Bontrager's paralysis is my fault, and for that, I am sorry. I confess my sin before you and before God."

Did one corner of the bishop's mouth rise the tiniest of amounts?

Elam drew in another breath. "And I was wrong to go to the press with Naomi's story after both you and she had forbidden it. Like Abraham with Hagar, I rushed ahead of the Lord, wanting to give Him a helping hand instead of waiting for Him to bless the auction. Of that sin, I also repent before you and before God."

All the air rushed out of Elam's lungs, and he hunched his shoulders, never taking his sight from the bishop's face. Would he forgive him?

Yet a heavy board lifted from his shoulders, from his chest. A rush of air filled him. Did it matter if any man forgave him when the Lord already had?

The bishop stroked his beard and gazed at Elam long and hard. "Are you sincere in your repentance?"

"Ja." Hadn't he sounded like he was genuine? "Every word I said, I meant. All this time, I've been an impetuous and reckless young man. I understand now that forgiveness must first come from the Lord. That His cleansing is the most *wunderbaar* gift of all." He blew out a breath.

"I see." Bishop Zook's gaze didn't waver for a moment. "What you've done is very serious, Elam. You weren't a member of the church when you had your truck, but you caused a disastrous accident that had serious consequences."

"I'm aware of that. Yet Aaron doesn't hold any bitterness toward me. He has forgiven me. And forgotten my sins against him."

"The more present problem is your unwillingness to submit to my authority. Do you want to be baptized and join the church?"

"*Ja.* That is why I've come to confess to you today."

"As a member of the Amish church, you would be under obligation to obey my instructions, no matter how unfair or unjust you think they are. If you have any reservations about that, then I suggest you not join. To be placed under the *bann* is a most difficult thing for a family. And a church."

"I understand."

"You aren't doing this just to get into Naomi Miller's good graces, are you?"

"*Nein,* not at all. I'm doing this for myself alone." But how would Naomi react to his baptism?

Bishop Zook nodded. "This is a matter that I must think on and pray about. One that I don't take lightly, and you shouldn't either."

"I never would."

"Give me time. I'll let you know later what my decision is." Bishop Zook stood up and brushed the straw from the back of his pants. "Now, let's go get a slice of Martha's crazy cake. She makes the best I've ever tasted, say not?"

How would Elam swallow while his future remained unclear? If only the bishop would hurry up and make his decision.

The warmth and conversation of the bakery swirled around Naomi as she kneaded the dough that would become a loaf of seven-grain bread, turning it over and over. Like she rolled the idea of loving Elam around in her mind.

Because she did. More now than ever. When they were engaged before, they'd both been young and maybe not truly ready for marriage, at least not to each other. She turned to Rachel, who kneaded dough for cinnamon raisin bread. "Do you ever wonder about if life happened differently?"

"What do you mean?"

"Like, what if the accident never happened and I had married Elam?"

Rachel blew a loose strand of hair from her face. "You wouldn't have Joseph."

Naomi sucked in a breath. "You're right. I never thought about that."

"God has His reasons and His ways. They aren't ours to know."

What would her life be like without Joseph? Not to see his sweet smile in the morning? Not to hear his laughter when his grossdaadi made faces at him? Not to smell his sweet powder smell when she held him close? "That's true. God has His reasons and His ways. And maybe He means for me to have a new life now with Elam."

Rachel stopped her work and turned to Naomi. "I've watched you the past week or so, and you seem happier. More at peace. Is that because you've made a decision about him?"

"I don't know. Trusting him is hard. Surrendering completely, you know. If I commit to him, I want it to be with my whole heart and for the right reasons. And I don't want to doubt him, not ever again. That isn't the way to build a marriage. If I can't do that, I have no right to be joined to him."

"What are you going to do?"

"I told him the other night that there couldn't be a future for us. But I said it because I was scared."

"Is it time for you to let go of that fear, leave what happened behind, and step out in faith?" Rachel's words were soft but demanded an answer.

As if he'd heard them talking about him, Elam strolled into the bakery. All of the women turned toward him. Many of them still held a hardness toward him. But what had started as an impenetrable wall between her and Elam melted like the ice on a warm spring day. When she saw him now, her heart didn't ache, but it fluttered in her chest.

"*Gut morgan*, everyone." He wound his way to the side of the large table where Naomi stood. "Is there a pie I can buy to take to work with me? I want to treat the crew on the job site."

"You're very early this morning. We aren't even open yet."

"I have to get to work."

"Take your pick, then." She nodded in the direction of the wire racks in the front room where the customers lined up for their goods.

He made his selection, a crust loaded with blueberries and topped with crumble, and came back to her. "Will you walk me out? I have something I want to discuss with you."

"Just give me a minute." She set the dough in a greased bowl, covered it and set it in a warm place to rise. Struggling to keep up with his long strides, she followed him outside.

The wind rattled the branches in the trees. Elam studied the sky for a moment before turning his attention to her. He gazed at her, intense, and breathed through his mouth.

What was it? Was he leaving again? Her pulse raced.

"I went to the bishop about a week ago."

"Oh." She couldn't draw in so much as a puff of air.

"We had a long talk. About the past and the future."

Wouldn't he just come out and say what he needed to tell her? That the other night was their last goodbye. That he was walking away from her once more.

He rubbed his cheek. "I went to him asking for forgiveness for everything I've done. The accident. Leaving. Going to the papers. All of it. It felt so *wunderbaar*. Even though I know God has forgiven me, I still want the people around me to do the same. And I want to be baptized."

The world tilted. Did Elam see the pulse pounding in her neck? "And what did the bishop have to say?"

"He hasn't given me an answer yet. Who knows what that means? I can only pray that he will accept my confession."

"That would be *gut* for you if he did." Her tongue stuck to the roof of her mouth.

"And maybe for you. Is there any hope at all for us? You said the other night there wasn't, but I have to ask one more time. You've forgiven me, and I'm so grateful for that. Could you consider…maybe…loving me again?"

She trembled. Could she? Really, she didn't have to ask herself the question. She knew her answer, even though she'd denied it to herself. Rachel was right. The time had come to take a step forward.

"I've done a lot of thinking since that night by the side of the road. I discovered that I do still love you,

Elam Yoder. That hasn't changed. This time, though, my love is more cautious, more mature."

He nodded and caressed her cheek, a shiver shooting through her. "You know I never stopped loving you. Each and every day, I thought of you. You're what drew me back."

"I'm glad you came. But I hope you aren't doing this for me." She touched his forearm, tingles racing up her own. "You need to do this for yourself. To find your own peace and your own place here."

"That is why I went to the bishop."

"And what happens if he refuses to baptize you?"

"Do you think he will?" He shifted his weight from one foot to the other and back again.

"I don't know."

"If he doesn't, what happens to us'?"

She couldn't look him in the eye but gazed at the leaves dancing in the wind. "You know I can't leave my home, my family or my church. This is where I belong. They have been so kind to me since Daniel died. They've helped me with Joseph. How can I walk away from this place where I belong?" She bit her lower lip. If he left, only little pieces of her would remain.

"Then I won't ask anything of you until I hear from Bishop Zook. But know this. I love you. I'll never stop loving you." He hopped in his buggy and clicked to his horse.

For the longest time after he left, she stood staring at the spot where he'd turned out of sight. "I love you, too, Elam Yoder."

Chapter Twenty-One

In the dimming daylight, Elam slid open the barn's big door, his muscles straining with the task. He stepped through the opening, the sweet smell of hay and the pungent odor of cow manure welcoming him. He'd missed this while he was gone. He moved to the back of the building where the truck sat covered with a tarp. He drew it back and examined his vehicle. The body shop did an expert job. Even though he knew where the damage had been, he couldn't tell the truck had ever been in such a terrible accident. No dents, no dings, no scrapes.

Before he sold it, he'd have to give it a thorough cleaning, inside and out. Maybe buy one of those pine-scented cardboard trees to hang from the rearview mirror to get rid of the farm stench. And then wash his hands of it forever.

He opened the door and retrieved the key from under the floor mat, the metal of it cool and smooth in his hand. When he'd driven it last, it had been fine, but he should probably at least change the oil and check the tire pressure before he put a for-sale sign on it.

After taking a deep breath, he slid into the driver's seat

and turned the ignition. The truck roared to life. He pushed the gas pedal a few times. The engine hummed. Good. Maybe he wouldn't have to do any other maintenance to it.

Just as he was about to turn the truck off, Naomi entered the barn, Joseph in her arms. With the dying light behind her, she was beautiful. He couldn't breathe. She loved him. If only the bishop would see fit to restore him. Then they could be married. He forced in a lungful of air.

What he wanted most in the world stood just outside his grasp.

She came to the driver's side of the truck, and he cut the engine and slid out. "I'm surprised to see you here. What brought you by?"

She gave him a shy smile, the light reaching her eyes, almost violet to complement the color of her dress. "I was at the store for a few things Mamm needed, and I saw you go into the barn. You piqued my curiosity when you started the engine." Joseph wriggled and gasped for breath. "I don't know what drew me inside. You, possibly?"

His heart somersaulted. Was she flirting with him? "I'm glad you did." His words came out in a croaked whisper.

"Have you heard anything from Bishop Zook?"

"Not a word."

"This waiting is hard." She stepped closer, so close that Joseph reached out and grabbed his shirt.

Never had she been so beautiful, a tendril of chestnut hair escaping the bun at the base of her neck, curling around her collarbone. He leaned closer and gave her a gentle kiss, her lips soft, tasting of sugar. Better than he remembered.

What was he doing? He straightened and backed against the truck. "I'm sorry."

"I'm not."

His head swam. "You don't have anything to be sorry about, like I do. I shouldn't have started something we might not be able to finish. You can't leave, and I might not be able to stay. More than anything, I want to build a family with you. If the bishop won't baptize me, that won't be possible. I refuse to hurt you that way again." His chest ached.

She nodded. "Then we have to pray that the bishop will allow you to join the church. Because if you left, I would miss you very much. Maybe even more than before."

He groaned and rubbed his temples.

"I wish there was something I could do."

Joseph reached for Elam, and he took the *bobbeli* from his mother. Better for him to hold the baby. Then he wouldn't be able to take Naomi into his arms. "There is nothing to be done. All we can do is wait for the decision."

She glanced away, studying the length of the truck. "Were you going somewhere?"

"*Nein*, just making sure it still ran. I'm going to sell it. That's something I should have done long ago. When I first got back. It's a reminder of an awful time in my life. Our lives."

"But you did get me and Joseph to the clinic when he was so sick, so something *gut* came of it."

He blinked as he stared at her, her eyes wide in her heart-shaped face. This was a different Naomi. Not the sorrowing, frightened, closed-in woman of a few months ago.

"I never even thanked you for that."

"There was no need for you to. I was glad to help."

"You've been nothing but *gut* to us, and all I did was treat you badly. In fact, I have a surprise for you to make up for that. Simon and Sylvia have agreed to let you use their barn to start your business."

"You arranged that for me?"

She nodded. "To show you my appreciation for what you've done for us and to make up in a small way for the hurt I caused you. I shouldn't have shut you out the way I did. When you came to me after the accident, I should have listened to you. Maybe I could have spared you some pain. Perhaps things would have been different."

"*Denki*. I can't thank you enough. That you should do this for me." He swallowed hard. "I'll be able to start sooner than I dared to hope. What has changed you?"

"Aaron. Daniel. And God. Mostly God. Aaron shared a verse with me. About God blotting out our sins and remembering them no more. That is what true forgiveness is all about. When I realized that, I was able to let go of the past. Everything. The accident. You leaving. Daniel dying. I'm ready to embrace the future."

His throat constricted. "But that future might not include me."

Naomi bent over the green bean plants, the pods full and ripe. She snapped several off and dropped them in the basket beside her. She, Mamm and Laura had a great deal of work ahead of them, canning this haul of beans. But eating them cooked in bacon fat in February made all the hard work worth it.

She stood and worked a kink out of her back. Elam's words from yesterday rang in her head. If the bishop refused to baptize Elam, he wouldn't stay. And she wouldn't go. She couldn't. Everything she knew, everything she held dear, was here. Even with how much she loved him, she would never leave.

He had told her there was nothing they could do but

pray. *Ja*, that was a *gut* thing to do, for sure and certain. Was it the only thing?

Maybe there was something else. Maybe there was a way she could influence the outcome. She brushed off her dirty hands, stepped over the ruts in the garden and went to the house.

Mamm didn't even glance up from her blackberry jam. "Done with those beans already?"

"I'll finish them later. I have an errand to run right now. Can you watch Joseph for a while more?"

"Of course I can. You don't even need to ask. Where are you going?"

"It's sort of private. I'd rather not say. At least not right now."

At this, Mamm did turn to her. "What is going on? You've been different the past few days. Almost...well, almost glowing."

Naomi covered her mouth and shook her head. "It's your imagination."

"I think it has something to do with a certain young man."

She shrugged.

"Be careful."

She kissed Mamm's cheek. "I must get on with my errand. I'll see you later." She washed her hands and slipped off her dirty apron before harnessing the horse to the buggy. Coneflowers and daylilies bloomed along the side of the road, a riot of purple and orange.

She didn't have far to go to get to her destination. In short order, she pulled into Bishop Zook's driveway. She brought the horse to a halt. Martha, crouched over the beans in her own garden, stood and waved to her. "Come, come, tell me what's brought you by today."

Naomi scrambled across the garden, silk drooping

from the corn stalks, little green tomatoes clinging to the plants. "Your garden looks *wunderbaar* this year."

"The Lord blessed us with plenty of rain." Martha laughed. "I'm glad there wasn't much water toting needed this year."

"You're right."

"Let's go in the house, and I'll put on the coffeepot."

"I've actually come to speak to your husband."

"*Ach*, just like Elam a week or so ago. I think you'll find Reuben in the tack room. Come inside first, though, and take a thermos of coffee with you. No one should have a chat without at least a coffee cup in their hands."

That statement just about summed up Martha Zook. Since there was no point in arguing with her, Naomi got the thermos and two cups and went to find the bishop.

He was in the tack room, just as Martha said, oiling the reins and harnesses. She knocked on the door so she didn't scare him.

"Naomi, what a pleasant surprise. To what do I owe this visit?"

"I need to talk to you about something. But first, I've brought coffee from your wife. She said we couldn't talk without it."

Reuben chuckled, the melody like a deep wind chime. "That sounds like my Martha. Have a seat and pour us each a cup."

Once they each held a steaming mug, the bishop leaned back, the old wooden office chair creaking, and crossed his legs. "What is it you want to talk to me about? I can almost guess why you're here."

"And you'd be right. Elam told me he stopped by not too long ago to confess and to request to be baptized. I've come to ask that you grant his request."

Chapter Twenty-Two

The Englischer popped the hood of Elam's truck and bent over the engine, examining the belts and checking the oil and transmission fluid levels. "Nice and clean. When was the last time you said you drove it?"

"A few weeks ago. But I just changed the oil, and it runs good." Elam held back the excitement in his voice. A potential buyer for his truck after only one day for sale.

The man flipped off his baseball cap and scratched his shaved head. "Has it ever been in an accident?"

Elam swallowed hard. "Yes." The word squeaked by his lips.

"How bad was the damage?"

"The front passenger side was pretty mangled. But the body shop did a full repair. It's as good as new."

"I'm going to have to think about it." The man meandered around the truck one more time.

Nein, Elam needed the man to buy the truck. Right here and now. Where had this urge to be rid of the vehicle as soon as possible come from? Like some force had hit him from behind and propelled him forward. "There isn't a scratch on it now."

"It is in good shape." The man chomped on a piece of gum. "But it sounds like it was a serious accident. What happened?"

Why had Elam pushed? Now he had to explain. He drew in a deep breath. "I hit a tree while I was on my cell phone."

"So why are you getting rid of it?"

Elam almost laughed at the absurdity of the question. "I'm joining the Amish church, and we're not allowed to have cars. That's the only reason." And he didn't mind giving up his truck. Not anymore. They were fast, dangerous and only got you into trouble. Much better to stick with a horse and buggy. People got hurt in those, certainly, but not like in cars.

The man stood facing the truck's grille, legs akimbo. "That accident makes me nervous."

"It wasn't the truck's fault." Elam grinned.

The man, Payton, chuckled. "I suppose not. But a damaged frame is a concern. It makes the truck less safe in the case of another accident."

Elam nodded. He fidgeted with the hem of his jacket.

"Well, let me sleep on it. I'll be back if I decide to go with it." Payton turned toward the barn's entrance and took five steps in that direction.

"I'll take a thousand dollars off the price." The words slipped from Elam's mouth before he could check them.

Payton stopped and rubbed the back of his neck. "I don't know. You're tempting me."

Gut. In this case, temptation was a very *gut* thing.

"But I still want to think about it."

"Fifteen hundred dollars discount if you buy it today.

That's my final offer." Elam hugged himself and held his breath.

Payton turned around. "Your final offer?"

What if he walked away? He wouldn't come back. Elam would lose this potential buyer. But maybe the man was testing him. "Yes. It's more than a fair price."

A slow smile spread across Payton's tanned face, and he stuck out his hand to shake Elam's. "You have yourself a deal. I'll run to the bank and be back with your money in about an hour."

Elam released his breath in a slow stream. "I'll have it ready to go for you then."

Payton was as good as his word. An hour later, Elam signed the title over to him, took the cash and stood at the end of the driveway as Payton drove the black pickup down the street, over the hill and out of sight.

He covered his face and breathed in and out. A knot that had kinked his stomach for a long time loosened. Like closing out the year on financial statements, he could shut the cover to this part of his life and start with a clean record book.

He fingered the money in his pocket. Even though he'd given Payton a hefty discount on the vehicle, Elam still possessed a wad of cash. Maybe he could buy Naomi something. But as a Plain woman, she didn't need anything. Perhaps it would go a fair way in a down payment on a house for them and Joseph. That was a *gut* idea, but not the right thing to do with the money.

Ja, there was one person this money belonged to. Elam strolled to the barn and hitched up the buggy. From now on, this would be his only means of transportation. He smiled and gave a one-note laugh at the way Naomi had held on to the truck's seat for dear life when he drove her to the clinic. She wouldn't have to do that in the buggy.

Because it was Friday, Naomi would be at the bakery, not at home, and that was a *gut* thing. Today he didn't pull into the Bontragers' driveway to see her. Instead, he parked near the wood shop and entered.

Naomi's daed pounded a dovetail joint together.

Elam stepped farther in, holding the envelope in his hand behind his back. "Hello."

Her daed peered up and harrumphed. "Thought I told you never to come back."

"Actually, I came to see Aaron. Is he around?"

Leroy nodded in the direction of the back room. "But don't bother him long. He has work to do."

"I won't." Elam followed the pungent stench of varnish to where he found Aaron staining a long dining room table. He whistled. "That's beautiful."

Aaron glanced up for a moment and grinned before returning his attention to his work. "*Denki.* I can see a large family gathering around it for special meals like Thanksgiving and Christmas." A wistfulness tainted his words.

"You do exceptional work. I take it you haven't told your daed about our business venture yet."

Aaron concentrated on the job in front of him. "I haven't found the right time for the announcement."

"You can back out if you want. We don't have to go through with the deal."

"I will. Tell him, I mean."

"He told me not to keep you, so I won't." He handed the envelope to Aaron. "This is yours. It's not much, but I hope it helps you in some way."

Elam spun around and hurried through the room, the

main shop and outside. He had almost made it to his buggy when Naomi crossed the street from the bakery. "Elam, I didn't expect you."

"I came to see—"

"Joseph has a doctor's appointment. Frank should be here any minute."

"Elam." The gravel crunched under the wheels of Aaron's chair.

Elam's heart pounded faster than a galloping horse.

Naomi glanced between Aaron and Elam. Elam's face resembled that of a fresh January snowfall. Aaron's was as red as a September sunset.

"Elam, wait." Aaron, breathless, motored across the yard. "I can't take this from you."

"*Nein*, I want you to have it." Elam stepped into his buggy.

Naomi went to him. "What's going on?"

"Nothing. This is between me and Aaron." He turned to her brother. "And don't say anything to her about it."

Naomi's windpipe closed, and she stomped her foot. "What are you talking about? Will someone please tell me?"

Aaron arrived at the buggy, sweat pouring from under his straw hat and down his face. In his hand, he held an envelope. "I don't know why you're giving this to me, but it belongs to you."

Naomi snatched the envelope from her brother. Elam reached out to grab it away, but she stepped back.

"Please, don't open it. This doesn't concern you."

She hesitated a moment. Elam widened his eyes and shook his head.

"Go ahead, Naomi." Aaron nudged her. "See what's in it."

She lifted the flap. Elam groaned. She gasped. "What is all this?"

"It's a lot of money. Money he gave me and told me was mine."

Naomi turned to Elam. "Is it his?"

"In a way, *ja*." Elam did little more than whisper. "It's my money, and I want him to have it. By rights, it belongs to him."

Naomi furrowed her brow. "Will one of you explain?"

Aaron shrugged. "It'll have to be him, because I don't understand myself. What do you mean that it belongs to me?"

"I sold my truck."

Naomi almost missed the soft-spoken words. Her mouth went dry. "You sold it?"

"Ja."

"It's gone."

Elam nodded. "And I can't say I'm sorry about it."

She couldn't stop the smile from stretching across her face. "Thank God. We can say goodbye to that chapter in our lives. Close the door and lock it. But what does this have to do with the money?"

"Those are the proceeds from the sale. Every penny the man paid me."

Aaron's mouth opened, but no words came out.

Naomi spoke for him. "Why?"

"It was me and my miserable truck that put him where he is today. Where he always will be."

Naomi drew in a breath to speak, but Elam raised his hand to stop her.

"Your family has gone through an awful time, in large part because of me. You have enough expenses with Joseph's care. I want to help. To ease your burden in whatever small way I can."

Naomi's knees buckled, and she leaned against Elam's buggy to stay upright. "You did that? For us?"

He touched her cheek, his fingertips cold against her warm skin. "No, *Liebchen*, I didn't do it for you, or for Aaron, or even for myself. I did it for God. He has given me so much. I have no right to keep the money. It was money that should never have been spent on an item I should never have bought. In the Englisch world, they call that coming full circle. It just means that everything is back to the beginning. To the way it should be. At least as much as it ever will be."

She couldn't stop the tears that tracked down her face and dripped from her chin. If only Aaron weren't looking, she would kiss Elam right then and there. Instead she grasped him by the hand. "You are a *gut* man, Elam Yoder. I am sorry I ever doubted you. *Ich liebe dich.* I love you." Was it possible for a heart to overflow with such emotion?

Aaron backed up his chair and headed toward the shop. "You two need some time alone." His chuckle faded as he went inside.

Elam kissed the palm of her hand. "This is why I didn't want you to find out. Because I knew you would get weepy."

"Is there anything wrong with that?"

"*Nein*, but I don't want you to get your hopes up. I still haven't heard from the bishop."

How could she ever live without this man in her life? She bit her lip. What was most important to her? "I—"

"Don't you ever, ever say it. Because I could never ask it of you."

"But you sold your truck. What happens if the bishop says no? And you gave your money to Aaron."

"I will have the business I'm starting, so I'll be fine. God will provide. He always does."

"But—"

"Please, don't say anything more. You have to get Joseph to the doctor, remember?"

She swiped the tears from her eyes just as Frank's white van pulled up the driveway. "I need to go." By the time she finished getting the words out of her mouth, Elam had already clucked to his horse and was on his way toward the street.

She stood as still as a deer in the woods that knows he's been spotted and stared as the orange caution triangle on the back of his buggy disappeared.

At the banging shut of Frank's van door, she jumped.

"Are you just about ready to leave? Where's that handsome son of yours?"

"I'll go get him." She turned to the house.

"Naomi, wait."

At Daed's voice, she spun around again. "I'm late for Joseph's appointment."

"I want to know what is going on between you and Elam."

She glanced in Frank's direction, and then back at Daed. "I can't go into it now. Can we talk later?"

"You can be sure we will."

Chapter Twenty-Three

In the glow of the gas lantern light, Naomi sat in the rocker in the living room, Joseph in her lap as she lulled him to sleep. Daed sat across from her in his big recliner, the family's German Luther Bible in his hands, Mamm and Laura on the couch, Aaron in his chair in the corner, near the wood-burning stove. Would they still gather like this when she moved next door? These nights would be a thing of the past if she married Elam.

If. The question hung over her head.

Daed leafed through the pages, searching for a passage to read for family devotions. He found the spot where they left off last night, and intoned the words of Scripture. Naomi rocked to the cadence of his speech.

What if she lost Elam? Could she stand the hole he would leave in her heart? Once he had been ripped from her. A second time might leave a wound from which she would never recover.

She scanned the room. Laura fidgeted with the hem of her apron and tapped her foot. Always on the go, she had a hard time sitting still every evening for the Bible reading. Sunday services were pure torture for her. The same for Samuel, who wriggled more than Joseph.

Beside her, Mamm sat with her hands folded on her lap, gazing at her husband, never wavering. Solid and steady, that was Mamm.

And Aaron, sitting straight in his chair, focused on the darkness outside the window, wise beyond his years. Was he as truly happy and content as he led the world to believe?

If the decision came down to Elam or her family, could she choose? If she could but split herself in half and be both places at once.

Daed coughed. He had finished the reading. The rest of her family bowed their heads in silent prayer. She followed suit. *God, please soften the bishop's heart. Allow us to be together here, in this place I love the most. I can't make this decision myself. Don't let me have to make it.*

The family stirred, and she opened her eyes. Daed rose to get ready for bed.

Aaron fidgeted and then spoke. "Can everyone stay for just a minute more? I have something to announce." His eyes didn't twinkle, and no smile lifted the corners of his mouth. He rubbed the arms of his wheelchair. What was coming?

Daed returned to his chair, and Mamm settled on the couch again. Laura shook her head. "Will this take long?"

"As you know, Elam came to see me this afternoon."

"Is that all this is about?" Laura stood.

Mamm pulled her down. "Listen to your brother without interruption."

"*Ja*, that is what this is about. He told me he sold his

truck, the one involved in the…accident. And he handed me an envelope. In it was all the money from the sale of his vehicle. Thousands of dollars."

Mamm gasped. Even Daed sat forward. "Why would he do such a foolish thing?"

"It's not foolish. He wants to help our family. He knows we have more than our share of doctor expenses. Even though the auction brought in plenty, this will keep us from dipping into the medical fund and leave more for others. That's the kind of man Elam Yoder is."

Daed frowned.

"And there's one more thing. In a few weeks, I'm going into business with him. He's starting a firm that makes outdoor furniture, and I want to be part of it. He has agreed to make me a partner."

"I will not have you leaving the family business to take on a venture with that man." Daed raised his shoulders and puffed out his chest. "Who will work with me?"

"You have Solomon. And in a few years, you'll have Samuel. They are more capable than I am."

"But I need you."

"You don't. With the little I do, you won't notice I'm gone. I'd like to try a different job, one that utilizes more of my skills."

Daed grunted, his eyes narrow.

Naomi jumped to her feet, startling Joseph awake. She shushed him, and he closed his eyes again. "Before you say anything, Daed, I agree with Aaron and think you should allow them to work together. Elam made a mistake. That was almost four years ago already."

"A mistake that was as much my fault as his. I told him to call ahead for pizza. If I hadn't done that…"

Daed slapped his thigh. "I will not have you blaming yourself for what happened."

Naomi stared at Daed. "Then you shouldn't blame Elam either. It's time to we moved past this. Isn't that the way of our people?"

"*Ja*, but—"

"No more *buts*. Remember the story from years ago about the shooting at the West Nickel Mines School in Pennsylvania? Families had children, little girls, who were gunned down there in cold blood. But that very night, in the midst of their grief, they visited the shooter's family, to offer them comfort in their loss."

"I recall that. You don't have to remind me." But a bit of the gruffness left Daed's voice.

Naomi, still clutching Joseph to her, kneeled in front of Daed. "Then how can we do any less? We still have Aaron with us. If they could see past their own tragedy to others' pain the same night it happened, shouldn't we be able to do that after so much time? And I happen to know that Elam went…" She bit her tongue. Maybe he didn't want the world to know.

Daed cupped her chin. "What has he done?"

She lowered her gaze.

"Tell me."

"He went to Bishop Zook and confessed all his wrongs. Everything. The accident. The papers. He's asked to be baptized, but the bishop is still making up his mind, weighing whether or not Elam's confession is sincere. And I went to see the bishop myself."

Daed drew his brows together. "Why would you do such a thing?"

"Because I love Elam, and I know he's changed. He's not the same person who left here in disgrace. In the time he was away, Elam grew up. Gone is the rash young man he used to be. He's wise, thoughtful and the most caring man I've ever met. His confession is a true repentance. That's what I told the bishop, and I asked him to accept Elam and baptize him."

"You love him?"

Naomi turned toward Mamm, who wiped a tear from her eye. "*Ja*, I do, very much. I haven't come to this conclusion quickly or easily. But once I let go of the past and truly forgave Elam, the bitterness and the grief disappeared and left only love for him."

Aaron leaned forward. "It's past time for us and everyone around here to embrace him into the fold. If God can forgive us, can't we do the same with Elam?"

Naomi turned back to Daed. "Can't you find it in your heart?"

Daed gave the smallest of nods. "Convicted by my children. *Ja*, you are right. It is time to count our blessings and not dwell on the things of the past."

Now, if only the bishop would make up his mind.

Never before had the sight of Elam's green-roofed white farmhouse looked so *gut* to him. Not even the day he'd come home after being gone for so long.

With the height of the summer upon them, the construction boss worked the crew extra hard. They had enough orders to keep them more than busy until the snow flew. And then there were the details to put together to start the new business in August. Elam yawned and stretched as Vern pulled into the driveway. If he could get a decent night's sleep, that would help. But all day and all night, he tossed and turned. What if the bishop refused to baptize him? What if he lost Naomi for a second time? He wouldn't be able to bear it. He'd be forced to leave this place and start over where he would forget about her.

As if he ever could.

He'd tried that once. And failed.

He'd done all that was possible. Now it was time to leave his future in the Lord's hands. A hard thing to do.

A buggy sat near the barn, and not one that belonged to any of his family members. Perhaps a friend of Mamm's had come to visit her.

Elam slipped from the van. "Thanks, Vern. I'll see you tomorrow."

Vern waved as he backed down the drive. As Elam climbed the steps to the porch, his stomach twisted. His lunch must not have agreed with him.

Mamm greeted him at the door. "I'm glad you're home. You look exhausted. But never mind that. You have a visitor. He's with Daed in the living room. Wash up and go see him."

"Aren't you going to give me a clue?" Elam worked to smile.

She shook her head, though a light shone in her green eyes. "Come and get the dirt off yourself."

Like he was a little boy again, he went to the sink in obedience to his mamm. He splashed cold water on his face. That woke him up. After drying his hands on a towel, he meandered to the living room, taking his time, his middle clenching and unclenching. Daed sat in his favorite, well-worn brown chair next to the window.

On the plain blue couch sat Bishop Zook.

Elam's lungs shut down and dizziness scrambled his head. "Bishop, it's *gut* to see you." Enough small talk.

They both knew why the bishop had paid a call. "I assume you made your decision about my baptism."

"Have a seat, Elam."

This couldn't be good. If the bishop had accepted his confession, he would have come right out and said so. He wouldn't stall. Elam sat and clasped his hands together to keep them from trembling.

The bishop crossed his legs. "I appreciate your coming to see me and repenting of your sins. You have a tendency to be rash, but I hope you have learned your lesson."

"I have. From now on, I will think through each of my decisions very carefully, and weigh every possible outcome before I act."

"Naomi visited me several days ago."

"She did?" Why?

"*Ja.* You are a blessed young man to have a woman such as her to love you."

Heat crept up Elam's neck. "That's for sure and certain."

"And such a wise woman at that. She spoke well of you and had such a humble and compassionate heart. She made me stop and take a good look at myself and how I was thinking about forgiveness. And about how I was treating you."

Had she overstepped her bounds with the bishop? Gone too far? Not that he would ever blame her for trying. He loved her all the more for it.

"Given everything I've heard from both you and Naomi and from talks I've had with Aaron, the elders and I have come to the conclusion…"

Blood pounded in Elam's ears.

"…that your confession was sincere. We agree to

baptize you and welcome you to our church, if you are still sure that is what you want."

Had he heard that correctly? "You're accepting me back?"

The bishop nodded. "*Ja*, I am."

The one good corner of Daed's mouth turned up into a grin. "I'm happy for you, son."

Mamm, who must have been in the room the entire time, came to him and enveloped him in a hug. "Thank God, you are truly home for *gut*. No more wandering for you."

A surge of energy rushed through him, like the time he'd shocked himself on a frayed drill cord. "*Denki*, bishop, *denki*. I cannot thank you enough. We will set the date very soon. As soon as possible. But right now, I have to go somewhere. Please excuse me."

He raced from the house. As fast as his shaking hands allowed him, he harnessed the buggy horse and set off. He urged Prancer down the street at a rapid pace. All the way, he rehearsed what he would say and how he would say it once he arrived at his destination.

Chapter Twenty-Four

Naomi stood at the kitchen sink washing dishes, up to her elbows in suds, when a buggy raced up the driveway. She shivered. Something must be wrong for whoever drove to be so wild. Hadn't they had their share of problems and trials? Couldn't they have a period of peace and rest?

Behind her, Joseph, who had been playing on the floor, cried. She grabbed a dish towel and dried her arms then picked up her son. She kissed his round cheeks and his high forehead. "What's wrong, my *bobbeli*? Don't worry. Whatever has happened, Mamm will keep you safe." His surgery still lay in front of him. She squeezed him, and he protested louder. "*Ach*, I'm sorry."

A rapid pounding sounded on the door. Mamm and Daed read *The Budget* in the living room, and the others, well, who knew where they'd gone to. Jiggling Joseph on her hip, she went to the door, trembling as she turned the knob.

And then she stumbled backward against the wall. "Elam." She clutched her chest. Something terrible must have happened for him to fly up the driveway at break-neck speed. "What's wrong?"

He grinned. Grinned? "Nothing is wrong, *Liebchen*, absolutely nothing." Light danced in his eyes. "Get your sweater. We're going to take a walk."

"Don't scare me like that. With the way you worked that horse, I thought we had another tragedy on our hands. All that for a walk? But why?"

"Grab a blanket for Joseph, too. He should come with us, I think."

"Again, why?"

His smile vanished, and he stared at her, his eyes hard, though his features remained soft. She squirmed.

"Don't you trust me?" His voice was a breathy whisper.

"Of course I do."

"Then let's get going."

"The dishes need to be finished."

"I'll help you when we get back."

"But—"

"Naomi, please."

His behavior was out of character, even for him. What was going on? She shrugged and sighed. "Fine." While she pulled on her sweater, Elam wrapped Joseph in a fleecy blue blanket. The summer evening held an uncharacteristic chill.

This was crazy.

Naomi popped into the living room, and Mamm glanced up from her reading. "Elam is here. We're going for a quick walk and taking Joseph. We won't be gone long. I'll finish the dishes when I get back."

"Have a *gut* time."

Daed glanced up, his lips pinched. To his credit, he didn't forbid her to go.

They set off from the house along the lane that led to the fields and the woods behind. Elam walked so fast she had to almost run to keep up with him. "Slow down. What is your hurry?"

He halted, color rising in his cheeks. "I'm sorry. I forget sometimes that my legs are so much longer than yours." He pointed to the trees ahead of them. "Look at how the setting sun is brushing them with fire. Now I know why the Amish don't have many pictures and such in their homes. Look at the beauty God gave all around us. That is what He wants us to appreciate."

"That's a fancy way of saying the leaves are pretty."

He chuckled, low and steady, like rolling thunder. "You are right." He clasped her chilly hand in his warm one, and they walked on for a while.

"So why did you really bring me here?" Joseph bounced in her arms and clapped his hands.

"He has a new trick I see."

"*Ja*, he claps all the time now. But in a short bit, he's going to start fussing. It's almost his bedtime."

They wandered down the path toward the little stream. This time of year, it still babbled over the rocks. Not for much longer. When midsummer's dry spell inevitably arrived, it halted the brook's gurgling.

Once they reached the water, he sat on the trunk of a downed tree and pulled her beside him. Was he shaking? Maybe something really was wrong.

"You are the most beautiful, the sweetest, the most remarkable woman I have ever met in my life. Do you remember the last time I brought you to this spot?"

She glanced around at the trees, their green leaves

forming a canopy over them. *Ja*, this place held a certain familiarity. When she'd been young, she had come here all the time and splashed in the water and made mud pies. Mamm would scold her when she came home with dirt streaked down her apron, the hem of her dress wet.

And when they'd been courting, Elam brought her here often, stealing a kiss or two from her. But the last time...

She sucked in her breath. Tears clogged her throat. "The last time you brought me here was when you proposed."

He nodded, stared at her and licked his lips. "When I came home from work today, a visitor waited for me."

She raised her eyebrows as Joseph tugged on her prayer *kapp* strings. Her heart hammered.

"The bishop."

Her hands sweated. "Has he made his decision?"

"Ja."

She turned from Elam, unable to bear the pain in his eyes when he told her the bishop refused to baptize him. "And?" The word came out on a puff of air.

"I'm to be baptized as soon as possible."

Elam's breath on her neck sent shivers down her spine. She spun to face him. "He did? Oh, really?"

"Ja, ja." That silly grin spread across his face again. The grin she loved more than anything in the world.

"That's *wunderbaar* news. The best ever."

He slid close to her and pulled her against his chest. *"Ich liebe dich*, Naomi. I love you more than ever. More than when we were here the last time. I brought you here for a special reason. Because I want to ask you an important question."

Joseph snuggled against her. "What is that?" Was this really happening a second time?

"Will you marry me? I promise to love you and Joseph and always take care of you and him and—"

With a soft kiss on his lips, she shushed him. "*Ja*, Elam Yoder, nothing would make me happier than to be your wife."

Joseph gurgled and sighed. Elam laughed. "I would say he approves of the arrangement." His voice caught. "I'm so proud that I'll be his daed."

"He can't be any happier than I am at the moment." If God blessed her any more, her heart would burst.

Epilogue

"Happy birthday, my sweet *bobbeli*." Naomi pulled Joseph from where he stood in his crib, kissed his plump cheek and set him on the floor. On his hands and knees, he rocked back and forth.

Without warning, Elam snuck up behind her and encircled her waist. "You won't be able to call him a *bobbeli* much longer. Look how big he's getting."

She turned in her husband's arms and kissed him. Oh, what a surprise awaited him if her suspicions were correct. By Joseph's second birthday, he would be a big brother. But today was Joseph's day. A time to celebrate his life and his health, how he endured the surgery and was now a robust little boy. "He's going to love the little chair you made for him."

"I hope so. That can be another line for my shop. Outdoor furniture for children."

"What a *wunderbaar* idea. Already God is blessing your business. Joseph is going to be thrilled with the train Aaron is giving him, even though he isn't walking yet to pull it around. And I can't wait for his reaction to the cake I'm making."

"I think you're more excited about the party than Joseph." He chuckled, rich and full and deep.

Just like their life now. She touched his bearded cheek. "How could I have ever doubted that you're the man God intended for me? I can't imagine my life without you."

He bent over and kissed her, pulling her close, squeezing her until she ran out of breath and had to pull away. She swatted his bicep. "What will my parents think if they come over and find us like this?"

"They'll think we're a very happy newlywed couple, that's what."

He smooched with her once more before she slipped from his embrace, laughing. "I have to get dinner ready before our families arrive. And since Joseph now has three sets of grandparents, it's going to have to be a big meal."

"Your fault for marrying me." He tugged on her prayer *kapp* string and kissed her on the cheek.

On the floor at their feet, Joseph gurgled, but she gazed at her husband. How could one woman be so blessed?

Elam grabbed her by the shoulder and shook her. "Look at Joseph. Watch him go."

Sure enough, there went Joseph crawling across his bedroom floor toward the door. She couldn't squelch the squeal that burst inside her. "He's crawling. See that? He's doing it." At the room's threshold, she scooped him up and bear-hugged him. "You're such a big boy."

"Don't leave me out." Elam wrapped both of them in an embrace.

For a moment, Naomi closed her eyes. Denki, *Lord, for this family.* When she opened her eyes, she drank in the sight of her husband and her son. "Come on, you two. Time to celebrate."

* * * * *

PLAIN OUTSIDER

Alison Stone

To Mom, with love

The Lord is my strength and my shield;
my heart trusted in him, and I am helped:
therefore my heart greatly rejoiceth;
and with my song will I praise him.
—*Psalms* 28:7

Chapter One

The headlights on Deputy Becky Spoth's patrol car illuminated the lines on the deserted country road. Some of her fellow deputies complained about the overnight shift, but Becky had grown to like it. There was something calming about patrolling the quiet roads devoid of cars or horses, or more important, people. It gave her a lot of time for quiet reflection while still providing a means to pay the mortgage. She appreciated her job now more than ever when just a few days ago she wondered if she'd ever be out on patrol again.

That was the thing about this job. Things could change on a dime. The radio that had been silent most of her shift suddenly crackled to life as if to prove her point. "Report of a break-in on Robin Nest Road. How far away are you, Deputy Spoth?"

She didn't have to give the location a moment's thought. She had grown up in Quail Hollow and knew all the windy roads and farms, even the ones the town didn't see fit to mark. That was the thing about a small town. Everyone knew everything about everything and everyone.

"I'm a mile out." Despite a year as a deputy, her stomach bottomed out and her mouth grew dry. Would she ever get used to answering calls, especially alone at night? All the officers in the sheriff's department traveled solo, but backup was usually only a moment away.

Backup. More than once over the past couple weeks, she wished she hadn't been the first to arrive to help Deputy Ned Reich subdue a young Amish man, an incident that had turned the sheriff's department upside down.

Had turned the small town of Quail Hollow, New York, upside down.

Forcing the distracting thoughts out of her mind, Becky weighed the pros and cons of turning on the patrol car's lights and siren. She didn't want to give the possible intruder a heads-up that a sheriff's deputy was on the way, a chance to get away. But she didn't want to surprise some unsuspecting driver. She stretched across to the control panel. *Flick.* Lights. No siren.

The engine revved under the weight of her foot on the accelerator. The power of the patrol car never failed to impress her, especially for a woman who didn't get her driver's license until she was twenty-five.

The first hints of pink and purple pushed into the black night sky as she drove toward Robin Nest. The only homes out this way belonged to the Amish. Perhaps a young Amish boy had been sneaking home after a night of shenanigans. A lot of the Amish youth went to Sunday singings and for some, the fun stretched into the early morning with unsuspecting parents who might glance outside at the most inopportune time and mistake their son for an intruder.

But that raised the question: Who called the sheriff? The Amish preferred not to deal with law enforcement.

And there was the issue of a phone, but even Becky realized that some Amish were adapting to the modern world by allowing phones and cell phones in a limited capacity. Like a landline in a barn or a cell phone strictly for work purposes. She doubted she'd be seeing an Amish family sitting around the table at the diner in town all staring at their cell phones anytime soon. A bit of a slippery slope, all the same.

As Becky's patrol car crested the hill, the headlights from an oncoming car blinded her. Instinctively, she jammed on the brakes as the approaching car veered into her lane. She gripped the wheel tightly and braced for impact, a prayer crossing her lips.

The tires skidded on the pavement. She swerved. The patrol car careened off the road and plowed into the nearby field, stalks of corn slapping at her windshield, her entire body jostling. The vehicle finally came to a hard stop and her seat belt dug into her chest. She let out a breath on a whoosh and slumped into the leather seat. She pried her fingers from the steering wheel and thanked God she was in one piece.

She contacted dispatch with her current predicament, then released the seat belt. She pushed open the door against the corn stalks. With heightened awareness, she stepped out into the field, her boots sinking into the soft soil. Her first concern was the other driver. Had he had a medical issue? Was he drunk?

The night air smelled thick, the combination of rich soil and burned rubber. She squinted against the glare of the red and blue patrol lights.

Plodding through the soil, she pushed the cornstalks out of the way. The other vehicle had stopped, positioned across the road, its extinguished headlights pointed toward her. A shadow of a figure sat motion-less in the driver's seat.

Is he watching me?

"Hello, are you okay?" she called, nerve endings prickling to life. Where was her backup?

The headlights flipped on and her hand instinctively came up to block the bright beams trained on her.

"Turn your headlights off, sir." She cocked her head, straining to see past the blinding lights.

The high beams flashed on and she jerked her head back. *What in the world?*

Her other hand hovered over her gun. *You've got this. You're trained for this.* She took a step back. Crops didn't exactly provide protection, but they could pro-vide a hiding place if necessary.

"Step out of your car," she ordered, keeping her tone authoritative and even, like she had practiced. Becky was jacked up on adrenaline from nearly getting hit head-on, but the mood had shifted from apprehension to determination. She had a job to do.

The man was watching her. Toying with her. She planted her feet in the soil, ready to draw her gun. Her legs felt like jelly, but she ignored the sensation. Nerves came with the job. She had been trained to fire a gun and hit a target. She had never shot another human being and prayed tonight wouldn't change that.

"Out of your car now!" she ordered, feeling her en-tire body tense.

The engine of the car fired to life, the sound rum-bling through her chest. The tires spun, spewing the acrid smell of burned rubber. She fought back a cough, keeping her sharpened attention on the vehicle. The tires gained purchase and the car backed up, stopped abruptly, then raced down the road, back in the direction it had come.

Becky's shoulders sagged and she drew in a few deep breaths. Staring toward the vehicle, she waited a moment, anticipating another drive-by. The early-morning chirping of birds seeped into her consciousness before she allowed herself to let down her guard. *He's gone.* She strode back to the patrol car and flipped off the flashing lights. She pressed her shoulder radio and said, "ETA on the tow truck?"

"Five minutes," the dispatcher asked. "Everything okay?"

"Yeah," she said, a not-exactly truthful reply, but a necessary one. A person couldn't show weakness on this job. Not if they wanted to be seen as competent.

Becky gave the dispatcher what limited information she had on the car that ran her off the road. Maybe they'd pull him over, figure out what his problem was.

Becky leaned against the trunk of her patrol car and ran a hand across her clenched jaw. She didn't know who ran her off the road, but she suspected he had known exactly who his target was.

Her.

This wasn't exactly how Becky had envisioned her first shift back at work. The tow truck driver insisted he could drop her off in front of the sheriff's station before taking the vehicle to the repair shop to make sure mud from her off-roading adventure wasn't clogging anything up. She was pretty sure he had been more specific with some technical terms, but she had tuned him out after the second time he appeared to be hitting on her. Like that never happened before: a guy hitting on a female sheriff's deputy.

Sorry, not interested.

"Stop. I'm going to get out here," Becky said, growing impatient as he debated with himself whether he'd be able to weave the tow truck through the narrow parking lot adjacent to the employee entrance.

"No problem." The young man stopped and gave her a silent stare while she scooted out of the cab. Her foot didn't reach the ground and she almost missed the running board, which would have added insult to injury. It wasn't exactly a good shift when a deputy returned with her patrol car trailing behind her.

She didn't bother giving the tow truck driver instructions because she suspected her boss already had. After determining that his deputy was okay and that the call on Robin Nest was a false alarm, the sheriff had instructed her to report to his office the minute she returned.

On solid ground, Becky smoothed out her uniform shirt. She watched as the tow truck lumbered away, its engine chugging as the sun poked over the horizon. The day shift deputies had started to arrive.

Just great.

Becky might have been imagining it, but several seemed to give her the side eye as they strolled toward the employee entrance, and she suspected it had nothing to do with her going four-wheeling in the cornfields with a patrol car.

She sighed heavily. She had hoped her first day back on patrol was going to be a smooth transition after a rough week. Apparently not.

Fighting the urge to fidget with the cuffs of her sleeves, she approached the entrance. She had wanted to go straight home, take a hot bath and get some solid sleep. But she had strict instructions to report to the sheriff.

Becky walked at a steady pace. She squared her shoulders, determined to prove to anyone who might be judging her that she was confident and self-assured, despite the mud caked up in the wheel wells of her vehicle. She frowned, realizing her driving abilities weren't the only thing her fellow officers would be questioning. Several had voiced their displeasure when she filed her official report last week against a fellow officer who had been placed on a long-term suspension while the department continued their investigation.

The memory of the sudden brightness of the headlights blinding her earlier this morning while she stood in the cornfields knotted her stomach. Could the anger of one of her fellow officers have turned to retribution? To show Becky just how wrong she had been to point a finger at another officer? To make sure she knew her place not only as one of the newer deputies, but also as a woman?

Support fellow deputies. Don't testify against them.

Someone had left that note for her last week on her windshield, but she didn't think it applied in this case. She couldn't ignore when a fellow deputy crossed a line.

She brushed at her white uniform sleeves, convincing herself that yes, she had done the right thing. A law-enforcement officer didn't have the right to beat up a young man, even if he had led him on a high-speed chase, barely missing a child crossing the street after getting the mail.

Becky slowed, allowing the first rays of morning sun to warm her face and the buzz of her nerves to settle a bit. An arm reached around her and grabbed the handle of the station door, surprising her.

"Oh, sorry," Becky muttered, not realizing she had been blocking the entrance. She glanced up into the serious face of Deputy Harrison James, the only deputy with less time at the Quail Hollow Sheriff's Department than she had. But she wasn't naive to assume his lack of time in this department meant he had less experience. Everything about him screamed skill, confidence and an "I don't care what anyone thinks of me" vibe. Three qualities Becky admired.

Three qualities she would like to purchase in bushels right now. If only that was a one-click option online.

Harrison nodded in a silent greeting and pulled open the door for her. He was standing so close she could see the flecks of yellow in his brown eyes.

"Thank you." Becky averted her gaze and stepped through the door and he followed behind her. The brief exchange had probably been the longest one she'd had with Deputy James. He wasn't exactly the chatty type. More like tall, dark and brooding. Considering the mood she was in of late, she could relate.

"No problem," he said, his voice low and gruff. They walked slowly across the small lobby, waiting to be admitted into the secure office area. Deputy James frowned as he pressed the buzzer. He looked like a man who hadn't had his morning coffee. But at least he hadn't had the kind of morning she'd had.

The interior door buzzed, and Harrison once again opened the door for her. "Tough shift?" His comment startled her.

"Um, yeah." Heat fired in her cheeks as she smiled meekly and jabbed her thumb in the general direction of where she'd climbed out of the tow truck. "Someone ran me off the road."

His brow furrowed. "Did he stop?"

"At first, but he took off once I got out of the vehicle."

Harrison looked like he was going to say more when Becky heard a stern voice calling her name.

"Looks like the sheriff's looking for me."

The corners of her fellow deputy's lips turned down. "Don't let me hold you up."

Reflexively, Becky checked her collar, making sure her uniform was in place. Sheriff Thomas Landry tapped the door frame before disappearing back inside his office. No deputy made the sheriff call them twice.

Becky forced a cheery demeanor for Anne Wagner, the sheriff's administrative assistant, as she passed. They had been peers before Becky had finished her training and become a deputy. Anne raised her eyebrows and returned a smile, a cross between friendship and *I hope everything's okay*. No one liked to be on the new sheriff's bad side. He had only been elected six months ago, and by all accounts, he was tough. All his officers toed the line or paid the price.

Exhibit one: Deputy Ned Reich, the deputy Becky had testified against.

"Good morning, Sheriff." Becky lingered in the doorway, hoping this would be a quick chat along the lines of "How was your first day back?"

"You've had better mornings, I'm sure," the sheriff responded, his tone calm and even. In the short time she had worked with him, he seemed unflappable. As cool as his demeanor in the ubiquitous political commercials that littered the airways: "Vote for me, Thomas Landry, for sheriff. The kind of transparent leader Quail Hollow needs." The department was still trying to reshape its image after one of their own had been convicted in a twenty-year-old murder of a young Amish mother.

"Yes, but it's all part of the job," she said. "Anyone find the car?"

"We haven't located the vehicle that ran you off the road yet, but everyone has the description."

"It was hard to see. Sedan. Early model. Maybe a B in the license plate. Isn't very descriptive, I know, but it was dark."

He waved his hand. "Glad you're okay. Probably some punk on a dare. Turns out the call to Robin Nest was a dead end, too." He shook his head. "Like we have nothing better to do than respond to crank calls."

"You think someone was dared to play chicken with a patrol car?" Becky asked in disbelief.

The sheriff leaned back and crossed his arms. "Or someone had too much to drink. Or maybe someone thought our country roads would make a great speedway. Easy to lose control." He shrugged. "We'll get to the bottom of it."

Still standing in the doorway, she glanced over her shoulder. The deputies were still wandering in for the start of the day shift. "I'm not exactly the most popular person around here." But how could she suggest that one of her fellow deputies might be out to get her without sounding paranoid, or at the very least, like someone who wasn't a team player?

The moment to offer a possible culprit passed and the sheriff gestured at her to come farther into his office. "Close the door."

Becky's heart sank. *Close the door.* Nothing good was ever said behind closed doors, unless it involved a raise or a promotion, neither of which she was in line for.

"I'm afraid I have bad news," the sheriff said.

Chapter Two

"Bad news?" What more could possibly go wrong?

Sitting behind his mahogany desk, the sheriff forced a tight smile and held his hand out to Becky. "Have a seat."

Becky wanted to refuse the seat, hoping that whatever he had to tell her could be said while she was standing, but her knees felt warm and wobbly. Swallowing hard, she moved around to the front of the chair and lowered herself into the seat as he requested. "What's going on?" She hoped her crossed ankles, hands politely folded on her lap and her square shoulders exuded outward confidence. Inside she felt like puking.

The sheriff tapped the pads of his fingers together and seemed to be looking right through her, as if collecting his thoughts. "I know you've been having a hard time since the Elijah Lapp incident."

"Yes." Short of leaving her Amish family, the past week had been the hardest of her life. When she took the oath to uphold the law, she never thought it would include speaking out against one of her fellow deputies.

"You've been under tremendous pressure," the sheriff said with a reassuring tilt to his mouth.

"Yes." Becky swallowed hard, feeling a bit like she was being interrogated again. Like she had when she answered questions about The Incident. That was how she had begun to think of it. A young Amish man had led Deputy Ned Reich on a high-speed chase and only stopped when he bailed out of his car in the hopes of making a getaway on foot. Fueled by adrenaline and a well-known bad attitude, Deputy Reich had quickly caught up with the man and beaten him to within an inch of his life. By the time Becky—Reich's backup—arrived on the scene, the young Amish man was on the ground and Ned was driving his fist into his face. Becky had stared at the ceiling each night wondering what would have happened if she hadn't come by to put an end to the beating.

Even now she wondered how she had been able to stop the fight. The events of that afternoon blurred into an adrenaline-fueled haze. She thanked God she had the strength and inclination to do something.

Becky bent back her fingers on one hand in a nervous gesture. Once she became aware of it, she dropped her hand, only to absentmindedly pick it up and start again.

She had left the Amish because she felt like she had a bigger calling—to help people outside the small Amish community. But she was beginning to think this job was going to be the death of her. She never imagined small-town policing could be such stressful work.

The sheriff picked up a cell phone that had been face down on his desk, then put it back down again. "New evidence has come to light."

"New evidence against Deputy Reich?" A part of her

was relieved. The more independent evidence against Ned, perhaps the less they'd have to rely on her testimony when it came to his trial. For now she had only testified in the confines of the department, providing enough information to keep Reich out of uniform for the foreseeable future. Maybe forever, depending on what additional evidence the sheriff had found. She hated this situation, but if she could find a spark of hope, this was it. Maybe her life would get back to normal and her fellow officers wouldn't treat her like a traitor.

The sheriff shot her a subtle gaze that chilled her to the core. She had misread this entire situation. "What is it?" Her body seemed to be hovering over her.

The sheriff touched the corner of his computer screen, adjusting its angle so she could see it. He clicked a few keys on his keyboard and a video frame popped up. The sheriff clicked the arrow button and an image of Ned pummeling the Amish kid while he was down on the pavement came into focus. The familiar uneasy feeling swept over her. The video had been taken from her dash cam on her patrol car. She wanted to look away, but didn't. *Couldn't.* There was a reason the sheriff was showing her this video, the same video she had seen play over and over again during her testimony against the man.

Her heart raced, just as it did the afternoon the events unfolded. Just as it did every time she had to relive the moment. She ran her hands up and down the arms of the chair. "I've seen this video more times than I can count, sir. Are we looking at something new?"

The sheriff cut her a quick gaze. "Hold on." He moved the mouse and scanned over a few files. Perhaps he had shown her the wrong video. "Here it is."

This time when he clicked on the arrow, another video played. She slid to the edge of her seat as the familiar scene played out from a new angle. One she had never seen before. She shot a quick glance to her boss, then back to the video. This time she appeared on the screen. She had out her baton. Nausea swirled in her gut.

"Stop. Stop. Stop." Her terrified voice could be heard in the video. She had her baton raised, much like Ned had his fist raised moments ago in the other video.

"What is this?" Her voice cracked.

"Someone took a video with their cell phone."

She stared at the screen as if watching someone else. A million memories from that day assaulted her, but this particular one escaped her. As she approached, Ned dragged the man behind his patrol car. This was when her dash cam lost coverage. But this video caught more, like a second camera on a movie set. This time Becky could be seen marching toward where the two men had disappeared.

The sheriff stopped the video and pointed to a part with the tip of his pen. "What are you doing here?"

"Um—" she stared at the computer screen until it went blurry "—I'm raising my baton."

"What did you do with your baton?" The sheriff moved the pen away from the screen and covered the mouse with the palm of his hand. He clicked on Play. On the video, she was commanding that they stop.

Who? Her fellow officer? The man getting beat?

She blinked rapidly. "I needed to help…" The next word got caught in her throat. Did she need to help Ned? Her fellow officer? Or had she been determined to save the young Amish man?

"Who were you going to help, Deputy Spoth?" He hit Pause again.

Becky sat ramrod straight on the edge of her seat and squared her shoulders. She had the answer. The question was easy, right? "I had to stop the fight. I had to get the driver safely into custody and away from Deputy Reich. The situation had turned out of control."

"Would you say you'd do whatever it took to stop the fight?"

"I'm not sure what you're asking." She flinched, then turned to stare at the screen, her digital form frozen with an anguished expression on her face. Becky may have been fairly naive because of her upbringing, but she studied people, knew how to respond. She was a quick learner and she wasn't going to allow the sheriff to get her to say something that could jeopardize her career.

The sheriff clicked Play. Video Becky walked authoritatively toward Reich's patrol car. She could be seen with her baton raised. To hit someone? Then she saw nothing.

On the video, someone muttered and then gravel came into view as the person took off running through what looked to be cornfields while still recording on their phone. Then the video came to a quick stop and the screen went black.

"I don't understand." A hot flush of dread blanketed her skin.

The sheriff sighed heavily and leaned back in his chair. It groaned under his weight. "This video was submitted to Deputy Reich's lawyer."

"Who?" The single word came out in a squeak. She

cleared her throat. "Who turned it in? Why not turn it in to the department?"

"We're working on that. The lawyer said it was from an anonymous source. The witness claims you hit Elijah Lapp on the head with your baton, thus ending the fight and potentially leading to the young Amish man's cracked skull."

Cold dread washed over her and she thought she was going to be sick. "Wait…what? No. That's not…" The memories of that day were disjointed, but she didn't hit Elijah. No way.

"Deputy Spoth," the sheriff said in a soothing voice, but she was having none of it.

"This is all a misunderstanding. I didn't hit anyone with my baton. I used it to pry the men apart. That's why I had the baton out." It was all coming back to her now in a flood of formerly suppressed memories. Or was she grasping for the truth? Was she confused? Had she done something regrettable in the heat of the moment? She blinked slowly. The walls of the room closed in on her. She tugged on her collar. "You can ask Ned." As soon as the words spilled from her lips, she realized the futility of it. Why would Ned help her after she testified against him? Cost him his job? She looked up and met the sheriff's even gaze and knew she didn't stand a chance to talk her way out of this.

"Ned's lawyer insists that you landed the final blow that cracked Elijah Lapp's skull. Ned's lawyer provided the video."

"But…"

"Reich's been with the sheriff's department for twenty-five years." The sheriff glanced at the closed door behind her, as if to make sure he wouldn't be overheard. "Between you and me, he's a hothead, but he's never gone this far."

"We can interview Elijah." Becky leaned forward on the edge of her chair, feeling like all the oxygen had been sucked from the room.

"Elijah has no memory of the incident." The sheriff's calm, cool demeanor only served to morph her initial fear to white-hot anger. "He's recovering at home and his family isn't allowing anyone from the sheriff's department to speak with him."

"I can't believe this."

The sheriff held up his hand. "I don't believe you hit the young man."

Hope straightened Becky's backbone, only for her to be immediately deflated with the sheriff's next words. "Despite what I think, I can't ignore this video. I ran for sheriff on the pledge that this office would be transparent and not allow any wrongdoing. This community has a reason to mistrust the sheriff's department after one of our own was arrested for murder."

Becky grew dizzy. "That was so long ago."

"But the perception that the sheriff's department protected him has hurt us." The sheriff shook his head. "We must regain the trust of the community."

"But—" Her world was sputtering out of control.

"Until we can clear you, you're suspended."

Becky stood to leave when the sheriff held out his hand.

"I'll need your gun and badge."

Deputy Harrison James climbed behind the wheel of his patrol car and turned the key in the ignition. He took a minute to adjust the AC vents, directing them toward his face. It was going to be a scorcher today. But hot in the country was never the same as hot in the city.

Fighting crime in the city was a whole new ball-game when the temperatures rose. Tempers spiked in direct proportion. And the concrete buildings held the heat. Here, the soft wind had a chance to reach a person across the large open spaces giving him time to think before he threw a punch or pulled the trigger.

Most of the time.

He thought about the deputy he had chatted with on his way into the building at the start of his shift. He wondered if her shell-shocked expression was a result of being run off the road or if the tight lines around her eyes were the aftereffects of the incident splashed all over the news. It was probably a combination of the two.

Harrison knew what it was like to have personal business laid out for public consumption. That was a big part of why he had taken a job with the sheriff's department in Quail Hollow. He never thought the small-town sheriff's department would be dealing with a case of excessive force. But he supposed people were people and bad decisions could happen anywhere. He had come here to get his head on straight and he hoped he could keep his distance from any interoffice drama. He wanted to do his job and go home at night with a clear conscience.

Such as it was. He carried a lot of guilt with him regardless.

As Harrison pulled out of the back lot of the sheriff's department, he noticed Deputy Spoth standing next to her personal vehicle. The petite blonde had caught his eye more than once, and not because she had arrived in a tow truck at the end of her shift this morning. And not simply because she was a woman—he had worked with plenty of female law-enforcement officers before. He noticed her because she seemed different. Almost too meek to do this job. Too nice. Yet she had somehow broken up a fight on the side of the road that, by all accounts, could have led to the death of a young Amish man. That was how he had interpreted the reports. Mumblings suggested other deputies thought differently. Not that he was willing to get involved in a heated debate.

Didn't concern him anyway.

Harrison didn't envy Deputy Spoth's position. Not all law-enforcement officers could understand how a fellow officer could testify against them. Some would silently support their fellow officer no matter what.

One side was right. One was wrong. Clear lines.

He had done that with his brother. Harrison had only seen his side of things. Had let his brother know of his disapproval under no uncertain terms. Had purposely alienated his brother in hopes that he'd realize the error of his ways. Had seemed like a good idea.

Everything had always been clearly black-and-white—until life served him up some bleak gray.

Harrison squeezed the steering wheel and shifted his focus to the female deputy standing by the open driver's side door. She had her hands planted on her hips and a frustrated expression on her face. At first he thought she was still carrying the weight of her rough shift in her posture until he dropped his gaze to the two flat tires on her personal vehicle.

He pulled up alongside where she was parked, jammed the gear into Park and climbed out, allowing the engine and the AC to run. The deputy glanced up at him with an unreadable expression on her face.

"What's going on here?" he asked.

The woman held out her hand toward her car. "Someone slashed all four tires." Her cheeks filled with air, then she huffed in frustration. "Apparently, the number of people I've managed to irk has grown."

Harrison crouched down and ran his finger along the clean slice in the rubber. "Man…" He angled his head toward the row of patrol cars across the parking lot. The heat was pulsing off the blacktop surface and he could feel the sweat forming under his uniform shirt. "I can put a call in to a local garage."

"I already did. They're on their way." She dropped down on the curb and rested her arms on her knees, letting her hands hang limply. "Looks like bad things really do come in threes."

He narrowed his gaze, not sure what she meant.

"Patrol car towed in. Flat tires." She ticked the items off on her fingers. "Got suspended."

"Suspended? Why?" He thought she had come out smelling like a rose after her testimony against the other officer.

"New video." She didn't need to elaborate; her participation in the most talked about case was well known. "Apparently enough to make them question my involvement."

"Really?" He ran a hand across his chin, reminding him that he should have shaved this morning. "How so?"

"The video's not clear-cut, but a person with something to gain could suggest I used my baton on Elijah Lapp." She shook her head, clearly dejected. "That's exactly what Deputy Reich's lawyer is doing. He's using the video to spread the blame. It's a mess."

"Who sent the video in?"

"Good old anonymous." She closed her eyes briefly and drew in a long breath, before finally meeting his gaze. "And now I'm out of a job."

She pushed to her feet and pulled out her cell phone from her duty belt. She walked around to the back of the vehicle and snapped a photo. "Don't let me hold you up. Pretty sure it won't do you much good to hang out with me."

He walked around to where she was standing to see what had caught her attention. He raised his eyebrows, surprised she seemed so calm. *Is fattgange* was written in soap on her back window. Gibberish as far as he could tell.

"What does that say? Anything?"

"It's Pennsylvania Dutch. You know, the language the Amish speak."

He hitched a shoulder. He had been here for less than a year, but other than a few bits and pieces here and there, he mostly heard the Amish speaking English, perhaps with a touch of an accent. "What's it mean?"

"Go away." Her tone was flat.

"I'm just trying to help." Harrison held up his palms and took a step back, not sure what he had said to offend her.

For the first time, the young woman's mouth curved into a grin and she laughed, adding to his confusion. "No, that's what *is fattgange* means. Go away. In Pennsylvania Dutch."

Harrison scratched his head and couldn't help but

laugh at himself. "Sorry, I haven't picked up much Pennsylvania Dutch yet, beyond the basics."

"You'll learn a little here and there, but most of the adults speak English. That is, when they want to talk to you. The Amish, as a rule, don't care to deal with law enforcement. The only problem you might run into is with little kids. Most of them don't learn English until they start school. But it's not likely you'll run into an Amish child without one of their parents or older siblings around."

Harrison nodded. "Yes, they mentioned that in my training." What little training the small-town sheriff's department had provided. He frowned. "You think an Amish person vandalized your car?"

"I don't know what to think. The car has been parked here all night on the edge of the parking lot by the trees. Pretty easy for someone to sneak in and out without being seen." She ran a hand across the top of her head. Her long blond hair had been braided, then pinned over her head, almost like the Swiss Miss girl. Something told him she was holding back, as if she had her suspicions as to who had vandalized her car.

"Go inside and report this. I'll wait. Give you a ride home."

"Are you sure?" Skepticism flickered in her eyes as she glanced toward the sheriff's station, then at him.

"Yes, go." He reached into his wallet and pulled out his business card and handed it to her. "My cell phone number's on here. If you come out and I'm not here, call me. I'll swing by and pick you up." He had no idea how long the report would take.

She took the card and slipped it into her back pocket. Harrison watched the deputy cross the parking lot to the station. He sensed, rather than saw, another patrol car approaching. He tugged open his patrol car door and the cold air from the AC hit his legs. The car inched past, coming awfully close to his open door, and stopped. Harrison squinted, unable to see the officer's face due to the brim of his hat.

The window slid down. Harrison tilted his head to see inside. The officer had his wrist casually slung on top of the steering wheel, blocking the name tag on his chest. Dark sunglasses hid his eyes.

"A little advice for the new guy."

Harrison wondered how long he had to be here before he was no longer the new guy. He gestured toward the driver to get on with it even though he didn't want his advice.

"Stay away from the chick. She's toxic."

Harrison crossed his arms and glared at the deputy, struggling to place him, then finally remembering his name: Colin. Colin Reich. Ned's son. No wonder he had it in for Deputy Spoth.

"Thanks for the tip." Harrison's tone was even. He had seen office politics take down the best of them. He had no plans to stir the pot. A noncommittal answer was best.

Behind the wheel, Colin saluted him in a mocking gesture, as if he suspected Harrison was going to do his own thing regardless. The man wasn't wrong.

"Don't say I didn't warn you," the deputy muttered before closing the window and driving away.

Chapter Three

"Where do you live?" Harrison asked Becky as he put the patrol car into Drive.

"Out on Asbury Road past the Millers' farm."

He cut her a sideways glance. "Mind telling the new guy where the Miller farm is?" Before she had a chance to answer, he lifted his hand in resignation. The locals often gave directions by landmark and if he didn't want to be forever known as the new guy, he had better figure it out. "Why don't you just holler when I need to make a turn? Sound good?" He gestured with his chin toward the road. "A left out of here?"

"Yeah." Her tone sounded as flat as the four tires on her car still awaiting the tow truck in the parking lot. A part of him wondered if whoever was taking their frustration out on her was doing it not just because she testified against another deputy, but because she was a woman. Despite the calendar year, a lot of guys still believed in the good old boys' club.

Harrison drummed his fingers on the top of the steering wheel as he slowed to look both ways before he pulled out of the parking lot and onto the road. "Everything go okay when you reported the incident?" The sheriff seemed like a pretty solid guy, determined to make a strong showing in his new position.

"Yeah, I guess."

His gut told him not to ask, not to get involved. But he couldn't help himself. "What does that mean?"

"Apparently, I've attracted some unwanted attention, including getting run off the road this morning."

This kind of behavior really ticked him off. Negligent drivers. Probably out drinking.

"The sheriff wanted to dismiss it as reckless driving on some back country roads, but now this…" She lifted her shoulders and let them drop. "Here, turn at the next road. It's quicker." She tugged on her seat belt and continued on about the sheriff. "If he hadn't already suspended me, he probably would have after my car was vandalized. I'm attracting the wrong kind of attention. The sheriff would probably claim a few more days off would be for my own good. Department morale seems at a low."

"Does the sheriff think it's someone in his department?" He scrubbed a hand across his face.

"Not that he'd ever say. But I wouldn't put it past Reich himself. He's a loose cannon." Becky ran the palms of her hands up and down the thighs of her uniform pants.

"His son works here, too." Harrison thought back to the officer who drove by slowly, warning him to avoid Becky.

"Doesn't help. All the other deputies will feel more loyalty to the Reich family than to me, unfortunately."

"You going to be okay?" He stared straight ahead as fields of corn whipped by on either side of them.

"Yeah." What else could she say? She wasn't exactly going to pour her heart out to him. He was a stranger.

"You need to hire a lawyer," he said matter-of-factly.

She shifted in her seat to partially face him. "You really think so? Isn't that expensive?"

"It might be too costly *not* to hire a lawyer. You need someone looking out for your best interests." He wished he had seen that his brother had got the help that he had needed instead of allowing his anger and embarrassment to put a rift between the two of them. "The sheriff's department has had a publicity nightmare after the beating incident. The video from your dash cam made it onto all the news stations from Buffalo to Cleveland. If this new video gets out, depending on what's on it, this story is going to grow legs and find its way into all the news cycles again. The sheriff's department will do anything to get out of the spotlight, even if that means throwing you under the bus."

"You can't be serious." She swept her hand across her mouth and eyed him wearily. "This is a small-town sheriff's department, not some big city."

"Office politics are office politics."

"But I didn't do anything wrong."

"Does the latest video support that statement?" His gut told him she couldn't be violent, but in an altercation, you never knew. Adrenaline and fear did things to people.

"Yes… I used the baton to separate the men." Becky tugged on the strap of her seat belt. "Reich's lawyer gave the sheriff a video of me approaching the men with my baton raised." She cleared her throat. "The rest of what happened is unclear. Whoever recorded it took off running, but…" She paused, rubbing her temples vigorously as if reliving the moment. "I used the baton to brace Reich and pull him off the kid. I didn't hit anybody. I mean, if I hurt anyone with the baton, it would be when I forced it against Reich." She blinked a few times. "I can't believe this mess. I only became a deputy because I wanted to help people. Now everyone is going to think I've turned evil." Her turn of expression sounded odd.

"Take a deep breath." He wanted to reach out and touch her hand, but decided against it. "Hiring a lawyer is a good idea, especially for the innocent." Well, for anyone. "Don't fight this alone. Reich has a lawyer," he added, if she needed more convincing.

"I don't know," Becky muttered. Before he had a chance to respond, her cell phone chimed. She yanked the phone from her duty belt and checked the number. "I should get this."

Harrison listened to a one-sided conversation. Obviously, someone Becky knew personally was in distress.

He reached over and touched her arm and mouthed. "What's going on?"

"Hold on, Mag." She held the phone to her chest. "My sister wants me to stop over. She's concerned about a neighbor's dog. *Again.*"

"Where does she live?"

"It's okay. I don't want to impose on you any more than I already have."

"I don't mind. I haven't had any calls anyway."

"Um, okay." Then into the phone. "Hang tight. I'll be right there."

Becky directed Harrison toward a house nestled among a cluster of Amish homes. "Right up here. Park on the road along the cornfields. Better if they don't see the patrol car."

"Are you going to tell me what this is about?"

Becky scratched her head. "My sister. She's worried about a neighbor's dog that ran onto the property. It's been an ongoing concern. The dog is hungry and not well cared for. We've suspected abuse, but I've handled it unofficially, returning the dog to his owner after they promised they'd take better care of it." She frowned. "Obviously, that's not working."

"Wait." Harrison angled his head to look up toward the home. A buggy was parked by the barn. An Amish family obviously lived here. "Your sister?"

"*Yah*, my sister." A twinkle lit her eyes. He had a feeling the amplified Amish inflection was for his benefit.

"Oh…" It was his turn to sound confused. "You grew up Amish?"

She pointed to her nose and said, "Ding. Ding. Ding."

"Oh… Do you want me to wait here, then?" Harrison asked, suddenly feeling a little discombobulated. *Amish? Really?*

Becky hesitated for a moment. "That would probably be best."

"Okay, I'll do that. I'll be right here." Now he was repeating himself, completely caught off guard by her revelation.

Becky climbed out of the patrol car and strode along the road and cut in between the cornfields, as if to go in undetected. He had read somewhere that the Amish shunned those who left their ranks. Perhaps Becky was sneaking in because she wasn't welcomed.

Harrison rubbed the back of his neck, replaying in

his mind all the events that had transpired since he had held the door at the station open for Becky this morning. He hadn't had much interaction with the deputy since he'd moved here less than a year ago, but he would have never guessed former Amish worked as deputies. Were there others?

Now the warning in Pennsylvania Dutch to "go away" made a little more sense. But how a woman went from Amish to sheriff's deputy was beyond him. Maybe it was time he finally learned a little more about the Amish. And maybe Becky was just the person to teach him.

Becky strode up the dirt path between the cornfield and the neighbor's property. She undid the buttons on her cuffs and rolled up her sleeves, hoping to look a little less official in her sheriff's uniform. It was early enough that perhaps her parents would be too busy with chores to notice their wayward daughter had snuck in to meet with her younger sister out back by the shed.

She hoped.

But if she did run into them, she wanted to downplay the fact that not only had she jumped the fence, but she had also joined the sheriff's department. Her parents didn't need to voice their displeasure. It was a given, not that either of them had even discussed it directly with her. It was kind of hard to confront someone when you didn't talk to them.

When Becky got to the shed without being discovered, she heaved a sigh of relief. She didn't think her day could get any worse.

Until it had.

Mag—short for Magdaline—was sitting with her

back pressed against the shed, a mangy dog in her lap. At seventeen, Mag was the youngest of the Spoth family children. Three brothers separated the bookend sisters, two of which were already married. Only Abram and Mag still lived at home.

"Hi, Mag." Becky crouched down and her heart dropped when she saw the pain in her sister's eyes. Becky gingerly touched the dog's matted hair. An unpleasant aroma wafted off the unwashed dog in the summer morning heat. Becky had to stifle a groan. "This poor dog found his way over here again, didn't he?"

Mag nodded, her lower lip trembling, making her appear much younger than her seventeen years and reminding Becky of the preteen she had left behind almost six years ago when she decided the Amish life wasn't for her. But now Mag was straddling childhood and the woman she would soon become. Would she choose to be baptized Amish or break their parents' hearts as Becky had done? Mag was a big part of the reason Becky chose to stay in Quail Hollow. Sure, she left the Amish, but she couldn't abandon her sister completely. Her three brothers had each other. Mag had no one.

Becky inspected the dog; open sores covered the pads of his paws. "He needs medical care."

"I know." Mag sniffed. "Are you going to make me return him, like last time?"

Becky looked toward her childhood home. She didn't see any sign of her parents. "*Dat* and *Mem* would want you to return him. He's not ours." Even as she made the argument, she wasn't convinced, especially since the owner had obviously ignored her warning to take care of his pets.

"But he's just a little puppy," Mag said, her words trembling as she fought back tears.

"No one can treat an animal like this. There are laws against it." Rage thrummed through Becky's ears as she grew more convinced that she couldn't hand over this dog to their neighbors. Not again. "Let's go talk to the Kings." The culmination of a few very bad weeks had suddenly reinforced Becky's spine with steel. At this exact moment, she didn't care about the consequences, not if it meant protecting this puppy.

"*Dat* won't like that." Mag suddenly had cold feet despite her fierce need to protect the dog. "I'll get in trouble for being disobedient." Their father had told Mag to stop meddling in their neighbor's business the last time the dog had wandered over. Becky heard the story secondhand when the sisters met in town for a quick cup of coffee. Their father wouldn't have liked that, either, but he had never expressly forbidden it.

"I'll take the blame. There's nothing they can do to me," Becky said. A look of admiration crossed her sister's delicate features, something Becky both cherished and dreaded. She didn't want to be a negative influence on her sister. Their parents also worried about her influence. Becky wasn't welcome at her childhood home. Shoving the thought aside, she held out her hand and helped her sister up. "Let's go."

Magdaline walked alongside Becky, holding the dog in her arms, the fabric of her long dress swishing around her legs as she rushed to keep up.

Becky slowed and held out her arms. "Hand me the dog. I'll confront Paul. You don't have to get in trouble."

Paul King, the owner of the farm next door, and Becky weren't strangers. Far from it. But with their vastly different lifestyles now, they easily could have been. Not so long ago, he had driven her home in his courting wagon more times than she could count from Sunday singings. He confidently laid out the plans for their future, while silently she made plans for her own.

Their more recent exchanges had been over this very same dog. Paul obviously wasn't caring for the animals on his farm. Perhaps since his father had died and Paul had become the sole man of the house, he had let things slide. However, this time she wouldn't hand over the dog and leave. She wanted to see for herself what was going on at her neighbor's farm.

"It's okay, I'll take the dog over and talk to him," Becky repeated.

Mag held the dog closer, reluctant to let him go.

"Mag, I don't have all day." The sun rising higher in the sky was making her sweat in her deputy uniform. "Give me the dog and I'll handle the situation."

Mag lowered her eyes to the puppy nestled in her arms. "But if he takes the dog back, he won't be cared for. Even dogs are God's creatures."

A sense of pride filled Becky. Her sister had far more spunk than she had at that age. However, she feared that kind of grit would get an Amish *youngie* in trouble more often than not.

Becky tugged on the hem of her untucked uniform shirt. She'd hate to see what she looked like after the day she'd already had.

And it was still early.

Becky touched her sister's sleeve. "The truth is, since the dog belongs to Paul, it's very possible that we'll have to give him back. But there are laws against inhumane treatment of animals. I can…"

Her suspension. What could she really do while suspended?

"We'll figure this out. But first, I need to see what's going on next door. Give me the dog." She smiled encouragingly. "Go home. I don't want you to get in trouble with *Dat*."

Mag jutted out her chin and pressed her lips together, the picture of defiance. "No, I'll go with you. I'll get back before *Dat* and *Mem* find out I'm gone."

A little twinge of guilt zipped through Becky. She didn't mean to encourage her sister to disobey her parents, but deep in her heart, she couldn't imagine her parents would want to let the treatment of this dog to continue unchecked. Animal cruelty was the only way this dog could have sores on his body and matted fur. "Let's hurry up, then, so you can get back to your chores."

"Okay." Her sister seemed to cheer up a bit. Big sister to the rescue.

Becky hoped she didn't look as ruffled as she felt, but she wanted to make a serious impression on Paul. He needed to take better care of his animals. Maybe the threat of interference from law enforcement would make him fall in line, but somehow she doubted it. He'd seemed unfazed the last couple times she stopped over. The sheriff's department walked a very fine line when it came to dealing with the Amish. They wanted to respect their right to live separately while making sure laws were followed.

Becky followed the small path that led through a crop of trees to the Kings' house. Memories of a life lived so long ago came floating back. Memories she'd rather forget because they made her nostalgic. As a teenager, she used to run along this path to visit her friend Amy. And later when she started dating her friend's older brother, Paul, back when she thought her life would be like her *mem*'s and all the female ancestors before her.

Now, Paul, and his wife, Mary Elizabeth, owned the farm, his mother living with them in the *dawdy haus*. Paul's brother Amos still lived there, too, but was rumored to be getting married soon. And her friend Amy had married an Amish boy and moved across town like a good Amish girl. Actually, Amy's husband was the cousin of Elijah Lapp, the Amish boy who had been beaten by Deputy Reich. Elijah had ditched his car in front of Amy's house in hopes of taking cover in their barn, or so the gossip went.

Such was life in a small town.

Becky shook away all the memories pelting her as she came to a clearing on the Kings' property. She slowed and turned to look for her sister, who had fallen behind. The dog seemed content curled up in Mag's arms despite being jostled as she ran to catch up.

When they reached the barn, Becky held up her hand. "Wait here while I look inside. I'm not going to hand the dog over this time without seeing the living conditions." Most Amish kept their pets outdoors.

Becky pulled open the door and slipped through the small opening. It took her eyes a few minutes to adjust to the shadows. The smell of hay and manure, although unpleasant, wasn't unfamiliar. She was grateful she was no longer responsible for mucking out the stalls. A little pang of guilt poked her because she had left her sister and brother behind to do her chores.

The guilt ebbed away as curiosity took hold. From the far end of the barn, she heard mewling sounds, as if a small animal or animals were in pain. Blinking, her eyes adjusted to the darkness.

Something moved in the shadows.

She pulled her flashlight from her belt and directed its beam toward the heartbreaking sound. The eyes of at least a dozen dogs in a small cage glowed under the light. She reeled back on her heels with a gasp.

"What are you doing in here?"

Becky spun around. Paul lifted his hand to block the light that hit his hardened expression under the wide brim of his straw hat. He gritted his teeth. "Get that out of my eyes, woman."

Instinctively, Becky lowered her hand, but didn't turn off the flashlight. Paul had a short fuse when things didn't go his way. She remembered the sinking feeling she had as they discussed something regarding their future and his anger when she disagreed. He had fully expected her to be subservient as his wife. And why not? They both had grown up with similar role models in their homes.

Becky didn't see that for her future. She had her own ideas. And from somewhere deep within, she had mustered the courage to leave. Sometimes she wondered how.

Resisting the urge to shine the beam back into his eyes to make a point, she gestured toward the door. "Come with me."

She strode past him into the bright sunlight and around to the back where Mag was standing out of sight. "Why is this dog—any of those dogs—not being cared for?"

Some of the bluster disappeared as his mouth worked, but no words came. The uncertainty in his eyes made her believe that he didn't know what to say. Perhaps he actually felt shame for the condition of the dogs.

"You didn't answer my question. Why are you here?" Paul tried to regain the upper hand.

Surprisingly, Mag spoke up. "Your dog wandered over to my farm again. He came through the woods." She spoke so softly she was difficult to hear above the dogs that had started barking in earnest at the commotion.

"This one keeps escaping." Paul reached out to grab the dog from Mag's arms. Mag pulled away and gave him her back, obviously determined not to relinquish the dog.

"I see stubbornness runs in the Spoth family." Paul huffed and crossed his arms. "Give me my dog. You said yourself it came from my property." It didn't seem to register with him that this was the very same dog they had previously returned on two separate occasions. How many dogs did he have in that cage? How had this one been fortunate enough to escape on more than one occasion?

A look of terror—of realization—crossed her sister's eyes and she took off running down the driveway, the awkward gait of someone holding on to something dearly as her gown slapped at her skinny legs.

"Mag!" Becky called out to her. She shared a brief exchange with Paul and an idea hit her. "I'm not going to hand over the dog like last time."

Paul smirked, as if her threat was meaningless. "I think you have enough trouble not to go borrowing more." His hard-edged stare made her speechless. "I read the papers. What are you going to do, beat me up?" He laughed, the sound scraping across her nerves. He held out his hand as if to touch her, and Becky stepped back, out of his reach. "You must be scrappier than I thought."

Rage roiled in her gut, helping her find her voice. "Let me buy the dog," Becky offered.

"What are you talking about?" Paul said, growing angrier. "Just leave. That's what you wanted from the beginning, to leave the Amish, so don't come back here in your uniform and try to tell me what to do. You have no say over me. You, of all people, should know that." Paul strode down the driveway toward her sister. "She better give me that dog."

Protective instincts kicking in, Becky rushed after Paul. "You will *not* take that dog from my sister. Do you hear me?"

Paul spun around and glared at her. Seizing the moment, she reached into her pocket and pulled out the two twenties she had stuffed in there before the start of her shift last night, before her world was once again upended. She never knew when cash would come in handy, for lunch, for someone down on his luck, or for offering her former boyfriend forty bucks for his dog.

"I'm buying the dog." She jammed the money in his direction. "Isn't that why you have so many dogs in a cage? To sell them? I'm buying this one." That had to be the reason. The sheriff's department had answered complaints regarding suspected puppy mills among the Amish, but she had never come across one. Mostly, she had hoped the reports were false. How could a kind and gentle people be anything but loving toward God's creatures?

With a sour expression on his face, Paul swiped the

money out of her hand. "Keep the dog. Now, get out of here."

Becky stared at Paul for a long moment, as if trying to decide her next move. She didn't have too many options legally right now because of her suspension, but he didn't know that. Maybe the threat of intervention by the sheriff's department was enough for him to clean up his act.

"Take care of those dogs. They need a clean, warm place to stay." Becky pointed to the barn. "Someone will be out to inspect the animals in the next day or two."

A muscle jumped in Paul's jaw. "What did I ever do to you?" Like always, he tried to turn things around. Cast the blame elsewhere.

"Take care of those dogs," she repeated, not bothering to soften the hard edge of her tone. The sun beat down on her, making her sweat. Becky hustled to catch up with her sister at the end of the driveway. Once there, she touched her sister's shoulder. She could feel her trembling. "Come on, sweetie. The dog is ours."

"Really?" Mag lifted her watery eyes. "But, what's *Mem* and *Dat* going to say when I show up with a dog?"

"Don't worry." Easy for Becky to say when, in fact, Mag had a very good point.

Just then, she noticed Harrison's patrol car pulling up on the side of the road. He must have been watching for them. He climbed out of the patrol car.

"Everything okay?" With a concerned look on his face, he gently petted the dog in her sister's arms, as if inspecting it for injuries. This tender gesture touched Becky's heart.

"Yes, it is for now." She shot him a "we'll talk about it later" look. Then she gently scooped the dog out of her sister's arms. "I'll take care of the dog. Once he's all better, maybe *Dat* and *Mem* will let you keep him. Okay?"

"Okay," Mag repeated quietly, not seeming so sure. Becky understood the feelings of helplessness and lack of control while on the cusp of adulthood, especially among the Amish.

"I promise I'll talk to our parents about the dog."

Mag looked up with wide eyes. "Might be hard if they're not willing to talk to you."

Becky ran a hand down the dog's matted fur. "One step at a time."

Becky turned to steal one last glance at the Kings' property. Paul had disappeared, but his wife, Mary Elizabeth, stood on the porch and stared at them, clutching something to her chest. A light breeze ruffled the Amish woman's long dress. A whisper of something—nostalgia, déjà vu, relief, maybe?—made Becky tremble as a vision of what most certainly would have been her future flashed before her eyes. But it wasn't her life. She had broken up with Paul. She had left the Amish, her family.

Yet, still, on this sweltering day, she couldn't help but feel shadows of her past stretching out to claim her.

Chapter Four

Harrison cracked the windows on the patrol car, but kept the AC cranked up. Their newest passenger needed a bath and Harrison needed a little fresh air, but it was too hot to forgo the AC all together.

Harrison remained quiet after Becky had climbed into his patrol car. They watched her sister until the blue fabric of her dress was no longer visible from the road. Becky seemed satisfied that she had arrived safely home.

It was then that Becky told him about the dogs in deplorable conditions in a cage in the barn. She had convinced him to take her home and to worry about the animals later. That she'd figure something out. He imagined she had had enough for one day and it was barely midmorning.

He agreed.

For now.

It wasn't until he got to the first intersection that he asked for directions to her house. Between cooing reassuringly to the dog on her lap, Becky pointed out where to turn. When they arrived at her house, she thanked him and got out.

Something about dropping her off without further comment didn't seem right. He climbed out of the patrol car and strolled toward the porch where she struggled to hold the dog and fish out her door key from a bag slung over her shoulder.

"Do you need a hand?"

She seemed to regard him for a minute, before handing off the dog. He held his breath as the poor dog, through no fault of his own, smelled like…he couldn't even put it into words.

He crouched down and set the dog on the porch. The dog seemed to know this was his chance and bounded down the stairs and across the yard. Becky turned around and made an exasperated sigh.

"Hold on, I'll get him." Harrison hustled down the steps and caught up with the dog when he thankfully slowed to sniff around a tree. "Come on, you. I don't think you realize what a good thing you've got going here," he muttered to the dog. "Anyone who takes in a mangy mutt like you has to have a good heart."

When he looked up, he was surprised to find Becky standing a few feet away watching him. A hint of a smile whispered across her lips. She blinked slowly, exhaustion settling in around her eyes. "Thanks. I'll have to call the vet and then see about getting a leash and supplies for my new friend. And a bath is in order, of course."

"Listen, I have to get back on patrol, but I'd be happy to stop by after work. I know your car's out of commission. I could drive you into town and pick up a few supplies for your new roommate."

Becky rubbed her lips together as if she had just put on Chapstick. "I can't impose. You've already helped me out a ton today."

Harrison tilted his head. "I don't mind." He glanced around her house and property. She had a well-maintained Dutch colonial house with a large front porch set back among the trees on a wide stretch of property. "You're kinda stranded out here until you get new tires." He shrugged, trying to act casual. He wasn't sure why getting her to accept his offer of help felt like a challenge. A challenge he wasn't willing to lose. Becky was certainly not like the women he was used to dating. His ex-girlfriend was, well, the opposite of Becky, not that he was looking for a date. He supposed the need stemmed from his desire to help out a fellow officer while she was down and out.

That was all.

Something I should have done for my brother.

"You never realize how much you take your car for granted until you don't have one." She smoothed the matted fur on the dog's head. "I do need supplies for…" She bit her lower lip. "I really should come up with a name for this guy." The dog playfully chewed on her hand. Becky looked up and laughed. "Chewie?"

Harrison couldn't help but smile. He hadn't had a dog since he was a kid. Seemed like much simpler times. Back then his little brother had thought Spot was a good name for their dog who, for the record, didn't have any spots. "Okay, Chewie, why don't you and your owner get inside where it's cooler?" He put a hand on the small of her back and led her toward the house. "I'll be back at four. We can grab a bite to eat first."

"Okay, as long as it's not too much trouble." He

sensed Becky was giving him every possible out, but he didn't want to take it. He didn't like what had happened in the parking lot at work. If someone had the nerve to vandalize her car within a hundred feet of the sheriff's department, what would they be willing to do at her isolated home?

Most men and women in law enforcement were good, honest, hardworking people, but it wasn't unheard of for someone—out of a sense of misplaced loyalty, perhaps—to go after another person if they felt they had betrayed their own.

He wondered if this was the case now. Was someone getting back at Becky for testifying against a fellow officer? Or did this have to do with something else from her past? Harrison didn't know her at all to make the determination. But he hoped he'd let her get close enough to find out.

"Running errands with you is no trouble at all," he said as he glanced around her cozy house after she opened the door and they stepped into the small foyer. He hadn't made the time to decorate his place, unless you counted a couch and a large-screen TV as decor. He took a step toward the door. "I better get back on patrol. Lock up."

Becky paused and looked up at him. Something swept across her gaze that he read as a mix of confusion and perhaps a touch of fear. "Do you think that whoever nearly ran me off the road this morning or sabotaged my car would come to my home? I have no idea if the incidences are related, but I want to believe it's someone blowing off steam. Right? Not someone with real malice." Perhaps sensing the wistfulness of her words, she shifted to a more somber tone. "Ned Reich has been a deputy for a long time and he *does* have a lot of friends. Do you think they're trying to get back at me for ruining his career?"

"You didn't ruin his career. He's responsible for that."

Becky shrugged and wrapped her arms around her middle.

"It doesn't feel right to me." He debated how much to tell her, but at the same time, he reminded himself that he was talking to another law-enforcement officer, not a poor damsel in distress. He needed to be up-front with her. "It could be someone loyal to Ned. Maybe even his son. But you've had some negative press lately, too. So that extends the suspect pool. And if this new video is as bad as you say it is, it might lead to other people trying to take matters into their own hands. For all we know, this video could be going viral on the internet."

All the color seemed to drain from Becky's face. She touched her hand to her forehead. "Like a friend of Elijah Lapp's?"

"Perhaps. It's too early to tell." Standing in the small foyer, he tapped the decorative finial on the railing post with his closed fist. "You need to be careful."

"You're right. I will be." She pressed her hand to her duty belt as if she was checking for her gun that wasn't there.

"They took your gun?"

"And my badge." But he had a feeling she was more concerned about her gun right now.

"Do you have other firearms in your house?"

Becky jerked her head back. "You really think I'm going to have to shoot someone?"

Harrison rubbed his jaw. "I don't know what's going

on here. But a weapon might help you sleep better at night."

She bent down and touched Chewie's head. "I'll sleep better once the truth comes out. I had nothing to do with the young man's injuries."

Harrison nodded and reached for the door handle, making a mental note that she had never told him if she had a personal weapon. "I'll pick you up after my shift."

Later that day, while Becky excused herself to wash her hands, Harrison stared out the front window of the diner overlooking the sidewalk in the center of town. It was one of those rare summer days in Western New York that could give cities south of the Mason Dixon a run for their money. Many families—both Amish and *Englisch*, as he learned he was called—were out in full force, despite the heat rolling off the cement.

He supposed it beat a foot of snow.

The charm of Quail Hollow was growing on him, but he doubted he'd stay here, or anywhere, for the long haul. When he took this job, he took it because he needed an out. An out from Buffalo. An out from everyone who was checking in on him. An out of his own head where all his mistakes replayed on a constant loop.

But so far, he had only managed to get away from his hometown and his well-meaning friends. His nagging thoughts and guilt, not so much.

His cell phone buzzed. Normally he'd ignore it since he was off duty, but he had set a few things in motion today that he wanted to follow up on. "Deputy James," he said after accepting the call.

"Yeah, Harrison, it's Timmy. I took a drive out to the Kings' farm."

"How'd it go?" Timmy Welsh, besides being a deputy, was assigned to animal control, a tricky job in a town where most of the animal owners didn't want anything to do with law enforcement.

"Conditions were pretty bad. The sheriff told me to give Paul King a written warning. Tell him to clean up his act. I threw in a few threats on my own accord. Told him I'd be back and not to be surprised if I took the animals. Most Amish don't want to run afoul of the law. That usually does the trick."

"Thanks, I appreciate it."

"Sure thing."

Harrison ended the call, figuring Becky would be pleased with the latest developments.

He turned toward the voices. Becky was chatting easily with the waitress at the counter. Since he had dropped Becky home early this morning after work—her last shift for a while—she had undone her braids and gathered her hair into a long ponytail. It hung down her back almost to her waist. He blinked away, realizing he was staring. It wasn't any of his business how long her hair was or how nice it looked.

Becky turned slowly and glanced at him as if sensing his appraisal. A small smile hooked the corners of her mouth. He acknowledged her with a quick nod and turned his attention to the plastic menu in front of him. Despite having been in town for a while, he had never sat down in the diner to eat. He preferred to cook at home. Or maybe he just preferred to not deal with people outside of work.

He was still trying to figure out what it was about this woman that made him break all his rules.

When Becky slid into the bench across from him

and brought with her a clean scent, maybe cucumbers, maybe something else, he suspected he partially knew the reason he was inviting her to dinner, even if he wouldn't admit it to himself.

"Sorry," she said, "just wanted to say hello to Patty."

Harrison nodded, but didn't say anything. He had a close circle of friends back home, but he couldn't imagine what it would be like to grow up and live in the same small town his entire life, where *everyone* knew your story. Where you'd actually stop to catch up with the waitress at the diner. Where people knew that you grew up Amish and left to become a deputy. Where soon they'd learn you were suspended.

Didn't sound too appealing, actually. He had experienced his own version of that in Buffalo after his brother died. It was a relief to go someplace where people didn't feel sorry for you.

Harrison opened his mouth to ask her what it was like to grow up Amish, but he found himself dropping his attention to an image of sunny-side-up eggs on his menu. He didn't like when people pried into his past and he should give her the same consideration.

Becky tapped the edge of the menu on the surface of the table. "Have you decided what you're having? The burgers are good."

Harrison set the menu down. "Then a burger it is."

"Oh, make sure you save room for dessert. They have the greatest shoo-fly pie."

"Just by the name alone, I know it's good."

Becky's eyes flared wide. "You've never had shoo-fly pie? How long have you been in town?" She didn't wait for an answer. "Oh, you're in for a treat." Her animated expression surprised him. She seemed so quiet, reserved, when in uniform. "A few different Amish families provide pies to the diner. When I was old enough to take the horse and wagon myself, I used to come in here and sell pies. Gave me some pocket money for when I decided to become a rebel." Her eyes flashed with excitement at the memory.

Harrison had a hard time imagining a bonnet covering her pretty hair. He had so many questions about the Amish, but he suspected those were questions for a second or maybe third date. His words skidded in his mind as if on a bullet train and someone flipped the brakes.

Easy boy, this wasn't a date. First, second, third or otherwise.

Oblivious to the commentary running through his head, Becky leaned forward and pulled a piece of paper out of her back pocket. "I have a list of things I need for Chewie. They should have most of them here in town." She smoothed out the wrinkled paper on the table.

"No regrets?"

Her brows snapped together, then smoothed. "About taking Chewie?"

He raised his eyebrows.

Becky waved her hand. "I didn't have much choice. The sweet dog needed a home. I have one. And the vet said she'd make a house call tomorrow."

Harrison liked her way of thinking, but in his world, few things were straightforward. "We can grab those things, sure. Shouldn't be a problem. By the way, I got a call from Deputy Welsh while you were washing your hands." She furrowed her brow, so he continued. "He works animal control. He stopped by the Kings' house and gave Paul a written warning. Said he'd be back to check in on the dogs."

"That's good." She bit her lower lip. "But I don't imagine Paul thought so."

By the way she referred to the owner of the property, Harrison suspected she had a personal relationship with the Kings. Of course she did; she grew up on the farm next door. He wanted to ask her how being former Amish impacted her job. In some areas, it must help, in others, they must look at her as a traitor.

Just then the bells clacked against the glass door of the diner. A shadow of concern crossed Becky's features. Harrison shifted in his seat to glance behind him to whatever had caught her attention. Two uniformed deputies strolled into the diner. Harrison recognized one as Colin Reich, the son of the suspended officer and the man who had warned him to steer clear of Becky.

Harrison gave them a subtle nod. "Evening, deputies."

Young Reich had his thumb looped through his belt as he sauntered past their table and glared at them. He must have signed on to work a double. He slid into the booth directly behind Becky. Her face grew red and the enthusiasm that was in her eyes when she was discussing her list of dog supplies had been replaced by something else. Fear? Regret?

The second deputy muttered a quick, "Hello," with a strained smile. The unspoken sympathy in his eyes suggested not all deputies were squarely behind Deputy Ned Reich, but refused to speak up. Harrison imagined there'd be a lot of tension within the sheriff's department until the beating incident of the young Amish man by a sheriff's deputy was just a speck in the rearview mirror of the town's collective memory. Unfortunately for Becky's future, memories were long and some incidents tended to forever stain a career.

Harrison reached out, falling short of touching Becky's hand resting on the table. He whispered, "We can go someplace else to eat, if you'd like."

Her gaze hardened and she whispered, "I didn't do anything wrong. I'm not going to run away with my tail between my legs."

From their adjacent table, Deputy Colin Reich made a disparaging remark about Becky. Harrison started to slide out of the booth. He wasn't exactly sure what he was going to do. A fist to the throat came to mind, but doubted that would do anyone any good, least of all, Deputy Reich. Before he had a chance to add his name to the suspension roster, Becky touched his hand gently. Her pointed glare stopped him in his tracks.

"Let it go. It's not important."

"How are you so calm about all this?" he said in a hushed whisper.

"How's it going to look if I'm involved in another altercation?" She shook her head. "Nope, I'm going to have to have faith that this is all going to work out."

She had far more faith than he had.

Becky unlocked the door to her home as Harrison lugged in the pet supplies. She raced to the mudroom and opened the door. Chewie was curled up on a temporary bed of blankets. He got up slowly and wandered over to her, skepticism evident in his eyes.

Becky crouched down and gently patted his head. "Poor guy, still trying to figure out who to trust, huh?"

"Where do you want the supplies?" Harrison stood in the doorway to the mudroom.

Becky glanced over her shoulder. "The kitchen is fine, thanks. Put the things on the counter. I'll have to make room in the cabinets."

She heard Harrison set the items down, then sensed him hovering in the doorway again. "I don't know if it's a good idea for you to be out here alone," he said, his voice thick with concern.

Becky slowly stood and stretched her back. "I'm not alone. I have Chewie." The little dog barked up at him, as if to say, "Yep, she has me."

Harrison ran a hand across his mouth, obviously not pleased with her quip. "Why do I think he'd lick an intruder to death?"

Becky shrugged and crouched down and touched the dog's head. "We'll be fine, right, Chewie?"

Becky crossed her arms, suddenly feeling very tired. It had been an exceptionally long day. She usually slept for a few hours when she arrived home from the night shift, but today, she couldn't quiet her mind in order to rest. Only now that she was back home did she feel the full weight of her exhaustion. And strangely enough, she was grateful she didn't have to work tonight.

"I'll walk you out," she said.

Harrison studied her, apparently recognizing when he was being dismissed. He paused at the door. "Are you sure? I can stay and help you get Chewie cleaned up."

"No, the utility sink is in the mudroom. There's hardly room for me." She blinked away the grittiness of her contact lenses. "Thank you for offering. I do appreciate everything you've done."

"Okay." The hesitancy in his voice knotted the tangle of nerves in her belly. Did he really think she was in jeopardy in her own home?

"Don't worry. I'll lock up." She ran a hand down her ponytail and twisted it around her hand. It still felt strange after two decades of wearing her hair in a neat bun. Lifelong habits die hard. "I am a sheriff's deputy, after all. Well, I think I still am. I'm trained to handle the bad guy." The humor in her tone didn't ring true. She cleared her throat and forced a reassuring smile. "Really, I'm fine." She ushered him toward the front door.

"Okay, goodnight." He glanced over his shoulder as he stepped out onto the porch. "You have my number if you need anything."

She waved. "Yep." She had pinned his business card to the bulletin board in the mudroom before she changed out of her uniform earlier today.

Becky stood in the doorway and watched until Harrison drove away. She closed the door and turned the lock, not something she was in the habit of doing. She flopped down on the couch and Chewie jumped up next to her. She ran a hand down his matted fur and turned up her nose. "You really are a stinky guy, aren't you?"

Groaning because she couldn't put this off any longer, she pushed off the couch and grabbed the gentle pet shampoo from the counter and wandered over to the utility sink. What was she thinking? A hose outside would be much easier. And faster.

She tapped her fingers on her thigh and recalled the big metal tub stored in the shed. She stared at the little guy at her feet. "Okay, you win." She reached into the bag and pulled out the new collar and leash. "Come on. Let's get you cleaned up."

Outside, the evening sun was still hot. Perfect weather to wash a dog. She unhooked the hose from the stand by the porch and dragged it toward where Chewie was digging in the dirt next to the steps.

"You're going to be a handful, aren't you? Stay there, I'll be right back." Becky hooked his leash around the railing for good measure, then wandered to the shed. The strong smell of wood baking in the sun hit her when she threw open the doors. The metal tub she had considered using was filled with topsoil. "So much for that," she muttered to herself.

She shut the doors and crossed the yard. She unwound the leash from the porch railing and led Chewie away from the steps. She didn't want a mud puddle at her back door.

She blinked a few times as her contacts grew cloudy. "I should have put on my glasses before coming out here." She blinked a few more times, trying to clear her vision. She let out a long sigh, looking forward to her evening on the couch. Looking forward to cuddling up with her freshly washed dog.

She held Chewie by his new collar and soaked him with the hose. She reached over for the shampoo and struggled with the cap. She let go of his collar and twisted the lid and took a whiff of shampoo. "This will make you smell like a new doggy." Becky laughed at herself. In only a few hours, she had become one of those people who talked to dogs. She figured it was okay as long as he didn't answer.

With two hands, she lathered up Chewie's fur. He seemed to be enjoying himself. After he was nice and soapy, she adjusted the attachment on the hose while blinking against her compromised vision.

Ugh, these contacts.

She pressed the sprayer and a sharp stream of water

hit the earth near Chewie's head, spraying some dirt. The puppy startled and with a yelp, ran toward the edge of her property bordered by woods.

Becky dropped the hose and started after him. "It's okay. I won't hurt you. Come on, Chewie."

She swiped the back of a soapy hand under her nose. A sharp pine needle scratched the underside of her foot. "Oww," she muttered to herself. *That's what I get for wearing flip-flops out here.*

Blinking rapidly, she slowed, fearing she was chasing her skittish dog deeper into the woods. "Chewie, come on, buddy," she called in her best "I'll never hurt you" voice.

Leaves crunched in the shadowed depths of the woods indicating steps heavier than Chewie's. During the fall, hunters often encroached on or near her property. But it wasn't hunting season. Maybe someone was hiking nearby.

Yet, she found herself frozen in place, listening hard against the competing sound of her roaring pulse in her ears. Her gut told her to run. Get inside. Lock the door. Her heart told her she couldn't let Chewie get lost in the woods. The poor dog had been through enough.

Pushing past her fear, she called again to her dog. "Come on, Chewie. Want a treat?"

With the offer of a treat, a little wet ball of fur came bounding out from behind a bush. "There you are!" The rush of relief made her eyes water.

She bent down to scoop him up when a crack sounded over her head. All her training kicked in. Adrenaline zinging through her veins, she gripped Chewie tighter and pivoted toward the house. Staying low, she bolted up the porch steps, praying that if they took a second shot, their aim would be equally bad as their first one.

Chapter Five

Becky slammed the mudroom door and turned the dead bolt and pressed herself flat against the wall. Her chest heaved as Chewie's wet fur soaked through her T-shirt. "You're okay," she cooed into her puppy's ear. No one was getting in. They were safe. Since she was a female sheriff's deputy living alone, she had taken precautions to secure her home with solid locks and an alarm system. But until now, she had never felt the inclination to use them.

She set the trembling dog down on the tile floor. He excitedly jumped at the door, his claws clacking as they left smeared prints wherever they touched, including her shirt. His incessant yapping did nothing to settle her frayed nerves.

Standing off to one side of the door, Becky pulled back a corner of the curtain and peered outside. She squinted into the heavily shadowed woods and couldn't decipher one tree trunk from the next or determine if, in fact, the shooter still lay in wait. She blinked again, frustrated with her contacts.

Yap. Yap. Yap.

She reached down and distractedly petted Chewie's head. "It's okay. It's okay. Shhhh…"

Yap. Yap. Yap.

She strained to hear above the noise of the dog and her racing heart. Were those more shots fired in the distance?

She glanced out again. Still nothing. Nothing that she could see. She bit her lower lip, debating what she should do. She wasn't helpless. She was a sheriff's deputy.

Who was suspended.

Without a gun.

Grumbling her frustration, Becky grabbed her cell phone from on top of the dryer and dialed 91 before pausing with her thumb hovering over the last 1. The harsh expression on the face of Deputy Colin Reich, the son of the officer she had testified against, came back to haunt her from earlier at the diner. In her heart, she knew most of her fellow deputies were good men and women, but someone obviously had it out for her.

Who could she trust?

Did she dare call dispatch to send a random deputy to help her? Would they?

Her gaze drifted to Harrison's business card tacked to the bulletin board over the washer. She stared at it for a second. She hated to bother him, but what choice did she have?

The crack of distant gunfire sounded above Chewie's incessant barking. She bolted upstairs and to her bedroom window, careful not to make herself a target. The tree branches swayed, playing tricks on her tired eyes. She ran to the bathroom and popped out her contacts and slid on her glasses. She returned to the window, still unable to see anything out of the ordinary.

More shots. They sounded far off. Not like the one that pinged off the bark near her head. She swallowed hard. What was going on?

With trembling fingers, she dialed Harrison's number and lifted the phone to her ear.

"Harrison." He picked up on the second ring, a coolness to his voice. She didn't take offense because of course, he didn't know who was calling.

Becky made a quick decision to play it cool. "It's Becky Spoth. Sorry to bother you," she rushed on, before he had a chance to say anything, "but something's come up." She hustled back down the stairs while she was talking. She opened the door to the mudroom and Chewie jumped up on her leg and barked frantically as if to say, "Don't ever leave me alone again." She patted his head reassuringly, trying to quell his barking.

"What's wrong?" Concern laced Harrison's voice.

"Hold on. Chewie's being loud. Let me see if I can get him to quiet down." She sat on the floor of the mudroom and pulled Chewie into her lap, ignoring the smell of wet dog and mud. He nuzzled into her damp shirt and settled in, his tiny, wet body quivering. "I was outside trying to wash the dog and a shot ricocheted off a tree near my head."

"Where are you now?"

"In the mudroom." She cleared her voice, not wanting to sound helpless. "I still hear shots, but they're farther away."

"I'll be right over. Stay inside. Away from the windows. Hold tight."

Becky ended the call. Chewie licked her chin. She

gave him a cuddle, glad for the company. "You're the cutest dog ever, but boy, do you stink." She ran her hand across the back of his sudsy fur.

Tilting her head up, she could only see the tops of the trees through the window. Pushing off the floor, she stood while Chewie danced around her feet, probably figuring they were headed outside again. "Not yet, buddy. Not yet. Let's see if we can finish your bath in the meantime."

After double-checking the lock on the door, she ran the water in the utility sink next to the washer until it turned warm. "Okay, let's get you cleaned up." Becky lifted the squirming dog into the large sink and held his collar while she sprayed him and washed the shampoo out of his fur. She shut off the water and Chewie shook his entire body, showering Becky and her glasses with droplets of water.

She couldn't help but laugh. She grabbed a towel from on top of the dryer and rubbed his fur while she had him contained in the sink. She plucked him out of the tub and set him on the floor. "Good as new."

Becky cut a glance toward the door and wondered what was taking Harrison so long.

Harrison grabbed his keys from the counter and ran out the door of the nondescript one-story house he rented on the edge of town. The real estate agent said it was within walking distance to schools and when she realized he was single, suggested it was a perfect fixer-upper. He wasn't in the market for either. He just needed a place to lay his head between shifts at work and this place was good enough.

Harrison sped to Becky's house. Once he arrived, he

did a quick jog around the perimeter—all appeared secure—when he heard shots in the distance. It sounded like they were coming from the south. Running toward his truck, he hopped in and called Becky. "Everything okay?"

"Yeah, are you here?"

"I am. But hold tight. I'm going to check the property behind yours. I heard shots in that direction."

Becky assured him she was fine, so he raced off to the quiet country road that ran parallel to her road. He slowed and pressed the button on the arm of his door. The automatic window whirred down. Crickets and birds chirping filled the gaps between the silence. Clouds of insects came to life as the sun settled on the horizon. He cruised slowly, searching the fields for any signs of people or cars.

A shot rang out.

His heart jackhammered as he pressed the accelerator. About a quarter mile up, he found some young men in a field. The ones who noticed him pull up in his personal vehicle seemed disinterested, which thrilled Harrison because that meant he probably wouldn't have to give chase. He wasn't in the mood. His hand brushed his personal weapon he kept in a holster under his shirt as he climbed out of the vehicle.

Then, on second thought, he pulled the gun out and held it down by his thigh. He'd want to react quickly if things went south. Someone obviously had a gun. His sneakers sank into the soft soil as he strode across the field toward the men. The earthy smell reached his nose, a mix of rich soil and dried vegetation.

As he got closer, he heard laughing. Males. Late teens. Early twenties. One was holding a rifle at his shoulder aiming it at a row of bottles set up on an old, run-down Amish buggy.

"Put the gun down!" Harrison called, planting his feet, ready to respond if need be, but man, he hoped he didn't have to. As far as he could tell, these good ol' boys were just having target practice.

The kid with the gun turned, still holding the gun up on his shoulder.

"Lower your weapon!" Harrison started to lift his.

The kid quickly laid the rifle down on the grass and held up his hands. "Easy man. We're just shooting some bottles."

Another kid, this one empty-handed, took a step back; a worried expression flickered across his face. "Who are you?"

"Deputy James." He scanned the faces of the four young men standing in front of him. It appeared that they only had one weapon and it was on the ground. "Any weapons besides that one?"

"No," one of the guys mumbled.

"Do any of you own this property?"

"No, we're just using it for target practice. No one cares," a second answered, not bothering to hide his annoyance.

"Why here?" The proximity to Becky's place unnerved him.

The same young man shrugged. "Someone suggested it. It's just some field. We ain't hurting anybody."

Harrison pulled out his wallet and quickly displayed his identification before stuffing it back into his pocket. "I had a report of shots fired." Better leave it vague. He didn't want one of these guys harassing Becky. *If* they already hadn't. "Are all you guys good shots?"

"What's that supposed to mean?" One of the teens seemed to take great offense, as if Harrison had questioned his right to carry a man-card.

"Anyone decide to take a few shots out in the woods? Maybe have a shot get away from you?"

Another guy came forward, ready to complain when Harrison held up his hand. "Let me see your identification."

"What the...?" But they all got out their wallets and Harrison took a snapshot of all their licenses. It wasn't exactly protocol, but since Harrison was off duty and no one complained, he figured he'd get away with it.

Harrison pointed at the teen who had the gun when he arrived. "You have a permit?"

"Yeah." Another young man pulled out a piece of paper and showed it to him.

"Okay." Harrison kept an eye on the guy with the rifle until he had it safely packed away. As they turned to leave, Harrison added, "I don't want you guys using this land for target practice anymore." He lifted his phone to suggest he had their names and addresses if he wanted to cause them trouble.

He waited until they piled into an older model pickup truck, two guys hopping in the back. Then he turned toward the woods, trying to determine if he could see Becky's house from here. The dried leaves crunched under his muddy sneakers as he made his way through the trees. Something caught his attention in his peripheral vision. Adrenaline surged through his veins. He slowed his pace. There shouldn't be anyone there, right? He had already found the source of gunshots.

Something felt off. Or maybe it had just been a long day. He swatted at a cloud of tiny insects swirling around his sweaty head. He squinted into the dense woods as the evening light faded.

Nothing.

Maybe it was deer. A fox. Anything could be out here.

He kept trudging forward, pushing aside sharp branches and stepping over fallen trees, until he reached what he suspected was Becky's house. It wasn't until he got around the front that he knew for sure. Before he had a chance to knock, an incessant barking sounded on the other side of the door.

A curtain fluttered at the picture window overlooking the porch. A second later he heard the locks on the front door. Becky's concerned face appeared in the crack before she pulled the door open wide. Chewie ran out and jumped on his leg. He crouched down and petted the dog. "Nice guard dog, here."

"If I hadn't bent over to grab this little guy, I'm afraid you wouldn't be talking to me right now." The memory of the bullet zinging past her head and striking the tree sent renewed terror skittering down her spine. God had been watching over her today more than once, that was for sure.

Becky straightened and stepped back into the entryway, studying her front yard and the road beyond that. She really was isolated out here, but she loved her house. Loved her independence.

She just didn't love feeling vulnerable.

"Come on in," she said to Harrison.

He paused and looked down. She followed his gaze to his mud-caked shoes. He kicked them off before stepping inside.

"Did you find anyone?" she asked, trying to read the serious expression on his handsome face. A five-o'-clock shadow darkened his jaw, making her wonder what he'd look like with a full beard, not that she was interested in a man with a beard. She could have stayed Amish for that.

"I discovered some guys conducting target practice in the fields on the other side of the woods behind your house."

"That explains the muddy shoes." She sat down on the couch and patted the cushion next to hers.

Chewie hopped up on the couch, did a little circle and settled in next to her. She laughed and dragged a hand down his almost dry fur. "That wasn't meant for you. But good thing you're cute. And clean." Then to Harrison, "I think there's still room on the couch if you don't mind sitting on the other side of Chewie."

"Don't mind at all." When he sat, Chewie gave Harrison a quick, almost possessive glance, then settled his head down on his new master's thigh.

"Yeah, I cut through the woods from that field to your yard." He ruffled the dog's fur.

"What are you thinking? Someone was a bad shot?"

"I'm not sure what to think. I'll want to go out and see where the bullet hit the tree. See what it looks like. Maybe we can determine the make and model of gun. But first, I have something to show you." He leaned forward and pulled the cell phone out of his back pocket. "I asked them all for identification."

"They gave it to you? Even though you weren't in uniform?"

"I'm convincing that way." A small smile quirked the corners of his mouth. His imposing six-foot-plus frame probably had that effect on a lot of people. As a petite woman deputy, she had to work at commanding authority. Her meek upbringing in the Amish community did nothing to aid her there, either. She was proud of how assertive she had become, but like anything, she was a work in progress.

Harrison clicked a few buttons on his smartphone and held it out to her. "Take a look at their photos on their licenses. Take note of their names."

She took the phone from his hands. Their fingers brushed in the exchange and she caught his concerned gaze. She stared at the screen and didn't recognize the first guy, swiped her finger across the screen and looked at the next. Until she had scrolled through all four images.

"Do you recognize any of them?"

She twisted her lips and studied the screen. "Number one looks a little familiar. I probably saw him around town. Tyler Flint." She said the name out loud, as if it might jog her memory. She adjusted the screen to make the image bigger. *Neh.* She swiped to the next two photos. Jeremy and Todd weren't familiar, either.

Then she swiped to the last photo and studied it for a bit longer. "Lucas Handler looks a little crazed, but I wouldn't want anyone judging me by my driver's license photo. His name's not ringing any bells. None of them are." She handed him his phone. "What did they have to say?"

"They seemed annoyed that I was breaking up their fun."

"What's your sense? Do you believe it was an accident?" Chewie was perfectly content on the couch cushion between them, but Becky pulled the puppy into her lap and stroked the length of him, needing the distraction. How many near misses could she endure in one day and still delude herself by claiming it was "just an accident"?

Harrison sighed heavily. Not exactly encouraging. He reached over and rubbed Chewie's head playfully. "He cleans up nice."

"Yeah. I finished his bath in the sink in the mudroom after I realized it wasn't safe to go outside." She buried her nose in his fur and inhaled his clean scent. "He's much better." She picked up a paw and inspected it. "I think he'll be fine. I'll feel better once the vet stops over, though."

"He seems at home here."

Chewie's presence calmed her nerves. "I promised Mag she could have him if my parents agreed."

"Are you regularly in touch with your family?"

"How much do you know about the Amish?"

"Not much, but I'm learning." He straightened and held up his hands, perhaps thinking he had said too much. "I don't mean to pry."

"No, it's okay." She leaned back into the cushions of the couch and continued to stroke the dog's fur. It felt good to open up to someone. "I think the Amish invented tough love." She laughed quietly, but knew it didn't sound as breezy as she had intended. She always felt a little skittish when people asked about her past. Perhaps she felt like they were judging her.

Perhaps she was the harshest judge of all.

She drew in a deep breath and continued. "If I had been baptized, they would have shunned me. Basically ignored me and kept me separate until I realized the error of my ways."

"But you were never baptized?"

"No, not in the Amish faith, so technically, I'm not being shunned, but they do like to keep me at arm's length. They don't want me to be a bad influence on my sister." She shook her head. "I also have three brothers. Two are already married and Abram still lives at home, but apparently, they're mostly worried about Mag."

"I know it's none of my business, but wouldn't it be easier for you to leave Quail Hollow? Make a fresh start somewhere else?" he asked. The spark of curiosity in his warm brown eyes touched her. He sounded like he was a man who had perhaps run away from something himself.

"I don't want to abandon my sister. That's why she has my phone number to call me if she ever needs anything. My dad has a phone in the barn for his woodworking business. He makes end tables and such to supplement my family's income."

To say "my family" seemed disingenuous. Her father had turned his back on her the minute he had learned she had jumped the fence. Despite the heartache, she had made the right decision. She loved and respected her Amish family and neighbors, but she felt a calling beyond the life she would have been allowed to live as an Amish woman.

God had called her to another life.

Becky continued to run her hand down the length of the dog, feeling like she had said too much. Harrison didn't need to hear all the details of her life. Simply put, she had left the Amish, but she hadn't allowed herself to leave Quail Hollow or her sister behind.

"Is that why you came to Quail Hollow?" she asked, needing to change the subject. "To get a fresh start?"

"Something like that," he said, his answer curt. Now she understood why he was reluctant to ask her questions. He hadn't wanted her to do the same.

"I guess I'm the one who's prying," she said, trying to lighten the mood.

When he smiled his entire face transformed. She almost didn't recognize him as the same serious man whom she saw around the station. "You're not prying. Just not much of a story to tell."

Somehow she doubted that, but let it drop.

Harrison pushed to his feet. "I want to take a closer look out back."

Together they went outside and found the bullet in the tree. He dug the slug out of the trunk with a pocketknife. Palming the bullet, he followed her to the back porch. The concerned look on his face sent prickles of unease washing over her skin.

"What is it?" she asked.

He gently took her by the arm and led her into the house and locked the mudroom door behind them.

Harrison pulled his gun out and set it on the kitchen island. "I'm not going to insult you and suggest you can't take care of yourself, but I'd feel better if you had a gun and I know you had to turn yours in when you were suspended. And you never answered me about having a personal weapon, so I'm assuming you don't..."

Her gaze drifted to the weapon then back to his face. He seemed to be looking right into her soul.

Becky swallowed hard. "You don't think the shot out back was an accident?"

He placed the bullet on the counter. "This didn't come from a rifle."

"I don't understand."

"The young men I talked to claimed they had only been shooting a rifle. If they had another gun, they didn't want me to see it."

Becky gripped the counter, feeling unsteady. Slashing tires as a warning was one thing, but firing a weapon in her direction? "Do you think they meant to scare me or kill me?" Her voice broke over the last two words.

"As far as I'm concerned, anyone who fires a weapon toward another human being has got to understand the risks."

"What do I do now?" Her breath came out shaky. "It all seems so hopeless."

"We need to take this information to the sheriff so the department can start an official investigation."

"What if this causes more problems for me?" Becky simply wanted to get her job back. Not be the focus of yet another investigation.

Harrison took a step closer to her. "You're not responsible for this. You can't blame yourself. You've done whatever you've needed to do." The intensity and concern in his voice unnerved her, almost as if it was personal to him.

"If I had kept my mouth shut…" She broke eye contact and studied the floor.

"You did the right thing. I won't let anything happen to you."

Chapter Six

A short time later Harrison crossed Becky's dark front yard and reached out to shake Sheriff Landry's hand. "Thanks for coming out, Sheriff."

"Of course." Landry adjusted his belt on his blue jeans. Harrison's call had caught his boss when he was off duty, probably at home watching TV with his wife and two young children, judging by the family portrait on his credenza behind his desk. Some people actually had lives outside of work.

"Come in. Becky's inside." Harrison turned and led the sheriff into the house. Becky was standing inside the doorway, holding Chewie.

"Hello, Sheriff," she said, quietly. If her bloodshot eyes were any indication, all the recent events were wearing on the young deputy. "Let's talk at the island in the kitchen." She quickly met Harrison's gaze. They had left the bullet on the counter, evidence that the young men weren't telling the complete truth.

The three law-enforcement officers settled in around the island. Harrison explained the situation to his boss, who seemed taken aback. "You mean to tell me someone tried to shoot you?" His question sounded pointed, accusatory, almost, and Harrison wasn't sure why. Maybe he was reading too much into it.

"It seems that way, sir. If I hadn't bent down to pick up the dog, I'd hate to imagine…" Becky leaned over and set the dog down on the floor, perhaps to allow herself a moment to pull herself together.

The sheriff leaned back on his stool as far as he could without falling off and crossed his arms over his chest. "Why didn't you call the sheriff's department immediately?"

Becky's face grew flushed and she started to stammer before she paused and composed herself. "I had Deputy Harrison's number. I didn't want to make a big deal out of it if it turned out to be nothing."

The sheriff's gaze drifted to Harrison and then back to Becky. Was he trying to figure out their relationship? "I'm glad you reached out to me now."

Becky trailed a finger along the edge of the counter. Feeling the need to rescue her, Harrison spoke up. "I got identification from each of the men doing target practice."

The sheriff rubbed his jaw slowly, probably trying to determine if Harrison had followed procedure, but at this exact moment, Harrison didn't care. He placed his phone on the table and opened the photo app. He slowly scrolled through the photos, watching the sheriff's face. If he knew any of the young men, he wasn't letting on.

The sheriff scratched the side of his head roughly. "Send those photos to my email address. We'll start an official investigation." He planted his palms on the island and stood.

"Great," Harrison said, standing to join his boss.

"When I ran for sheriff, I campaigned on a platform of transparency." He seemed to puff out his chest. "I can't have my deputies running off on their own."

"I only called Harrison because I could trust him," Becky said. Her posture slumped and she blinked slowly as if realizing the implication of what she had said. Harrison wanted to reach out and squeeze her hand, reassure her, but he knew now was not the time or place.

The sheriff slowly turned to look at her. "Are you saying you don't trust the other deputies? Has anyone given you reason not to trust them?"

"I think Becky's afraid of backlash after testifying against Deputy Reich," Harrison said. "There's definitely been a coolness within the department toward her."

Becky held up her hand. "I can speak for myself." Harrison detected a hint of a tremble in her voice.

"Is that true?" The sheriff stared at her. "You think one of my deputies is out to get you?"

"I do feel like some of the officers wish I had kept my mouth shut. That's all." She fisted her hands and placed them in her lap. "I have a hard time believing one of them would hurt me."

"I'm glad to hear that." The sheriff sat back down and rested his elbow on the island, his posture more relaxed. "Let me assure you that anyone who harasses you will be dealt with severely." Sheriff Landry gave her a stiff smile showing all his teeth, reminiscent of his big face plastered on the billboard during the election. "I know this is hard for you, but you have to trust that the department will conduct a thorough investigation regarding the video."

"How long will it take?" Becky asked. "I'm eager to return to my job."

"I know you are," the sheriff said. "But there's more than one investigation to be done. I have to make sure we do this right."

"I didn't strike Elijah Lapp. I used the baton to break up the fight. To pull the two men apart."

The sheriff seemed to consider this for a moment. "Then our investigation will reveal that." He stared at her pointedly. "We have to allow the investigation to run its course. I know it's hard, but we have to do everything aboveboard. This way we can put this to bed once and for all."

Harrison recognized himself in the sheriff. Prior to his brother's death, he had been about rules, procedures and everything being black-and-white. But sometimes a strict adherence to rules meant compassion was lost. Meanwhile, real lives were being affected. Possibly ruined.

"Do you understand, Deputy?" the sheriff asked Becky, a hint of condescension in his tone.

"Yes."

"Good." The sheriff stood and adjusted his belt.

Harrison walked him to the door. "I can talk to the young men tomorrow." He wanted to see for himself why they didn't tell him about a second gun.

The sheriff slowed at the door and turned around. "I think it would be best if I have one of my more seasoned detectives follow up with that."

Harrison's head jerked back and he opened his mouth to protest when the sheriff held up his hand. "In an effort to be transparent—" there was that stupid word again "—I think it's important that someone not connected to the case conduct the interviews."

"What are you talking about?" Harrison glanced over his shoulder to make sure Becky was out of earshot. He was ready to plead his case.

"Trust me on this." The sheriff opened the door and left, leaving Harrison baffled.

"I suppose that went as well as expected." Harrison turned around. Becky stood in the doorway to the kitchen with Chewie in her arms. She stroked his back methodically.

"I suppose." Harrison replayed the conversation in his head. Something about this didn't feel right. It wasn't that he didn't agree with the sheriff that an official investigation should be conducted, he just hated being squeezed out of it.

"You need a lawyer." Sheriff Landry was going to protect his department no matter the cost. Becky had to look out for her own interests. If the sheriff was going to keep Harrison from helping Becky in an official capacity, he'd do whatever he could on a personal level.

"I don't know. Doesn't that make me look guilty?" She ran a hand down her long blond ponytail.

"You need to protect yourself."

"How does that work? I grew up Amish. We didn't use lawyers."

"You've told me before that the Amish don't care for law enforcement, either. Look at you now." He crossed the room and brushed his knuckles across the back of her arm, trying to encourage her. Reminding her that she was in a whole new world and had to play by new rules.

"How would I go about finding a lawyer?"

"I have a friend in Buffalo. I'd be happy to take you. He'll make sure your interests are protected. He'll fight for your job."

"Do you really think this is necessary?" After an extremely long day, Becky's skin looked ashen under the kitchen lighting.

"I have off the day after tomorrow. I'll see if I can get you an appointment then." Harrison tilted his head and forced her to meet his gaze. "I promise I'll be here for you every step of the way."

"Why would you do this for me?" Becky asked quietly, evidently still unsure. Her shoulders sagged in apparent defeat. Chewie lifted his head and licked her chin as if sensing she needed a little moral support.

Harrison needed for her to know this was far from over. That she had rights. That everything would work out. That she wasn't alone. A sadness whispered through him because he hadn't made this same show of support for his brother.

"I have my reasons," he said. "I hope you'll let me help you."

While sitting in the driver's seat, Becky flipped down the visor and stared in the mirror. She ran her finger along the darkened flesh under her eyes. "Ugh…" Another sleepless night, but at least she had her car back. The garage had returned it to her this morning with four new tires and detailing. Gone was the ominous warning in Pennsylvania Dutch to go away that had been scrawled on her back window.

That part of the vandalism puzzled her. Had a clever deputy known just enough Pennsylvania Dutch to threaten her and remind her of her place in society in one fell swoop? Or had someone from the Amish community really been harassing her? Friends of Elijah Lapp certainly had motive if they were following the press or the rumor mill, but she hated to think her Amish neighbors had run this far outside the law. Outside the *Ordnung*, the rules that the Amish district strictly followed.

Becky shoved the thought aside and jammed the key into the ignition and fired up the engine. She adjusted the AC to high and stuck out her lower lip and blew the wisps of hair that had escaped her ponytail from her face. Another sweltering day.

Fearing she'd go crazy if she spent another day cooped up in her house, Becky put the car in Reverse and backed out of the driveway. The vet had come to the house this morning and given Chewie some medication for the sores on his skin, but other than that, she said he was healthy. Now Becky's new companion was curled up on his cushy bed in the mudroom while she ran some errands. Errands that couldn't wait another day, especially if Harrison insisted she hire a lawyer.

Becky was a smart woman. She had made it this far in life on her own; she could certainly find a quicker way other than lawyers and lawsuits to put this mess behind her. She didn't do anything wrong and she wanted her job back. She couldn't shake the idea that lawyers were only for the guilty.

Mustering all the confidence she had, she drove to the farm near the sight of the brutal beating. She purposely waited until after the midday meal. If there was even a spark of hope that her old friend, Amy Miller, would talk to her, it would be if her husband John was out in the field.

Becky parked next to a cornfield, her car hidden from the house and the men working in the fields. The heat from the pavement blasted her cheeks. She plucked at her T-shirt, suddenly feeling underdressed. Nothing could make a former Amish woman more self-aware than showing up at an Amish home dressed in jeans and a T-shirt. Why hadn't she thought this through? Probably because as soon as the vet left, Becky wanted to leave, too. Before she lost her nerve.

As the gravel crunched under her sneakers, words like *humble* and *modest* from scripture pinged around her brain. Just because she had chosen to leave the Amish didn't mean she had chosen to disregard all of their teachings. She tugged on the hem of her T-shirt, pulling it down over the waistband of her jeans. She admired the Amish for their simple lives and their love of God; however, their way wasn't the only way to God. She wished their teachings allowed them to see that.

Becky pushed the swirling thoughts aside. Thoughts that always crowded in on her when she dealt directly with her Amish neighbors. Sometimes she did wonder if moving away from Quail Hollow would be easier than constantly confronting her past.

Taking a deep breath, she climbed the steps to the porch, and the slats creaked under her weight. The smell of something delicious wafted out through the open window. It made her nostalgic for home. Squaring her shoulders, she turned back toward the road and focused on why she was here: to find a witness to Elijah Lapp's beating. Someone to clear her name. She should have done this right away, but the sheriff had advised her against it.

From the porch, she searched the road. Other than

a fifty-foot clearing in front of the house, the scene of the altercation was obscured by the crops. Any witness would have had to walk to the end of the driveway. And from what she remembered from the chaotic scene, several people had. Tenting her hand over her eyes, she leaned back and stared up at the well-kept house, at the second-floor window. Her heart jackhammered when she saw an Amish woman staring down at her.

Amy.

Becky forced a smile and lifted her hand in a friendly greeting. She and Amy had grown up together and had been good friends until Becky decided to leave. Whereas Amy had followed the path set out for a young Amish woman: baptism, marriage and children.

Amy disappeared from the upstairs window and Becky waited, wondering if her former friend was going to come to the door. Becky scanned the landscape, holding her breath that John wouldn't appear and chase her away before she had a chance to talk to his wife.

Becky lifted her hand to knock, when the door flew open. Amy averted her gaze as if looking straight at Becky would somehow be breaking the rules.

"Hi, Amy."

Amy finally met Becky's gaze. "*Gut* afternoon. May I help you?" Becky should have been used to the stiffness and formality when it came to dealing with the Amish now that she was in law enforcement, but she and Amy had been the best of friends. Laughed together. Shared secrets together.

Perhaps Becky had made a mistake by not sharing the biggest secret of all. But that would have been an unfair burden to place on a friend. Neither Amy nor

Mary, her two dearest friends, knew the plans Becky held in her heart.

Becky clasped her hands together, purposely trying to act meek, the opposite of what she had been trying to do since she left the Amish. She wanted her friend to see the girl she used to be, but jeans and a T-shirt certainly didn't help.

"Nice to see you," Becky said. "Can we talk?"

Amy's hesitant gaze drifted to the field. "I'm not sure what we have to talk about." Her words came out hard-edged.

"How is Elijah?" The young Amish man beaten at the side of the road was her husband's kin. Reports suggest he bailed out of his car at this location in hopes of taking refuge at his cousin's farm.

"He's recovering at home." Her tone suggested the unspoken words, "no thanks to you."

Becky wanted to ask if he talked about the incident, but she wanted to ease her way into the topic. And part of her was afraid of what he might have said.

"I was wondering if you could help me."

A crease of concern lined Amy's forehead below her white bonnet. "I don't see how I can."

"Were you home the afternoon Elijah was hurt?" It sounded more benign this way. Passive, as if there was no way she could have had an active hand in his injuries.

"*Yah*, I was home." Amy's eyes clouded over with an emotion Becky couldn't quite pinpoint.

"Did you see anything?" Becky twisted her clasped hands and her stomach knotted.

"*Neh*, I was settling the baby."

Shame heated Becky's cheeks. In another lifetime, she would have made a quilt for her friend's baby or at the very least, brought over food for the family. "Congratulations. I heard. A baby girl."

Amy nodded and a smile lit her face like it used to when they were girls and giggling over a shared story and lunch. "She looks just like John." She shook her head, a twinkle brightening her eyes. "Poor kid." But she didn't mean it. She was pleased that the child resembled her husband.

"I'm sure she's beautiful. Maybe I can see her sometime…" Becky left the question hanging, knowing that as long as she was an outsider and law enforcement, she wouldn't be welcomed into her friend's home. Not as a cherished friend. She cleared her throat, getting back to the topic at hand. "Did John see anything?"

A mask descended and Amy seemed to bristle. "Perhaps you should wait until he comes in from the field. You can talk to him yourself. Other people from the sheriff's department have been here, you know." She plucked at the folds of her skirt. "We want life to go back to the way it was, *yah*."

"The sheriff's department is trying to make sure justice is done." Becky's mind drifted to the chaotic events of that fateful afternoon. "I remember a lot of people watching. Did you know who was here?"

"*Neh*, the baby keeps me busy."

Was she hiding something?

"A video surfaced from that day and I was trying to figure out who took it."

Amy pinched her lips and shook her head again. "You're best to look for someone from your world. It's doubtful the Amish would be taking videos. You know that."

Becky also knew that plenty of Amish, especially

the *youngie*, bent the rules during their running around time. But she didn't want to press her friend. Bowing her head, she finally said, "I'm desperate. I need help. The sheriff's department thinks I hurt Elijah and I need to find witnesses to prove that I didn't. Otherwise, I could lose my job."

Amy's face brightened. "If you lost your job, would you come back?"

"Come back?"

"To the Amish. You could confess your sins to the bishop. I'm sure they'd welcome you back as long as you confessed." The hopefulness in her friend's tone broke Becky's heart. She missed her friends. But not enough to return. She wasn't sorry for leaving, so confessing in front of the Amish community, asking for forgiveness, would be a greater sin.

Becky gritted her teeth and stepped back. The wood slat on the porch let out a loud groan. She hadn't come here to confess. She wasn't interested in returning to the way of life she had run away from, but she needed to be careful not to offend her friend.

She needed friends, not that Amy would count herself among them.

"Thank you for thinking of me, Amy, but I'm happy with my life." Mostly. Becky threaded her fingers and finally worked up the nerve to ask the question she most feared the answer to. "Does Elijah remember what happened?"

Amy shook her head tightly. "I have not asked him." She lifted her head with a steely gaze. "We want to move forward."

Becky opened her mouth to say something and a baby cried from somewhere in the house.

"I have to go."

"Okay…but if you hear anything, can you let me know?"

Amy stood with her mouth pressed into a grim line before saying, "To be in the world, but not of this world. You don't need to be trapped by the evils of the world." She reached for the door handle. "Perhaps you should think about returning to us. Our hearts are open to forgiveness."

A tenet of the Amish faith was forgiveness. Becky understood this because she grew up with it. Love your enemies. Leave vengeance in the hands of God. Whenever a tragedy struck the Amish community, their ability to readily forgive their transgressor often made the national news alongside the crime itself. Forgiveness was their duty.

Becky gave her friend a quick nod, acknowledging she had heard her, but she wasn't willing to comment. What could she say? Was her community ready to forgive her for leaving the Amish? Or did Amy think Becky needed forgiveness for hurting one of their own?

Chapter Seven

Later that day, Harrison parked his truck in Becky's driveway and crossed the yard to the front porch. The grass, dry from a long stretch of no rain, crunched under his footsteps. He had run home just long enough to change his clothes after his shift. He could have called Becky, checked on her over the phone, but if he was being honest with himself, he wanted to see her in person. Make sure she was doing all right. She seemed defeated after the visit from the sheriff last night. As if her chances of returning to work anytime soon were slim to none.

Harrison jogged up the steps and decided he'd act casual, pretend he wasn't genuinely concerned with her state of mind.

If only I had checked on my brother.

If only I had listened to my gut instead of my pride.

Harrison was determined to be there for Becky, but since they were simply working acquaintances, he'd have to be subtle. He could claim he was in the neighborhood. Tell her in person about the appointment he had set up with his lawyer friend in Buffalo. He laughed to himself. No way was anyone ever "in the neighborhood" when you lived out in the sticks.

Harrison plucked at his shirt, wondering if this heat spell would snap anytime soon. He lifted his hand and did a quick little knock, sounding out a rhythm. *Really casual.* Deep within the house he heard Chewie barking. He turned and studied the road from the vantage point of the front porch. Heat rose from the pavement, but a nice breeze whispered through the leaves in the trees surrounding the property. It was peaceful out here. Quiet.

He turned back toward the house, listening for footsteps, something to indicate Becky was coming to the door. Nothing. A small knot formed in his gut.

Where is she?

Her car was in the shop. She couldn't be far. He jogged down the porch steps and walked around the property, hoping he'd find her outside even though he had warned her that staying inside was safer.

The sudden stillness made the fine hairs on the back of his neck stand on edge. He scanned the house and property. His attention stopped at the tree line, the heavy shadows mocking him. He wondered if the sheriff had made any progress in investigating the young men conducting target practice yesterday. Harrison had taken the liberty to use their identification to look up each of the men in the system. None of them had records. *Maybe* it had been an accident. Maybe one of them, for whatever reason, had been reluctant to produce the gun used during the wayward shot. Maybe that was the reason. Nothing more. *Who's going to admit to being reckless?* They could face charges.

Harrison climbed the two steps to the back door and knocked. Chewie barked wildly, his nails scraping against the door. Harrison cupped his hand on the glass on the back door and through the gauzy sheer curtain he could see the dog's tail wagging wildly. "Hey, buddy," Harrison said, "where's Becky?"

The interior door from the kitchen to the mudroom was closed. Had she gone out somewhere and put Chewie in the mudroom for safekeeping?

A new thought crept into his subconscious. He stepped away from the glass and took a deep breath.

He had gone to his brother's home under the guise of a wellness check. He pounded on the door. No answer.

Just like now.

Harrison tilted his head from side to side, trying to ease out the tightening between his shoulder blades.

He had been called out to Officer Sebastian James's home because everyone knew they were brothers. "Thought you'd want to know. He didn't show up for his shift," dispatch had told him in a somber tone as if they already suspected the worst.

Part of him wanted to tell her Seb wasn't his problem anymore. That once Seb chose drugs over job, over family, he was on his own. Harrison no longer wanted to hear the constant barrage of questions.

"How's Seb doing?"

"Glad to hear he got through rehab and got his job back. This drug epidemic is out of control. Sorry your brother got wrapped up in it. Looks like that's all behind him now."

Wrapped up in it? As if his brother hadn't slid that first needle into his arm. As if it wasn't a choice.

But his brother had sworn he was done with it. Drugs were in his past.

Harrison clenched his jaw as he jogged down the

porch steps and around to the front of the house, trying to dismiss the images that haunted him.

Seb, his little brother, slumped against the bathroom wall with a needle in his arm. His eyes staring absently at the pink tile of their childhood bathroom. Where Seb used to have to use a stool to reach the sink to brush his teeth.

The hot sun beat down on Harrison's head. He scratched his eyebrow and paced the gravel driveway, wishing Becky would answer the door.

How did anyone move past this kind of tragedy?

He let out a long, slow breath, trying to calm his rioting emotions. Everyone wanted to know why he left Buffalo to be a cop in Quail Hollow, some small town in the middle of nowhere.

This was why.

He thought distance would ease the pain. Make him forget. He suspected some of his friends knew the reasons, but he never talked about them. Working among the deputies in Quail Hollow who didn't know his back-story was easier than constantly seeing the sympathy in his fellow officers' eyes.

Harrison had come to a lot of conclusions since his brother's untimely death. People made choices, sometimes with disastrous consequences.

Some people stood by their family and friends no matter what. Harrison was ashamed to acknowledge he wasn't one of those people. Now he had to live with the guilt.

Life isn't black-and-white.

If he had listened to Seb when he first came to him. If he hadn't enacted tough love when it came to his brother, would he still be alive?

Harrison second-guessed himself every step of the

way until he finally had to walk away from a job and a home he shared with his brother.

Until he found himself in Quail Hollow on the porch of a rookie deputy, worried that perhaps she had succumbed to the pressure. Found an escape.

That's Seb. Not Becky.

A trickle of sweat rolled down his forehead and a weight pressed on his chest. From the short time he had grown to know her, he sensed she had no one to rely on. As it was, she was straddling two worlds. Neither were welcoming.

Nothing would change until she cleared her name.

"Don't leap from point A to Z, buddy," he muttered to himself, realizing he was letting his past experiences get the best of him.

He strode to his truck for his cell phone. One quick call and he'd know where Becky was. Dilemma solved.

As he stood with the truck door open, he heard a car approaching. He hadn't realized he'd been holding his breath until the car slowed and turned into the driveway.

Becky.

She climbed out and angled her head, a look of surprise widening her eyes. "Did I forgot you were coming?"

"No, not at all." He was finally able to breathe. "I stopped by after my shift." He held out his hand, trying to act casual. "You got your car back."

Becky patted the roof. "Yes, they dropped it off this morning. Feels good to have wheels again."

"That's great." If he had known, he wouldn't have conjured up the worst-case scenario. Perhaps he had further to go in his recovery than he thought if his mind went spiraling out of control at the first sign of trouble.

The gravel crunched under her sneakers as she walked past him toward the front door. "Want to come in? Get something to drink? I can't believe how hot it is outside." Her cheeriness seemed forced.

Harrison followed her through the house and into the kitchen. She opened the mudroom door and Chewie leaped out as if sprung from prison. She playfully rubbed his head, then went to the fridge. "Iced tea?"

"Sounds great."

She filled two glasses and handed him one, seeming to study him with a watchful gaze. Then suddenly, she looked away and snatched the leash off the hook. Chewie ran over to her, eager to go outside. "I need to let the dog out."

Drink in hand, he followed her to the back porch. She let the lead out so the dog had a lot of space to wander without getting away. She leaned a hip on the railing. "I should consider getting a fence, if I'm going to keep Chewie. Or I suppose I should approach my parents to see if Mag can keep him."

"I sense you're reluctant to talk to your parents."

"That's a story for another day." She rested an elbow on the railing. "Is there a reason you stopped by?"

"I made an appointment with a lawyer in Buffalo for you."

She worked her lip and he fully expected her to refuse or at least be evasive, but she looked up at him with resolve in her eyes. "Okay."

Harrison scratched his jaw. "Why the change of heart?"

She laughed. "Didn't you tell me I needed a lawyer?"

"Yeah, but, I figured you'd push back."

Becky plopped down on the back steps and Chewie bounded over, nuzzling her thigh. Harrison sat on the step, one above hers.

Becky threaded the slack leash through her fingers.

"I have to do something or I'll go stir-crazy here." She flicked him a quick glance over her shoulder, then turned her attention back to Chewie, who was sniffing around a tree trunk. "I stopped by the farm next to where Elijah Lapp was beaten."

Harrison clenched his jaw. "You shouldn't have…"

"My friend, my former friend, Amy Miller, lives there."

"I didn't realize that." Harrison watched her bend and twist the leash.

"I'm tired of waiting to get my job back. I had hoped Amy would vouch for my character. Perhaps she had witnessed the events of that day." There was a faraway quality to her voice. "She knows the real me. I'd never hurt anyone. But she's not going to help me. Her desire to stay separate and punish me for leaving the Amish is stronger than our friendship ever was." There was a brittleness to her voice.

"Perhaps she didn't see anything. Maybe you're reading too much into it." He tried to reassure her.

"She believes she's doing what she needs to do because they love me and want me to come back."

Hadn't Harrison felt the same way about his brother? *If he sees how angry I am, he'll stop. If he knows I won't be there for him, he'll make recovery stick.*

Becky absentmindedly fluffed the fur around Chewie's snout. "Unless I want to lose everything I worked for, I need to help myself. And if that means hiring a lawyer…" She pushed off the steps and turned to face him, swiping the back of her shorts. "What time is the appointment?"

The next day, Becky met with the lawyer for forty-five minutes and his reassuring nature allowed some of the tension to ease from her shoulders. Maybe she wasn't alone in this. She had rights and this lawyer would fight for them. For the first time since Elijah ended up in the hospital, she felt like she had a plan. Felt like she was being proactive and not waiting for someone to make a decision on her behalf.

The lawyer opened his office door and Harrison quickly stood. He had used his day off to drive her to Buffalo and then sit patiently in the waiting room. He looked handsome in khaki pants and a navy golf shirt. She still couldn't figure out why he insisted on being so helpful, but she appreciated it.

"Everything okay?" he asked.

"It's good to know I'll have someone pushing for reinstatement on my behalf." Becky glanced at the lawyer.

"I'll do some digging and we'll get moving on this." The lawyer shook her hand, then Harrison's. "Meanwhile, you have my phone number if you need me, Deputy Spoth."

Becky drew in a deep breath. How strange that she had grown up on a small farm in Quail Hollow and now she had business in a law firm in a glass skyscraper in Buffalo. "Thank you."

As Harrison and Becky headed toward the elevator, he asked, "So, it went well?" He pushed the down button.

"Encouraging. Definitely." She smoothed the lapel of her business jacket.

"That's good. The sheriff's department has to understand you're going to fight for your job. I get the sense the sheriff doesn't want any problems and he might be dragging his feet on getting you reinstated. He's afraid of making the wrong decision, so he's not making any."

"That's a pretty strong assessment of him."

Harrison rocked back on his heels. "I'm good at reading people. He's new and he doesn't want to jeopardize his reputation. You've heard him going on and on about transparency." He shook his head. "He's into the politics of it all."

Becky took off her suit coat and draped it over her arm. "I just want my job back."

The elevator doors slid open and they stepped into the car. The smell of perfume from a recent passenger lingered in the small space. "My head tells me this is the right path, but a part of me worries I'm handling this all wrong. What if I'm building a wall between myself and the sheriff?" Hugging her jacket to her chest, she turned to face him. "Won't this make working for Sheriff Landry harder?"

"That's what they want you to believe. There's a procedure for these things. They know the rules and they're hoping you'll go it alone. Once they know you have representation, they won't play fast and loose with the rules."

"I thought I was a rule-follower." She had proved herself wrong when she left the Amish. The doors opened on the lobby floor. Prior to leaving the Amish, she often wondered what the inside of one of these fancy buildings looked like. Once when she was younger, their family had hired a driver and a van and had taken a rare trip to Niagara Falls. She was in awe of the world outside her own. Maybe that was when her curiosity began. A great, big world existed out there.

She often wondered if her parents regretted that trip. Regretted showing her a life outside of Quail Hollow.

As Harrison and Becky crossed the marble lobby, a few women dressed in business suits pushed through the glass revolving doors. Becky ran a hand down her jacket self-consciously, getting the sense that hers had been bargain basement while theirs probably cost more than a few of her paychecks. One of the women, carrying a coffee, strode confidently in their direction.

Again, Becky's mind drifted to all the lives she had never lived, could never imagine living. Was it easier or harder to find joy in life once you knew about all the opportunities in this great, big world? That was probably why the Amish shunned those who left.

Curiosity was contagious.

The woman seemed to take interest in Harrison and slowed down. She waved to the other women. "I'll see you back in the office." The woman's gaze then dropped to Becky, a small smirk tugging at the corners of her pink lips. "Harrison…" The intimate nature of the way she said his name caught Becky's attention.

"Hello, Courtney," he said. Was that a muscle twitching in his jaw?

Courtney tilted her head. "What brings you to my building?"

"Some business on the tenth floor."

"Legal trouble, huh? No lawyers in little ol' Quail Hollow?"

"The one I needed works here." He gently touched Becky's arm. "This is Deputy Becky Spoth. Becky, this is an old friend of mine, Courtney Ballston."

Courtney extended her hand and Becky shook it. The woman's keen inspection made Becky feel like she was pressed between glass slides.

Feeling like she was intruding on a private moment, Becky greeted the woman, then turned to Harrison. "I'll meet you outside."

He handed her his truck keys. "I'll meet you in the truck."

"Okay." She took the keys, gave Courtney a polite smile and strode toward the door. The air was hot, but it felt good to be outside instead of in the sterile confines of the shiny marble lobby.

With the weight of the key fob in her hand, she strode toward the parking garage across the street. It still amazed her that structures existed for the sole purpose of parking cars.

She laughed to herself. Would she ever get used to the outside world? She pulled open the door to the stairwell and the smell of garbage and standing water assaulted her. Jogging up the steps to the second floor, she thought about her conversation with the lawyer. He had told her she had a few options regarding her job, and one included suing the department. He said he'd contact the sheriff's department and request a copy of the video. See if they could authenticate it. Apparently, videos could be edited to appear one way when things were actually another. Was that what had happened?

Becky couldn't remember every detail from the event because of the adrenaline coursing through her system, but she didn't strike Elijah. It wasn't in her nature. Maybe if someone had altered the video like the lawyer suggested, this could be all over. She'd get her job back.

What if that only proved the video was real? Apprehension sloshed in her gut, extinguishing her momentary flicker of hope. Since the entire event wasn't captured on video, she'd need to find a witness. And her friend Amy who lived near the incident wasn't talking.

Frustration weighing her down, Becky pushed open the stairwell door on level three. She had to blink to adjust to the heavily shadowed parking garage She should have paid more attention when they got out of the truck, but she had been following Harrison's lead while simultaneously trying to quiet her rioting nerves. She had never dealt with a lawyer before. And she hadn't anticipated having to locate the truck in the parking garage on her own.

Becky held out the key fob and pressed the lock button. The chirp of Harrison's truck echoed somewhere close by. She followed the memory of the sound to the next row over. She pressed the button again and saw the red brake lights flash.

Her heels—which she wasn't used to—clacked on the cement parking garage. The interior felt claustrophobic, especially to someone like Becky who had grown up on a farm.

A flush of dread she couldn't explain washed over her. She quickened her steps and checked over her shoulder. *No one.* But her imagination was full of all sorts of crazy notions.

It's just the stress.

When she reached the truck, she clicked the unlock button this time and heard a click-click. She reached for the door handle, when footsteps rushed toward her. Before she had a chance to react, a solid body slammed her into the side of the truck. Pain ripped through her hip and ribs.

She opened her mouth to scream, when a hand clamped over her mouth, making it impossible.

"You're dead," a deep voice growled.

As terror shot through her veins, the words of the bishop came flooding back, a cautionary warning she had refused to heed.

There is evil in the outside world. We must remain separate.

Becky should have listened. It was time for her to pay for her sins.

Chapter Eight

"New girlfriend?" Courtney asked after Becky pushed through the glass doors and disappeared across the street to the parking garage.

"Becky's a deputy in the Quail Hollow Sheriff's Department," Harrison said, wishing he and Becky had made it out of this building before Courtney had returned from lunch with her friends. He should have known better than to come here, but Declan Atwal was one of the best lawyers he knew, not to mention they were friends from law school.

Courtney's gaze drifted to the elevator. "And you brought her to your buddy Declan's office because she's in trouble." She sighed heavily. "I thought you went to Quail Hollow to get your head on straight." She lifted a perfectly groomed eyebrow, obviously suspicious of his motives. "Getting wrapped up in someone else's drama isn't going to help. You have to learn how to get out of your own way."

"Nice to see you, too, Courtney." Harrison didn't bother to hide the sarcasm in his tone. Their relationship had fractured even before his brother's death. But it was Seb's death that had sealed their fate. Harrison clung to the guilt that he had left his brother swinging in the wind. Whereas Courtney refused to live her life with any regrets and couldn't understand Harrison's. His brother had made his own choices and suffered the consequences, however dire. This clarity certainly made Courtney a fantastic litigator. She was a bulldog with a bone, never deviating from her mission. She had told him more than once, "You can't let your feelings get in the way."

"I'm worried about you. I thought I'd hear from you once you left Buffalo." The compassion she tried to force into her tone sounded more like condescension. He had been gone nearly a year and she hadn't bothered to call or text, either. "I expected even if you didn't want to stay in touch with me, you'd stay in touch with someone here. *No one* has heard from you."

"I'm fine. I've been busy. Don't worry about me." He hated that he sounded petty.

"I do worry about you." She leaned over and pushed her empty cup into the garbage can. The lid shut with a clatter as she pulled her hand away quickly. "We all do."

"I appreciate it. Well, nice seeing you."

He started to turn to leave when she reached out and brushed her fingers gently across the back of his hand. "You don't have to stay in exile. You could always come back. Practice at the law firm." Harrison had decided to become a police officer after a stint with the prosecutor's office. That had been a sticking point from the beginning with Courtney. She had always envisioned two professionals, dual incomes, two point five kids, *if* they had kids. Perhaps he hadn't been the one who had been fair. He shouldn't have changed the course of their lives midstream.

Or he should have been up-front about what he wanted in life from the beginning. He wanted to follow in his father's footsteps. He only had the courage to do that after his father's passing. But he could have never predicted the derailment of his life after his brother's death.

"Practicing law is not for me."

"You should give it another try," she said, exasperated. They had been through this many times before they officially broke up.

"That's not what I want to do. And you know it."

"You're not still blaming yourself for Seb's death. It wasn't your fault."

"I should have been there for him." He averted his gaze, not wanting to risk that all-too-familiar look of sympathy he always got. "Listen, I need to go." Becky had to be wondering where he was. He hadn't meant to keep her waiting this long.

"Oh yeah, I'm sure you don't want to keep your girlfriend waiting." Courtney's tone was drenched in sarcasm with a hint of jealousy. She always had a way of reading his mind—claimed she knew him better than he knew himself—but today he wasn't in the mood to engage.

"Nice seeing you, Courtney. You look good." She always did.

Courtney hesitated a moment, the look in her eyes suggesting she was calculating something, but then thought better of it. "I need to get back to work." She lifted her hand and wiggled her fingers at him. "Don't be a stranger."

He nodded and turned toward the exit. Why did he feel more like a stranger here now than he did in Quail Hollow? At least there he didn't have to pretend he was something he wasn't.

He pushed through the glass revolving doors, then jogged across the street toward the parking garage. When he opened the door to the stairs, a man dressed in black with a mask over his face burst through the door, narrowly avoiding a collision.

"Hey!" Harrison yelled, before his mind jumped to Becky. He gave a quick glance toward the fleeing man, then decided Becky was his first priority. He started up one flight of stairs before he heard squealing tires. He jumped out of the stairwell onto the second floor and just missed the taillights of his vehicle speeding down the ramp.

Had someone stolen his truck?

Or was Becky driving? Going after the guy dressed in black?

Harrison made a split-second decision. He spun around, reentered the stairwell and bolted down the stairs and burst out onto street level. He hoped that Becky was behind the wheel of his truck and not stuffed into the back under a tarp or—another horrible thought darted through his mind—sprawled unconscious on the hard concrete three stories up.

Pumping his arms, he reached the exit of the parking garage and found Becky yelling at the attendant to lift the tollgate or she was going to plow through it. Harrison flashed his badge and the baffled guy who didn't make enough money to deal with this kind of stress, entered his little glass building and the tollgate suddenly lifted.

Harrison jumped into the passenger seat and braced himself against the dash. "Care to tell me what's going on?"

"Did you see a guy dressed in black running away from the parking garage?" Becky leaned forward on the steering wheel, peering down the road, one way, then the other, her eyes wide. Her breath labored.

"Go to the right," Harrison suggested. "I saw him bolt out of the stairwell and take off toward the park."

The wheels on the truck squealed on the pavement. Becky gripped the steering wheel tightly, praying she didn't crash or run into a pedestrian. Flooring it on the country roads was one thing; here in the city was something altogether different.

Frustration rolled over her as they sped past parked cars and office workers returning from lunch. Her gaze darted all around her. "You see him?"

"No."

She slowed, realizing he could be anywhere. And it wasn't likely that he'd be running down the street with his mask on. It was sweltering out and besides, a knit ski mask would be like a neon sign blinking, *I'm guilty. I'm guilty.*

She pulled over and jammed the gear into Park. "He's gone."

"I'll put a call in. The local cops can investigate. The parking garage has to have cameras."

Harrison made a call and gave the local police a description.

Becky shifted in her seat, then ran a hand down her long ponytail. "I was walking to the car when that guy jumped me from behind."

Harrison ran his gaze down the length of her. "Are you okay?"

She waved her hand in dismissal. "He didn't know he was trying to mug a sheriff's deputy who had training in self-defense." She winced at the memory of his nose crunching under a swift blow with the heel of her hand. Direct hit. "A few strategically placed strikes and he took off." She shook her head in disgust. "I thought about going after him on foot, but I had on these stupid shoes. How do women even get around in these? My feet are killing me." The flow of words spilled out on a wave of adrenaline.

"You're okay? Are you sure?"

"Yes, of course." She tapped the center of the steering wheel with her fist. "I wish I'd caught the guy. He'll probably wait for the next victim in some dark parking garage. Creep."

"Becky..." Harrison seemed to be waiting for her full attention.

She turned to him. "What?"

"Did you ever consider that you were the target?"

She furrowed her brow. "Here? In Buffalo? I don't..." Her shoulders sagged and she plucked at her sweaty blouse. She once again remembered that trip to Niagara Falls as a young Amish girl and how her parents had warned her of the dangers. To always be vigilant. Evil lurked in the outside world. Wasn't that what this was about?

The ubiquitous evil the Amish talked about.

"No, he couldn't have been targeting me. Quail Hollow is a good hour's drive from here."

"We can't rule it out. Maybe someone followed us

here. If they attacked you in Buffalo, maybe they hoped it couldn't be traced to the events in Quail Hollow."

With the adrenaline subsiding, a sadness settled in her heart. "This is getting out of control." She needed air. She pushed open the truck door and stepped out onto the pavement.

"Where are you going?"

"I want you to drive home. I need to let my nerves settle."

Harrison climbed out of the passenger seat and met her around back. He took both of her hands in his and forced her to look into his eyes. "You're fine. You did great fending off your attacker. They'll think twice before coming after you again if it wasn't a random event."

They both knew it wasn't.

Becky swallowed hard and nodded. "Thanks. All my training has paid off." She just wished it didn't have to.

Back at her house, Becky leaned her hip against the kitchen center island and winced. She was a little sore from the attack, but grateful that was all she was. *Thank God*. She flipped open the lid of the Chinese take-out container. She peeked at the beef and broccoli and drew in a deep breath. "I've never had Chinese food. It smells wonderful."

Harrison unloaded the other little white boxes and plastic containers, taking a moment to bend down and pat Chewie's head. "You're not serious."

She lifted a shoulder in a half shrug. "They don't have a Chinese restaurant in Quail Hollow and I guess the times I've been away from here, there were so many other options to try."

He stared at her for a long minute as if he were looking through her. "I can't imagine what it was like grow-ing up Amish."

A piece of broccoli fell off the spoon she was hold-ing and plopped onto the counter. She picked it up and tossed it onto her plate. "Not much to imagine. What you see is what you get." She sat down on the other side of the island. She grimaced when her hand hit against the counter. She examined her fingers. The heel of her hand was already turning a shade of blue from where she made contact with her attacker.

Harrison sat down next to her with his plate. "Are you sure you're okay?"

"Yes, I'm fine. I can't say the same for the guy."

With his fork dangling over something that looked fried and wonderful, he said, "Tell me exactly what he said."

Becky wiped her napkin across her mouth and closed her eyes, recalling the feel of his sweaty hand on her mouth. His hot breath whispering across her ear. "You're dead."

Harrison pushed his rice around with his fork. "I hate to think someone from Quail Hollow followed us today. What did Sheriff Landry say when you called him?"

"I gave him all the details. He said he'd follow up here, but it was now an issue for the Buffalo Police De-partment." She shrugged. Before leaving Buffalo, they had filed a report at the station and had driven home in mostly silence. "I feel like the walls are closing in."

Harrison set down his plastic fork and reached out and covered her hand. "I'm going to help you get through this."

She flinched. "I didn't do anything wrong, but I'm

suffering the consequences." She slid her hand out from under his. "I'm the one without a job."

"Not for long."

"You don't know that," she said accusingly.

"You're taking all the right steps. You'll get your job back."

"The rules seem arbitrary." She picked up her fork and poked the branches of the broccoli. "I thought the hardest decision I'd ever have to make was behind me. Leaving the Amish was tough, but at least within their community, everyone knows the rules." She tilted her head. "A person might not like the rules. But everyone knows them." She lowered her voice. "Maybe I made a mistake by leaving." A knot formed in her stomach and she suddenly wasn't hungry anymore.

"Why did you leave?"

She looked up slowly, a bit surprised by his question. Most people wondered, she realized that, but most didn't ask.

"I felt like I was living a life that wasn't mine." She swallowed hard. "From the time I was a little girl, I'd look around the farm, at my mother, and wonder if this was all life had to offer." Heat suddenly swamped her face and she turned away. "Forgive me. I don't mean to disparage my mother. She's a good woman. But I'm not built like her. I never found satisfaction from cooking, cleaning and taking care of a husband." She shook her head. "Even now it makes me twitchy. I wanted to be on my own. There's a big world out there." She cut him a sideways glance. "A big world out there," she repeated, "but I decided to stay in Quail Hollow."

"You don't have to defend your decision to me." He

spoke like he had experienced what it was like to live a life that didn't feel like your own.

"I feel like I've had to defend my decision to everyone—including myself—every day since I left." She unwrapped a little bag and looked inside to find a small roll. She didn't want to be rude and lift it to her nose to smell it. "What is this?"

"A vegetable egg roll. Try it. If you don't like it, I'll finish it." He smiled and her heart fluttered a bit. She quickly lowered her gaze. When she had left the Amish, she had vowed she'd forever be independent. If she wasn't willing to be tied down to the Amish way of life—which included marriage—why would she do it outside when she was free?

Her hand fluttered around the hollow of her neck and she wondered if freedom wasn't all that it was cracked up to be. Maybe the reasons the Amish had so many rules was to protect the people from themselves. From all the worldly temptations.

She took a bite and set the roll down on her plate. After she swallowed the mouthful, she said, "I thought I'd be happier once I left the Amish."

Harrison leaned in close. "Don't mistake your current mood for how things are always going to be."

She slowly lifted her eyes to his. "You sound like you're speaking from experience."

"Yeah, you met Courtney today. We were engaged."

"Oh." Becky wasn't sure why she suddenly got a twinge of…was it envy?

"We met in law school. I never felt like I was where I needed to be. I grew up the son of a police officer and always thought that wouldn't be enough. I worked for the prosecutor's office for a few years, but after my dad died, I decided to follow in his footsteps." A corner of his mouth curved into a smile. "Courtney called off our engagement because she wanted to be married to a lawyer. Not a cop. She thought my next stop should have included a fancy corner office."

Becky studied his face. "Are you happy being in law enforcement?"

"For the most part."

"For the most part," she repeated. "Does this have something to do with why you left Buffalo and came here?" Becky asked, feeling a bit like she was being nosy. Her mother would have scolded her to mind her manners, but Becky had always been inquisitive. It was why she was here and not content to marry Paul and live in the Amish way. She had felt the walls closing in on her when Paul expressed his interest. She was grateful—and amazed—that she had been strong enough to leave before their engagement was published.

"It's a long story." Harrison moved around a piece of white rice on his plate.

Becky leaned back and held up her hand. "I ask too many questions."

"I don't mind, but I don't want to bore you."

"I'm willing to listen," she said. She owed him that much after everything he had done for her since this mess started.

"Well, the short version is that after I left the prosecutor's office, I became a police officer. I had a strong sense of right and wrong while convicting the bad guys. Now I had a chance to work as a police officer, taking criminals off the street." He lowered his voice in frustration. "I wanted to get in there, get my hands dirty."

"Sounds admirable."

"It can be. But sometimes it takes more than determination. It takes compassion."

Becky scrunched up her nose. "For the bad guys?"

Harrison put down his fork and rubbed his temples as if something pained him. "Sometimes someone we think is the bad guy just doesn't see any other way out."

Harrison glanced up even though he wasn't sure he could look Becky in the eye. She seemed too trusting.

"What happened?" She reached over and placed her hand on his forearm.

"Shortly after I joined the police force, my mom got sick. She told me to keep an eye on my little brother, Seb. He was a rookie officer." Even now referring to his brother in the past tense was like a punch to the gut.

Becky brushed her thumb back and forth in a soothing gesture across his arm. He wondered if she even realized she was doing it. He had noticed her doing the same thing when she held Chewie.

Speaking of which...

Harrison glanced around to find the dog curled up, sleeping on his bed in the corner of the kitchen. A part of him hoped the dog would jump up and save him from spilling his guts. He didn't want Becky to start looking at him like his friends did back in Buffalo.

Poor Harrison. His brother overdosed. He *found him. Did you know that? It must have been awful. Needle still in his arm.*

He stared off into the distance and ran his palms up and down the thighs of his pants, trying to shake that last horrific image of his brother. Apparently sensing his distress, Becky said, "You don't have to talk about it. Not if you don't want to."

He found himself drawn to her compassion. "I do." He hadn't realized that until he said it out loud. Even though he had only grown to know her over the past few days, he wanted to share this part of his life with her. He felt a certain connection to her.

He no longer felt alone.

"My brother Sebastian got involved with illegal drugs after he got hurt on the job. A back injury led to painkillers led to heroin use."

To her credit, Becky kept her expression even. He had learned to anticipate judgment, as if a person who used drugs didn't deserve compassion.

He had been one of those people.

"When I discovered his drug use, I employed tough love. Told him to knock it off. Told him he was bringing shame to the family name."

"I'm sorry," Becky whispered, still offering a comforting touch to his arm.

"Instead of pushing him away, I should have been there for him."

"I'm sure you did your best."

"But I didn't. He died less than a week after returning to work. He had made it through rehab. He had been doing well. But I still acted cool toward him. I wanted to let him know he hadn't been forgiven. He had to work for it. That I had zero tolerance for his drug use." He ran a hand across his mouth. "Who did I think I was? I'm not perfect." He shook his head. "Maybe if he knew I was in his corner…"

"You didn't know…" Her voice trailed off.

"I should have known." A muscle ticked in his jaw. "I was the one who found him in the bathroom of our childhood home." He plowed a hand through his hair and he suddenly felt sick, just as he had done every time he remembered the pallid color of his brother's skin.

Becky didn't say anything; she just looked at him with that pained expression all his friends back in Buffalo gave him.

"I found a journal he kept in rehab. There were pages and pages about me and stuff we did as kids growing up and how he missed me and wished I would support him more."

Harrison sniffed and fought to hold the rest of his emotions at bay. "Seb made a huge mistake getting involved with drugs, but I didn't do anything to help him."

Becky cleared her throat softly. "We all do the best we can. You didn't know how this would end."

"I should have. As a police officer, I've seen it enough. But I was more worried about appearances. How his drug use reflected poorly on me. On our family. I was terrified of enabling. Like, if I relented, he'd think I was okay with it."

He pinched the bridge of his nose. "Biggest mistake of my life and unfortunately, there's no redo on this."

"You need to forgive yourself."

Harrison pushed the stool away from the kitchen island and carried his paper plate to the garbage can. He stepped on the foot pedal and the lid snapped open. He tossed his plate in, then turned back to her. "I don't know if I can ever forgive myself. I can't even bear to live in the house where he died. To run into our mutual friends. To see his old locker at the police station downtown." He rubbed his jaw. "I thought moving here would get me out of my head. But clearly it hasn't."

Becky set down her fork and stood. She approached him cautiously as if he might spook. He imagined how he looked standing there. "I'm sorry you had to go through all that. Perhaps you need to find faith to find peace."

He bit back a laugh, something that came automatically when people suggested things like prayer, faith—what did that mean anyway? "Faith? Where was God when Seb shot up on the bathroom floor?" He clenched his jaw to stop from spilling out all the arguments for why *faith* was not going to help anyone. Yet, as strongly as he felt, he didn't want to offend this sweet woman who was only trying to help.

"You didn't deserve that," he said quietly as he stepped around her. "How did you keep your faith after everything you've gone through? I mean, how can you not be resentful that your so-called God-fearing parents ignore you? What kind of hypocrisy is that?"

Becky radiated a calmness he didn't understand. "My parents are good people. They think that by giving me the cold shoulder, I will return to the Amish way. It is meant to be redemptive. They want me to come back into the fold." Becky tilted her head, forcing him to meet her gaze. "Just like you did what you thought you had to do for your brother."

Harrison groaned at the comparison.

"You could have never anticipated the outcome," Becky continued. "You thought Seb would make the right decision and give up drugs."

"I should have anticipated a relapse." Harrison wasn't ready to acquiesce to her argument.

Becky shook her head. "I'm not trying to compare drug use with running away from the Amish, but one thing we have in common are family issues. My family loves me and you loved your brother."

"I did."

"We all do the best we know how." She snapped closed the lid on a takeout container. "If you ever want to take me up on going to church, you know where to find me. I find it keeps me centered when everything around me is falling apart. I may have left the Amish, but my Christian faith is strongly intact."

Harrison slid the takeout container from her hand and leaned down and brushed a kiss across her cheek. Becky jerked back in surprise. Before she had a chance to respond, he said, "Thanks for being a friend. I haven't had many since moving to Quail Hollow."

"Anytime," she said breezily, clearly uncomfortable. He hated that he had made her feel that way. "Um, do you think you'll return to Buffalo?"

"I still own my parents' house. I suppose I could find another police job either in Buffalo or the surrounding communities." He shrugged. "I haven't given it much thought, but I also never thought Quail Hollow would be long-term. I needed to get away."

"I know that feeling." She took a step back and spun around and returned to the task of closing containers and snapping on lids to the Chinese takeout. "You know, it's me who should thank you. Without your introducing me to your lawyer friend and—" she lifted a container "—Chinese food, my life would be far drearier." She opened the fridge and started stuffing containers inside.

Becky's movements suddenly seemed manic as if she was trying to be cheery. It made Harrison wonder what he had said. Perhaps he had shared too much.

Chapter Nine

The next day, Becky sat on the couch with Chewie curled up by her side. She had the blinds drawn against the gorgeous sunny day. It was easier to pretend her life hadn't gone off in a ditch this way. She didn't have many friends as it was and certainly the ones she had in the sheriff's department thought she was toxic. Even Anne, her closest friend and assistant to the sheriff, hadn't returned her phone calls.

Her memories drifted back to the conversation she and Harrison shared last night over Chinese food. In a way, they were kindred spirits. Both struggling with life's circumstances and family issues. The one difference: Harrison was truly alone. All his family had since passed. Hers was on the other side of town, choosing to pretend she didn't exist.

All except Mag.

She wasn't sure which was worse.

TV remote in one hand, she flipped through the stations, getting tired of all the shows she didn't feel like watching.

After recent events, this was the only way she felt

safe, cocooned in her house. Harrison had called her this morning to check in on her and she feigned cheeriness. She rambled off a long list of things she planned to do around the house that she never had time to do when she was working full-time. Yet, here she sat on the couch feeling too blah to move. She didn't want him to feel like he had to come by to check on her. He had already done too much. She shouldn't be depending on him. And she didn't want to be his "get over his guilt" project because he hadn't been there for his brother.

That's harsh. The man's genuinely concerned about you.

She turned up the sound on some all-hours news station to drown out the constant chatter in her head. Eventually, she began to doze. Her dreams were wild and disjointed. Stress did that.

Something startled her out of a dream—she might have been in pursuit of a speeding car or maybe she had been walking across a muddy field sinking up to her knees. Sitting up slowly and wiping the sleep from her eyes, she tuned in to a quiet knock on the door. Chewie, who had apparently also been sleeping next to her on the couch, lifted his head, looked at her, then looked at the door, then put his head back down. She couldn't help but laugh and patted him playfully on the head. "Some guard dog you'd make."

She squinted at the clock on the cable box and realized it was too early to be Harrison, unless he decided to stop by during his shift. Untucking her legs from under the blanket, she stood and shook out her right foot that had fallen asleep. Running a hand through her hair, she walked slowly toward the front window—Chewie in tow—and was surprised to find a horse and buggy in her yard. Chewie hopped up and rested his paws on the low windowsill and growled at the horse. "Now you jump into action," she joked, even though she wasn't in a jovial mood.

"This can't be good," she muttered. Becky paused at the mirror in her front hallway and glanced at herself. Dressed in sweats and a T-shirt with a messy bun, she had most definitely seen better days. She didn't want word swirling around the Amish community that she was falling apart. The bishop would probably use her as a cautionary tale. "Nothing good happens when you succumb to worldly pressures."

A familiar shame washed over her. *Be humble. Don't worry about what others think of you.*

A soft knock sounded again and Becky had to make a quick decision. Ignore the door or open it to see who was here.

Curiosity got the best of her.

She pulled open the door and sucked in a breath. "Mary Elizabeth." Paul's wife. The last time Becky had seen Mary was when they rescued Chewie from his horrible living conditions on the Kings' farm. Her old friend had been watching her from the porch when she left.

A thought suddenly slammed into her and she had an irrational urge to scoop up Chewie and hide him in the mudroom, but the fool dog was barking his head off at the horse. It wasn't like Becky could hide him now.

Mary bowed her bonneted head and clasped her hands together. Pink blossomed in her cheeks. Apparently, her old friend had found her house, but now that she was here, she couldn't find the words.

Becky stepped back and held out her hand. "Would you like to come in? I could make tea."

Mary studied her with cautious eyes. "I shouldn't." Her gaze scurried around the porch as if she feared she'd be discovered. "Can we talk out here?"

"Sure. Hold on." Becky closed the door over and ran to get Chewie's leash. She hooked it onto the ring of his collar and met Mary on the porch. She followed Chewie down the steps and stood on the walkway while Chewie sniffed and explored every inch of the yard that he possibly could within the parameters of his leash.

"I see the dog is doing well," Mary said, her voice soft.

"Yes. He seems happy." She studied her old friend. "What brings you here?"

Mary started wringing her hands again. "They came and took all the dogs away this morning."

Becky nodded, hiding her relief. "The dogs needed to be cared for. You must realize that."

"*Yah*, I do. And Paul does. He's too proud to admit we got overwhelmed. We never meant to let the conditions get so bad. After Paul's father died and we had a rough crop season, he thought it would be a way to make a little extra money." She turned her back to Becky, the hem of her long gown brushing against her black boots.

"Animal control will make sure they're cared for. It'll be fine."

"*Yah*, but I'm worried about my family. Will the sheriff's department take Paul away? He was only trying to do right by his family."

Becky tightened her grip as Chewie tugged, trying to chase a bunny under the tree but was foiled by the leash.

"Everything will be okay," Becky said reassuringly,

but really, she had no idea what if any charges would be made.

"We heard *Englischers* liked puppies and were willing to pay *gut* money. We never…" She bowed her bonneted head. "We never meant to mistreat the dogs."

"What did the deputies say after they collected the animals?"

"I don't know. Paul told me to stay in the house." Mary's eyes grew wide. "I don't know how any of this works. I could never imagine the farm without him. We've already had a rough year." Every possible emotion flickered across her face as she considered the worst possible scenario.

"Don't borrow trouble."

"Can you talk to the sheriff? Make sure Paul isn't arrested? You can do that, *yah*?"

Becky dragged the toe of her sneaker along the edge of a paver. She wasn't sure how much she could do now that she was suspended, but her heart went out to her friend.

She took a chance. "I've been suspended from my job."

All the color seemed to drain from Mary's face. Her skin tone matched her bonnet. She turned away, then turned back around. "Was it because of the incident with Elijah Lapp?"

Becky studied her friend's face. *Does Mary know something?* A slow *whoosh-whoosh-whoosh* filled Becky's ears and she chose her next words carefully. "The sheriff is trying to sort out what happened. A video suggests I was more involved than I claimed." Her pulse spike with the injustice of it all. "But I'm innocent. I never hurt Elijah. I need a witness to come forward to support my claim." Her mouth grew dry, making it difficult to swallow.

"A witness?" Something about the way Mary said the two simple words niggled at Becky's insides. Anticipation buzzed her nerves.

Mary does know something.

"Can you help me?" Becky pressed her lips together, trying not to say too much. Trying not to scare her skittish friend.

Mary folded her arms tightly over the white bib of her pale gray dress and began to pace. "Maybe we can help each other." She flicked her gaze at Becky, then back down to the grass.

Becky waited.

"Paul's brother, Amos, was there the day Elijah got hurt. I'm sure he'd come forward as your witness if it meant protecting his brother."

A mix of hope and disbelief washed over Becky. "Does Amos know what happened?"

Mary drew up her shoulders and let them fall. "I heard Amos and Paul talking. Amos showed Paul the video."

"When did this happen?" Becky felt light-headed.

"Last week."

Becky's stomach bottomed out. "Are you sure?" Last week? Becky had only been suspended a few days ago.

"*Yah*, definitely. We had to clear out the barn for Sunday service and they were standing in the corner looking at something on Amos's phone."

"Do you know if Paul or Amos sent this video to anyone?" Deputy Reich's attorney had supposedly received it anonymously. Had Paul turned it over in an effort to get back at her for harassing—as he called it—

him over the dogs? That had been an ongoing source of confrontation even before the Elijah incident. The video might have been the perfect ammunition Paul needed to get back at her.

Becky pressed a shaky hand to her forehead. If Paul thought the video would hurt her, how did Becky think Amos could help her now? A headache started behind her eyes, realizing the futility of it all. Unless… Unless, she thought to herself, Amos saw something the video hadn't captured. Maybe he could testify that she hadn't struck Elijah with her baton.

Nerves knotted her stomach. "Did Paul turn that video in to anyone? Maybe the lawyer representing the other deputy?"

"I don't know," she whispered.

"Why would Amos help me if he took the video? If he turned it in…" She scratched the top of her head. "He never came forward before. Why would he help now?"

"The men stopped talking when I approached, but I got the sense that Amos saw more than he videotaped." She studied the palm of her hand for a moment before continuing. "I know we lead very different lives now, but I know you'd never hurt someone."

"Thank you." New hope blossomed in Becky's chest and made her jittery. She had to act on this. "I need to talk to Amos. Get him to come forward." She watched Mary's face, praying that her friend might pave the way.

"Then you'll help Paul?"

"I'll see what I can do."

Mary's eyes brightened. "Really?"

"I can't promise you anything, but perhaps since the animals are now safe and healthy, he can pay a fine.

Nothing more. I'll have to see. I don't have the power to make this decision."

"Denki." Mary nodded enthusiastically, perhaps overestimating Becky's influence.

"Don't tell Paul or Amos that you spoke with me, either," Becky said. She wanted to track down Amos this afternoon and use the element of surprise.

"Yah. I better go. I need to get dinner ready. Paul will be hungry." Without saying anything more, Mary turned and hustled toward her buggy, a woman on a mission. She unwound the reins from the light post near the end of the driveway. She hopped up on the buggy and flicked the reins. The horse began his steady trot.

Becky stared after the horse and buggy long after it disappeared, the *clip-clop-clip* ringing in her ears.

"Come on, Chewie. Time to go in." Her new companion bounded up the steps and sat down at the front door. Becky opened the door and the cool air-conditioning washed over her.

She unhooked the leash and patted Chewie on the head. He curled up on the couch. He lifted his head as if to beckon her. She plopped down next to him. The dog was great company, but she missed true companionship.

In just the past few days, she had talked to two Amish friends. Girls with whom she had shared a past. Her childhood hopes and dreams. She had missed their friendship. Was her past beckoning for her to return? Had she made a horrible mistake by leaving the only people who ever truly supported her?

She snapped off the TV and hugged her legs to her chest. She sat in silence save for the occasional jangle of Chewie's collar. She reached across and picked up her cell phone and texted Harrison.

Have lead on witness to Elijah's beating. Care to go with me?

She stretched to put the phone down when it chimed.

Yes, don't go alone. Pick you up after shift.

At the end of his shift, Harrison stopped by the sheriff's office. He was hoping for an update on the investigation into the Elijah Lapp beating as well as any news regarding the young men conducting target practice behind Becky's house.

Harrison lingered outside the office door, waiting for Sheriff Landry to finish up a phone call. He didn't want to appear to be eavesdropping.

Landry hung up the phone and looked up. "How can I help you?"

Harrison stepped inside the office and closed the door. "It's about Deputy Becky Spoth," he said, sitting down. He didn't want Landry to feel on the defensive.

Landry braced both hands on either side of his desk as he pushed back in the large leather chair without standing up. "I can't talk about the investigation. It's ongoing."

"I understand the difficult position you're in."

Landry sighed and slumped back in his chair as if he had finally found an ally. "This is the last thing I wanted during the first year of my tenure as sheriff." His gaze drifted toward the door as if someone might overhear his confession.

Harrison cleared his throat. "Deputy Spoth needs support. I haven't known her for long, but I understand she grew up Amish." Harrison was reluctant to reveal his growing relationship with Becky for no other reason than to respect her privacy.

"Yes?" The curious inflection in the single word suggested the sheriff wanted to know what one had to do with the other.

"Becky walked away from her community and she no longer has their support." Harrison drummed his fingers on his thigh, feeling a current of anxiety. "Now she doesn't feel like she has the support of the department." In a sense, she was being shamed from all sides. Harrison imagined that was how his brother felt during his downward spiral before his death.

Landry sighed heavily. "She's in a tough spot. She testified against another officer and then a video surfaced suggesting she may have been just as guilty."

"Is that what you believe?" Harrison struggled to keep his voice even. "That she's guilty?"

Landry steepled his fingers and placed his elbows on the desk, and gave him a bland, non-committal expression as if debating which path would have the least negative effect on his career. Protecting one's own backside seemed to be a natural political instinct.

"The video is damaging to her story," the sheriff said evenly.

"We can't…" Harrison braced his hands on the arms of the chair to stand, then decided to lean back. *Deep breath. Control your anger.* "Any chance there are other witnesses? Someone who saw more than the video showed?" He wanted to get the inside dirt before meeting with Becky and discussing her possible witness.

Landry ran a hand over his mouth. "The deputies have canvassed the community. Nothing. The Amish are tight-lipped. I don't imagine it's going to be easy, especially since Becky used to be one of them. They already view her as a traitor."

"What would it take to get her back in uniform, because we both know she's innocent in this."

A corner of the sheriff's mouth twitched. "She's going to have to be patient as we investigate."

"Do you really think—" he stopped short of calling her Becky "—Deputy Spoth is a bad deputy?" A growing anger pulsed in his veins at the sheriff's cool indifference, or so it seemed.

Landry lifted his palms. "I don't. But it's hard to dispute a damaging video."

Harrison cleared his throat. "The video shows nothing." He had seen a copy floating around the department.

"It's inconclusive. We can't have it blow back in our faces if she's found guilty. We can't appear too soft because she's a woman. Or former Amish. This needs to be done by the book."

"Investigate, then. Do what you need to, but in the meantime, also be aware that someone is trying to hurt Becky."

"Hurt?" The sheriff jerked his head back. "She reported that someone slashed her tires in the lot here. It's certainly not a common occurrence, but it's not rare, either. We live in a small town. Teenagers get bored." He leaned forward, resting his forearms on the desk. "They do stupid stuff."

"You can't blame this on kids will be kids."

Landry's brows snapped together. "And the Buffalo incident can't be related to this."

They didn't know that for sure. "What about the incident in her yard when she almost got shot?" He struggled to keep his frustration in check.

"Some young men were having target practice. They neglected to show you all their guns." The sheriff seemed to be able to explain everything away.

"Did anyone follow up with them?" Harrison couldn't find anything in the system, but the deputy in charge of the investigation could have looked deeper into their stories.

The sheriff flattened his hands on the desk. "Nope. Nothing. I'm thinking that's a dead end."

Harrison stared at him a long minute, deciding how to proceed on that. Is this what small-town policing was like?

"Listen," the sheriff said, having gone back to tapping the pads of his fingers together, "I know you want to help, but we have to be careful. We have to root out bad deputies, otherwise it makes the whole department look bad. Quail Hollow is still reeling from one of its own murdering a young Amish mother."

"That happened decades ago." Harrison had only recently moved to Quail Hollow when news broke of the arrest of a former undersheriff in the murder of a young Amish mother over two decades ago. Allegations that the sheriff's department didn't know how to police their own were splashed all over the news from Buffalo to Cleveland. Now it seemed Becky would pay the price for stricter policing among their own.

"The truth was hidden for a long time. As the new sheriff, my campaign promise was to be transparent. I can't shirk my duty because it's tough. People have long memories."

Harrison had the same convictions when it came to

his brother. Tough love and all that. Sometimes living with the effects of your convictions was harder than having the convictions in the first place.

"We'll follow up on everything, Deputy James," the sheriff said, a dismissal clear in his tone. "Best if you stay out of it. It seems you might be biased."

Heat flared in his ears, but he bit back his temper. "Deputy Spoth needs to be cleared sooner rather than later."

Landry held up his arms with his wrists together, miming that his hands were tied. Harrison took it as an excuse to do nothing.

Harrison pushed to his feet. "Sometimes *someone* has to stand up for what's right, even if their hands are tied."

Landry got to his feet. The cords straining in his neck suggested he, too, was holding back the full force of his temper. "Are you suggesting I'm not doing my job?" He tapped his index finger on the desk repeatedly for emphasis. "I'm the sheriff here. My job is to find the truth. Not fly off the handle because I don't think one of my female deputies is capable of excessive force." He lowered his voice to a low growl. "They want equal rights, now they have them and can't handle the consequences."

It was Harrison's turn to narrow his gaze. "I'd almost think you had something against women in the department."

The sheriff's eyes widened, looking like he had been offended. "I don't care if my deputies are male or female. I only care that they do their jobs." He paused for effect. "This department can't afford another black eye."

Harrison turned toward the door, then turned back.

"In your efforts to protect this department, don't forget to focus on protecting the people that work within it."

The sheriff leaned back and crossed his arms, the expression revealing his barely contained rage.

As soon as Harrison pulled up the driveway, Becky ran across the lawn and hopped into his truck. She was glad to see he had changed into jeans and a T-shirt, because it would make approaching Amos King easier. He might talk if he felt less threatened.

She still couldn't believe she had a potential witness.

"Thanks for coming," she said. "I would have followed up on this myself, but your lawyer friend said I shouldn't do anything to stir the pot regarding my case, and this definitely feels like stirring the pot." She resisted reaching out and tapping his arm, she was so excited.

Harrison put the truck into Reverse. "Where to?"

"Let's try the church parking lot on Main Street. I've seen Amos with his friends riding skateboards down there. It's worth a shot. This way we don't have to confront him at home in front of his brother, Paul."

Harrison pulled out onto the road and headed into town. "So Amos is part of the King family?"

"Yes. Amos is Paul's younger brother."

"Interesting. There are only a few degrees of separation around here."

"You don't know the half of it."

"Tell me what happened. This Amos kid took the video, but his brother Paul turned it in anonymously to give you grief because you've been on him about the dogs? Did I get that right?" Becky had shared the events of this afternoon over the phone.

"Mary didn't say Paul turned it in, but it had to be him. Amos doesn't have any ill feelings toward me. There's no reason." She searched her memory, but couldn't come up with anything.

When they got to the church, sure enough, a handful of young men were using the stairs, railings and parking curbs to do stunts.

"Pull over here. I don't want them to take off if they see us coming," Becky said.

"Do you see Amos?" Harrison asked.

Squinting, Becky leaned forward. The early-evening sun was right in her line of vision. A tall guy leaped off the stairs and landed on his skateboard, rolled a few feet before spinning around to watch a friend repeat the stunt behind him. His blunt-cut hair poked out from under a Buffalo Bills baseball cap. The frayed edges spoke of its age.

"The kid on the right. I think that's him. Come on." She pushed open the door without waiting for him.

When Becky was within a few feet, she called Amos's name. He stepped on the back of the skateboard and it popped up into his hand. "Yeah," he started to say, rather coolly, until recognition sparked in his eyes. "Hey, Rebecca." If she wasn't watching him so closely, she might have missed the color growing in his cheeks.

She pointed at his skateboard. "You're pretty good at that." Amos was a handful of years younger than Paul. He had always looked up to his brother while Paul seemed to dismiss him. She supposed that dynamic was fairly universal, Amish or not, big brother to little brother.

"I want to talk to you about a video."

Amos tucked the skateboard under his arm and

dipped his head. His bangs hid his eyes. "I don't know what you're talking about," he mumbled with the lilt of Pennsylvania Dutch.

"I think you do." Becky took another step toward him, then she suddenly changed tactics. "I'm hoping you can help me." She also hoped all the times she had been nice to Paul's younger brother would pay off here.

The other three boys stopped doing stunts in the church lot long enough to watch them. "We're just chatting," Becky said in her best reassuring tone. "You guys can go about your business. All I want to do is talk to Amos."

One of the kids' eyes suddenly lit up and he pointed frantically at her. Was that admiration she detected in his eyes? "You're the lady deputy who beat up Elijah."

"Are you basing that on something you witnessed firsthand?" Harrison asked, speaking up before Becky had a chance to find her voice. Regardless of her innocence, would she forever be known as the "lady deputy who beat up the Amish kid"? She tried to hide her frustration by squaring her shoulders and never taking her eyes off Amos's friend.

"No, um…" The kid started to stammer. "I saw the video. It went viral. Totally awesome." If violent videos were deemed awesome, Becky feared for the next generation. She clenched her teeth, fighting the urge to school the young men. There was nothing awesome about it. But she couldn't risk Amos shutting down.

"Did you post the video online?" Becky asked.

"No, but I recorded it." Amos pushed the gravel around with the toe of his sneaker. He probably had a stash of clothes and shoes at a friend's house that he changed in and out of as he left home, not wanting to get any grief from Paul or Mary. Amos was the last unmarried King. From what Becky's sister had told her, Amos was supposed to be baptized and married later this year. He certainly didn't act like a young man preparing for baptism and subsequent marriage in an Amish community. "And I sent it to a bunch of people, too." He looked up with a hint of regret in his eyes. "It was just a video."

Just a video that had ruined her life.

She drew in a deep breath to calm her rioting nerves. "Okay, so someone alerted Deputy Reich's lawyer about the video. That can't be undone. But I could use your help, Amos." She took a step closer, forcing him to meet her gaze, reminding him who she was. "Did you see the entire incident with Elijah?"

"Yah." He looked up, a wary look in his eyes.

Her mouth went dry. Had she found her witness? *Please, Lord.* She held her breath and dared to ask him the question. "Did you see me hurt Elijah Lapp?"

Amos shook his head slowly. *"Neh."*

"What did you see?"

Amos rubbed his nose vigorously. "You used a stick to pry the deputy off Elijah. When you pulled him off, he landed on you, but you scrabbled out from under him and forced him back down."

"You saw all this?"

"Yah, when I was running away. The video caught the ground, but I didn't take my eyes off the fight. By the time I got to the Millers' barn, the other patrol cars and the ambulance had arrived."

Thank you, Lord.

"What were you doing at the Millers' farm?"

"They hired me to do some extra work."

Becky considered all this. "Would you be willing to come down to the sheriff's department and give your testimony?"

"Oh, man. I don't know. I'm supposed to be preparing for baptism. How am I going to explain having a cell phone and taking videos? The bishop won't think I'm serious about committing to the Amish."

"I'll do all I can to protect you. I need your help."

Amos looked like he was going to be sick.

"Please, Amos. The truth needs to be told. Someone is trying to hurt me and I'm afraid it's because they think I hurt Elijah."

Amos opened his mouth to protest, but Becky's smile seemed to disarm him.

"Someone slashed my tires. Someone shot at my house."

"I don't know anything about that. I just took the video. That's all. I promise."

"Of course," Becky said. "And I'm sure you had nothing to do with the dogs in your family's barn."

Amos's eyes lit up. "No way. That was all Paul. I told him it was a bad idea. I'd leave the cage open at times, letting them get away."

That explained how Chewie got out.

"Besides," Amos added, seeming skittish, "the deputies took the dogs away."

"I know," Becky said.

"But why did you show Paul the video?" Harrison asked.

Amos's gaze skittered over to him. "I showed it to a lot of people. And it was on the internet."

"Have you heard any rumors about me?" Becky

calmly drew his attention back to her. "Perhaps some-one wanted to get back at me for hurting Elijah?"

Fear flickered in Amos's watchful brown eyes. *"Neh."*

Harrison tapped the screen of his cell phone and brought up the photos of the four men shooting targets behind her house. "Do you know these guys?"

Amos stared at the screen. *"Yah*, I've seen them all around town."

"Where exactly?" Harrison pressed.

Amos explained how he knew each of the guys and added a bit on whether he liked them or not. Becky and Harrison both let him keep talking, figuring he might unwittingly reveal something important.

At one of the photos, Amos said, "That kid is the sheriff's nephew."

Harrison jerked his head back. "Interesting. What kind of kid is he?"

Amos hitched a shoulder. "Tyler seems all right. Us guys don't really discuss much."

"Is he a troublemaker?" Harrison asked.

"Depends on what you call trouble." Amos smirked. "From where I come from, riding a skateboard and doing stunts could be construed as trouble."

"Has Tyler been in any kind of trouble?" Becky clar-ified.

"All I know is that he grew up in Buffalo and his mother sent him to live with his uncle, the sheriff, to straighten him out." Amos pulled off his hat, adjusted the bill and stuffed it back down on his head. "I imag-ine that means he got into some kind of trouble back home. That's all I know."

"Thanks." Becky shot Harrison a quick gaze. Not

wanting to scare Amos off, she handed him a business card. "I could really use your help. Call me if you're willing to come in as a witness."

"Ah, man," he groaned again, but she could tell he was softening. He'd come through for her; she just knew it.

"If you don't want to deal with me, go directly to the sheriff's department and ask for the sheriff." Becky touched Harrison's elbow. "Let's go."

When they reached the car, Becky said, "I think he'll come around."

Harrison nodded. "I hope so. But why didn't the sheriff tell me Tyler was his nephew when I showed him his photo?"

A knot tightened in Becky's gut. "Does this mean we can't trust the sheriff?"

"It means someone's holding out on us. It means we have to investigate ourselves. We can't leave it to the sheriff's department."

Chapter Ten

"We're going to have to look into the sheriff's nephew," Becky said as Harrison drove her home.

"I ran all four guys' names through the system. Nothing came up."

"Mind if I look at the photos again?" Becky asked.

Without taking his eyes off the road, Harrison took his phone out of the cup holder and handed it to her. He pressed his thumb on the button to unlock it. "Go to the photo app."

"Mind if I send the images to my phone?"

"Go ahead. Just not quite sure what we're going to uncover since none of them have records. Someone needs to start talking."

"Amos is a start." She pressed her lips together. "Should we go to each of these guys' homes? Talk to them directly?"

Harrison scrubbed his hand across his face. "Let me see what I can dig up on the sheriff's nephew first. If we start asking too many of the guys questions, they might start talking to each other and shut down. Then we'll get nowhere."

Becky sighed heavily. "I feel like we're already getting nowhere. I'm—"

Her phone rang in her hand as she was saving the photos she had sent to her phone, stopping her midsentence. "It's my sister. I better get this."

Becky lifted the phone to her ear. "Hi, Mag."

"Bec-ky." her sister said her name on a sob.

Becky's heart dropped to her shoes. "What's wrong?"

"Paul said they're going to kill all the dogs they took from his farm and *Dat* told me it was none of my business and—"

"Stay where you are. I'll be right there."

"But *Dat* is mad. He'll be mad I called you."

Anger pulsed through her veins. "I'm sorry, but this has gone on long enough. I'll be right there." The thought of her sister alone in the barn, crying her eyes out while talking on their only landline, broke Becky's heart. She remembered feeling so alone and adrift while growing up on the Amish farm with no one to talk to. She didn't dare share her deepest thoughts about leaving.

Becky ended the call before Mag could argue. She looked over at Harrison, who cut her a gaze, then turned his attention back to the road. "Mind making a pit stop?"

"Whatever you want."

It took less than ten minutes to get to her family's farm. "Want me to park on the road, so my truck's not visible?"

"No, pull right into the driveway." Defiance laced her tone. "I don't care who sees us. They have no right…"

Becky jumped out of the truck before she finished her sentence. She jogged over to the barn and found Mag sitting on a hay bale in the shadows. The fading light of the setting sun created long lines across the barn floor.

Becky sat down next to her sister and put her arm

around her shoulders. At this moment Mag seemed so much younger than her seventeen years. She stiffened for a fraction before accepting the gesture and resting her bonneted head on her sister's shoulder.

"Tell me what happened?"

"The deputies took the puppies this morning."

"Paul wasn't taking care of them. You know that." She nudged her sister's shoulder affectionately. "And now I'm blessed to have Chewie."

"That's a silly name for a dog," Mag said distractedly.

"But appropriate." Becky lifted an eyebrow.

Mag shook her head, and her lips started to quiver again. "Paul told me that the deputies put the dogs into bags with rocks and drown them."

Shock pulsed through Becky's veins. She didn't think she could be any more angry with anyone ever than she was with Paul right now.

"That's not true. No one's going to hurt those dogs. They'll make sure they're cared for and then they'll search for homes for them."

"He said you'd lie about it. He said they had to drown them because they don't have resources to care for so many puppies." She drew in a shaky breath. "He said he was getting around to cleaning up the cages. That he would have made things right. That it was my fault the puppies would get drowned."

Mag's grief-stricken words bounced around Becky's brain. "I can't believe—" She couldn't think straight. She wanted to run over to the Kings' farm and give Paul a piece of her mind. How dare he strike terror into Mag's heart with his lies? Was he that angry at her that he'd take it out on her sister?

Mag sat up and swiped at her cheeks. "You have to get the dogs back. I'll never forgive myself if they kill them."

"They're not going to kill them." A horrible realization swept over Becky. Her sister believed Paul over her own flesh and blood. Mag believed an Amish man instead of her own sister, an outsider.

The reality of the moment settled on Becky's lungs and made it difficult to breathe.

She took a moment to compose herself, fearing if she spoke, her sister would hear the hurt in her voice. Her sister didn't need any more guilt heaped on her already aching heart.

"Let's talk to my friend Harrison. He knows the man who picked up the Kings' dogs. He can assure you that they'll care for the animals until they find new homes." Becky stood and held out her hand to pull her sister to her feet.

"How do I know he's not lying?" Mag stood without taking her hand.

"You're going to have to trust me."

In front of Becky's childhood home, Harrison waited by the truck. After a short time, he saw two shadows emerge from the barn. As they got closer, he noticed Becky had her arm around her crying sister.

"Everything okay?" he asked.

"No, it's not." Becky's words came out clipped and he could tell she was angry. Maybe even a little hurt. "Can you call Deputy Timothy Welsh? I need him to assure Mag that the dogs confiscated from the King property will be better cared for than when they were caged up next door."

"Yes, sure." Harrison's gaze drifted to Mag and then

back to Becky. As he was entering "Welsh" in his contacts on his smartphone, a crash made all three of them jump.

A tall, thin man with a long beard emerged from the house, the force of his exit slamming the screen door against the side of the house. He didn't slow down for the woman scurrying behind him as he strode across the hard-packed earth toward them. A dent ringed his hair and forehead where his hat once sat. Harrison could easily assume this was Becky's father.

"What's going on here?" he demanded, his voice gruff, his jaw set for battle.

Mag refused to meet her father's gaze. Her chin trembled. "I-I called Becky to see if she could get the Kings' dogs back. I don't want for them to be drowned."

"Your sister has done enough." Mr. Spoth pointed at Becky, then the truck. "Get out of here."

The hurt in Becky's eyes cut through Harrison. He understood what it was like to have a family ripped apart.

"Dat," Becky said, twisting her hands in front of her, then letting them drop and squaring her shoulders. She returned her father's unwavering gaze. "We're going to make a phone call to assure Mag that the animals are okay. Then I'll go."

Mr. Spoth's nostrils flared. "You had no right to interfere in Paul's business. You chose to leave. Your life isn't with us. Now go."

"Sir," Harrison said, daring to step forward. "Your daughter and I were worried about the well-being of the dogs. We had a responsibility to make sure they weren't being mistreated."

Mr. Spoth laughed harshly. "Responsibilities. My daughter knows nothing about responsibilities. We raised her to choose baptism and marriage within the Amish community. Then she shamed us by leaving in the middle of the night. She doesn't care what goes on around here. You have been corrupted by outside influences." Mr. Spoth blinked slowly. "We can't have her infecting our other daughter with her dangerous attitudes. She shamed us. We don't want anything to do with her unless she comes back to openly confess with a contrite heart."

Becky audibly gasped as if she had been sucker punched, but she didn't speak up to defend herself. Harrison assumed long-established father-daughter boundaries were at play here, not allowing her to find her words. To speak up against her father.

Familiar feelings crowded in on Harrison's heart, making him share Becky's shock, but not at her father's outburst, but at his own actions, not unlike the harshness of her father. Harrison understood the feelings of hurt and shame that allowed a person to alienate someone they loved. He lived those emotions with his brother.

Harrison couldn't stay silent.

"I'm not Amish, sir, but I can assure you I understand family and how important it is."

Mr. Spoth turned his head, his strong profile outlined against the purples and oranges of the evening sky. His posture suggested he wanted nothing to do with Harrison, but he hadn't walked away, either. Harrison's gaze drifted to the porch where Mrs. Spoth stood very still, as if afraid to move.

"I know what it's like to be disappointed by a family member. I know what it's like to push them out of my life. To try to get them to see the error of their ways." Harrison coughed to clear the emotion from his throat.

"Unfortunately, I know what it's like to lose that person forever. And I'm not talking because he moved across town. My brother is dead and I did nothing to help him before he reached that point."

He felt Becky's warm hand on his forearm, but he couldn't meet her eyes. His heart was racing in his ears.

"I am sorry for your brother, but you are not Amish. You could never understand," Mr. Spoth bit out.

"Perhaps," Harrison conceded. "But you have your daughter right here. She's made a decision you don't care for, but she's trying to help the daughter that is here. I suggest you accept the offer in whatever way doesn't offend the rules you live by. But I imagine your God is the same God my mother taught me to pray to, and He'd want you to accept your daughter for who she is."

"Perhaps you forgot your lessons, son. The fourth commandment says honor your father and mother. Our daughter shamed us."

Becky squeezed Harrison's arm. "Let's go." She turned toward her sister. "I promise you the dogs are okay. I'll call the deputy who picked them up and check on them." She walked around to the passenger side of the vehicle. "Trust me."

"Good night," Harrison said curtly, and climbed into the truck and slammed the door.

Becky slumped into the passenger seat of his truck and snapped on her seat belt. Her heart was racing so hard she thought it was going to jump out of her chest. She had never had a confrontation with her father. Not like that. Since she left, their relationship was nonexistent or if their paths accidentally crossed in town, he pretended he didn't see her.

Sadness and anger threaded around her middle and made it difficult to breathe. She focused straight ahead, ignoring the hard stare of her father as Harrison did a wide U-turn in the driveway and pulled out onto the main road. She tried not to notice her mother in the shadows of the porch, slump-shouldered and silent. Always silent.

"I probably should have kept my mouth shut. I'm sure I didn't help any," Harrison said, his voice low and somber.

She shifted in her seat to face him, the shadow of a beard on his jaw. The urge to reach over and cup his chin and reassure him was strong, but she wasn't that kind of person. She was a person who had grown up Amish, with conservative values, who was now struggling to fit into her new world. Yet feeling like she was doing a miserable job at that, too.

"Thank you for sticking up for me."

"I didn't mean to be disrespectful. It's just…" He stared straight ahead, letting his words trail off. "It bothers me that he won't acknowledge you when you're right there."

"It's their way. We've talked about it. They hope I'll come back." She curled her fingers around the edge of the seat. "Are you really that angry with God?" It made her heart sad to hear the words he had chosen when confronting her *dat*.

Harrison's Adam's apple bobbed as he seemed to consider her question.

"I didn't mean to pry. You don't have to answer."

"I suppose I can't get past why God would let my brother die in such a horrible…" He shook his head.

She threaded her fingers together. "I'm sorry you're

hurting. Everyone has free will. To make choices. Your brother made some horrible decisions. You can't punish yourself for the rest of your life because of *his* choices."

"I thought I was doing the right thing by showing my brother how mad I was." He stared straight ahead at the road, but he seemed lost in thought.

She reached across and touched his arm. "You can't undo what's already happened. If your brother was anything like you, I don't think he'd want you to punish yourself for the rest of your life."

"No." The single word wasn't convincing. "Do you ever regret leaving?"

Harrison's question surprised her as much as the answer that sprang to her lips. "Lately I've wondered. The Amish are all about community. I felt the sheriff's department was also a supportive community until I really needed that support. Then everyone disappeared. Even my friend, Anne, the sheriff's administrative assistant, has stopped returning my calls. Everyone I thought was a friend has disappeared." She laughed, a mirthless sound. "But then again, others have shown friendship when they didn't have to." She squeezed his arm. "Thank you for that."

"Of course." Harrison cut her a quick gaze before returning his attention to the dark country road. "Would you ever consider going back?"

"To the Amish? No, I couldn't be happy living in the Amish way. I know that for certain. Despite everything." *I've come too far. Yet, not far enough.*

The reality of that pained her heart. She was like an orphan without a home. "I guess that means I have to work extra hard to clear my name."

Chapter Eleven

The next day Becky was determined not to sit around feeling sorry for herself. Chewie was a big help with that. "Come on, let's go outside. Get some air."

She hooked his leash on his collar and he charged ahead toward the back door. He bounded down the steps and over to the tree line. A hint of unease whispered across the back of her neck. Would she ever feel safe again? Or would she forever be looking over her shoulder?

She said a silent prayer that the sheriff's department would find the person who was harassing her. Maybe then she wouldn't feel so jittery.

"Maybe it's time to weed the flower beds," Becky said to Chewie. "Get this place looking nice." That was one thing she loved about being independent. She had her own house that she could maintain. And she could do the chores when and if she felt like it.

She bent down and wrapped the end of the dog's leash around one of the posts on the railing. She tugged on it to make sure it was secure. She opened the small shed and found her gardening gloves. She tapped them together and little balls of dirt sprinkled to the ground. She studied the shelves until she located the long tool with a pronged end used for weed removal. "What else do I need?" She tucked a paper compost bag under her elbow, then closed over the shed door.

Standing directly on the other side was Deputy Ned Reich. Based on his expression, she wasn't sure who was more surprised.

"Ned," she said, her voice cracking. The man she had testified against. The man who had beaten an Amish man to within an inch of his life.

"I didn't mean to startle you," he said, his expression now stoic.

Her heart thrummed in her ears and she swallowed around a too-tight throat. Could she beat him to the back door? She cut a sideways glance to Chewie, who seemed more interested in sniffing around the base of a tree than her predicament.

Ned lifted his hand toward the house. "I rang the doorbell and knocked, but no one answered. I saw your car in the driveway, so I thought I'd walk around." He stuffed his hands in his pockets and rolled back on his heels.

Despite his nonthreatening manner, her instincts were to grip the long, metal tool tighter. He seemed to sense that and his gaze dropped to her white-knuckled fist.

"I assure you, you don't need that," he said in a deep, even tone, but something in his eyes gave her pause.

Becky eased her posture, trying not to show fear. Her thoughts raced and she swallowed hard. She stared back at him with what she hoped was a neutral stare. "How can I help you?"

"I suppose I could say you've helped enough." He ran a hand over his face. "But that's not why I'm here. I wanted to let you know that I've talked to Sheriff Landry."

"I didn't think anything was going on right now with your case."

"It's not about that. Well, it is, but not anything official right now. I needed to take responsibility for what I did."

Becky blinked rapidly, trying to make sense of what he was saying.

"I know I'm a hothead. I've always been a hothead. But I need to take responsibility. I can't let you continue to pay for what I did."

"Really?" she whispered, not sure if she had given voice to the single word.

"Your only crime was rolling up on the scene as my backup. You weren't involved in the beating—" he tilted his head "—except for breaking it up." A hint of amusement flashed in his eyes as if he had sensed the irony of his words.

Becky pressed her hand to her chest and the tip of the weeding tool tapped her chin. "Why? Why come forward now?"

Ned scratched his eyebrow and studied the ground for a moment before lifting his gaze and meeting hers. "I've destroyed my career and I'm feeling pretty down and out." He cleared his throat as if he was touching on stuff that he didn't usually discuss. "And my lawyer encouraged me to see a counselor regarding anger management." He hitched a shoulder. "Thought it would look good when it came to the trial—that I was seeking counseling and truly sorry."

"Are you?"

A muscle twitched in his jaw. "I'm sorry I let it get to this, yeah." He twisted his lips into a wry grin and ran his palm over the back of his neck. "In talking to the counselor, I realized it wasn't fair to you. You seem like a good person. I'm going down, but I can't take you with me."

"Thank you." Becky set her gardening tool on the shelf in the cabinet, then peeled off her gloves.

"I just came from the sheriff's office and thought you'd like to know. I expect my lawyer won't be happy about it." He cleared his throat. "But I truly believe now, looking back, that you've saved me from facing more serious charges." He shook his head as if reliving the event that had changed the course of both their lives. "I was so angry. I saw how close Lapp had come to hitting that kid crossing the road… I would have killed Elijah Lapp if you hadn't intervened."

"Thank you for letting me know," she said. "What did the sheriff say?" *Does this mean I'm getting my job back?*

"He took my statement. Didn't fill me in on his next steps. I suppose I won't ever be privy to his plans." He shrugged again and took a step backward as if ready to retreat.

"Do you want to come in for an iced tea?"

Before he had a chance to answer, her cell phone in her back pocket rang. Her first instinct was to ignore it, but something told her to answer it. "Can you hold on one second?" She pulled it out and glanced at the display and then Ned. "It's a call coming from the sheriff's department."

"Take it," Ned said. "Maybe it's good news."

"Hello." Becky listened intently while the sheriff confirmed what Ned had told her. For some reason she didn't feel the need to tell the sheriff that Ned was standing right in front of her.

Just when she thought the sheriff was finishing up, he said, "Amos King came in today, too."

"He did?" Becky took a step back into the shade. The top of her hair had grown hot from the sun.

"Told me he witnessed the whole thing. Confirmed much of what Ned had said."

Becky didn't know what to say.

"I'm not sure who this lawyer you hired is, but he's pulled a few rabbits out of the hat for you."

Something about his comment made her bristle. The sheriff hadn't exactly been forthcoming when it came to investigating the incidents following her suspension. From the start, his focus seemed to be on keeping his own reputation intact. She struggled to keep her tone even. "My lawyer had nothing to do with the two individuals who came forward."

The sheriff didn't say anything, so she continued, "Any news on my slashed tires or the shooting behind my house?" She felt Ned's gaze on her, even with her back to him.

"Working on it." Becky imagined him tapping the pads of his fingers together like he always seemed to do when he was giving her a speech in his office. "Maybe a witness will wander in and solve the case for me." Becky didn't miss the hint of derision in his tone.

Ned started to walk away and she held up her finger, indicating that he hold on a minute. Then into the phone, "When can I return to work?"

"I need a few days to fill out paperwork. I'm thinking Monday."

"Monday would be great. See you then." Becky ended the call, not giving him a chance to prolong her return to work any longer.

"Your suspension has been lifted?" Ned asked, a hint of relief in his voice.

"Yes. I go back Monday. Apparently, another witness came in today and confirmed that I only used the baton to pry you and Elijah apart."

Ned plowed his hand through his unkempt hair. Now that Becky thought about it, he looked like he had just rolled out of bed. Or off the couch. A little part of her could relate. The world could get awfully small when you lost your job under these circumstances. She wondered where Ned would go from here.

"I'm glad to hear it." He sounded sincere. "I'll let you have at it." He gestured with his chin toward the shed and her gardening tools.

Before he had a chance to walk away, she asked, "What now?"

"Ask for mercy. Probably have to find a new job."

Becky opened her mouth to say sorry, then clamped it shut again. Apologizing couldn't be her default answer. She had nothing to be sorry about. "Do you have a good support system at home?"

Ned laughed and his overall demeanor changed. "Now you're sounding like my shrink."

"I know what it's like to be left out in the cold."

"Well, my home life is a little messed up. I've never been much good on that front either. I'm afraid marriage number two is on the rocks." He took a deep breath. "And I'm sure you know my oldest son. He's a deputy."

Becky nodded, but didn't say anything.

"He's turning into a hothead like me. You'd think I'd serve as a cautionary tale. He better learn to check his emotions before he ruins his career and any relationship he might have."

Despite the mess this man had created for her, she felt compassion for him. Forgiveness. "Come in out of the heat. I have iced tea."

Ned held up his hand. "No, thanks. I really should go." He averted his gaze briefly, then looked at her, a sadness in his eyes. "I hope things work out for you."

"I hope things work out for you, too."

Apparently, the Amish tenet of forgiveness hadn't been something she had left behind when she jumped the fence.

"Are you ready to go back to work tomorrow?" Harrison lifted the glass of icy-cold lemonade to his lips and glanced over at Becky, her one leg folded under her in the rocking chair on her front porch. Chewie rested at her feet. In the front yard, a cloud of insects swirled over the grass, back lit by the purples and oranges of another gorgeous sunset.

The past few days since her name was cleared, he and Becky hadn't talked much. He figured he didn't have an excuse to visit. But now, with a return to work looming, he had taken the opportunity to stop by. To see how she was feeling.

Becky ran her hand up and down the arm of the chair. "I'm nervous. Feels almost like the first day."

"You shouldn't be nervous. You're a good deputy." He set the glass down on the table between them. "You stepped in and protected a young Amish man. You did what was right."

Becky used her toe to rock back and forth. She looked over at Chewie, careful not to crunch his tail under the rockers. "People will always associate me with the beating. People tend to only remember what they want to remember."

"You can't control what other people think."

She lifted an eyebrow as if to say, "Whatever." She traced a line of grain in the wood on the arm of the chair with her index finger. "I wonder if they'll ever find out who was harassing me. The sheriff claimed it would probably settle down now that a witness had come forward. He thinks it was someone trying to get back at me for hurting Elijah, but now that I've been cleared, they have no reason to come after me." She tilted her head and ran her fingers through her long ponytail. "But the sheriff assures me they're still investigating."

"They won't let someone get away with it."

"No, I suppose not. I wish everything could be wrapped up so these reporters stop calling me. They're like vultures."

"Crimes among the Amish are big news."

"Unfortunately."

"It'll die down." Harrison reassured her.

Becky stifled a yawn and Harrison stood. "I should get going."

"Sorry." She bowed her head. "I didn't mean to be rude by yawning."

"I hope we can still be friends."

Becky crossed her arms, but didn't meet his gaze. She slowed her rocking. "Of course we can be friends." She stressed the word *friends* a bit too heavily. She wasn't interested in dating, so it didn't come as a surprise. "I appreciate all you've done for me." Pink blossomed in her cheeks.

"I didn't mean to make you uncomfortable…" Harrison was never this tongue-tied. "I hadn't made an effort to get to know people before now and I'm glad I took the time with you." They locked gazes. "It'll be nice to have a friendly face while I'm in Quail Hollow."

"You plan on leaving soon?" Some emotion he couldn't pinpoint flickered across her features.

"No, not soon, but I can't avoid the demons of my past forever. I'll have to go back to Buffalo. Clean out the house." He took a deep breath. "Maybe even beg for my old job back." He shrugged. "Find a new one, maybe? But I'm not in a hurry. I'd like to make sure whoever's harassing you is punished."

"I'd feel much better knowing they had someone in custody." She stood and tugged at the hem of her T-shirt.

Harrison brushed the back of his hand across the smooth skin of her arm. "Remember you're not alone." He bent and planted a kiss on her forehead. Then he stepped back and the space between them was charged with electricity.

Something caught Chewie's attention and he bolted from the porch. Becky darted in an attempt to catch the leash when a shot rang out. Instinctively, Harrison moved to protect Becky, pushing her down and toward the house for cover. A piercing pain radiated up his arm.

"In the house," he yelled at her. "Get in the house."

Her eyes grew wide with fear. As he shoved her toward the door, she pushed back, craning to see around him. "Chewie!"

Despite her resistance, Harrison opened the door and

shoved her inside and slammed the door. "Stay away from the windows."

"Chewie's going to get lost." Frantic, she reached for the door handle.

"No." He lifted his hand to stop her. "We need to make sure it's clear." That was when he noticed blood running down his arm.

"Oh no…" All the color drained from Becky's face and suddenly he felt nauseated himself. "You've been hit. Sit." She pushed him against the wall and guided him to a seated position. "Stay put." She raced to the kitchen and returned with her cell phone and a dish towel.

She handed him the towel. "Hold this against the wound." Then she ran to the front of the house and peeked out the window. She glanced down at her phone and dialed. "This is Deputy Spoth. Shots have been fired at my residence." She rattled off the address. "Deputy James has been hit. Send an ambulance. Be cautious. Active shooter."

She ended the call, then ran back to Harrison. She took the dish towel from him and pressed it to his arm. "They could be hiding anywhere. There are too many trees around." As she crouched in front of him, he found himself studying her bright, blue eyes filled with concern. "Are you okay?"

"I think I'm okay." A buzzing started in his ears and he immediately realized that he had spoken too soon.

Becky pulled the towel back from his arm and twisted her mouth.

"Not much for blood?" he asked, trying to make light of the situation.

"Um, no…" She grimaced. "You'll need to go to the

emergency room for sure. This isn't a do-it-yourself wound. The ambulance should be here soon."

The glass on the front window exploded. Instinctively, Harrison pushed to his feet and moved them both toward the center of the house. "Stay away from any windows." He glanced around, anticipating his next move if the shooter tried to gain entry. "Where's the gun I left you?"

Hunched over, Becky scrambled upstairs to retrieve the gun from the safe in her bedroom, careful to stay clear of the windows. The sheriff had returned her gun and badge on Friday in preparation for Monday. Holding the weapon at the ready, she positioned herself next to the broken window on the first level of the house. Making sure she didn't create a target, she peeked out of a corner of the window, her gaze scanning the heavily shadowed yard. The gunman could be anywhere.

And Chewie was nowhere in sight. She prayed he was hunkered down behind a tree. But the silence unnerved her. She expected him to be barking, at the very least.

"You okay?" she hollered to Harrison, who was sitting against the wall in the dining room.

"I've been better," he said, then muttered something she couldn't quite make out. "See anything?"

"No. Nothing." Her hand holding the gun felt sweaty. "The shooter could be hiding anywhere in the woods next to the house or across the street." The exhaustion she had felt sitting on the porch had been replaced by a buzz of adrenaline. No way she'd sleep tonight. "Where are you, Chewie?" she whispered, growing more worried for her furry friend.

"He'll show up," Harrison reassured her.

Becky shot Harrison a quick glance, then went back to peering out a corner of the window. "I hate to think someone would hurt him."

"Don't think about that."

"Hard not to. Chewie's the only one who has been by my side this whole time."

"What am I? Chopped liver?" Harrison joked, obviously trying to add levity to a tense situation.

She laughed, appreciating his efforts. Her muscles strained from staying hunched down by the window, careful to only peek out at the very bottom lower corner.

Just then a little fuzzy ball of fur emerged from the shadows and bounded up the porch steps. She fisted her hands to keep from jumping up and throwing the door open for him. She watched until she couldn't see him any longer from her position on the floor. The next moment she heard him clawing at the door. When no one answered, he started yipping. The dog wouldn't stop until she let him in.

"I have to let Chewie in."

Becky locked gazes with Harrison before crawling past the window. He got up with a groan and held out his arm. "Let me."

Her gaze dropped to the dish towel pressed to his wound. It was soaked with blood. Her stomach did a little flip-flop and she immediately felt queasy. There was a reason she wasn't a doctor, besides the exorbitant cost of higher education. Suddenly she felt a little thoughtless that she had been more worried about Chewie than the man who took a bullet for her.

She studied Harrison's face while Chewie scratched at the door. Even in the heavily shadowed room, she could see the color draining from his face. "You need to sit down." She guided him against the wall and it scared her when he didn't put up a fight as she eased him to a seated position.

He closed his eyes, seemingly resigned. "Don't make yourself a target."

"Not in my plans." She pressed her palm to his clammy forehead before rushing to the front door. Crouching low and standing against the wall, she twisted the lock and opened the door just enough to allow Chewie to slip through. Becky slammed the door shut again and turned the lock.

Becky gave Chewie a quick once-over. After assuring herself he wasn't injured, she hustled back over to Harrison, who now seemed disoriented and gray.

Becky cupped his cheek. "Ambulance is on its way. You're going to be okay. Just hold on." Her mouth went dry and she was too numb to feel anything.

And as if an answer to her prayer, she heard sirens in the distance. "You're going to be okay," she repeated. "Just hold on."

Chapter Twelve

A buzzing sounded in Harrison's head as myriad disjointed images flashed behind his eyelids. The distant sound of an overhead paging system pulled him up through a dark tunnel to a bright light.

He opened his eyes and immediately slammed them shut. *Very* bright light. Painfully bright light. The long line of fluorescent lights burned through his eyeballs.

Where am I?

A shadow crossed his face and he tried to pry his eyes open again. This time he was rewarded with Becky's pretty but concerned smile. She spoke in a reassuring tone, "You're okay. You lost a lot of blood, so you need to relax." Her warm hand on his shoulder grounded him. "You just got out of surgery. They removed the bullet from your arm."

"Ah," he groaned. It was all coming back to him. The gunshot. Scrambling off the front porch. Hunkering down in her house. Chewie barking at the door. That was the last thing he could remember.

"How do you feel?" she asked.

"I've felt better," he said. "Did they catch the trigger-happy guy?"

"No, but the sheriff's department is looking for him."

His brain ached as he tried to figure out who might still have it out for Becky. Ned had come forward, admitting he had used excessive force when he beat Elijah. Basically, his clearing Becky's name should have taken her off the target list of any of Elijah's friends, and certainly the officers in the sheriff's department would feel less animosity toward her, knowing that Ned took responsibility for his actions.

However, those who shot at innocent people while they sat on a front porch weren't exactly rational thinkers.

And feelings died hard.

Or aren't any of these events connected? Unable to think straight, he lifted his hand to rub his eyes when he realized he was attached to an IV.

Maybe there had been developments while he was unconscious. "Does anyone have any idea who could have done this?"

"Nothing yet. Believe me, I'm going to make sure this is a top priority now that I'm back at work. The sheriff may not let me personally investigate this one, but I'll be in his face every day. Demanding updates." If Harrison wasn't loopy on pain meds, he might suspect Becky was upset. *Very upset.*

"Are you okay?" he asked, his voice hoarse.

Becky turned and dragged a hand through her ponytail. He studied her profile until she finally turned back to him, biting her lip. "You shouldn't have dived in front of me."

He reached out to touch her hand resting on the

side rail, when she pulled it back slightly, causing him to miss. His fingertips brushed hers, but his arm felt too heavy to try again. He wanted to tell her that he wouldn't have been able to look at himself in the mirror if she had been hurt because he couldn't protect her.

Like he hadn't protected his brother. But his mind was too foggy to explain all that to her, at least coherently, without sounding like a lovesick fool.

Is that what I am? I hardly know her.

He pushed up on one elbow and grimaced.

Becky placed her hand on his shoulder. "Don't strain."

"Water, please." His eyes moved to the pitcher on the bedside table. Becky picked up the cup and held the straw to his lips. The water felt cool going down his throat. "It's not safe for you to be alone." Even as he said the words, he knew they didn't sound right. She was a sheriff's deputy.

He closed his eyes briefly and bit back his frustration. He wanted to be back on his feet so he could protect Becky.

"I'll be fine. You know I'm not helpless."

He knew, but he didn't like it. "When do I get out of here?"

"You'll have to wait until the physician comes in. They wouldn't tell me much. Privacy laws and everything."

Harrison plucked at the ribbon on his hospital gown at his neck. "Where are my clothes? We need to get out of here."

"You're not going anywhere until the doctor releases you." She patted his chest in a familiar gesture he was growing to like. "Blood ruined your shirt. Maybe I can run by your house and pick up fresh clothes so you have something to wear when you do get released?" She sounded a little bit like she was appeasing him.

"I don't want you driving to my house alone."

"Are you afraid I'll riffle through your sock drawer?" She laughed. He liked it. She didn't do it nearly enough.

"It's not—"

"I know what it is. But I'm a deputy. I can protect myself."

He tried to let the reality of that settle in, but his thoughts were hazy.

She cocked her head and seemed to be studying his face. "If we're going to be friends, you're going to have to get used to that idea. You're not going to go on patrol with me, are you? Protect me from all the bad guys?" Her pink lips twitched before she drew in a deep breath. "Don't treat me like I'm helpless." She leaned in and whispered, "This is exactly part of the reason I refuse to get involved with a fellow officer. There's that whole chivalrous thing going on. Then it gets…complicated."

"That's not what this is about. Someone's out to get you. They shot at you while we were sitting on the porch."

"They shot at *us*," she said evenly.

"I don't recall having made any enemies in Quail Hollow," Harrison said.

"Our jobs make us targets. I have been trained to protect myself." She walked around to the other side of his bed and picked up a plastic bag on the chair. "Are your house keys in your pants pocket?"

"Should be," he said, letting his head sink back into his pillow and fighting a battle against his drooping eyelids.

He heard a jangling as her shadow crossed his line of vision behind closed eyelids. "I'll grab your clean clothes. Will I find them in your closet? A dresser?"

"Folded. Top of dryer. Laundry room off the kitchen," he said, realizing despite his protests she was going to leave and get him clean clothes. The only consolation was that he might get out of here faster.

"Why doesn't that surprise me?"

"At least they're clean *and* folded." He laughed, then yawned.

She patted his chest again. "Sleep. I'll be right back. Maybe you'll have word from the doctor by then."

"Okay." Next thing he knew he was drifting off to sleep. He hadn't even remembered Becky slipping out the door. A rapping sounded on the door frame of the semiprivate room in recovery. He opened his eyes to find the sheriff standing there, hat in hand.

He blinked against the light, confused and disappointed that this was the face greeting him and not Becky.

"You caused some excitement around Deputy Spoth's place."

"Is she here?"

The sheriff glanced around the room. "No, I haven't seen her."

Harrison felt for the bed controls and raised the head of the bed so he could sit up and get a better read on the man he didn't fully trust, not after he lied—or technically omitted—that his nephew was one of the men shooting targets behind Becky's house.

The only people who kept secrets were those who had something to hide. And Harrison didn't like it one bit that someone had been targeting her house again today. A part of him wondered if he had dropped the ball by not pursuing the tip on the sheriff's nephew days ago. But Ned's confession and Becky's reinstatement made following up seem less urgent. Had he been wrong?

"Did they find anyone?" Harrison sniffed, trying to ignore the pain pulsing through his arm where the bullet had ripped through. Absentmindedly, he touched the bandage, wondering when the doctor would be in here to give him a full report. He needed to get out of here.

"Not yet, but they're canvassing the woods." The sheriff's expression didn't give anything away.

"Think you should run another check on the four guys who were doing target practice last week behind Becky's house? See if all of them are accounted for?"

A subtle flinch skittered across the sheriff's face. So subtle that Harrison would have missed it if he hadn't been studying his superior.

The weight of her gun on her hip provided a sense of security as Becky strode out the emergency room exit of the hospital while keeping her focus on her surroundings. Fortunately, hospital security had allowed her to keep her weapon. She had lost track of time and was surprised by how dark it was.

Of course, it was close to ten o'clock at night.

Fortunately, the parking lot was brightly lit and a security guard was stationed at the entrance to the ER.

Becky rolled back her shoulders, surprised at how stiff she had been holding her posture while she was waiting for Harrison to wake up after surgery.

Thank you, Lord, for watching over him.

They had only known each other for a short time and

she hadn't allowed herself to process the jumble of emotions she was feeling. She couldn't deny they had grown close. Closer than she realized until the thought of him not waking up made her feel empty inside.

She didn't know what to do with these feelings. Perhaps their bond had been made stronger because the two of them had very few people to rely on, other than each other.

She had a tough time reconciling her emotions. She had always seen herself as single. Independent. Not leaning on anyone. Wasn't that the point of leaving the Amish?

Was it?

She glanced both ways as she stepped off the sidewalk and crossed the parking lot between two parked cars. She couldn't stop thinking about how devastated she would have been if the gunman had killed Harrison. Or were her emotions born out of relief, pure and simple, that he hadn't died on her account? It wasn't like she had tons of experience dating. Paul King had been her only suitor when she was still Amish, and back then, it was like following a prescribed script.

Could she and Harrison have a future? Not likely if he was going back to Buffalo at some point.

Shoving aside the distracting thoughts, Becky held out her key fob and unlocked the door to her car. She surveyed the area to make sure no one was around before climbing behind the steering wheel.

As she pulled out onto the road, her car felt a bit sluggish, but it wasn't like she was driving a brand new vehicle. She glanced down at Harrison's address again.

She picked up the piece of paper and a loud, clunky sound made her stomach drop. "Oh no," she muttered as she clutched the steering wheel with both hands, crumbling the paper. The entire vehicle rumbled beneath her and she had a hard time steering.

She scanned the road around her, grateful there were no other cars around. The car sputtered and putt-putted until she had to pull over on the side of the road.

Groaning, she pushed open the door. She reached down and released the hood. She climbed out and walked around to the front. Steam poured from under the hood. As much as she knew about caring for a horse and making sure he didn't get overworked, she knew next to nothing about cars. But she did have roadside service and a cell phone. Better to call them than get burned by the steam.

She walked around to the passenger side, opened the door and grabbed her cell phone from the passenger seat. Just then, a pickup truck pulled in behind her. A young man with a baseball cap tugged down low climbed out. "Got a flat?" Something about the lack of emotion in his tone made her skin crawl.

She watched him cautiously, feeling the weight of her gun on her hip, hidden by her T-shirt. Something about him set off alarm bells. However, by all accounts, he was just a good Samaritan, offering help. But out on the deserted country road, alone, at night, was enough for her to exercise caution.

"No, I broke down." She waved him off. "I have roadside assistance. I'll be fine. I already called them," she lied, as a matter of self-preservation. She didn't want the stranger to know how truly vulnerable she was.

"I hate to leave a little lady like you out here on the side of the road all alone at night. I'll wait with you."

"No need." Her stomach quivered. She let her hand

slide over the butt of her gun and her fingers twitched. Even though her instincts were screaming to pull out her gun and point it at him to protect herself, she was suddenly doubting herself.

Doubting all her training.

Tomorrow she would finally have her job back as a deputy and she couldn't risk a run-in tonight that might make the news.

Off-duty deputy shoots good Samaritan.

But if she let her guard down and something bad happened, she'd make the evening news, too, but for far more permanent reasons.

"Didn't catch your name?" She tried to sound casual.

"Don't believe I gave it." A corner of his mouth twitched in the moonlight.

The *clip clop clip* of a horse coming over the hill caught her attention. Based on the shift in body language, it had caught the young man's, too.

The Amish man in the wagon pulled back on his reins. Becky's heart slowed to a dull *whoosh-whoosh-whoosh* when she recognized her married brother.

Thank God.

"Hello, Levi." A long time ago they had been close. Now, because she had left the Amish, she had only seen his wife and two young kids from a distance. While out and about in town, they had silently greeted each other with a subtle head nod. Maybe someday they'd be allowed to be closer. When more time had passed.

"Ah, Rebecca. Your fancy car isn't quite so reliable." His eyes were heavily shadowed by the brim of his hat and she couldn't tell if he was joking or not. He liked to tease her when they were growing up. At the time, it frustrated Becky, but what she'd give now to go back to a simpler time when he was razzing her about how her pie wasn't as good as their *mem's*.

"I'm afraid my car's *not* very reliable." She wondered if her brother could feel the tension. Would he understand the edginess radiating off her wasn't due to their estranged relationship?

The man who had stopped to help her came up behind her. She was angry at herself for letting her brother distract her. For allowing the stranger to approach her from behind.

"Do you need help?" her brother asked.

"No, we're fine," the man said as he stood a fraction too close, pressing something hard into her side.

"Um…" A tingling started in her fingertips and raced up her arms.

The man whispered, "I have a gun. If you don't want your Amish friend hurt, tell him to leave."

"Are you sure?" her brother asked again. "I can drop you off at home."

"No, no, it's fine." She fought to keep the panic out of her voice. "You better hurry home to your family. I'll be fine."

Her brother seemed to stare at her for a long moment before flicking the reins. "Come on, Brownie."

Becky nearly cried at the sound of her former horse's name. She waved and forced a bright smile, if for no other reason than to protect her brother. She refused to bring any more grief into her family's lives.

As the sound from the horse's hooves grew more distant, she lifted her hand slightly, an attempt to grab her own gun. But the man was a step ahead. He snatched her wrist and twisted her arm up behind her. His hat tumbled off in the tussle and landed at her feet. Pain radiated through her shoulder and back. Before she had a chance to spin around and free herself, he pressed a gun into her side. Then handcuffed her wrists.

"I know what you're capable of. This time, instead of me getting a bloody nose, you'll get a bullet in your side."

Becky tugged on her handcuffs and bit back her frustration. The parking garage in Buffalo.

This man had attacked her, but she had been much quicker at defending herself. Her brother's arrival, his offer of help, had actually made her vulnerable. Her attacker wasn't going to be thwarted so easily a second time.

Now she was at his mercy.

"What do you want?" she asked, hiking up her chin, refusing to let him see her fear.

"What do I want?" he said in a mocking tone.

She jerked away from his grasp and spun around. Despite having her hands bound, she got up in his face. "I'm not going with you." Her pulse roared in her ears. And that was when she recognized him. A flush of dread washed over her and the ground swayed.

He lifted the gun to her forehead. "I've got nothing to lose. Try me." The dead look in his eyes drove his point home.

"Okay. I'll go with you. Don't hurt me." She had to buy time. She had her cell phone in her back pocket. Maybe he'd forget. Maybe he wouldn't pay attention long enough for her to text Harrison. Tell him who her harasser was.

But why was he doing this to her?

He took her gun and shoved it in his waistband. His fingers dug into her forearm as he forced her around to the back of his truck. He opened the tailgate and made her climb in under the canvas stretched across the bed. "Try anything stupid and I'll kill you."

She swallowed around a too-tight throat and nodded briefly. She lifted one leg and put her knee on the tailgate and hesitated. Hopping up while her hands were handcuffed behind her back posed an additional challenge. The sound of a car approaching made him shove her inside quickly and he slammed the tailgate, sealing her between the hard metal of the truck and the soft canvas of the bedcover.

She listened hard. His footsteps crunched on the gravel. He opened the door. Slammed the door. The engine started.

Her arms ached as she slid her cell phone from her back pocket. On the bed of the truck, she twisted awkwardly to see the screen. She was grateful for backlit screens. With trembling fingers, she texted the most important thing first:

Lucas Handler.

Send.

Kidnapped. Blue Truck. GMC.

Send. Send. Send.

Each message she got off was a small victory. Breadcrumbs leading to her location.

The truck slowed and Becky rolled back on her elbow, painful bone-to-metal contact. The engine still purred. Car door slammed. Heavy footsteps. Running.

The cell phone grew slippery in her sweat-slicked hands.

The tailgate flew open. She tried to hide the phone under her shirt, but with her hands bound, she was too slow. He ripped the phone from her hand and threw it across the road.

Had he noticed what she had done?

Lucas Handler, one of the young men conducting target practice behind her house had kidnapped her. And now Deputy Harrison James knew.

She prayed.

"I don't think we need to worry about those young men. I checked them out personally. They're good kids," the sheriff said, rubbing a hand across his jaw.

Harrison gritted his teeth, trying to contain his growing anger and wishing he had full use of his left arm. "And you know this because one of them is your nephew."

The sheriff jerked back his head. "How did you...?" Letting his question trail off, he seemed to change his approach midsentence. "That has nothing to do with anything."

"Why didn't you tell me Tyler Flint was your nephew the minute I showed you his identification? The absence of transparency—" he spit the sheriff's favorite word back at him "—makes me think either you or Tyler has something to hide."

The sheriff seemed to slump as he took a step back and then lowered himself into the hard plastic chair. "My nephew's a good kid. Just impulsive. My sister sent him to live with me. Straighten him out. He's got a scholarship to college next fall if he can keep his nose clean his senior year."

"You interfered with an investigation so your nephew wouldn't get into trouble?" Anger pulsed through Harrison, making him sharper despite the meds in his system. All the color seemed to drain from the sheriff's face. "What else haven't you told us?"

The sheriff ran a hand over his short haircut. "Nothing. Nothing at all."

Harrison hated that he was stuck in this hospital bed when all he wanted to do was rip the IV out of his arm and... *Grrr...* "You let politics get in the way."

The sheriff squared his shoulders and looked every bit like the man running for office. "There is no indication my nephew did anything. There was no need to stir up trouble."

"Your omission makes me wonder what else you're not telling me."

A muscle ticked in the sheriff's jaw.

A ding sounded from the plastic bag hanging over the hook at the back of the door. Worried that it might be Becky, he pointed at it. "Get my phone."

The sheriff shot him a glance, probably surprised his subordinate didn't say please. However, considering their exchange, he no doubt realized he better do what Harrison had asked. *Now.* The sheriff stood, grabbed the bag and tossed it into Harrison's lap.

With one hand, Harrison found his folded up jeans and dug out his cell phone. He glanced at the display. He squinted at the screen, trying to figure out what Becky meant by "Lucas Handler."

Then the words that came through next send terror pressing into his heart: Kidnapped. Blue truck. GMC.

The roaring in his ears drowned out all the other sounds in the small recovery room. He swiped his hand across the screen and pressed call. The phone rang and went to voice mail.

"Call me."

"What's going on?" the sheriff asked.

"Becky just texted me. Now I can't reach her." Harrison called the number again and waited. Again, her voice mail.

Harrison didn't like this one bit. He flipped back the thin white hospital bedspread and gritted his teeth when pain shot through his arm. He hesitated a fraction of a moment before sliding the IV out of his hand. He gave the raw flesh on the back of his hand a quick glance before swinging his feet over the edge of the bed.

"Whoa, whoa. I don't think you're supposed to get up." The sheriff held up his hands as if he was going to try to stop him. *Not likely.*

"Not only am I leaving, but you're driving me."

Chapter Thirteen

Every body part that came into contact with the steel bed of the pickup truck ached as the crazed driver made sharp turns and hit ruts. Becky would probably be black-and-blue all over tomorrow; that is, *if* she lived to see the sunrise.

No, she'd live. She *had* to.

She bit back a yelp as the truck turned, apparently off the smooth main road and onto a side road, maybe a driveway. The vehicle bobbled over each and every rut. Where was he taking her? She wished he had stuffed her in the backseat and not the back of the pickup, then maybe she'd have a chance to talk him out of this. As it stood, she just had that much longer to imagine her fate.

"You'll be fine," she whispered to herself. The sound of her voice calmed her. "You're a trained sheriff's deputy." She drew in a deep breath as the truck came to a sudden stop and she banged her head on the bump out from the wheel well. She yanked on her wrists, hoping against hope that the handcuffs had come loose.

She tried to stretch her legs in the cramped space but it was of no use. She'd have to comply with his commands until she got her feet under her and her hands free.

She found herself holding her breath. Listening.

Car door slammed.

Footsteps. Growing fainter.

What does that mean? Is he leaving me here?

A trickle of sweat trailed down her forehead and into her ear. She wasn't sure what terrified her more: being left trapped in the truck breathing in the stale smell of vinyl mixed with soil or being dragged out to some unknown fate.

A bubble of panic welled up and threatened to consume her.

Stay calm. You'll be fine. She pressed her eyes shut and did something she should have done immediately. *Dear Lord, protect me. Keep me clearheaded. Let me see the way out.*

Taking calming breaths, she listened harder. The sound of a car passing. Fast. They weren't too far off the main road.

Footsteps again.

The tailgate creaked as he lowered it. Fresh air and moonlight flooded the space. Becky did her best to act calm. Keep this kid calm.

"Where are we?" she asked, trying to take in as much as she could as he gripped her forearm and yanked her out of the truck. Unable to get her feet under her fast enough, she fell to her knees.

Annoyed, Lucas wrenched her to her feet. "Hurry up." He glanced around as if he feared someone was about to find them.

She prayed that meant they weren't in a remote location.

Nothing struck Becky as unique. Trees, country road, small house hunkered in the shadows. Nothing to pinpoint her location. "Is this your house?" She avoided calling him by his name. That was her secret. She feared his reaction if he realized she knew his identity.

When he didn't answer, she asked again. "Do you live here?"

"No, but someone I want you to see does," the kid said, surprising her with an answer of any kind.

"Are they home?"

"He's supposed to be, but he didn't answer the door." He sounded genuinely disappointed.

"Do you know who I am? I'm a sheriff's deputy. You'll be in a lot of trouble for kidnapping a law-enforcement officer."

The kid scoffed. "If you were much of a deputy, you wouldn't be so easily kidnapped."

"How'd that work out for you in the parking garage? Nose still hurt?" She took a shot at his self-confidence. He seemed to be deflated after learning no one was home. Had he kidnapped her on a dare? Wanted to show someone what he had done?

He glared at her for a long minute before his expression shifted. "You won't catch me off guard again." He tugged on the handcuffs and pain ripped through her raw wrists. "Now look who has the upper hand."

"People will be looking for me."

"Maybe." He seemed disinterested. "But will they find you in time?"

He pushed her up two steps to the front porch. Their footfalls sounded loud on the wood slats as if they were the only people around for miles. Keys jangled and he pushed past her to unlock the door.

He grabbed her forearm and shoved her inside. The place smelled closed up. Like someone had been away for a few days, at least. Lucas went to the keypad and entered the alarm code.

"Who lives here?"

"Shut up." He shoved her and she bumped against the hall table. A collection of photos fell over like dominos. Behind her, the kid flipped on a light. A photo of Ned Reich stared back at her. He was standing with a woman, a little boy next to him. The portrait of a happy family.

A flush of dread washed over her. She willed herself to be calm. "This is Ned Reich's home. How do you know Ned?" Her entire scalp tingled and she struggled to swallow.

Lucas flinched, but he set his jaw and glared at her, remaining silent.

She tried again. "Who is this little boy in the photo? You?"

"Shut up." Lucas's expression was hard. Angry. "Do I look like that snot-nosed kid?"

"Why are we in Deputy Reich's house? That's where we are, right?" Was this some form of retribution toward her and Deputy Reich for their involvement in the Elijah Lapp incident? Or had he brought her here as punishment for her role in Reich's suspension? The pieces didn't quite fit.

She studied his face. The dead look in his eyes made icy dread pool in her stomach.

He grabbed her by the arm again and shoved her into the family room at the back of the house. A kitchen was visible on the other end. It was what she heard her Realtor call an open concept. All the ways *Englischers* lived baffled her when she first left the Amish. The Amish had clean, well-maintained homes, but all these extras were perplexing to her, even now.

She had to lean back on her hands because of the handcuffs. She shifted, trying to find a comfortable position. Lucas paced in front of her as if he had miscalculated something. His growing agitation was rubbing off on her. Making her skin buzz. She needed him to be calm. *She* needed to be calm.

"You should have never been made a deputy. You're not competent." He pivoted and turned back around. He plowed a shaky hand through his straggly hair.

"What did I ever do to you?" The words flew from her lips before she could call them back.

"You took my job." He kicked a stuffed animal that got in his way. Becky imagined a well-loved pet lived somewhere in this house.

She studied him carefully, realizing there was no rationalizing with an irrational person. She couldn't have taken his job any more than Harrison had taken his job. After all, Harrison had been hired after her. But for some reason he had focused on her as the guilty party. Why? Because she was an outsider? A woman? Because she had drawn his attention with all the news coverage of the beating of Elijah Lapp? Had he targeted her because he felt she was a symbol of everything that he felt was wrong with the system? Was he on a mission to hurt Deputy Reich, too?

After leaving the Amish, Becky had immersed herself in newspaper and online articles about the world around her. A world she had been living in, but hadn't been a part of. Initially, she had her doubts. Wondered if she made the right decision. The evil around her made her fantasize about running back to the insular world of her family. But God's calling to live a different life had been louder than the whispers of uncertainty buzzing in her ears as she tried to fall asleep each night those first few lonely months.

Now after all that, is this where I'm meant to die?

She couldn't accept that. She wouldn't. God hadn't placed her on this difficult journey to have it end here.

"Are you mad at me because of the incident with Deputy Reich?" She kept her tone soft, inquisitive.

The man's fingers flicked and closed, flicked and closed as he paced in front of her. He was growing more agitated, leading her to believe she was on the right track.

"Are you looking to get back at Deputy Reich and me for hurting Elijah? Are you and Elijah friends?"

He squinted at her. His mouth was twisted in a mocking grin. "You'd make a crummy detective."

She stared at him a long minute. "Is Deputy Reich a mentor of yours?"

The man spun around and bent down and picked up one end of the coffee table. Candles, decorations and TV remotes crashed to the floor. She recoiled at the uncontrolled anger pulsing off him.

"He is my father. He is my father. My *father.*" His face grew red and spittle flew from his lips.

Becky blinked slowly, trying to let that register. This man was Ned Reich's son. This man was out for revenge against her *because of* his father.

She tugged at her handcuffs and feared the desperateness of the situation, but she forced herself to remain calm. Words came to her. "Then you know your father is a good man who made a mistake. He wouldn't want you to hurt me."

A muscle worked in his jaw. "How do you know what he'd want? You ruined his life." Lucas breathed in and out quickly through his flaring nose. His eyes darted around the room as if he was replaying her words in his mind. "A mistake? The only mistake he made was confessing. He needed to stay strong. Fight the charges."

"He's sorry. He told me as much."

"We're only sorry you testified against him."

"With or without my testimony, he couldn't explain away what happened in the video."

"You made everything worse." He glared at her and for a fraction of a moment, she thought he was going to charge at her. Instinctively, her stomach clenched. She didn't have her hands free to defend herself.

"Hurting me won't solve anything."

It was his turn to blink at her, processing her words. "If you hadn't responded to the call with your dash cam rolling, his life wouldn't have been ruined. If you hadn't been a witness against him. If you hadn't..." His voice bellowed in the confines of his father's house.

Becky opened her mouth to protest, but the rage flaring in his nostrils gave her pause.

"His life is ruined because of you."

Harrison jumped out of the patrol car the second it stopped in front of the address on Lucas Handler's driver's license. Holding his injured arm close to his side, he ran to the front door of a trailer with rust running down its white sides. The door swung open as if someone had been waiting for them.

"I'm looking for Lucas Handler."

The woman's eyes grew dark. "What's he done now?"

"Is he your son?" Harrison asked, trying to tamp down his frustration. The woman looked past him to the sheriff standing outside his patrol car. They had already called in Becky as missing. Possibly kidnapped. Other patrols were out looking for her. Harrison wouldn't rest easy until she was found.

"Who's asking?" The woman's gaze dropped to his arm in a sling. He had somehow managed to throw on his bloodied and torn shirt.

"I'm Deputy James." He touched his injured arm. "I had a little accident and I need to find your son."

She sighed heavily as if resigned to answering. "I don't know where he is."

"Has Lucas ever mentioned a Deputy Rebecca Spoth to you?"

The woman's thin eyebrows rose under her long bangs. "Is that what this is about? That Amish woman who thinks she can be a cop?" She crossed her arms tightly across her thin frame. A smug expression slanted her mouth. "She doesn't know her place."

Harrison clenched his jaw, knowing if he responded how he wanted to respond she'd shut down. And right now he needed to find Lucas.

And Becky.

"Do you know where Lucas might be?"

She shrugged. "Doesn't report in to me. Comes and goes as he pleases." She shook her head as if she never had any control over her son.

"How about Lucas's father? Could we talk to him?"

"His father's not in the picture. Never has been." The woman stared at him defiantly. She hiked her chin at the sheriff. "Why don't you ask the sheriff over there. He knows where Ned is."

"Ned?" Harrison's pulse roared in his ears. "Ned Reich?"

The woman gave him a self-satisfied smile. "Ned doesn't have anything to do with me or Lucas. I couldn't care less, but Lucas would do anything for his father. Not that his father would have anything to do with him. Rarely has. Stopped coming around as soon as he knew I was pregnant. The guy has a problem. Cheated with me on his first wife when his oldest son—Colin, he's also one of yours—was just a young boy. Swore he couldn't leave his wife until he found the next one. I heard he has himself another wife and boy. Apparently, we weren't good enough."

Harrison tried to be patient as the woman unraveled her unfortunate life story. "Has Lucas been in contact with Ned recently?"

"I don't know how Lucas spends his time. I'm not sure how to be clearer on that."

Harrison opened his wallet and pulled out his business card. He offered it to the woman, who took it reluctantly. "Call me if you see Lucas. It's important."

Harrison spun around and jogged over to the sheriff. "Did you know Lucas Handler is Ned Reich's son?"

The sheriff shook his head. "Can't say I was privy to that information."

"But your nephew is friends with him?"

The sheriff waved his hand in dismissal. "Kids just hang out. Doesn't mean they're best friends."

"Call Ned. Find out if he's with Lucas. Don't tell him what's going on." The sheriff did what Harrison asked even though the expression on his face suggested he wanted to do anything but.

Harrison still couldn't shake the feeling that the sheriff was hiding something.

He paced next to the patrol car while the sheriff made the phone call. A teenager around fifteen on a brown bike with motocross stickers plastered on the frame skidded to a stop on the gravel. "Are you here to arrest Lucas?"

Harrison studied the teen. "No, we're here to talk to him. Do you know Lucas?"

The kid roughly rubbed his nose. A large scab covered his elbow. "Everyone knows Lucas." The kid rolled his eyes. "But no one likes him."

"Why's that?"

"He's always mad. Going on about how he's going to become a deputy and come back and put us all in jail. He acts like he never did the stuff we do." The kid glanced around, acting skittish. "Nothing bad, just stuff like skidding on the gravel in front of his trailer. Playing our music loud. He once stole my friend's baseball mitt when he put it down to run in for a drink. Claims he never saw it." He shook his head in disgust.

"Any idea where Lucas hangs out?" Harrison asked.

"Mostly he hangs on the porch yelling at us. If he's not here, I don't want to know where he is."

"Thanks," Harrison said, then turned to the sheriff. "Find anything out?"

"Ned says he doesn't have much contact with his son. The son was the result of a stupid fling." The sheriff frowned. "His words, not mine. Never married the mother. The relationship has always been strained."

This pretty much matched what Harrison got from the mother.

Harrison ran a hand across his jaw. "Okay, so he's not with Ned. Wonder—"

The sheriff held up his hand. "Ned's out of town. Gone fishing up at Lake George. Just turned on his phone—was trying to go off the grid for a bit, but knew with everything going on regarding his employment that he better not go completely silent. Anyway, he had a notice on his home monitoring app. Someone entered his house here in town. Knew the alarm code."

"Couldn't be Lucas, right? Not if Ned doesn't have contact with his son. He wouldn't know the code," Harrison reasoned.

"Here's the thing. About a year ago Ned reached out to the kid. Thought maybe he was wrong in not being a father figure. Even had him dog-sit." The sheriff pushed up his hat. "But the dog wasn't well cared for and the two had a blowout. Haven't spoken much since."

"So, unless Ned changed the code, Lucas has it."

"Exactly. Ned never changed it." The sheriff reached for the car door handle. "Told Ned we'd check on his property. Told him not to call the house. We want the element of surprise."

Harrison pulled the passenger door open. "What are we waiting for?"

Becky studied Lucas from her seat in the corner of the couch. He opened and closed closets and drawers with short, jerky movements. She wondered if he was under the influence of something. His distraction never lasted long enough for her to make a move, especially with her hands in cuffs.

A few feet in front of her, Lucas opened the cabinet under the TV then froze as if he had remembered something. He slowly pivoted, glared at her with a distant expression, stood and then strode over to the door and opened it. Watching carefully, she slid to the front of the couch cushion and shifted her weight to her feet. Ready to pounce.

Lucas slammed the door. "His car's not here. I thought I heard it. I think he went fishing." A muscle worked in his jaw as his gaze locked on hers. He tilted his head and studied her, perhaps trying to read her thoughts, trying to figure out why she had positioned herself forward on the couch. Was he going to lash out at her? Make her regret her feeble attempt at overpowering him.

She slid back onto the couch casually. "Do you like to go fishing?"

"He only takes Noah fishing."

Becky licked her lips. "Is Noah the little boy in the photographs?"

Lucas practically snarled. "My half brother, not that anyone would know it."

"Maybe your father would take you fishing if you asked him to." Lucas seemed like someone who would be too proud to ask for what he wanted.

Lucas plowed a hand through his hair. "I need to see him. Show him what I've done for him."

"What have you done for him?" Her pulse whooshed loudly in her ears as she held her breath, waiting for the answer. Fearing the answer.

"I'm going to take care of his biggest problem." His expression was a mix of determination and anger. "He's finally going to be proud of me."

Becky slid forward on the couch cushion again, her heart jackhammering in her chest. "Hurting me is not going to solve anything. Can you please remove my handcuffs? It's hard to sit like this. My arms are aching."

He stopped and stared at her; his eyes looked blank, but something compelled him to grant her request. He put the handcuffs back on, but this time in front. She counted it as a victory. "Thank you," she whispered.

"Don't thank me." He couldn't seem to make eye contact. She wanted to get him talking, hoping to break down the wall around his heart.

"I can imagine you're sorry you ran me off the road and slashed my tires."

His gaze shot up to her face and he laughed. "Sorry? My only regret is that I didn't kill you when I had the chance." He made a gesture of a gun with his fingers and slowly lowered it to take aim at her head. "If my shot had been one foot lower, your brains would have been splattered all over your little dog. Don't think I'm a bad shot. The miss was intentional. Fear is a powerful motivator."

"Motivator?"

"To motivate you to leave my father alone."

Becky threaded her fingers and twisted. "Did your friends know what you were up to?" Maybe if she kept him talking she could buy some time. She wasn't sure at all if Harrison would figure out where they were. They had no idea Lucas was Ned's son.

An ugly smile pulled at his lips. "My friends?"

"Yes, Deputy James talked to four young men, including you, the day you almost shot me. The day you and your friends were having target practice behind my house." She watched as he scratched his neck viscously as if a mosquito had bitten him. "Did your friends know what you were up to? Were they in on it?" She wasn't sure why she was asking him, but the longer he answered questions, the less likely he would act on his wish to see her dead.

"They were clueless." He seemed to take pride in his proclamation. "I told them that nature called. I slid into the woods." He gave her an exaggerated frown as if he was recalling the events of that day. "I was going to shoot out a window in your house. Scare you back to the Amish farm where you came from. But imagine my surprise when you were outside." He made a shooting sound with his lips. "Bang. Bang. I waited until one of the guys took aim at a tin can, masking my shot. The bark exploded and the look of terror on your face was worth it. Hid the gun in a hollowed-out log. Went back to get it later. I'm not so stupid. Not sure why my dad is so hard on me."

Becky floated between fear of and sympathy for this truly lost young man. "You don't have to do this, Lucas. Let me go." She was going to add, "no one has to know," but it seemed rather cliché.

The doorbell rang.

Lucas swung his attention toward the front door and cursed under his breath. They both knew his father wouldn't ring the doorbell. Lucas held up his index finger to his mouth in a harsh hush gesture.

The sound of her ragged breath filled her ears. Should she yell out for help? Seconds ticked by, indecision weighing on her. She couldn't risk the safety of whoever was at the door.

The doorbell chimed again followed by a pounding.

"Lucas Handler, it's the sheriff. Open up."

"What the…?" Lucas darted over to the kitchen and grabbed her gun from the counter. Becky cringed at how carelessly he handled the weapon. Hated that it was her weapon he was going to use against the sheriff.

With a determined set of the jaw, Lucas stomped over to the couch and yanked Becky up by the front of her shirt. Her awkward forward momentum caused her shoulder to crash into his solid chest.

"Lucas," the sheriff yelled again, "we know you're in there. We're looking for Deputy Spoth. Come on, son. Your dad wouldn't want this."

Lucas's face grew red with rage. "You have no idea what my father wants. You fired him."

While Lucas directed his fury toward the front of the house, out of the corner of her eye Becky thought she saw a shadow in the yard. Hope blossomed in her chest. She made sure Lucas was focused on the front door, and she turned her full attention to the glass sliders in the kitchen. Harrison peeked around the corner, careful not to make himself a target, and gave her a reassuring nod.

Becky had to think fast. They were on the precipice of a major tragedy, of which she was going to be the star. She bowed her head and tucked her face into her shoulder. "I think I'm going to be sick."

Lucas seemed to snap out of it for a moment, long enough to register what she had said.

"Please, I'm going to throw up."

Lucas gestured toward the kitchen sink. "In there. I'm not cleaning up your mess."

Becky nodded contritely and took a small step backward. She needed him to believe she was weak. A victim. At this moment she chose to be anything but.

Panicked by the sheriff at the front door, Lucas left her to move about unchecked. He jogged to the front door and positioned himself against the wall, holding the gun in both hands now, down between his legs, his attention focused on a thin, smoked-glass side light running the length of the door. She prayed the sheriff stayed clear of the window, otherwise it would be a bullet from her gun in his gut.

Becky pivoted and walked slowly, so as not to draw attention to herself. At that exact moment the sheriff started pounding again. Lucas jammed a hand through his hair, his whole body trembling. An animal trapped in a corner with no hope of escape.

Becky let out a long, shaky breath, knowing they had reached a critical point.

As she moved toward the sink, she hustled past the slider, flicked the lock in one fluid motion. Her heart dropped when she noticed a bar reinforcement. Watching Lucas out of the corner of her eye, she released the bar and it dropped with a clack.

"What's that?" Lucas yelled, marching partially down the hallway with short, jittery steps.

Becky leaned heavily on a chair. "Sorry, I tripped." Holding her breath, she watched as Lucas shifted his attention back to the front door. She moved toward the sink. Her throat growing tight, she turned on the faucet and made like she was splashing water on her face, the entire time watching the situation out of the corner of her eye.

Harrison slid open the door and aimed his gun at Lucas with his one good hand. "Drop the gun."

Lucas's eyes widened and all the color drained from his face. He seemed baffled that the sheriff was at the front door while Deputy James had made it in through the back.

Becky grabbed a cast-iron skillet off the hook in the kitchen and crept through the dining room, emerging on the other side of the foyer with a clear sight of Lucas.

"Drop the gun!" Harrison yelled again.

The young man's fingers twitched near the trigger. His arm started to rise. Becky lifted the skillet with her two cuffed hands and ran at Lucas, clobbering him over the head.

Lucas crumpled to the ground in a heap of limbs and baggy clothes. Becky dropped the pan; her arms felt like JELL-O.

She turned to look at Harrison. He slid his gun back into its holster and without one note of surprise said, "Nice job." He opened the door to the sheriff. "There's your man."

The sheriff crouched down, picked up the gun and pressed his fingers to Lucas's neck to check for a pulse. "What did you do?"

"What I had to," Becky said, pointing with her thumb at the heavy skillet on the table.

The sheriff handed keys to Harrison and he quickly undid her handcuffs. He gently ran his hand over the tender skin of her wrist. "You okay?"

She narrowed her gaze at his bloodstained shirt. "I could ask the same of you."

He touched his wounded arm. "I'll live."

"I'll call an ambulance for our friend here on the floor." The sheriff stepped outside, leaving the door open.

Becky ran a hand across her face, her wrists still

sore from the handcuffs. "Honestly, I didn't know I had it in me."

"I did." Harrison pulled her into a one-armed embrace and for the first time since he had been shot on her front porch—which seemed like a lifetime ago—Becky allowed herself to take a deep breath. She rested her head on his shoulder, careful not to hurt his arm.

Harrison smiled at her. "You're one tough deputy."

"Thanks for providing a distraction so I could sneak up on him."

"My pleasure." She could hear the smile in his voice as his breath whispered across her hair.

"I think it's finally over for real. Lucas was the one harassing me, trying to get payback for his father."

Harrison stepped back and ran a tender hand down her arm. "I'm happy for you. But I'm sorry I wasn't there to protect you."

"You'll have to get used to it. I'm a deputy. Your job isn't to protect me."

He opened his mouth, but whatever he was about to say died on his lips as his gaze drifted to the door.

"Ambulance is on the way." The sheriff stood in the doorway, holding his phone. "They're going to want a full statement from you, Deputy Spoth."

"Yes, sir." But this time her statement would be the end of her problems and not the beginning.

Harrison gently took her by the hand and led her outside. She drew in a deep breath of the sweet night air. "I'm grateful God was watching over me tonight. And that He sent you."

"Me, too. I don't know what I would have done..." His words trailed off and she felt his steady gaze on her as the darkness and sounds of nature crowded in on them. "You know, you're not in this alone."

"No?" She looked up at him.

"All deputies need backup," he added breezily, as if their conversation had grown too serious.

Her quiet laugh had a shaky quality to it. "Are you offering to be my backup?"

"How about an offer of dinner instead?"

Heat warmed her cheeks. "After everything we've been through, you're asking me on a date?"

"You're not going to make this easy on me, are you?"

Feeling emboldened after everything she'd been through, Becky placed her hand on his chest and stretched up to brush a kiss across his cheek. "I'd love to go to dinner. But, let's keep it low key." Harrison didn't have plans to stick around Quail Hollow long term anyway, no sense making it more than it was.

The sound of sirens approaching filed the air. "Low key sounds perfect." He placed his hand on the small of her back. "Let's go inside before the mosquitos eat us alive."

Chapter Fourteen

A few days later, while back at work, Becky felt like she had never left. The one big change was that she was now on the day shift and her fellow officers no longer gave her the side eye. They no more tolerated rogue deputies than she had, but it took a few of the officers a while to realize former Deputy Ned Reich wasn't the good guy they thought he was. Even his son, Deputy Colin Reich, had offered her an apology for giving her a hard time. The entire sheriff's department wanted to move forward.

Becky hoped Ned would eventually find his way. He had admitted his temper got the best of him when it came to the beating of Elijah Lapp. Fortunately, Elijah was on the mend. Last she heard, he had moved to live with family in another Amish community. And Ned lost his job. But Becky felt deep in her heart that Ned was repentant. Perhaps he could eventually find his place in this community and rise from the ashes after he served whatever sentence he received for beating a man.

But that was his journey. Not hers.

The afternoon temperatures had still remained hotter than average for Quail Hollow, New York. Calls to the sheriff's department had thankfully been slow. As Becky crested the hill near her family's farm, she decided there were other fences she needed to mend before she'd be content to settle into her new routine.

Becky parked her patrol car along the road out of respect for her Amish family and neighbors. She called into dispatch to let them know where she was. She used the guise that she was checking on the Kings' residence after the incident with the puppies.

The hot sun beat down on her hat as she walked toward the Kings' barn. She held her shoulders back. She was done letting even a hint of shame color how she felt about her job as a sheriff's deputy. Her Amish family may not like it, but there was an element of pride for serving as a law enforcement officer. Despite their tenet of staying separate, even the Amish had to admit law enforcement had the entire community's best interests at heart.

As she approached the barn, she had a sense of déjà vu, yet it felt like a million years since she had rescued Chewie from his horrible living conditions.

Oh man, Chewie, she thought. The little guy had been a great companion. She supposed she had to ask Mag if she was expecting him to come live with her. Becky had promised her sister, but she would hate to see the little fur ball go. He was her only steady companion after she and Harrison decided to keep things platonic after their dinner date.

Becky supposed it was probably for the best. Despite her growing feelings for him, they both had different paths in life. She suspected he'd be returning to Buffalo soon anyway.

Out of the corner of her eye, she noticed someone running across the yard: her old friend, Mary Elizabeth.

"Becky, is something wrong?" Mary asked.

Becky shook her head. "No. I wanted to see how things were going."

"Fine," Mary responded stiffly. "Anything else?" Mary glanced toward the barn, perhaps a bit nervously, probably wishing Becky'd leave. Her friend had been terrified she'd lose her husband if he was arrested for mistreating the dogs. But that had been resolved with fines and the promise to not mistreat animals again. Becky wanted to believe the Kings had never meant to hurt the animals, but had quickly become overwhelmed with their puppy selling enterprise.

"I don't mean to cause any trouble for you. Please, if you ever need anything from outside the Amish community, consider me a friend."

Mary bowed her head briefly, then looked back up. "I'd like that." Her cheeks reddened as if her desire didn't match what the strict rules allowed. In her heart, Becky cheered the small victories. Their friendship could never be what it was, but maybe they could stop and chat at the market when their paths crossed. Becky would learn the names of her children. Maybe help the next generation know it's okay to reach out if they need help from an *Englischer*.

"Is Paul in the barn?" Becky asked, feeling like the silence had stretched into awkward territory.

"Yah." A line marred the flawless skin of her forehead.

"I'm just going to say hello." Becky gave her old friend a quick nod, then strode toward the barn before she tried to stop her. Becky found Paul brushing a horse.

He paused, looked at her with an even expression, then went back to his task.

Becky glanced around the barn. Gone was the cage holding the dogs. The space was tidy. The horses seemed well cared for. "How are you, Paul?"

"Fine." His eyes shifted skeptically. "Spying on me to see if I've broken your rules?"

Becky didn't answer, knowing he wouldn't take kindly to her patronizing him. "At lot has gone on in the community these past few weeks. Law enforcement and the Amish stay separate, but with the beating of Elijah Lapp and the intertwining of our families, that hasn't been possible." She took off her hat and touched her braids that were neatly pinned on top of her head. "I hope despite our past, there are no hard feelings. If there is anything I can ever do for your family, please let me know." Part of her hope for being a deputy and staying in Quail Hollow was to bridge the gap between the two worlds. A difficult task, for sure, but a necessary one.

"Yah." Paul's mouth twitched as if he wanted to say more, but he turned and went back to brushing the horse in silence. She'd have to take what she could get.

"Have a good afternoon." She spun on the heel of her boot and decided it was time to face her family because that was the fence she truly wanted to mend.

Becky cut through the path connecting the neighboring properties. When she was about thirty feet from her parents' house, a cute little white fur ball ran across the yard to greet her. Becky bent down and patted his head. "Well, hello there. Who are you?"

She straightened and glanced around. Mag came running out of the barn and stopped short when she saw her big sister playing with the dog. "Yours?" Becky asked.

"*Yah!* Can you believe *Dat* let me get him?" She glanced around and lowered her voice. "Sometimes I even sneak him into my room." Her parents had always believed animals belonged outside or in the barn.

"Does that mean you don't want Chewie?"

Mag's eyes widened. "I thought you loved him."

"I do." Becky couldn't contain her smile.

Mag's expression relaxed. "Well, *gut*, because now we both have dogs we love."

Becky was pleased that the dog situation had been easily resolved.

"Are *Mem* and *Dat* around?"

"In the house." Mag's gaze drifted to their well-maintained, nondescript home. A row of pale blue and gray dresses flapped in the wind on the clothesline. A sense of loss pinged her heart.

Will I ever get past the feelings of loss?

"And Abram?" Becky asked, forcing a cheeriness into her tone.

"He went to a cattle auction. Should be home later tonight." After hesitating a moment Mag said, "Come on in."

Words never sounded so sweet, but Becky wasn't naive enough to believe her parents, especially her *dat*, would feel the same way.

Mag led the way, the folds of her gown flapping against her legs. They found their parents in the kitchen. *Mem* at the stove. *Dat* at the table working on the reel of his fishing rod.

The sight, the familiar sounds, the fragrant smells, were like a punch to Becky's gut. She hadn't realized how much she missed family until she was back in the heart of her home.

Former home.

They both looked up at their daughters at the same time. Curiosity lit her mother's expression. Stoicism defined his.

"Hello," Becky said, feeling very much like the eighteen-year-old Amish girl who had left in the middle of the night. "Um… I got my job back."

Her father ran his hand down his unkempt beard. "I can see that," he said, indicating her crisp uniform. Even though they didn't discuss it, she suspected they experienced their share of shame over the news stories suggesting Becky had beat an Amish boy and for that, she was sorry. But she was even more sorry that their estrangement meant she hadn't had her family to rely on during the lowest point in her career.

They'd never understand their daughter's career. Harrison's handsome smile came to mind. He might have been the one to stand by her side moving forward, if only his plans included staying in town. Since they didn't, she couldn't risk her heart. She had already experienced too much loss in her life.

Becky quickly shoved thoughts of Harrison aside. "I was cleared of all charges in the Elijah Lapp incident." She needed her parents to hear it from her. To know that even though their daughter left the Amish faith, she hadn't abandoned the morals that they had instilled in her.

"*Yah*, I heard. I never believed you were capable of that," her mother said. She'd probably never realize how much those words meant to her oldest daughter.

"Is that what you came here to say?" her father said, wiping off the fishing pole with a rag.

"I want you all to know I'm here if you need anything." Her words were mostly for the benefit of her little sister. She never wanted Mag to feel as alone as Becky had when she was struggling with the decision to leave the Amish.

Her father mumbled something she couldn't make out while her mother returned to stirring whatever was on the stove, leaving it up to her husband to address this weighty matter. It was this need to defer to the male that had always stuck in Becky's craw.

Speak up, Mem, *tell me how you feel!*

Just because she felt a certain way didn't mean it was the right way. The only way. Generations of Amish women had lived happily on the farm as if no time had passed. However, Becky knew it wasn't the way she wanted to live.

"Well…" Becky fidgeted with the hat in her hands. "I better get back on patrol."

"*Denki* for stopping by," her mother said as if grasping for something to say.

"You're welcome. I look forward to seeing you around town." Becky would respect her parents' wishes that they remain separate and she wouldn't continue to stop by, especially since it seemed to make them uncomfortable.

"Our worry has always been for your sister," her father said, his voice low and even. He never looked up from the work he was doing. "We never wanted you to be a negative influence."

"I understand." She did. She just didn't like it.

"However, I have come to the difficult conclusion that I can no more force Magdaline to stay among the Amish than I was able to force you to return." He set down the rag he was using on the table next to his fishing pole. "It would make your mother happy if you could come for dinner on occasion. You were never baptized into the Amish faith, so I feel we have some leeway there. It couldn't be a regular occurrence, mind you. But a special occasion."

Joy exploded in Becky's chest and she did everything to contain her excitement. She didn't want to scare anyone off. "That would be nice," she said in the same self-contained manner in which her father spoke.

"It would be," her mother said, clutching a dish towel to her chest, light beaming in her eyes.

"I should go," Becky said, and turned toward the door, more pleased with the results of her visit than she could have ever imagined. The invitation had been an olive branch extended by her father.

Mag saw her out. She leaned in and whispered, "Eli Hoffstettler asked to take me home after singing." Her sister seemed giddy. Becky could tell she was bursting with the news. The who's-who of dating was usually done quietly and engagements were only published weeks before a wedding. Becky was thrilled her sister shared this news with her.

"Do you like him?"

Mag nodded her head enthusiastically. "I've liked him since he tugged on my bonnet strings the first day of school when I was six years old."

Becky squeezed her sister's hand. "I'm happy for you." It seemed her sister might find happiness among the Amish that she couldn't.

Becky walked toward her patrol car feeling a lightness she hadn't felt in ages.

* * *

Deputy Harrison James pulled his truck into a spot at the sheriff's station and climbed out. He had to get an update on his disability after getting shot in the arm. Two spots down, Becky pulled in with her patrol car. He'd be lying if he didn't admit he was happy to see her. He had purposely timed his visit with the end of her shift.

Harrison slammed his car door and called after her, determined not to let this get too awkward despite their decision to simply remain friends. "How's the day shift treating you?"

Becky slowed her pace and turned around, giving him a bright smile. He missed seeing her pretty face. "I like it. Finally get to live a normal life. Sleep when normal people sleep." If the fact she was beaming was any indication, she was right. The day shift agreed with her.

"Glad to hear it. Most of the calls seem tamer on day shift, too." He twisted his mouth and raised his eyebrows. "Mostly, anyway."

"True." She took a step backward and lifted her arm to the station where the deputies had to report before going home for the night. "Well, I better get moving, Chewie needs to be let out."

"You're a dog owner for the long haul?"

"Go figure." She shrugged, but he could tell she was happy about it.

"Have a good evening." She waved her hand casually, then turned to walk into the station.

He hustled to catch up to her. "I wanted to let you know I'm headed to Buffalo."

"Oh." Was that disappointment settling in the fine lines around her eyes?

"It's time I faced my past," he admitted. Long past

time. He patted his arm. "Seems like a good time, considering my arm will take a bit to heal."

Becky angled her head and the sun reflected in her bright blue eyes. She lifted her hand to block it, waiting for him to continue. When he didn't, she asked, "Are you coming back?"

"I don't know yet."

Her smiled seemed strained. "You'll be missed around here."

Harrison bent his head and scratched his forehead. "I need to sort through some things. Put my parents' home up for sale." His brother had killed himself in the bathroom. He'd never be happy there, but he couldn't avoid going back. He had to sell the house and move on.

"That'll be good."

"I agree. It's long overdue. I've been paying someone to cut the grass, shovel the snow and do a walk-through every few weeks to make sure everything is okay. Like no busted pipes or a break-in. But enough of that. It's time I went back."

"I've learned you can't find your way forward until you make peace with the past." She raised her eyebrows. She spoke from experience.

"Keep me in your prayers," he said before he had a chance to overthink it. Slowly coming back to his faith had given him some direction and peace.

A light came into her eyes. "I will. I'm confident you'll be fine." She took a few steps, then turned back around. "Don't be a stranger."

"I won't." But in truth, he wasn't sure what the future held.

Epilogue

Three weeks later...

Harrison slammed his locker door and twisted the combination lock. His arm had healed and he was allowed back at work. He had finished his first shift at the Quail Hollow Sheriff's Department, disappointed that he hadn't crossed paths with Becky. Maybe she had taken the day off.

He waved casually to a few fellow officers who were coming in for the second shift. When he had left Quail Hollow, he wasn't certain if he'd ever be back. Whether he'd see this place. These people. Sure, he had officially been out on disability, but in his heart, he knew there was a real possibility of calling in his resignation once he got bogged down with the details of settling his life in Buffalo.

Three weeks of cleaning out his family's home and sorting through all the possessions and memories gave him a lot of time to think. And most of his thoughts involved Becky Spoth.

After he had done his part to clear out his family's possessions, he had left the rest in the hands of a Realtor who would hold an estate sale and list the house. The rest could be managed by a quick visit to Buffalo to sign papers.

He had more important business in Quail Hollow.

Harrison pushed through the glass doors, and the afternoon heat hit his face. Soon, the temperatures would drop and everyone would be complaining about the cold.

He climbed into his truck and backed out. As he came around the corner, he noticed Becky's car parked where their adventures together first began. Curious, he slowed. Leaning forward against the steering wheel he searched for any sign of her.

A knocking on his side window startled him. He turned and saw Becky smiling at him. *Ah, that smile.* He pressed the lever to lower the window.

"Looking for someone?" she asked, a twinkle brightening her eyes.

"I thought maybe you had another flat."

"Oh, hush, things have finally settled down. Don't go trying to stir things up again."

Harrison held up his hands. "I wouldn't dream of it."

"I heard you were back."

"How?"

"Oh, a little birdie told me." He could only imagine. Word spread like wild fire in this small town.

"I had to be in court today."

"Anything to report?"

"Nothing I want to talk about. Time will settle everything." She rested her forearm on the ledge of his door. "I want to know about you. How's your arm?"

He held it up. "Good as new."

"And your trip home?"

"Good. I accomplished everything I needed to accomplish."

"Glad to hear it."

"You holding the fort down here?"

"Trying to. Rounded up the Hoffstettlers' cows that got out through a broken fence, gave a stern talking to some young boys who thought it would be more fun to steal a few apples from Mrs. Lapp's produce stand than pay for them…" She hitched up her shoulders. "You know, the usual fare."

"Sounds like things *are* back to normal."

"Yes, that's a very good thing." Becky stepped back from the door and jutted her lower lip to blow the hair off her face. Then she grew serious. "And you're back. I didn't know that you had plans to return."

"I didn't know myself when I left here. I did a lot of thinking while I was gone. I only got in late last night. I was due to report to work this morning." He studied her face. "I should have called you, but I wanted to talk to you in person."

"Oh?"

"I missed…this place." He didn't want to scare her off. They had agreed not to date, but he held out hope that perhaps they could revisit that possibility now that he was staying. But he didn't want to be presumptuous.

She raised her eyebrows in expectation. Her hair was pulled into a long ponytail with a few strands falling loosely around her face. "You missed this place, huh?"

He tilted his head to one side and studied her. "Yes, very much."

"Well, I think this place missed you, too," she said, pink blossoming on her cheeks. "And I thought maybe you'd like to hear about all the things you missed since you've been gone. Perhaps over dinner?"

"Dinner?" He smiled. "Something low key?"

"Absolutely low key. Tonight, if you're free."

He glanced at the clock on his truck dashboard. "I happen to be free." He kept his voice even.

"Great." She tucked her fingers into the back pockets of her pants. "See you in an hour."

"I look forward to it."

The doorbell rang and Becky quickly dried her hands on the dish towel after rinsing a cucumber for the salad. Chewie ran in circles and barked, probably more excited than she was. But unlike Chewie, Becky was going to play it down a little.

As she crossed the house to answer the door, she nervously wiped her hands on her capris. She had almost everything ready for dinner except for a few vegetables for the salad. She probably would have had everything ready except Chewie took his good old time getting around to doing his business outside.

Smoothing a hand down her top, she drew in a deep breath and leaned forward to open the door. Deputy Harrison James stood on her porch with a bouquet of wildflowers in his hand and a huge smile on his face. Her heart nearly exploded in her chest. In that moment she couldn't figure out why she had held him at arm's length for so long.

Well, she knew, but she also knew that events in life made you reevaluate your priorities. What you thought you wanted or didn't want could change a hundred times over a lifetime.

And then on one beautiful afternoon, God's plan lined everything up perfectly.

"Hello." He handed her the flowers. "For you."

She lifted the bouquet to her nose and inhaled. "They

smell wonderful." She stepped back to allow room for him to enter.

"Whatever you're cooking smells wonderful, too."

"I have homemade chicken pot pies in the oven and I just finished mashing the potatoes. I learned how to cook as a child, but I haven't made some of my favorite meals in a long time." Ever since she had left the Amish, she had been exploring new things. She had lost sight of her past. No more. Leaving the Amish didn't mean she had to abandon her roots. "I was putting together a salad, but you caught me before I finished."

Harrison followed her to the kitchen while she pulled a vase out from under the counter and filled it with water from the utility sink. He went over to the kitchen sink and washed his hands, then picked up the cucumber. "Slices okay?"

"Um…" Becky jerked her head back. "You don't have to do that."

"I know I don't have to do that. I like cooking." He slid a sharp knife out of the butcher block. "This okay? On the cutting board here?"

"Sure."

While Harrison sliced the cucumbers and then the tomatoes, Becky poured lemonade and put the rest of the food on the table.

The doorbell rang and Becky glanced at Harrison as if he might know who was stopping by. She hustled to the front door, surprised to find her mother standing there.

"Hello, Rebecca," her mother said.

"Um…" Confusion swirled in Becky's head. She looked past her *mem* to find her *dat* sitting in the buggy, reins in hand.

"I didn't mean to stop unannounced." She shoved the bundle in her hand toward her daughter. "I thought you might like this for your home."

Becky glanced down and recognized the deep greens and soft yellows of a quilt she had started as a teen. The back of her nose tingled. She had left home before she had a chance to complete the project. She fingered the finished edges, then met her mother's steady gaze. "I hope you don't mind," her mother said. "Mag and I finished it for you. We thought you might like it in your home. Soon, the nights will be getting colder."

Becky hugged it to her chest. "Yes, thank you." Her mind drifted to the soft green she had used to paint her bedroom. "It will match my bedroom perfectly."

"Gut." Her mother dipped her head shyly.

"Would you like to come in?"

Her mother quickly shook her head. "No, your father and I are on our way home. Mag and Abram are expecting us." She turned to walk away, then turned back around. "Perhaps another time."

"Yes, perhaps." Becky lifted her hand to wave to her father and was rewarded with a tip of his hat.

Harrison came up behind her just as her mother was pulling herself back up on the wagon. She closed the door and set the quilt on a bench inside the door. "They dropped off a quilt I had started to make when I was just a girl. My mother and sister took the time to finish it."

"That was nice."

"Yes, it was." She blinked away the emotions raining down on her. She fought to keep her voice from shaking. "I suppose we should eat."

"I put the salad on the table."

Becky dished out the rest of the meal and they sat

down across from each other. "I'm glad you were free for dinner," she said. "I had all this food and no one to cook for."

Harrison took a bite of the flaky pastry on the pot pie. "Oh, wow, this is good."

"Thanks." For some reason, she suddenly felt shy.

"How has work been since you've been back?"

"Good," Becky said, happy to be on neutral ground. "The sheriff has come out with more promises to be transparent after he…"

"Wasn't transparent."

Becky laughed. "Exactly. He had his nephew's best interests at heart. The kid hadn't done anything wrong in Quail Hollow, but in light of everything else going on, it just threw a wrench into our investigation. But regardless, I think Sheriff Landry has survived to sheriff another day."

"People often have their judgment clouded by family." Harrison dipped his head and rubbed the back of his neck. "I was so angry at my brother for getting involved with drugs. For bringing shame on my family—the memory of my father and mother—that I wasn't there for him. But I've come to peace with everything that's happened. I've learned to have faith thanks to you."

"I'm happy you've found peace." Becky reached across the table and covered his hand. "Sometimes part of that process means you have to make your own family."

Becky was grateful her family had allowed the ice to melt, including giving her the beautiful quilt, but they'd never be one of those families who got together for Thanksgiving and shared laughter and naps during the football game. It could never be that way with them.

Harrison pushed back his chair and came around to her side of the table and pulled the chair out next to hers. He sat down on the edge and leaned toward her. "I'd like to think that maybe someday you'd consider me family."

Becky's heart raced as she met his steady gaze. She cleared her throat. "You've been there for me when I had no one else."

He cupped her cheek with his hand. He leaned in and pressed his lips to hers, warm and inviting. He pulled back and studied her face. "I have no plans to go anywhere, if that's all right with you?"

Butterflies fluttered in her belly at the intense gaze in his eyes. "You'd think someone who was adventurous enough to leave the Amish and start a new life wouldn't get so nervous when it came to change, even good change."

"You've had a lot of changes in your life." He was so close she could see flecks of yellow in his eyes. "And I suppose over the course of our lives, there will be many more."

"Whatever lies ahead, it's good to know I'm not alone. I'm glad you're here." It was her turn to lean closer and press a kiss to his lips. He tasted like a home-cooked meal and the promise of the future.

She felt his lips curve into a smile against hers. "Me, too."

* * * * *

Love Inspired

Save $1.00

on the purchase of ANY
Love Inspired® or
Love Inspired® Suspense book.

Available wherever books are sold,
including most bookstores, supermarkets,
drugstores and discount stores.

Save $1.00

on the purchase of ANY Love Inspired® or Love Inspired® Suspense book.

Coupon valid until August 30, 2019.
Redeemable at participating retail outlets in the U.S. and Canada only.
Limit one coupon per customer.

52616381

Canadian Retailers: Harlequin Enterprises Limited will pay the face value of this coupon plus 10.25¢ if submitted by customer for this product only. Any other use constitutes fraud. Coupon is nonassignable. Void if taxed, prohibited or restricted by law. Consumer must pay any government taxes. Void if copied. Inmar Promotional Services ("IPS") customers submit coupons and proof of sales to Harlequin Enterprises Limited, P.O. Box 31000, Scarborough, ON M1R 0E7, Canada. Non-IPS retailer—for reimbursement submit coupons and proof of sales directly to Harlequin Enterprises Limited, Retail Marketing Department, Bay Adelaide Centre, East Tower, 22 Adelaide Street West, 40th Floor, Toronto, Ontario M5H 4E3, Canada.

U.S. Retailers: Harlequin Enterprises Limited will pay the face value of this coupon plus 8¢ if submitted by customer for this product only. Any other use constitutes fraud. Coupon is nonassignable. Void if taxed, prohibited or restricted by law. Consumer must pay any government taxes. Void if copied. For reimbursement submit coupons and proof of sales directly to Harlequin Enterprises, Ltd 482, NCH Marketing Services, P.O. Box 880001, El Paso, TX 88588-0001, U.S.A. Cash value 1/100 cents.

5 65373 00076 2 (8100)0 12422

® and ™ are trademarks owned and used by the trademark owner and/or its licensee.

© 2019 Harlequin Enterprises Limited

LICOUP47010